SMILE AND FLUSH AWAY

Johnson decided to answer Nature's call first.

The toilet gurgled ominously.

He opened his mouth and was about to articulate the words, 'Oh crap', when the irradiating sanitation unit back-flushed, drenching him with its contents. Unfortunately his prophetic words now, rather aptly, described the circumstance he found himself in.

Johnson, who in his time felt he'd experienced all that sanitation engineering had to throw at him, just sighed and continued with his examination.

And there it was: the pilot valve had been reversed…

But how could this be? Who would do such a thing?

1ST

EDITION

ABOUT THE AUTHOR

Nils Derrick was conceived in the year humankind first journeyed into outer space and, as such, considers himself to be a child of the Space Age.

After childhood's end he studied engineering at university, became an engineer and subsequently spent his time languishing in the doldrums of corporate middle management.

He now lives in rural England with his family and various animals, and dreams of life yet to be found, of travelling the stars and, at the end of his days, hopes to find heaven – though he suspects that is not what will be waiting for him on the other side.

smiLE
AnD flUSh AWAY

NILS DERRICK

To KAREN,

MAY ALL YOUR STARS LINE UP
IN CONJUNCTION,

DERRICK ☆

Published by
PLAIN STAR PUBLISHING LTD. in 2012
www.plainstar.com

SMILE AND FLUSH AWAY
A Plain Star book.
ISBN 978-1-908893-01-7

To Paula.

[1] Once Upon A Future…

Once upon a future, in a reality that lies far too far away to be probable, there lived an ordinary human. He led an ordinary life; he ate and he slept; he dreamt and he worked, plying his wares throughout the numerous inhabited systems of the Spiral Arm. And though many generations separate his time from ours, he was, in many ways, little different from you or I.

The human, whose name was Johnson, considered himself to be a sales representative. However, his employer, the Flush Away Corporation – a fabricator of less than lucrative sanitation products – insisted on calling him a 'customer-relationship and promotions' specialist, much to his annoyance.

He was informed that the acronym of this job title was designed to mildly amuse prospective clients. Suffice to say the job title had been created by the self-styled 'intelligentsia' of the Flush Away Corporation, namely its merchandising department, and was, in their own words, conceived to 'initiate the interpersonal framework necessary to generate an interactive discourse with the highest statistical probability of concluding a nett positive fiscal transaction'.

Johnson thought it must be good to work in the merchandising department – a department where you were paid to come up with, well, literally crap!

He was certain customers just invited him to their workplaces to crack a seemingly endless succession of jokes, puns and one-liners, all inspired by his job title. Oh, how he yearned for the time when his business holocard would have simply projected 'sales representative', but sadly that time had long since passed. Now it was all about 'Customer Affinity Cultivation' and 'Product Propagation', 'Focussed Networking' and 'Evolving Value'. It was a time when customers expected more than just the product they paid for. The balance of power had shifted: supply outstripped demand, and customers demanded someone to be there to satisfy their every need – whether that need was directly related to the commercial transaction or not.

In the words of his boss, Ms D'Baliere, the team was there to 'blow the customers' minds away'. To Johnson this seemed to be a corporate enterprise statement that could be easily misinterpreted.

The fact was, even after his all-too-frequent performance enhancement sessions, the most positive thing that could be said about Johnson's results was 'could do better'. And on those rare occasions he reflected on the matter he would see his all-important sales graph projected on the holoplay, and the look on Ms D'Baliere's face as she rotated the graph, trying to decide which way up it went.

Johnson sighed.

It had been his smooth-talking colleague, Chad Edger, who had helpfully suggested his current business lead to Ms D'Baliere. Chad had said he had so much potential business lined up that perhaps Johnson might be able to fit this particular lead into his schedule. Ms D'Baliere was overjoyed at this budding sign of teamwork, and Johnson, with nothing but empty slots in his schedule, had no choice but to accept Chad's generous offer.

Johnson knew as soon as he had stepped planetside that things weren't looking good. Whilst Old MacDonald's World's Insem-A-Sow Spaceport, sponsored by the planet's leading artificial inseminator of pigs, was suitably contemporary, the panorama of ramshackle buildings that confronted him wasn't. This was an agricultural planet, and an agricultural planet meant farmers, and farmers meant why spend when you could make do.

With a sense of impending disappointment Johnson got into the first waiting taxi-skyrider and requested to be taken to the headquarters of Old MacDonald's Wholesale General Stores.

According to the ever-talkative Talk-2-U taxibot his destination was located at the heart of Old MacDonald's Town, the planet's less than imaginatively named primary conurbation. Johnson sat back and relaxed, as best as he could in the taxi's Wipe-Me-Down-Easy seats, and decided to make the most of the journey.

Old MacDonald's Town wasn't quite the *conurbation* Johnson imagined it to be. In fact the use of the word 'town' was something of an exaggeration. Before he'd even managed to look up, the taxi-skyrider drew to a halt, its door slid open and the ever-talkative Talk-2-U taxibot announced his arrival.

Johnson appraised his destination. Before him loomed a large, ex-Space Corps, geodesic dome. From the tell-tale blaster marks it was evident that the building had seen active service at some point in its past, and the multitude of faded signs on its outer skin lay testament to the fact that the current owner was just one in a long chronology of second hands.

With true professionalism, born of countless, easily forgotten business appointments, Johnson managed to raise a smile and walk to the front door. Oddly the door remained shut, and for a while Johnson thought it wasn't working. Then he noticed the handle and an intermittent hololabel suggesting that all he had to do was turn and pull. How quaint. He turned and pulled, but the door remained firmly shut. Johnson then clasped the handle with both hands and, with a little more force than necessary, pulled again. Suddenly the door sprang open, causing him to stumble backwards in a rather ungainly and noticeably unprofessional manner. Johnson composed himself and, through his smile, took a resigned breath. He entered.

Inside, and Johnson was confronted by a warehouse full of containers, crammed upon racks, piled high to the ceiling. He stood and waited. And waited. He could hear a faint whirr and clatter. His patience came and went, and, finally, he called out, 'Is there anyone there?'

The faint whirr and clatter momentarily stopped, and then it grew louder. Eventually a timeworn Ever-On forklift bot emerged from the far end of the aisle, gently clipping the racks as it rocked from side to side. It was one of Forever On Industries many products from its Ever-On range and, as the corporation liked to remind everyone, it was 'forever on for you'.

The Ever-On forklift bot drew nearer. Instinctively Johnson took a step backwards. The term 'shiny and new' could only be applied to the exposed metal rents gained from its all-too-frequent scrapes with the warehouse's racks. The Ever-On forklift bot juddered to a halt. 'Forklift Bot TE... um, something, er... something, reporting, sir!'

'Thank you,' replied Johnson. 'I have an appointment with Mr Legrand, the proprietor. My name is Johnson and I represent the Flush Away Corporation.'

There was a pause. The Ever-On forklift bot whirred. 'Forklift Bot TE... um, something, er... something, awaiting your orders, sir!'

'An appointment, with Mr Legrand. My name's Johnson, I'm from the Flush Away Corporation,' repeated Johnson.

There was another pause. The Ever-On forklift bot whirred. 'Forklift Bot TE... um, something, er... something, awaiting your orders, sir!'

This conversation had clearly short-circuited. However, Johnson, ever the enduring sales representative, tried once more. 'Can you take me to see the proprietor? My name is Johnson and I represent the Flush Away Corporation. I have an appointment.'

'Location unknown, sir!' responded Forklift Bot TE... um, something, er... something.

Barely encouraged by this glimmer of partial sentience, Johnson decided to embark upon a new approach to overcome the Ever-On forklift bot's somewhat limited speech recognition: he would try as many key words as possible, 'Take, show, introduce, present; me, visitor, human; to the boss, commander, leader, chief, principal, person in charge, your superior.'

'Location unknown, sir!' came the all-too-predictable response from Forklift Bot TE... um, something, er... something.

With weary resolve Johnson tried a few more key words, 'Workplace, headquarters, command-bunker?'

The Ever-On forklift bot paused and, after much processing, a yellow

3

light flickered. It then sparked into action. 'Take visitor to command-bunker. Yes sir!' The Ever-On forklift bot then rattled and started to reverse along the aisle. Johnson followed, cautiously.

After what seemed to be a complete guided tour of every aisle in the warehouse, the Ever-On forklift bot arrived at a ramp leading down to a large, heavily fortified, hermetically sealed hatch. The words 'Command Bunker' had originally been stencilled on the hatch in a robust military typeface, but these had long since faded and were now overwritten in a barely legible hand-painted scrawl.

'Command-bunker, sir!' announced Forklift Bot TE... um, something, er... something.

'Excellent. Thank you,' said Johnson, relieved to have arrived somewhere.

'To hear is to obey, sir!' replied the Ever-On forklift bot, which, with a clang and a clank, rotated and disappeared back into the warehouse.

As Johnson tentatively descended the ramp he noticed a large metallic holocam on a flexible stalk sited above the hatch. It tracked his movements.

'Friend or foe?' rasped the holocam, as it focused in on him.

'Er, friend?' suggested Johnson.

'Computing.' There was an ominous pause and then the holocam concluded, 'You may enter.'

With a depressurising hiss the hatch swung open. Johnson stepped inside. The hatch closed behind him, firmly.

'Flush Away representative? Y'all had a good trip? Find us OK? Wanna' take a seat?' asked a voice in quick-blast succession, as Johnson adjusted to the neon-red half-light.

'Er, yes,' replied Johnson, unsure as to whether he'd answered all the questions correctly.

Behind a large, robustly constructed and apparently blast-proof workhub sat Mr Joshua Jeremiah Legrand, clearly identifiable from his framed image in full-dress uniform on the wall behind, and from the hand-carved wooden name plaque that took pride of place in front of him.

Mr Legrand was casually dressed in military fatigues and had adorned his workplace in suitably matching memorabilia. He was a vortex of activity. Holoplays flashed as he issued commands through a multitude of interfaces.

Johnson sat patiently.

After more than a few photon phases had passed, Mr Legrand commanded, 'In meeting.' The holoplays stopped flashing and there was silence.

Johnson decided to take the initiative and handed Mr Legrand his business holocard.

Mr Legrand lifted it up to a spotlight and read it aloud, thankfully ignoring Johnson's job title and any associated witticism, 'Irradiatin' sanitation products – not much call for them fancy things in these parts. Hm, though maybe, at the right kinda' price I might be able to sell some. Folks round here ain't gonna' pay good credits for one of them there irradiatin' sanitation units unless y'all can show 'em that it's cheaper than diggin' a hole.'

'I'm sure that...' began Johnson but Mr Legrand, keen to continue, did not want to be interrupted.

'Best start small. Seein' as y'all seems to be a nice 'n friendly type 'a fella' 'n not one of them there pushy sales representatives, I'd be willin' to take ten domestic irradiatin' sanitation units on approval, sale or return. Just send me the necessary. Thankin' y'all.' Mr Legrand sat back in his chair.

Johnson maintained his professional smile and tried not to roll his eyes. The commission on ten units 'on approval' would not even cover travel expenses. But before Johnson could start negotiating, Mr Legrand leant forward, pressed Johnson's hand and announced that the meeting was over, whereupon he returned to his now reactivated holoplays.

To Johnson's surprise his chair rotated and the fortified, hermetically sealed hatch, by which he'd entered, re-opened; clear conformation the meeting had ended. He hadn't even got out his Show-It-All holostrator, or used the obligatory 'Smile and Flush Away' catchphrase. He hadn't even left the customer with a Flush Away singing novelty toy.

With his earlier sense of impending disappointment now fully realised, Johnson stood up. There was little point trying to pursue further sales and so, still smiling, he said, 'Excellent, thank you for your custom. I'll get on it right away, sir.'

As he ascended the ramp, Johnson started to wonder about his good fortune, or more to the point, apparent lack of it. And as he walked he thought about Chad Edger who had clearly conspired to bring disappointment to his life, when it occurred to him that he didn't know the way out.

He decided to retrace his footsteps back to the command-bunker. It was a good idea – in theory. Unfortunately, after some time he found himself in an entirely new part of the warehouse that, unhelpfully, looked entirely like every other part of the warehouse.

He was lost.

'Hello, is there anyone there?' he shouted.

Silence.

Again he shouted and again there was silence.

Apply logic, that's all he had to do. And so another idea formed in his mind. If he walked straight in one direction he would come to the edge of the dome and then he could make his way around its perimeter.

Surprisingly, for Johnson, his idea worked. Though only after a time-

5

consuming, almost complete circumnavigation of the dome. With relief, and a certain amount of force, he pushed open the front door and emerged into sunlight.

'Ten units on approval!' He shook his head and, using his holocom, holoed a taxi-skyrider. Well, at least he would be able to seek consolation in a drink or two back at the Insem-A-Sow Spaceport.

* * * * *

The Stiff One drinks dispense machine had the better of Johnson. This outcome was never going to be in doubt, for the drinks dispense machine was a device that required a certain amount of mechanical aptitude to operate, and mechanical aptitude was not amongst Johnson's higher scoring life skills.

The Stiff One drinks dispense machine stood against the back wall of a small self service beverage emporium in the Insem A Sow Spaceport. It stood where it had always stood since its installation. It stood unmoved by Johnson's ill-advised kick. It had functionality, rationality and logic. It was there to serve and, given the right interaction, would fulfil its single design purpose without fault.

Johnson hopped about aimlessly, clutching his foot and muttering expletives. He had, literally, just set foot in the self-service beverage emporium when it had all started to go wrong. He felt frustration, pain and anger. He had tried to get a drink and, given a simpler set of operating instructions, was sure he would have been able to do so.

'Is this yours, dear?'

Johnson looked up to see an elderly female peering at him quizzically and holding out his holocom.

'Er, yes.' He searched for an explanation. 'I must have dropped it when I, um, stubbed my toe. Excellent. Thank you.'

'You should be more careful, dear. There are those who would have not given a second thought to taking it and using it themselves.' The elderly female then continued, 'I do not hold with that kind of behaviour myself. I was taught that a strong sense of morality is essential if one is going to lead a happy and productive life. "Do right by others and others will do right by you", that is the axiom by which I was raised and it has stood me in good stead for these many solar cycles.'

The elderly female was clearly keen to engage Johnson in conversation, even if it was somewhat one-sided. Then, sensing that he was incapable of escape, she sought to secure her intention. 'Let me have a look at that foot. You may have broken a bone. I was a medic during the last war you know.'

With surprise on her side, and the strength of a female half her age, she deftly pushed him onto one of the nearby chairs. Before he could react

6

she was unfastening his footwear and examining the suspect injury.

'Of course, it was very different then. Oh, such good times, and the stories I could tell you.' She expertly manipulated his foot, testing the bones and joints. 'I remember we were on patrol in the Rigel Quadrant. We were outnumbered ten to one with barely a star trooper left standing. And the bloodshed, it was hand-to-hand fighting you know, we couldn't charge our blasters fast enough and we had no serviceable combat bots left. I kept my star troopers patched-up though. There was hardly an injury that I couldn't fix with a swift amputation and a prosthetic. "On your new feet, star trooper", I'd say, "there's a war to fight!" I can see them now, desperate to get back to the front. Some of them were barely able to stand on their new artificial limbs and yet they'd try anything to leave my field hospital.'

Johnson could picture the scene all-too-vividly and worried whether his foot warranted amputation.

'Of course, I would never have had the time to give you this kind of examination then. It would have been straight into the Limb-O-Fix with you, my lad, and straight out with a nice shiny one-size-fits-all artificial leg. As good as new! Ah, by providence, no bones broken, just a bruise.' She seemed disappointed.

'Well, um, er, thank you for your help. It feels much better now.' Fearing that the elderly female may wish to take a second look, Johnson hastily added, 'In fact I think it's almost as good as new.' To demonstrate he stood and bravely smiled, disguising the pain that convulsed up through his leg.

'Yes, I think you're right. Then it's back to the front with you, star trooper!' she commanded.

Johnson was unsure as to whether this was humour or a direct order.

'I've got a starliner to catch. Going to visit my son and daughter-in-law. You know they haven't contacted me in ages so I thought I'd pay them a surprise visit.' And with a swift 'Goodbye' the elderly female smartly about-faced and marched off in the direction of her departure point.

Johnson collapsed back into the chair. It seemed to him that travelling was never quite the rich, carefree experience it promised to be. It was always fraught with little trials and tribulations, and by encounters with citizens you'd normally cross the walkway to avoid.

His starliner wasn't due for some considerable time. He then faced the monotony of the return passage, cooped up in a cost-efficient seat primarily designed to maximise passenger numbers rather than provide for their comfort.

He considered trying the drinks dispense machine again, but the more he thought about it the more his foot throbbed. Johnson decided to hang the expense and find a full-service beverage emporium for the more successful business traveller.

It was only a short hobble. The beverage emporium was sited on the main concourse and appeared to be fairly empty. Like every other service outlet it was themed and, like every other service outlet, it seemed to just not quite get the theme right. This particular one, Comrade Cosmonaut, was themed to Ancient Earth and was in the style of a Soviet tribal beverage emporium, with billowing red flags and upbeat martial tunes. He sat at one of the industrially fabricated tables. A Made-4-U serving bot appeared, sporting a faux-fur hat with a corkscrew and sickle motif.

'Greetings space voyager, welcome to Comrade Cosmonaut!' announced the Made-4-U serving bot, with something of a metallic accent. The Robo Labour Corporation, the bot's fabricator, stated in their promotional material that the metallic edge to their product's accent was there to give the customer that 'authentic robo experience' though, in reality, it was more a consequence of aggressive cost-cutting rather than design.

Having waited for and not received a response, the Made-4-U serving bot continued, 'Perhaps comrade space voyager would like a drink?'

'Pernodka,' demanded Johnson, forgoing any semblance of the usual politeness he displayed to all things living, sentient or otherwise. He needed a drink that delivered, and found that the traditional blended drinks did so rather more quickly than the genetically tailored ones that were currently the fashion.

The Made-4-U serving bot disappeared into the beverage emporium and re-emerged with a red tray bearing a tall plastiglass tumbler. It smoothly put a red star-shaped coaster on the table and then placed the tumbler in front of Johnson, announcing its contents. Motionless it awaited acknowledgement that the order had been fulfilled. Johnson eyed the tumbler, picked it up and, with one swift movement, downed its contents.

'Another Pernodka,' instructed an uncharacteristically impolite Johnson.

Taking the old tumbler and coaster, the Made-4-U serving bot disappeared into the beverage emporium and re-emerged with a red tray bearing another tall plastiglass tumbler. It smoothly put a red star-shaped coaster on the table and then placed the tumbler in front of Johnson, announcing its contents. Motionless it awaited acknowledgement that the order had been fulfilled. Johnson eyed the tumbler, picked it up and, with one swift movement, downed its contents.

'Another Pernodka,' repeated Johnson.

Taking the old tumbler and coaster, the Made-4-U serving bot disappeared into the beverage emporium and re-emerged with a red tray bearing another tall plastiglass tumbler. It smoothly put a red star-shaped coaster on the table and then placed the tumbler in front of Johnson, announcing its contents. Motionless it awaited acknowledgement that the order had been fulfilled. Johnson eyed the tumbler, picked it up and, with one swift movement, downed its contents.

And so the sub-routine of Johnson's consolatory drinking continued.

After many loops of this potentially infinite sub-routine Johnson decided to stop. With a full tumbler in front of him he simply acknowledged order fulfilment by saying, 'Thank you.' The Made-4-U serving bot then disappeared into the beverage emporium.

Johnson's holocom started to buzz. It must be time to make his way to the departure point. Johnson eyed the tall plastiglass tumbler once more, picked it up and, with one not quite so swift movement, downed its contents.

[2] A Trip Into Space

It was a long stand on the moving walkway to his departure point. Holovert after holovert projected out from the barrier-to-barrier holoplays, all promoting a common subject: farming. Johnson took little notice, though not through disinterest, for he knew it was important to understand his potential customers, but more because he was trying to concentrate on staying upright. That last drink had been a drink too many. It was always the same. After the first drink, the second simply followed to keep it company and then the third just added to the pleasure and, with time for a fourth, it was all-too-easy to lose count.

His holocom buzzed again as the moving walkway turned the corner into the departure point. Final call. Awaiting him was the usual assortment of business travellers, tourists and visiting relatives, all en route to their destinations.

The passengers began to make their way towards the embarkation ramp. Above, a holoplay projected the words 'Boarding Now In Progress', and the passengers trouped, single file, up the ramp. Johnson followed. A cheerful jump associate stood by the transit shuttle's airlock welcoming each and every one. She smiled at Johnson and wished him a pleasant trip. Johnson managed to half-smile back as he recovered his balance, after having duly tripped over the airlock threshold. The cheerful jump associate retained her smile, but marked Johnson as a potential problem passenger.

It was with great relief that Johnson fell into his allocated All-Ways self-forming seat.

'Sir, sir.' Johnson could hear a voice and felt himself being shaken.

The cheerful jump associate leaned over, trying not to breathe in the alcohol vapour. 'Sir, we're about to make ready for take off. If you could return your seat to the upright position and strap yourself in.'

'Er, yes, certainly, sorry about that, must have dosed off,' Johnson apologised, as he tried to adjust his seat.

'Yes sir, the other passengers had noticed, from your,' the cheerful jump associate's voice dropped to a whisper, 'snoring, sir.'

Johnson felt the red flush of embarrassment as he looked around, only to see his fellow passengers shaking their heads with disapproval. He fumbled the seat adjustment control and almost catapulted himself into the seat in front.

'Would sir like some help with his seat?' the cheerful jump associate asked rather loudly. 'Here, let me strap you in.' She grabbed the safety harness and yanked it tightly, causing Johnson to gasp for air as the belts dug into the fleshier parts of his body.

The cheerful jump associate beamed. 'All done sir, all safe and secure. We wouldn't like to see you fall out of your seat now would we, sir?'

'Excellent, er, thank you.' Johnson was sure the circulation to his legs had been cut off.

The cheerful jump associate just smiled and continued on her way to the rear of the transit shuttle, checking the other passengers. Johnson tried to loosen his harness, but the mechanism seemed to be jammed.

In front of him the holoplay ran through the transit shuttle's safety instructions, and projected details of the short journey to the waiting starliner.

There was a slight judder, the transit shuttle rotated in preparation for lift-off. The drives began to hum. The holoplay flashed the countdown in big dramatic numbers and, as ever, the children on board counted along, 'Five, four, three, two, one, lift-off!'

The lift-off was, for many, an anti-climax. The transit shuttle built up speed gently as it pulled away from Old MacDonald's World. The times of gut-wrenching, high-g acceleration were but a distant memory, as they had been followed, equally swiftly, by many solar cycles of compensatory litigation.

Johnson looked to the porthole and through it he could see the vista of the planet spread out below; the patchwork of fields and the clusters of habitation; a checkerboard of life; a farming world that he was now, thankfully, leaving behind.

The transit shuttle barely shook as it rumbled its way through the planet's atmosphere. The horizon darkened and, in one pulsar's pulse, the stars appeared. Below, the green expanse of Old MacDonald's World could be seen tinged with blue and encompassed by a single planetary ring glistening orange in the light of the system's solitary sun. Then, with the friction of the atmosphere overcome, all became silent.

For Johnson the sight of deep space, the colours, the infinite complexity of stars and the bottomless black emptiness of it all never failed to amaze. But it was also a sight that never failed to bring on an accompanying feeling of tumbling nausea, due to its disorientating vastness. And, as ever, after the feeling of amazement had passed, the feeling of nausea still remained. At least they'd soon rendezvous with the starliner.

The cheerful jump associate floated down the aisle, checking on the condition of her passengers. Transit shuttles were fondly called 'vomit comets' by their seasoned travellers and this one was no exception. For those *green* passengers, who had failed to reach for their regurgitation receptacles in time, the cheerful jump associate had a Go Suck portable suction pack – a product conceived and fabricated by Vacuous Industries. This she used to capture the regurgitated stomach contents that floated free from gravity's call.

Despite the thousands of solar cycles that had passed since the birth of space travel, the cure for space sickness still eluded the greatest endeavours of the scientific community. Although, that said, the absence of such a cure had created a sorely needed merchandising opportunity for Vacuous Industries.

The transit shuttle's drives began to hum again. The passengers' holoplays indicated that they were but a pulsar's pulse away from docking with the orbiting starliner. For the cheerful jump associate it was now a contest against the space-time continuum: as soon as the transit shuttle started to manoeuvre, any free-floating vomit would continue with its own momentum and, invariably, start *docking* with those unsuspecting, unfortunate passengers who happened to be on its trajectory.

As the cheerful jump associate passed, and had almost reached the end of the aisle, Johnson looked back and noticed something floating above him. Helpfully he pointed it out. 'Um, miss, there's some more.'

She turned, but before she had a chance to bring her Go Suck portable suction pack into play, the transit shuttle had started to rotate front end up. The securely strapped in Johnson realised that he was now on the free-floating vomit's trajectory – too late.

She smiled as she vacuumed Johnson. 'Oh, I am so terribly sorry, sir.'

*   *   *   *   *

Billy Bob Brown sat two rows back from Johnson, on the opposite side of the aisle. Throughout the trip he had watched Johnson fastidiously.

As the newest member of the Children Of The Soil, Billy Bob had volunteered for this mission. It was his initiation and he wasn't about to let his kinfolk down.

This was the first time Billy Bob had been offworld. In fact this was the first time any member of the Children Of The Soil had been offworld. Dressed in his ill-fitting best attire, he hoped to pass unnoticed among the other passengers, just another face in the cosmos.

The Children Of The Soil described themselves as organic fundamentalists. Their beliefs were rooted in the ancient philosophy of the organic agricultural movement. However, in the spirit of true believers, they took their belief in all things organic just that one parsec beyond. They aspired to a complete, balanced natural universe where all must come from the soil and all must be returned to the soil.

Charitably, they could be described as an unheard-of fundamentalist collective, driven to spread the organic word; a committed extended-family of disaffected brothers and sisters, cousins and second cousins.

Alternatively, they could be described as a misguided rabble, clearly demonstrating the consequences of what happens when there's too small a gene pool.

Whilst nominally democratic, the Children Of The Soil were led, without question, by a single-minded, charismatic, although possibly delusional, visionary who, whilst ably espousing organic principles, was inclined to get lost in the detail. His discourses veered from the broad, *The Overthrow Of Corporate Universisation*, to the narrow, *The Use Of Organic Sanitation Facilities*. This had the effect of causing his followers to directly associate these topics. And, whilst *The Overthrow Of Corporate Universisation* went over the heads of the majority of the Children Of The Soil, *The Use Of Organic Sanitation Facilities* was much more understandable. In fact *The Use Of Organic Sanitation Facilities* was understandable to such an extent that the more active members of the collective had started to take it as a basis to affect the organic revolution.

To date these anarchic activities had been random, ineffectual and largely unnoticed by the greater part of humankind. Their untargeted acts of insurgency: the blocked u-bends, loosened toilet seats and non-dispensing toilet Paperette dispensers were generally taken to be caused by that all-too-common shortfall of corporate endeavour; shoddy workmanship, and, as such, were considered by most to be the fault of the fabricators.

The leader of the Children Of The Soil, whilst revelling in his followers' fervour, decided that it was now time to escalate and focus their revolutionary activities. It was time to strike at the very heart of the corrupt corporate organisations whose attempts at what he described as 'unorganic universisation' permeated their lives.

The Children Of The Soil had watched Johnson from the very juncture in the space-time continuum he had landed on Old MacDonald's World. They'd learnt of his arrival from the youngest of their number, Amy Mae Legrand. She worked part-time for her Uncle, Joshua Jeremiah Legrand, who owned the wholesale general stores. He'd told her he was expecting a visitor, a Johnson from the Flush Away Corporation; a corporation that fabricated irradiating sanitation products.

And so it was agreed. Johnson was the perfect target: an offworlder who was part of the corporate universisation. Simply put: he was *unorganic*. The Children Of The Soil, or more specifically their leader – as is always the way in any nominally democratic movement – had decided to act, and Billy Bob was going to be the instrument of that decision.

Across the aisle, Billy Bob could see that Johnson had managed, at last, to release the safety harness that strapped him to his seat. Most of the other passengers had already made their way to the waiting starliner.

Johnson stood and gingerly headed for the transit shuttle's airlock. The combination of alcohol and the orbiting starliner's Hold-Me-Down gravity-simulation system made Johnson's head spin.

At the airlock, the cheerful jump associate smiled and hoped he'd had a pleasant trip. Johnson half-smiled back.

Billy Bob followed.

* * * * *

The waiting starliner, named Freedom Of The Stars, was an economy class, commercial interstellar starliner described by its fabricator, the Jetsui Corporation, as having the latest in economic gravity-simulation and propulsive systems.

Proudly designed and built, it was promoted as reliable, efficient and most importantly, to the starliner's operator, cost effective in terms of mass of living organism per parsec travelled.

The starliner was essentially a large tube. By rotating the tube, the starliner's passengers experienced the sensation of simulated gravity. Patented by the Jetsui Corporation, this low-cost Hold-Me-Down gravity-simulation system drew on the wonders of centripetal force.

To enable the starliner to jump from star system to star system, it was powered by the potent, but occasionally unstable, Gigastar propulsion system, also patented by the Jetsui Corporation. This was a propulsion system based on tried and tested matter-anti-matter technology, and was located on the central axis of the starliner. Fortunately, for the Jetsui Corporation's conception & evolution department, the matter-anti-matter technology ban, which encompassed all planetary-based uses, had yet to be extended to interstellar applications.

In addition, passengers could be safe in the knowledge that their protection, from the harmful radiation of the cosmos, was provided by an impenetrable outer layer – lovingly crafted from the best, and cheapest, space debris and scrap material available for acquisition by the Jetsui Corporation's acquisition department. Of course, a further bonus was that the word 'reconstituted' could be used in the starliner's promotional campaign.

The passenger deck and other life support areas, which formed the main tubular structure of the starliner, were sandwiched between this outer layer and another similar, inner layer of dense material. Although less well publicised, the inner layer provided protection from the Gigastar propulsion system, in the unlikely event that it should become unstable and explode.

There was considerable debate within the Jetsui Corporation as to whether this inner layer was strictly necessary. Using a complex cost-efficiency equation, derived by the corporation's fiscal department, it could be determined that the inner layer was an unnecessary expense. However, the litigation department – who always seemed to have the last word – deemed it to be necessary, given the litigious nature of the universe. And so the inner layer remained.

Inside, utilitarian functionality predominated; with 'No space wasted, no optimisation opportunity missed' according to the Jetsui Corporation's promotional department. The starliner truly was a design without equal, a design that would not have been what it was, were it not for the petty rivalry and in-fighting between the Jetsui Corporation's many and fractious departments. It was truly 'a marvel of budgetary interstellar engineering'.

A few coats of paint later, and christened Freedom Of The Stars by the Liberty Discount Star Line, the starliner lived up to its owner's pledge: 'If you're looking for freedom you won't find cheaper'.

Which was a thought that seemed to echo in Johnson's mind as he wedged himself into his allocated All-Ways self-forming seat, a seat that seemed to have retained the form of a thinner previous occupant, a seat that refused to reform to Johnson's somewhat larger frame.

The Freedom Of The Stars had the same thin veneer of décor as the transit shuttle, but without the portholes. And what particularly disorientated Johnson was, wherever you were on a starliner, the deck curved to a horizon that was just out of sight.

The return passage would take the good part of a planetary rotation, and Johnson needed sleep, but his head was still spinning, his mouth was dry and he desperately needed to answer Nature's call. As he stood he had to wait for a young male wearing ill-fitting attire – which had clearly been the height of fashion many seasons ago – to walk past. The young male seemed to look at Johnson as if he knew him and then hurriedly turned away.

Johnson joined the toilet queue, a queue that didn't appear to be moving. Up ahead he heard someone say those fateful words, 'Out of order,' followed by, 'Convenience, make me laugh, inconvenience more like. When is anyone ever going to design a john that works?'

Johnson dropped his head, for fear of being recognised for his trade. He, like the rest of the queue, turned and started to walk the length of the aisle to the next toilet only to be met by its similarly inconvenienced queue coming towards them.

'Out of order?' asked the head of the other queue.

'Out of order,' replied Johnson.

Then the commotion started; it transpired that all of the conveniences were inconvenienced.

Rodger, the jump associate in attendance, did his best to reassure and empathise with the needy passengers: 'I'm sure it's only a temporary malfunction and all will be back to normal momentarily.' And, 'If sir could just hold on a while longer.' And, 'Perhaps if madam would care to sit and cross her legs, I'm certain the situation will be resolved quickly.'

But despite his best efforts, Rodger sensed that the passengers were losing patience: their demands for an immediate solution were being requested in an increasingly threatening and belligerent manner. They were using language that, dare he say it, best belonged in the toilet.

How he wished for the elegance and refinement of the Silver Service Star Line, with their well-mannered clientele and fully-functioning sanitation facilities, and not the masses that were packed into this forever-malfunctioning interstellar cattle-car.

Finally, he managed to calm the ever-desperate passengers enough to say that he would go and speak to the jump engineer to see what could be done to rectify the situation.

Jump Engineer Olaf Gundersson had his feet up. Though bored, he was thankful for the recuperative time that a Freedom Of The Stars passage usually afforded. It enabled him to recover from whatever excesses he'd succumbed to during his previous planetfall, and it gave him time to dream. How he longed for the adventure of the Space Corps, the uniforms, the medals... the control deck's hatch swung open.

'Yes, yes, what is it? Can't you see I'm busy?' he said, hastily lowering his feet to the ground.

'Jump Engineer Gundersson, sir, the passengers are somewhat restless. All of the toilets appear to be out of order.' Rodger felt he had delivered the news in an appropriately professional way, without panic, whilst still managing to relay the gravitas of the situation.

Olaf Gundersson sighed. As jump engineer his function was to deal with any malfunction on board. Given that the roles of captain and navigator had long since been automated away, he was, by default, the senior officer on board. It was his responsibility to step up to command, and deal with any issues that arose. But in reality, the only reason he was on board was to show that the starliner's operators were demonstrating their legal 'duty of care'. In practice there was little he could do. In fact, Olaf Gundersson tried to remember the last time he'd been able to do anything and couldn't.

'I'm coming,' he said and, with all the enthusiasm he could muster, he stood and made his way to the passenger deck, with Rodger in tow. He walked to every toilet and outside each he checked the status display. Each one indicated 'Out Of Order' and had automatically shutdown, sealing its door. Then, after he'd inspected the last toilet, Jump Engineer Olaf Gundersson confirmed, officially, that all of the toilets were out of order.

'And?' Rodger prompted.

'And nothing, once they shutdown it's an in-dock-service job to repair them,' replied Jump Engineer Olaf Gundersson.

'You're not serious, are you, sir?' asked Rodger, all-too-aware of the rising consternation among the passengers and foreseeing the potentially messy consequences that may ensue.

'Perfectly serious, this is a job for trained specialists. You will just have to make other arrangements for the passengers.' Jump Engineer Olaf Gundersson then turned and headed off in the direction of the control deck, leaving Rodger open-mouthed.

Johnson, who'd realised that sleep would only follow relief, decided there was just one thing for it: he'd have to go and offer his professional help.

He arrived on the scene just after Jump Engineer Olaf Gundersson had left and found Rodger, the jump associate, debating whether to close his mouth or not.

'Can I help?' Johnson asked, and pressed his business holocard into Rodger's hand. 'I happen to know how these things work.'

Rodger looked down at the holocard and then up at Johnson. And, with the undisguised joy of a pilgrim looking upon a saint, said, 'If sir could make the toilets work I could not describe how grateful I would be.' And then, judging the mood of the gathering crowd, added, 'But if sir could just hurry.'

'No problem.' Johnson made his way to the nearest toilet, took out his holocom and selected the appropriate override routine. He passed the holocom over the toilet's display panel. The display status changed from 'Out Of Order' to 'Vacant' and the door slid open. He stepped inside and the door closed behind him.

Rodger turned to the gathered crowd. 'If I could have your attention for a pulsar's pulse, I would just like to say that everything is under control. The conveniences will be at your disposal soon. And I'd like to take this opportunity to thank you for your patience in this matter and assure you that relief will soon be at hand.'

Johnson decided to answer Nature's call first. He then operated the toilet's activation icon and waited to see what happened next: nothing. The core irradiating unit had failed to function. A few photon phases later, after he had taken the wall cover off and was examining the mechanism, the toilet gurgled ominously.

He opened his mouth and was about to articulate the words, 'Oh crap', when the irradiating sanitation unit back-flushed, drenching him with its contents. Unfortunately his prophetic words now, rather aptly, described the circumstance he found himself in.

'Well done, you've got it to work!' he heard Rodger exclaim from behind the door, together with much cheering and clapping from an almost relieved queue of expectant passengers.

Johnson stood back and the toilet's door slid open to reveal his soiled and somewhat fragrant form to those waiting outside.

'Not work exactly,' reported Johnson. 'It flushes, but not quite the right way.'

The expectant passengers, together with Rodger, hastily retreated.

Johnson, who in his time felt he'd experienced all that sanitation engineering had to throw at him, just sighed and continued with his examination. And there it was: the pilot valve had been reversed and the actuation sensor reconnected. But how could this be? Who would do such a thing? The reconnection of the sensor would have caused the 'Out Of Order' sign to come on, and any person then attempting to flush – well, Johnson could feel the results soaking through his attire. He took out his Total Tool universal wrench – fabricated under license by the Socket-To-You Corporation. It was a tool he always carried, but tried never to use for fear of the mechanical mayhem he may cause. With tool in place he reversed the valve back to its factory setting. And with eyes closed, and breath held, he operated the activation icon. Surprisingly, and without apparent fault, the irradiating sanitation unit worked. Johnson marvelled at his own abilities and then stepped outside, and dripped.

'It's fixed,' Johnson reported to Rodger, as the needy passengers looked on. 'We'll just need to clean it up in there.'

The passengers clapped and cheered, though from a distance.

'I'll summon the cleaning bot,' replied Rodger, whilst holding his nose.

Rodger enabled an icon on his attire and, from the rear of the passenger deck, a small, hemispherical Happy-Scrubby cleaning bot floated down the aisle, announcing that cleaning was in progress and warning that surfaces could be slippery. It disappeared into the toilet only to re-emerge a few photon phases later. The toilet was once again ready for use.

Eventually Johnson returned to his seat. He was wearing Rodger's spare full-dress uniform, complete with gold braid and epaulettes; his attire was drying in the galley. He'd defused the remaining toilets without further incident and, in time, everything returned to normal on the passage. At last he could get some sleep.

Sitting a few rows back, Billy Bob chewed on nothing in particular, deliberately and slowly. He was not happy. Not only had the Children Of The Soil's first interstellar strike at corporate universisation been thwarted, but also Johnson had become a hero, applauded by the rest of the passengers. This was not the intention of his mission.

Billy Bob continued to chew and, as he did so, he tried to do some thinking. What he needed was an idea, but for Billy Bob ideas were slow in coming and often disappointing when they arrived.

For Johnson the rest of the passage passed without incident. Rodger returned Johnson's attire, in a far-too-small complimentary toiletry bag, explaining that, unfortunately, it had shrunk, due to an oversight in setting the temperature controls of the galley's oven. By way of compensation, Rodger gave Johnson a form to be completed and, of course, his well-practiced customer service smile.

'Thank you,' replied a somewhat confused Johnson, who then asked, with rather more hope than expectation, 'it's not a practical joke is it?'

'Would that it was, sir, would that it was,' responded Rodger.

'Do you mean to say that I have to wear this-this uniform?' stuttered Johnson.

'I've had a word with the principal jump associate and, whilst it does contravene corporate regulations for someone other than jump crew to wear a full-dress uniform, she said that, in the circumstances, she is willing to overlook it this once, just so long as you don't try and impersonate a jump associate.' Rodger maintained his customer service smile throughout.

'Impersonate a jump associate,' repeated Johnson. 'Why would I want to impersonate a jump associate?'

'Oh, it has been known, sir. We've had several instances of passengers trying to disguise themselves as jump crew. It's the glamour you see, sir. They perceive it as a way to escape the humdrum of their ordinary lives, and there is no doubt that a smart uniform does turn heads.' Rodger's smile remained constant.

'Would you rather I didn't wear it?' asked Johnson.

'We did consider that scenario, sir, but the principal jump associate felt that a semi-naked male emerging from our starliner was not really the type of image we wish to present to the travelling customer.' Rodger's smile was unflinching. 'And, if sir could remember to return the uniform, together with the compensation form, we would be most grateful.' Rodger, and his smile, turned away.

'O-,' began Johnson, looking to the palm of his hand and the small complimentary toiletry bag containing his shrunken attire, and then he added, belatedly, '-K.'

[3] Land

Johnson's destination, Pacifica, was a planet almost entirely covered with water: and water, of one form or another, figured almost entirely in its climate. This had not been the intention when the planet was originally conceived: Pacifica was to have a multitude of small, sun-drenched islands, and, most importantly, a high beach-to-land-mass ratio. Unfortunately, following a series of long-running contractual disputes between the terraforming Creation Corporation and the sponsoring U-Tan-U Corporation, only one island was created; an island devoid of beaches and subject to constant precipitation in all its various forms.

With one small island, and one very deep ocean, Pacifica overflowed with humanity stacked in massive, high-rise skybreakers. Ironically the overpopulation, vast ocean and incessant precipitation were often cited for Pacifica's economic success: what else could you do on a rainy rotation with nowhere to go?

The transit shuttle descended through the atmosphere. Johnson looked forward to returning to his small cooperative and shutting out the rest of the known universe. His business trip had been a washout in more ways than one.

On landing, Johnson followed his fellow passengers along the disembarkation tunnel. He soon joined the flood of travellers that swelled the concourses of the U-Tan-U Spaceport, Pacifica's only spaceport – sponsored by the U-Tan-U Corporation, purveyors of personal colour enhancement products and associated apparatus for over a hundred solar cycles.

Everyone on Pacifica, colour enhanced or not, seemed to be busy. Everyone seemed as if they were late for wherever it was they were going, and everyone seemed to be going somewhere. Johnson, head down, soon merged into the crowd.

It would have been pure chance if Johnson had spotted the fly that buzzed overhead, and it would have been even more remarkable if he'd recognised that the fly was, in fact, an Eye Fly surveillance bot. But with no thought, other than to return to his co-op, he carried on, oblivious to the fly that followed.

* * * * *

It was the break that Operation Kicking Butt had been waiting for. Investigator Strait and his team had been monitoring the U-Tan-U Spaceport vigilantly for over half a solar cycle in search of 'leaf' traffickers. However, there had been little to show for their tireless endeavours, except for several profuse apologies to outraged passengers, and an unfortunate incident over the full-body search of a visiting goodwill ambassador from the Nova Vega Chamber Of Commerce – who just happened to be a personal acquaintance of the First Citizen Of Pacifica and had rather a large amount of credits in his possession.

It was after this particular *unfortunate* incident that Investigator Strait had been given a little pep talk by his chief of law enforcement, whose ears were still burning after his recent conversation with the First Citizen.

The pep talk, if Investigator Strait recalled correctly, ran something like this: 'One more failure and you and your team will be in deep trouble. Now get some results or you will be seconded to administrative duties in the archiving department for the rest of eternity. Have you got that clear?'

Whilst getting the gist of the chief's message, Investigator Strait's memory, which was selective at the best of times, seemed to have missed out the chief's many colourful and illustrative expletives.

Investigator William B. Strait was, as his name suggested, a straightforward male. He had been born of a law enforcement family, to become a part of the law enforcement community, and thus, a part of the law enforcement community he became. After twenty-five solar cycles of dogged persistence, he had risen through the ranks to become an investigator, but aspired for higher. Whilst the recent minor diplomatic incident had been something of a set back in his career, he felt that everyone had overreacted. It was all very well and good protecting the rights of innocent citizens, but in his experience they were only to be found once in a cerulean moon. Everyone was guilty of something: it was only a question of what.

At the outset of Operation Kicking Butt, he and his deputies had set up Sniff-A-Whiff sensors at all transit points in the U-Tan-U Spaceport. Every passenger had to pass by them. Even the slightest trace of that most accursed of narcotics, 'leaf', would be detected.

So when a jump associate, in full-dress uniform, had passed, and the sensor had gone off the scale, it was exactly what he and his team had been hoping for. Leaf, the drug that had afflicted humankind since the time of Ancient Earth, was clearly being smuggled onplanet by citizen or citizens unscanned: citizens who had managed to infiltrate the ranks of a star line.

Despite an overwhelming urge to take down the jump associate, with a swift deployment of his hardened Tactical Response Assault Patrol, Investigator Strait realised that it would be better to let this mere courier lead them to the rest of the lawbreakers and, hopefully, to the mastermind behind the leaf trafficking.

'Send in the Eye Fly surveillance bot,' he'd ordered, much to the disappointment of his Tactical Response Assault Patrol, who had already fixed their combat knives to their assault blasters in anticipation of fierce hand-to-hand fighting.

'Not now team; let's wait until he's led us to the rest of the lawbreakers. Then you can go in.' But this promise did little to quell the murmur of discontent that accompanied the unfixing of combat knives. Half a solar cycle was a long time to wait to draw blood.

* * * * *

The unsuspecting Johnson joined a queue for taxi-skyriders. It was raining. Water ran down the back of his neck.

Billy Bob stood behind Johnson. He'd almost lost Johnson in the crowded spaceport. It was only because Johnson was wearing the jump associate's full-dress uniform that he'd been able to follow him.

Billy Bob had never seen so many folks in all his life. He wondered how everyone remembered everyone else's name.

Back in the U-Tan-U Spaceport, the members of Operation Kicking Butt crowded round a holoplay. To their annoyance the suspect's image kept coming in and out of view as the Eye Fly surveillance bot moved from side to side, its artificial intelligence mimicking the behaviour of a common housefly. Unfortunately, once outside the spaceport, a statistically abnormal raindrop hit the Eye Fly surveillance bot and with one final buzz the holoplay went blank. The Eye Fly surveillance bot had met a watery end.

With contact lost, Investigator Strait acted quickly. He told the team they would need to revert to manual covert surveillance. There was an eager clamour to volunteer. The team aggressively jostled each other with arms raised, shouting, 'Me, me, me!' in a bid to be selected. This mission could result in the physical apprehension of a notorious leaf trafficker and, if they were really providential, hand-to-hand combat.

Investigator Strait eyed the expectant law enforcement deputies and then made his decision. 'Deputies D'Angelis and Gilbrae, you're selected.' The other members of the team grumbled with disappointment and, muttering under their breath, sat back down.

With the voice of command, Investigator Strait continued, 'Right then, D'Angelis and Gilbrae remember to keep your distance. This is covert undercover surveillance; I don't want the suspect spooked. We've waited half a solar cycle for this break.'

As Deputies D'Angelis and Gilbrae made for the door, Investigator Strait shook his head and added, 'Before you embark on your *covert undercover* surveillance activities may I suggest you take off the combat fatigues and body armour. Oh, and don't forget to leave your assault blasters behind. I think you'll find you'll blend in with the crowd more easily without them.' The other members of Operation Kicking Butt sniggered.

* * * * *

The queue crept forward and, in the ever-present rain, Johnson had become soaked. The epaulettes on his full-dress uniform had begun to droop and what had been pure white was looking decidedly patchy. Johnson took another step forward, but if anything the queue seemed even longer.

Whilst the nature of Pacifica's precipitation varied from intermittent drizzle to tropical downpour, what never varied was that it fell. Johnson often wondered why anyone bothered to employ weather forecasters on Pacifica. If you said it was going to rain you pretty much had a ninety-nine percent chance of being right. Though, given this meteorological certainty, what was surprising was why he invariably forgot to take any waterproof attire with him when he went out.

To try and keep warm Johnson put his hands in his attire, only to find something there: a package. He took it out and looked at it. The package was neatly wrapped but unnamed – clearly a gift or a present of some kind. Johnson put it back. He would return it with the uniform.

The queue took another step forward.

Behind and bored, Billy Bob decided to introduce himself to the female next to him in the queue. After all, it was the neighbourly thing to do.

'Hi y'all, I'm mighty pleased to meet ya',' said Billy Bob with an outstretched arm. 'Back where I come from they call me Billy Bob. What they'd call y'all, mam?'

The female stared at him blankly. Pacifica's inhabitants did not indulge in small talk, they were far too busy for that – or at least far too busy thinking about being busy.

'Mighty fine town y'all got yourselves here,' continued Billy Bob ignoring the stare. 'Ain't got nothin' like this back on Old MacDonald's World. That's where I was born 'n raised ya' know. Born 'n raised by my Ma 'n Pa, though I guess I was brung up by Philippa Sue; she's my oldest sister. I got me eleven brothers 'n sisters in all. There's Bart Bob, he's the eldest 'n helps Pa out on the farmstead with the almaakian cattle 'n all, 'n then there's Philippa Sue, she mostly helps Ma with the young un's now. There's Jimmy Bob, he tends the fields, 'n Drue Ann, she does the buyin' 'n sellin'. Then there's me. Judy Ann, Bella Sue 'n Johnny Bob, they're still in school, but they'll be leavin' soon as they're sixteen – cain't have too much help on the farmstead ya' know. The triplets, Hew Bob 'n Jamie Bob 'n Tom Bob, ain't but kids, 'n Ma's just had John Peter. He's the cutest baby ya' ever did see, with big sunflower-yellow eyes 'n barely a hair on his head. I got me some images, if y'd like to see 'em.' And Billy

Bob reached inside his attire.

At this point two taxi-skyriders landed. Billy Bob turned round, only to see the first taxi-skyrider take off and Johnson gone. 'Darn 'n damnation!' muttered Billy Bob and, remembering his manners, he turned to the female next to him and said, 'apologies for my cussin', mam, but I gotta' go.' Billy Bob then leapt into the second.

Across the way, Deputies D'Angelis and Gilbrae watched from their unmarked law enforcement skyrider. When the suspect got into the first taxi-skyrider they made to follow, but as quickly as they accelerated, they found their way blocked by the second taxi-skyrider coming to an abrupt halt. Deputy D'Angelis flashed his lights and shouted, but it showed no sign of moving.

'I'll be, we're blocked in,' said Deputy D'Angelis. 'Gilbrae you'd better go see what the hold up is.'

Deputy Gilbrae grunted and got out of their skyrider. As he approached the second taxi-skyrider, he could see its fare pounding on the interior partition. He manually released the door to hear the occupant shouting, 'What d' y'all mean, it ain't no destination? Ya' useless heap 'a no good scrap metal!'

Deputy Gilbrae decided to take control of the situation and pulled out his standard issue hand-zapper. 'You, out.' Deputy Gilbrae was a male of few words.

Billy Bob looked up to see the focussing lens of the hand-zapper. He knew a zapper when he saw one and quickly stopped pounding on the interior partition.

Deputy Gilbrae commanded the Happy-Cabby taxibot, at the controls of the taxi-skyrider, to pull over and, rather than create a scene, hurriedly marshalled Billy Bob into the back of his unmarked skyrider.

Deputy D'Angelis twisted the accelerator and sped off in the direction taken by the first taxi-skyrider. 'We're after him! I think he turned, up ahead, at the intersection of Armstrong and Main.'

Billy Bob remained quiet.

They weaved erratically through the commuting skyriders and then suddenly turned against the traffic control at the intersection. Billy Bob, who had his eyes firmly closed, was thrown across the seat.

'There he is, down there.' Deputy D'Angelis looked and dived down to pull in, a few skyriders behind their suspect.

To add to the commotion the rain became heavier and drummed hard on the roof. The ground traffic had come to a halt. Ahead, impatient drivers began flashing lights and shouting: patience was in short supply on Pacifica. Deputy Gilbrae leaned out of his window to see what the problem was.

Billy Bob, who was still lying across the back of the seat, opened one of his eyes and saw the door release. He reached for it and, to his surprise, found that the door was not locked. He slowly eased the release and quietly slid across the back seat. Outside he pushed the door to and, half-crouching, made his way through the stationary traffic to the walkway, where he disappeared into the crowd.

Johnson had also got out of his taxi-skyrider, just after it had turned onto Main. He'd decided it would be quicker to walk. As his taxi-skyrider pulled away, he'd noticed a skyrider turn against the traffic control, dive down to ground level and jostle through the traffic, though it too soon came to a halt. Strangely one of its occupants seemed to fall out of the back and half-crawl to the walkway.

The rain was falling harder and Johnson, fed up with getting wet, stepped into Stackit & Sellit, 'The store you can set your store by', to buy some waterproof attire. A short time later he emerged, sporting the latest in waterproof fashion; a military-style poncho conceived and merchandised by Pacifica's very own Honcho Poncho Corporation. The retail associate positively swooned when Johnson had put it on, 'Oh, it's so you, sir', he had said. Johnson had his reservations, not least because the poncho made him look like a small planetoid, but decided that it would serve its purpose and, unlike the jump associate's full-dress uniform, would keep him dry.

'We're in pursuit of the suspect, in traffic, five skyriders behind. Traffic not moving. Shall we storm the taxi-skyrider, Investigator?' requested Deputy D'Angelis through his skyrider's hololink.

'No. We need to let the suspect lead us to the rest of the lawbreakers.' Investigator Strait sensed the taste for action on the part of his team. 'Stay in your skyrider and that's an order, and don't let that taxi out of your sight.'

'OK Investigator.' Deputy D'Angelis turned to Deputy Gilbrae, who was leaning out of the window exchanging points of view with the rest of the stationary traffic by using his own *personally adapted* sign language. 'We have to stay in the skyrider and follow. No storming the taxi.'

Deputy Gilbrae slouched back in his seat. He hadn't joined the Tactical Response Assault Patrol to play escort to a leaf trafficker. Bored, he decided to interrogate their passenger. He turned, only to find the back seat empty and their passenger gone. He nudged Deputy D'Angelis, who also turned around and looked.

The deputies then looked at each other.

'I'll be, our passenger's escaped! The Investigator's not going to like this,' exclaimed Deputy D'Angelis. Then Deputy D'Angelis thought for a pulsar's pulse. 'What the Investigator doesn't know ain't gonna' hurt him. Anyway, I don't think that particular citizen knew anything. From his attire he just looked like some offworld scratcher who happened to be next in the queue.'

Deputy Gilbrae nodded.

The rain continued to pound and the traffic crawled forward. Deputy D'Angelis held station behind the suspect's taxi-skyrider, as it turned left onto Aldine and then left again back towards the U-Tan-U Spaceport.

'Our suspect's circling round. You know what? I think he's checking for a tail. Do you think he's spotted us?' asked Deputy D'Angelis.

Deputy Gilbrae shook his head.

'Then why's he going back to the U-Tan-U Spaceport?' continued Deputy D'Angelis.

Deputy Gilbrae, who treated all questions as rhetorical unless pressed, said nothing.

When the taxi-skyrider eventually arrived at the spaceport, an old male burdened with too much luggage got out.

'That's not our suspect,' observed Deputy D'Angelis.

His colleague looked across and shrugged.

*   *   *   *   *

'And it was then we realised he'd given us the slip,' D'Angelis concluded.

Deputies D'Angelis and Gilbrae were stood in front of Investigator Strait's workhub. Investigator Strait slowly switched his gaze between the two, but said nothing. Deputy Gilbrae stood perfectly still; Deputy D'Angelis started to shuffle from side to side feeling increasingly uncomfortable. The Investigator was not known for his sympathetic reaction to the bearers of bad news.

'Right then, I'm going to make this simple for you,' said Investigator Strait with the calmness of the eye of a solar storm. 'I don't want to see or hear from either of you again until you've found the suspect. If that takes the rest of your miserable careers so be it. Do you understand?'

Deputies D'Angelis and Gilbrae nodded.

'And you're waiting for?' added Investigator Strait.

Deputies D'Angelis and Gilbrae hastily left Operation Kicking Butt's incident-room accompanied by the silence of their fellow colleagues, who looked on only too relieved that they hadn't been standing before Investigator Strait.

*   *   *   *   *

Across the metropolis, Johnson was tired and hungry. However, thankfully, he was not wet, due to the waterproof qualities of his newly acquired poncho. And so, at last, he stepped into his one room co-op on the six hundred and sixty-fifth level of the Sun Rise Cooperative Skybreaker. Johnson found the name 'Sun Rise' somewhat ironic as no one in his skybreaker had ever seen the sunrise, for the skybreaker was overshadowed on all sides by a forest of much taller skybreakers.

One use of his Jet-Wet shower and a nutritionally balanced meal, or so it had said on the Ever Fresh Never Left packet, and he was sat watching a local newscast. Pacifica's law enforcement agency was requesting information. The Investigator in charge described how a male dressed in a jump associate's uniform was wanted for questioning after evading the authorities at the U-Tan-U Spaceport. The suspect was described as 'potentially dangerous' and under no circumstances should be approached by members of the electorate.

Johnson, disinterested, turned the holoplay off with a flick of his hand. He needed sleep.

[4] Bumping Into A New Friend

Rodger, the jump associate, tried to describe the pressure he'd been under: the out of order toilets, the angry passengers, the unhelpful jump engineer; but Mr Edger seemed less than understanding.

'So let me comprehend the incomprehensible. You gave him your uniform, with my package in it, and the last you saw of him was when he exited the starliner for the transit shuttle,' summarised Mr Edger.

'Everything seemed to go wrong, I just wasn't thinking: first the toilets had malfunctioned and then I shrank the male's attire. So lending my spare uniform to the poor male, who, by the way, had just saved me from lavatorial purgatory, seemed the right thing to do. It was only when my shift ended and I went to get changed that I remembered where I'd put the package,' explained Rodger, as best as he could.

Rodger sat back in his chair in the Algolian Starlite Lounge, the beverage emporium where Mr Edger had arranged to meet. Frankly it was a little sub-standard. Where had they found their interior designers? It was all too much. The designers had tried to mimic the ambience of a period Algolian solar-viewing gallery: high-backed faux-plastic chairs, simulated flashing-control-panels and a holographically emulated starscape. And as for the arbitrary sounding of an ear-splitting radiation alarm – with its associated drink-spilling vibration – this was clearly a touch too far. He was in no doubt; he could have done a much better job.

'You wouldn't happen to know who the male was, would you?' asked Mr Edger, just managing to control his exasperation with Rodger's incompetence.

'Now, I thought you might ask,' replied Rodger.

'And?' pressed Mr Edger, lifting his drink to his mouth.

'It just so happens that he gave me his business holocard.' Rodger reached inside his attire and handed the holocard to Mr Edger.

Mr Edger projected the holocard to himself, 'Johnson, customer-relationship and promotions specialist, Flush Away Corporation,' and almost choked.

* * * * *

Billy Bob was trying to work out where he was, as he wandered the walkways of Pacifica. Cousin Jez had provided him with an old map of the metropolis, which he said had been his mother's, and had neatly marked the location of the Flush Away Corporation's headquarters with a big red cross. Cousin Jez had said that using a traditional map to navigate by, rather than Billy Bob's own holocom, would not leave a digital trail –

whatever a digital trail was.

Billy Bob had been told that Johnson would go to work at the Flush Away Corporation's headquarters each sunrise, and so, next sunrise, he planned to be there too.

The metropolis sure was big. How could so many folks live stacked up on top of one another like mu chickens in a coop? Billy Bob held up his map and tried to get his bearings, but the skybreakers, the skyways and the walkways all looked the same; thronging with traffic and folks.

Uncertain and lost, he'd barely taken a step when he inadvertently tripped and found himself sprawled-out on top of a male in a wheelchair. Billy Bob quickly got back to his feet; the male smelt worse than a greater-toed swamp boar on heat.

'Beg pardon, sir.' Billy Bob had been brought up to be polite to strangers.

The male pointed towards the handwritten sign he'd been holding. Billy Bob leant across and picked it up. It read: 'War Vet • No Voice • No Legs'.

Sensing a charitable opportunity, the male held out his hand.

Billy Bob pressed the hand.

'Pleased to meet y'all. The name's Billy Bob. I guess you cain't tell me yours, but y'all seem mighty friendly to me. Most folks round here seem a might too busy to be neighbourly and pass the time of rotation – sure is a strange place.'

The male, a little taken aback at Billy Bob's interest in engaging in conversation, rattled a decapitated drink carton.

Billy Bob peered into the drink carton. 'Glad to see y'all got some credits there.'

The male pushed the decapitated drink carton towards Billy Bob and rattled it harder.

Billy Bob smiled. 'I'd be thankin' y'all kindly, but I got me some credits.'

Billy Bob then retrieved his map and stared at it. He rotated the map and stared at it some more. 'Sir, y'all wouldn't happen to know where we are?'

The male in the wheelchair shook his head and took the map. He turned it the right way round and pointed to their location.

'Being a vet 'n all I bet ya' learnt yourself map readin' in the Space Corps when ya' was lookin' after all them there animals. I wish I had me ya' kinda' education, then I'd really be able to help Pa on the farmstead. For now, I gotta' get me to this here red cross. Which way do y'all reckon I should go?' Billy Bob thrust the map back in front of the male's face. From behind it an outstretched arm appeared and pointed.

'Sure has bin' a pleasure passin' the time 'a rotation, but I gotta' go,

I got me a mission to complete. Take care y'all.' Billy Bob waved as he walked off. The male looked on and shook his head.

It was only when Billy Bob had disappeared from sight that Star Trooper Jonah Jones muttered something to himself about 'the ability to talk being no indication of intelligent life in this universe'.

With clear direction Billy Bob marched on, bumping and jostling his way through unsuspecting commuters as they returned from a shift at the workplace. Singularly focussed on the map, he held at arm's length, he strode forth. He passed over overpasses, walked along walkways and got conveyed by conveyers. Billy Bob was oblivious to all the folks around him. Without regard for his own personal safety he stepped out into traffic. He was oblivious to the scream of drives being thrust into reverse, the shouts, or the flashing of lights, as the traffic dived every which way to avoid him. All he could see was that red cross. He'd counted the grids on the map and was counting them down aloud as he traversed each intersection. Ten grids to go!

He was not to be distracted and, even as darkness fell and rain washed down the map, his count continued. He had reached 'eight' when he noticed that the red cross had started to run, and by 'five' it looked more like a stain.

'One!' he shouted as he came to the last grid and stopped. At last he'd arrived at his destination. Unfortunately the map was soaked through and had started to tear under its own weight. The red cross had simply vanished in a smudge.

He looked around. These skybreakers were spaced farther apart than the ones were when he'd started his journey, and they'd grown in height. When he looked up he saw that they just disappeared into the clouds. He stood and admired these up-lit towering edifices of mirrored plastiglass. And if he looked at a certain angle he could see a multitude of Billy Bob Browns reflected back and forth, a whole host of Billy Bob Browns. He was not alone!

About him, instead of the stacked layers of overpasses and underpasses, there were just ground-level walkways. And, instead of the barrier-to-barrier thronging mass of folks, there were small courtyards, neatly kept, with spurting fountains and naked statues that left little to the imagination. There was nothing like this on Old MacDonald's World – though he did wonder where folks grew their crops and kept their animals.

Returning to his limp, sodden map it was clearly of no further use in finding Flush Away's headquarters. He would have asked someone for directions, but there was no one to be seen, only the odd taxi-skyrider circled by high above, passing among the skybreakers. The rain had slowed to a drizzle. He thought he could smell newly cut grass. It reminded him of Old MacDonald's World and he decided to follow his nose.

It was some vegetation! At last, an open space, though overshadowed by the giant towering skybreakers it was an open space none the less. He found a bench and sat down.

Billy Bob didn't regret volunteering for this mission, and he didn't doubt that he could complete it; Billy Bob didn't have the capacity for self-doubt. He just felt a little out of his depth. Urban folk and their ways made no sense. They always seemed busy doing something, but what? He hadn't seen any crops or livestock.

He decided to put such thoughts aside and, with steadfast resolve, he stood up and went in search of the lair of his quarry. Johnson and that corporation he worked for wouldn't know what had happened to them by the time he'd finished with them! No matter what, he told himself, he'd complete his mission; he wasn't about to let Cousin Jez down.

*   *   *   *   *

Being sat in a wheelchair, that little bit closer to the ground, could often be an unpleasant experience for Star Trooper Jonah Jones, particularly if someone chose to break wind as they passed. But it wasn't the smell, Star Trooper Jonah Jones had smelt much worse than that, it was the memory the smell evoked.

Just one sniff and it would all come back to him in a flash.

He remembered the fighting had been vicious, intense and hand-to-hand. Unhelpfully their commander had explained that blasters could not be used, as they hovered above the atmosphere of Pongo Pongo: sulphides, methane and other gaseous hydrocarbons, together with a high oxygen content, made for a somewhat volatile combination. Stripped of their main weaponry, and all other potential sources of ignition, Jones and his fellow star troopers had to glide down through the bilious green clouds armed with hastily crafted clubs and pointed sticks. Barely able to see his hand in front of his face, he remembered trying to take his first uncertain steps on that planet's spongy surface. His every footfall pressed deep into the ground, releasing a small puff of noxious green gas with a loud flatulent sound that only served to alert the enemy to his position.

And then they were on him.

Oh, the horror...

The memory passed.

Drizzle turned to heavy rain and, even though he'd tried vigorously to extol the benefits of handing credits over, his 'patrons', as he termed anyone willing to give him credits for nothing, had long since pulled up their hoods and quickened their pace.

Star Trooper Jonah Jones picked up his half-empty, decapitated drink carton and started on the long push back to his makeshift shelter.

31

He had once owned a pair of artificial limbs, which the Space Corps had given him as part of his severance pay – after they'd accidentally amputated his legs. But somewhere down the line he'd lost them gambling, or was it when he'd been drinking? Anyway, what did it matter? He found that whilst his simple, if somewhat dilapidated, wheelchair was a pain to push; it proved to be an invaluable prop in extracting credits from Pacifica's inhabitants.

A few grids on and he rolled into One For The Skyway, a self-service beverage emporium with a timeless country and western theme that was said to date back to the era of Ancient Earth – if some scattered simulated sawdust, a pair of battered artificial saloon doors and an endless loop of traditional country and western tunes could be called a theme.

Jones inserted his rotation's takings into one of the many garishly coloured Stiff One drinks dispense machines, which, in return, ejected a couple of cartons of Drinkers' Delight. This particular drink was a heady mix of genetically tailored industrial alcohol and artificial flavouring substitutes. According to the fabricators, Scoff Enterprises, it was guaranteed 'To give the high, but at a low low price'. Jones thought that even the promotional line was cheap, but as long as it did the job what did he care?

As he rolled on he was always amazed how the tide of commuters would part in front of him without anyone actually seeing him. When he actively tried to collide with them, to create a charitable opportunity, they seemed to just neatly sidestep and continue on their journey as if nothing had happened.

He had tried flailing his arms, as if he was about to fall over, but this also failed to net him any commuters, although he did manage to collect the odd dropped waterproof.

He had tried the more subtle approach of simply running over their feet, targeting particular footwear in the belief that there would be a correlation between footwear expense and size of donation received. Interestingly, after several lunar cycles of trial and error, he found that the more up-market the footwear the smaller the donation proved to be. And targeting open-toed footwear, particularly those worn by females, tended to result in verbal abuse and the occasional retaliatory swipe rather than an actual donation.

'These urban types might think it's tough in their corporate career scramble,' Jones mumbled to himself bitterly, 'but they should try living off the slim pickings of charitable donations.'

He pushed on, frequently stopping to drown the rotation in another swig of Drinkers' Delight. Whilst he'd just about survived over the last few lunar cycles on Pacifica, it hadn't exactly delivered the lifestyle he'd expected when he'd first arrived here. It was time to move on and seek more fertile ground. The question was: where to go next?

*   *   *   *   *

By rotation's end Billy Bob's search for Johnson had resulted in nothing save wet feet and an urge to settle down until light. Unexpectedly he'd stumbled upon a strange-looking shelter hidden among some trees in the single open space he'd found. The frame was constructed from branches bent and tied together, like the hull of an upturned boat, and the whole thing was covered in waterproof attire.

After collecting some wood, he built himself a fire under the trees, pulled out some provisions from his backpack and sat down to eat. He could hear the fountains and the odd passing skyrider, but totality in totality it was mostly peaceful. The loudest sound was the fire, crackling and spitting in the rain.

It was when his thoughts started to turn to sleep that he heard an odd squeaking sound. The sound grew louder and louder until, through the trees, came the male in the wheelchair.

Billy Bob greeted Star Trooper Jonah Jones like a long-lost friend. Jones just glared; this was where he lived, he'd built it from the kind donations of his patrons.

'Pull yourself round the fire 'n share some 'a these here organic eta beans.' Billy Bob held out his pan and eating utensil. 'Sure is a surprise seein' y'all, how'd ya' find me?' Then Billy Bob thought for a pulsar's pulse. 'Course y'all ain't got no voice. Y'all have to forgive me for not thinkin'.'

Billy Bob decided to answer his own question. 'Guess it must be all that Space Corps trainin' needed to track them there animals. I tell ya', I got me a procyon hound dog back on Old MacDonald's World who couldn't find his own tail compared to y'all.'

Jones rolled his eyes, the thought of having to spend time listening to the mindless chatter of this offworld scratcher was about all he could take. He pushed past Billy Bob and rolled into his shelter, pulling the entrance flap – a rather elegant female's chromium-green waterproof – down behind him. He unfurled his ex-Space Corps Sleep Forever sleeping cocoon that, in the true spirit of military practicality, had the additional benefit of being able to double as a body bag – should circumstances require. But as Star Trooper Jonah Jones sought sleep, the shelter's entrance flap slowly parted.

'Mind ya' Simple, that's what I call that flea bitten mutt 'a mine, is always able to track down one 'a Ma's groundnut pies. I reckon he's got himself one 'a them there six senses when it comes to food. Ma, she makes the best groundnut pie this side 'a Old MacDonald's Town, or any side for that matter. It makes me drool just thinkin' about it.' Billy Bob paused for a pulsar's pulse. 'Did I tell y'all about the family farmstead back on Old MacDonald's World?' Another pause. 'I sure am missin' that farmstead. I was born 'n raised there by my Ma 'n my Pa. We got us some almaakian cattle 'n altairian sheep 'n pollux pigs 'n there's mu chickens 'n a couple 'a capricornus goats. We grows us plenty 'a crops too, mostly eta beans, but we got us some canopian corn 'n scheat wheat.'

Billy Bob reached inside his attire and unfolded an image. 'This here's the family: John Peter, he's but a baby, 'n there's Hew Bob 'n Jamie Bob 'n Tom Bob, the triplets. Next to them is Bella Sue 'n Johnny Bob 'n Judy Ann, all dressed in their finest, standin' in front of Drue Ann. That's me with Jimmy Bob 'n Philippa Sue, 'n Bart Bob is beside Ma 'n Pa.'

It was at this point that Jones decided Billy Bob's monologue was never going to end unless he did something about it, and, in a firm but restrained voice, he asked, 'By the stars, don't you ever shut up?'

Billy Bob's mouth hung open mid-word, frozen with surprise.

'Ba, ba-ba, ba-ba-but y'alls sign said ya' couldn't speak, I read it 'n that's what it said,' exclaimed Billy Bob in a single breath.

'You shouldn't believe all that you read. Now go away and let me sleep!' Jones concluded the conversation by closing his eyes and rolling over.

After a little hesitation, and in some confusion, Billy Bob withdrew from the shelter. It was only when he'd lain out under the trees by the fire that he began to wonder whether the male was a vet after all.

[5] And On The Second Rotation

A new rotation came to pass over Pacifica, and from the confines of his sleep-cot Johnson looked out of his co-op window. It was a view that never changed: for his was a view of the skybreaker across the way, and that skybreaker was, in turn, overshadowed by the next. In fact all Johnson could see was skybreaker upon skybreaker upon skybreaker, all greyed by rain.

However, on this particular rotation, had he been able to see beyond the skybreakers, he would have seen a rare and glorious sight emerge from across the horizon: a rainbow of colour filling Pacifica's cold grey sky and reflecting down over the ocean as Pacifica's bright blue sun rose, for once unobscured by cloud.

As Johnson lay he thought, with surprising optimism, that at least it was a new rotation. Then he remembered it was a workshift, and on a workshift he had to go to work. And then he remembered that, on this rotation, not only did he have to go to work, but he also had to report on the outcome of his business trip to Old MacDonald's World. His newly found optimism faded.

Johnson got up and began his routine.

The ritual use of his Palomine irradiating sanitation unit, with its Tell-It-To-Me technology – fabricated by Flush Away, of course – brought the same disappointing news. It recommended strenuous exercise, a new target weight and, recognising Johnson's drinking excesses, deleted all alcohol from his grocery call-off.

Johnson sighed. It was another working rotation. Using his holocom he selected his business attire from his wardrobe and got dressed. He chose plain grey, conformist, though with just a hint of individuality marked by a flash of colour on his lapel. And then he saw the white full-dress uniform draped over the back of the chair.

He remembered last rotation's events. Again he sighed. Well, he had no time to waste worrying over things he could not change. He put the full-dress uniform into a bag; he'd drop it back at the U-Tan-U Spaceport after work.

And, as with every rotation, he looked at the time, decided he was late and grabbed a carton of Go-All-Rotation – a stimulant-enhanced nutritional supplement drink. Johnson particularly liked this drink. Ironically, the Go-All-Rotation drink largely consisted of the by-products produced from the fabrication of the rather more alcoholic Drinkers Delight product, a fact that was much to the delight and profitability of Scoff Enterprises.

As his co-op door slid shut behind him, Johnson wondered whether he'd forgotten anything. He shrugged and walked on to wait in the lobby for the express skyvator where he, and his fellow commuters, would each look at the time, hoping to speed the skyvator's arrival.

And, as with every rotation, the express skyvator took an eternity to descend. It was quite a feat to share a small space with twenty others and not to catch anyone else's eye, but somehow he and the rest of his fellow commuters had perfected this to an art form.

And, as with every rotation, everyone was too busy to speak.

On the walkway below he joined the throngs of commuters, but then he stopped. He looked up and wondered where the rain had gone. Was it just waiting to catch him out? This time Johnson had remembered to bring waterproof attire, and not just any waterproof attire; this time he had his new military-style poncho draped over his arm.

*   *   *   *   *

For once Star Trooper Jonah Jones awoke with his particles fully charged. He'd decided that this rotation was going to be a rotation for change; time to move on to where the stars shine more brightly. But as he pulled open the entrance flap to his shelter, he saw Billy Bob sat with his back to him, attending to last sunfall's rekindled fire.

Jones decided to make a break for it, and he almost made it.

'Mighty fine mornin'. Y'all should 'a seen this here sky change with the sunrise; sure was a beautiful thing with all them colours 'n all,' said Billy Bob without turning round.

Jones cursed his squeaking wheelchair.

'Made us some food.' Billy Bob held out a plate of refried organic eta beans.

Jones let his hunger overcome his better judgement and wheeled forward to accept the plate. Unexpectedly, the organic eta beans were good and Billy Bob gladly put more onto the plate. It was an improvement over Jones's usual sunrise ritual of draining any last drops of Drinkers' Delight he could find in the previous rotation's discarded cartons.

After he'd finished eating, Jones began to notice that Billy Bob was starting to act a little strangely – that is even more strangely than he'd observed so far.

Billy Bob was scurrying around, looking behind trees, under bushes and through the undergrowth. Then, when Billy Bob appeared to be satisfied that everything was as it should be, he turned to Jones, leant forward and in a quietened voice said, 'I got me a proposition for y'all.'

Jones was now a little concerned.

After a further furtive glance to either side, Billy Bob continued, 'How'd y'all like to be part 'a my mission?'

Jones felt a certain amount of relief that Billy Bob's 'proposition' was in the realms of the simply idiotic. Clearly Billy Bob was a few altairian sheep short of a flock.

'And what mission would that be?' asked Jones politely, deciding to play along.

'I cain't tell y'all everythin' 'coz it's a secret mission, but I sense y'all's the kinda' fella' who's used to goin' on a mission without askin' questions, bein' military 'n all,' clarified Billy Bob.

Jones continued to feign interest: it wasn't as if he had anything better to do, and he asked, 'A secret mission?'

Billy Bob drew even closer and whispered, 'Yep, top secret. I've bin' sworn not to tell no one by Cousin Jez.'

'Cousin Jez?' Jones enquired tentatively, though in the back of his mind he knew he'd regret knowing the answer.

'Cousin Jez, he's our leader. He's the only son 'a Aunt Mary, who's my Ma's younger sister. She's real bright, reads lots 'a books 'n talks funny. When she was young she went offworld to do some more schoolin', but she got herself pregnant 'n had Cousin Jez. Caused quite a scandal they say. Ma says we ain't to talk about it, on account 'a Jez only havin' one parent 'n all – if you know what I mean. Anyways, Cousin Jez is real bright too, but he didn't want to get no offworld schoolin', due to something called,' and Billy Bob closed his eyes and devoted his whole body to recalling Cousin Jez's words, '"Inherent corporate indoctrination" or the like. Cain't say I rightly understand, but Cousin Jez sure seems sure enough.'

Jones tried to digest what Billy Bob had said, but was still in the firmament as to Billy Bob's 'mission'. It was going to be a long, long rotation. 'Forgive me for not entirely following what you are saying, but your Cousin, Jez, your leader, has sent you on a mission and you want me to help you, but the mission is top secret so you can't tell me what you want me to do?'

'Yep,' confirmed Billy Bob, using surprisingly few words.

'No,' replied Jones, in answer to Billy Bob's request.

'No?' asked Billy Bob.

'Yep, no!' concluded Jones.

There was silence. Time passed and then, much to Jones's amusement, Billy Bob had some kind of heated debate with himself. Eventually the debate ended, and Jones wondered who, if anyone, had won.

'If I tell y'all about the mission y'all's gotta' swear, on ya' mama's life, not to tell no one, not under torture, nor interrogation, nor after too many of them there drinks,' said an agitated Billy Bob, pointing to a pile of empty Drinkers' Delight cartons.

'OK, I promise,' replied Jones.

'On ya' mama's life?' pressed Billy Bob.

'On my mama's life,' repeated Jones, whose mama had long since died.

'Cousin Jez says we're,' Billy Bob drew a deep breath and, without moving, recanted, '"Ideologically dedicated to organic principles and the overthrow of corporate universisation. Our mission is to spread the organic word and bring about the collapse of the unorganic corporations that infest the universe with their attempts to enslave the very masses they are meant to serve in themedom."'

Jones was open-mouthed. He would never have believed that Billy Bob could recite a sentence with so many long words in it, even if the sentence was completely nonsensical.

Billy Bob leant even closer and showed Jones the image of Johnson he had been given by Cousin Jez. 'This is my target.'

*   *   *   *   *

One consequence of drinking Go-All-Rotation nutritional supplement drink was the need to, as it were, 'go'. And thus Johnson, on arrival at Flush Away's headquarters, had to hastily use the visitors' convenience.

Inside, the irradiating sanitation unit, a rather tired and now obsolete Vesuvius model – with its Suck-It-From-Me technology, left the user in no doubt that any deposit left had been vaporised, by making a disconcerting, ground-shuddering noise when operated.

For Johnson this toilet, whilst being a place of obvious relief, was a place of solitude, a place of contemplation, a place where he could sequence his thoughts before facing the workshift. Others may have exercised, or meditated, perhaps taken some artificial stimulant or other, but for Johnson it was the emptying of his bladder, followed by a bowel movement, that satisfied. And after the all-fulfilling wipe using the corporate-embossed toilet Paperette – the ever-versatile paper substitute – he smiled a smile made in the knowledge that each sheet was printed with the corporation's name. For Johnson it really was 'Smile and Flush Away'.

Calmed and relieved, Johnson stepped into the workplace, with his new military-style poncho over his arm.

Chad Edger was waiting for him.

Chad just happened to be standing by reception, passing the time of rotation with the ever-delightful Miranda; Flush Away's long-suffering greetings associate. With a sparkle in his eye, he was telling her his tall tales, which he mostly told to inform others how wonderful he thought he was – though most wished he would go away and tell them to someone else. That was certainly the thought running through the ever-competent Miranda's mind. She greeted Johnson. She hoped his arrival would distract Chad enough so she could get on with doing something more interesting

– like work!

Chad's tall frame turned to face Johnson. Above a well-polished smile, and his evasive eyes, Chad's head gleamed. 'Hey Johnson! Like the attire, great stuff! Discount rotation at the ex-Space Corps surplus store?' And like a predatory denebian wildcat toying with its prey, the self-amused Chad threw his arm around Johnson, as he went to walk the long walk through their open plan workplace.

'Hello Chad,' replied Johnson without enthusiasm.

'Successful trip?' enquired Chad and his all-pervasive smile.

'Um, er, excellent. Thank you. The lead worked out, er, well. I've, um, achieved... positive primary market sector penetration on Old MacDonald's World,' replied Johnson, recovering from his initial hesitation to complete the sentence in a flurry of sales doublespeak.

'Great stuff, Johnson, knew you could do it!' Chad gave Johnson a firm slap on the back, almost winding him, and then loudly announced to the rest of the workplace, 'Hey, listen up team, Johnson's got penetration on Old MacDonald's World!'

The customer-relationships and promotions team rose, one-by-one, clapping. Johnson felt himself blush with embarrassment to the applause and congratulations.

'Hey, let's have an image to display of our soon-to-be employee-of-the-lunar-cycle,' urged Chad.

In a flash, before Johnson could say anything, one of his colleagues obliged, and an image of Johnson, with his military-style poncho, adorned the workplace.

'So, Johnson, don't keep us all in suspense, how many units?' Chad was going in for the kill.

'Um, er, ten,' spluttered Johnson and, hoping that no-one would hear, mumbled, 'on approval.'

'Ten thousand?' asked Chad.

Johnson looked at his feet.

'Ten hundred?' suggested Chad.

Johnson counted his feet.

'Ten?' queried Chad.

Johnson continued to count his feet.

'Ten!' concluded Chad and beamed, loudly.

The congratulations of the customer-relationships and promotions team stuttered to silence and, as they had risen, one-by-one they returned to their work.

Everyone, who was anyone in the sanitation business, knew that ten thousand units would have been an excellent result; a thousand units would have been a good sale; a hundred units was not worth the transaction time; but ten units, well, that was a humiliation.

Chad Edger shook his head, clearly failing to empathise.

'Johnson, when you tell her she's gonna' go supernova. Hey, look if there's anything I can do to help, you know, you just have to say – after all that's what teamwork's all about.'

Johnson was now certain that this rotation wasn't going to be a good rotation; Ms D'Baliere had emerged from her workspace, and reading a bundle of reports had asked, 'Who's going to go supernova?'

Chad casually ducked away, and sauntered off back to his workhub, leaving Johnson standing alone.

'Ah, Johnson, Old MacDonald's World report, my workspace, now,' instructed Ms D'Baliere.

[6] To The Bottom Of The Earth

Star Trooper Jonah Jones propelled his squeaking wheelchair with long, deliberate strokes. Billy Bob ambled alongside talking about his family, which was proving to be an apparently inexhaustible source of conversation, much to Jones's irritation.

Jones had decided to go with Billy Bob to Flush Away's corporate headquarters, and whilst he had not agreed to be part of Billy Bob's mission, he was interested to see how things might turn out. The headquarters were only a grid away. What else did he have to do?

The walkways were filling with look-a-like commuters, dressed in smart business attire. Star Trooper Jonah Jones and Billy Bob merged as unobtrusively as they could with the ebb and flow and, in a photon's phase, they stood – that is one stood and one sat – in front of the hub of Flush Away's corporate enterprise.

Steps rose up to a Marblesque colonnade. Out of this sprouted a skybreaker that tried to imitate a grand imperial building from Ancient Earth, a building that was of Roman tribal origin. Flush Away's corporate image-makers majored heavily on Roman tribal imagery. They felt any association with the tribe's undoubted sanitary and water-distribution achievements was too good an opportunity to miss. But miss it they did.

To a casual observer, the skybreaker looked like some sort of over-decorated themed resort complex. To the employees, it only served to remind them of the slavery of their corporate existence, the unrelenting gladiatorial combat of interdepartmental strife and, perhaps most of all, being thrown to the lions when it all went tragically wrong.

'Wow-wee,' commented Billy Bob. 'Sure is a mighty fine lookin' buildin'. Ain't got nothin' like it on Old MacDonald's World. What with them there columns 'n all this Flush Away Corporation must be one mighty powerful organisation.'

Jones couldn't help but feel that Billy Bob, the would-be fundamentalist revolutionary, didn't quite match up to his intended vocation.

'So, what are you going to do now then, Billy Bob?' asked Jones. Billy Bob was clearly distracted.

'Y'all wouldn't mind takin' an image, so I can show the folks back at the farmstead?' Billy Bob rustled his holocom from his backpack and handed it to Jones. 'Make sure ya' get all 'a this here skybreaker in.'

It wasn't quite the start to the mission that Jones had expected, but there again he hadn't been part of a plot to overthrow corporate universisation before. Billy Bob duly posed on the steps, as Jones asked him to smile.

'Why thank ya' kindly, sir.' Billy Bob put his holocom back in his backpack.

'And the next step on your mission is?' quizzed Jones.

'If y'all stay here 'n look after my backpack, I'm gonna' go inside, find me our target, 'n continue me this mission,' replied Billy Bob, with the naive determination of one who knows no better.

Shaking his head, Jones took the backpack. He then made his way over to a promising part of the walkway, took out his sign and began his rotation's work. He might just get some 'charitable donations' from some unsuspecting patrons. Perhaps this rotation wouldn't be a complete waste of time after all. As he turned to look back, he saw Billy Bob disappearing into the skybreaker, disappearing into corporate themedom.

* * * * *

Ms D'Baliere sat behind her workhub, engrossed in her bundle of reports. Johnson had entered quietly, perhaps too quietly for her to notice, and stood by the door. He was debating whether to make some sort of noise, to attract her attention, when her hand rose and pointed to a solitary chair in the middle of the room.

The chair was strategically positioned to be just far enough away from the workhub not to be able to draw up to it, and too far away from any other piece of furniture to be able to use that as a prop.

Johnson sat uncomfortably.

Ms D'Baliere continued to turn the pages of her reports. Johnson waited, trying to guess when she might stop. Just when she had finished one report, and it seemed she would talk to him, she started another.

Time passed and Johnson became uneasy.

Her hair was a perfect corporate cut, nothing out of place. Her business attire was as smart as the rotation it had been fabricated. Her face held that serious but pleasant business air that oozed professionalism. In short, she looked the model corporate employee.

'Good trip?' Ms D'Baliere asked, though she continued to turn pages.

'Excellent,' replied Johnson, remembering to keep his answer short and positive.

'Wonderful. Old MacDonald's World is a key market indicator,' said Ms D'Baliere. 'The demographic analysis predicts massive sector potential in agricultural communities. And, as such, we need to be first to market.'

'I can report that we've, er, achieved positive primary market sector penetration on Old MacDonald's World,' reported Johnson, unconvincingly.

Ms D'Baliere stopped leafing through the reports and her finger traced along a line on a particular page. 'I don't suppose you made an input error when you loaded the order for ten units on approval?'

'Um, no.' Johnson closed his eyes. Well, whilst his answer was negative, at least it was short, if a little, 'um', hesitant.

Ms D'Baliere appeared to contemplate his answer, for what seemed like an eternity to Johnson, and then continued. 'I've spoken to Chad. He believes that we've somewhat *under exploited* our initial market penetration and has agreed to stop off on Old MacDonald's World to see if he can help *you* speed the development of the deal.'

'Excellent.' Johnson opened his eyes and took a deep breath.

'And whilst he's sorting out Old MacDonald's World, I suggest that you cover the conclusion of a major deal he has been working on with the Creation Corporation on Nova Vega.' Ms D'Baliere let the news sink in. 'We need to learn to work as a team, and it would be good for you to get some major account cultivation experience.'

'Excellent,' repeated Johnson. Things were looking up!

'I must say I commend Chad for his teamwork. I'm sure a lesser team player would have protested and tried to prevent me from doing this, but Chad said he'd support you fully and that the more we work as a team, the better our results will be.' Ms D'Baliere looked Johnson in the eye. 'He'll brief you on the necessary.'

'Excellent, I'll get on it right away.' Johnson felt he'd worn the positivity out of 'excellent', though his short and positive answers seemed to have worked. He'd survived another rotation. However, in the back of his mind he began to worry that things were starting to go too well. It wasn't quite the outcome he'd expected from the meeting, and he did wonder why Chad was being so helpful.

Ms D'Baliere returned to leafing through her reports. The meeting was over.

Johnson stood and made to leave.

'I'm sure there will be no mistakes,' said Ms D'Baliere pointedly, and then added, 'remember we are a team: what are we?'

'A team,' replied Johnson as positively as he could.

Ms D'Baliere smiled with self-deserved satisfaction and Johnson left the room.

* * * * *

Billy Bob stood transfixed in the lobby of the Flush Away Corporation, amid a bustle of folks making their way to work. Its vast white Marblesque expanse outstretched before him: exotic plants, fountains and statues were organised in mock splendour. Ever-vigilant Ever-On security drones hovered above and, across the far side of the lobby, a small group had gathered around a floating sign, which flashed the words: 'Museum Guided Tour'.

As if in a daze, he looked up to see the grand circles of levels rising above him, with their plastiglass skyvators ascending to a magnificent atrium, through which he could see clouds rolling across the grey sky.

Then he recited word for word, though with little understanding, his mission: '"To spread the organic word and bring about the collapse of the unorganic corporations that infest the universe with their attempts to enslave the very masses they are meant to serve in themedom."'

Where better to inconvenience the conveniences than where Johnson would least expect it: at the headquarters of the Flush Away Corporation itself!

Billy Bob checked that he had the necessary tools hidden in the lining of his attire. He then made for the nearest skyvator.

'Welcome to Flush Away – the corporation that totally wastes your waste!' the skyvator intoned in a flawless accent. 'How may we be of service?'

Billy Bob had expected an icon to operate not a conversation.

Unsure of what to say, Billy Bob said nothing.

There was a pause and then the skyvator repeated its welcome, adding that it would be only too happy to help if assistance was required.

'I'm here for the tour,' blurted Billy Bob with uncharacteristic quick thinking.

'The next museum guided tour will begin momentarily. Visitors are requested to wait by the designated sign in the lobby, where a Tell-2-U tour bot will soon arrive to escort you and provide edutainment to heighten your experience. Please exit the skyvator.'

'Thank ya' kindly, mam,' replied an agitated but courteous Billy Bob.

'It is a pleasure to be of service, sir. Enjoy your tour,' responded the skyvator.

With relief, Billy Bob got out. The skyvator's doors slid shut silently behind him. He made his way across the lobby, towards the growing throng milling around the tour sign. It was then that the Tell-2-U tour bot drifted into view, its holoplay projecting the words 'Flush Away' in the correct designated corporate font.

'Valued customers, on behalf of Flush Away – the corporation that totally wastes your waste, let me welcome you to our headquarters here on Pacifica. I will be your guide for this magical journey through history: a journey that shows how convenience technology has developed through the ages. Please feel free to ask questions at any time.' The Tell-2-U tour bot spoke with no perceptible accent; it had been so designed in an attempt to be as innocuous as possible to all.

'Where's the john?' a voice from the crowd asked, and then started to laugh. This caused a ripple of mild amusement among some of the other tourists.

'Valued customers, conveniences for your convenience are clearly marked along the way. Currently, the nearest convenience is across the lobby,' replied the Tell-2-U tour bot, apparently oblivious to bad humour. 'Please ensure that you keep hold of all belongings and small children. The Flush Away Corporation can accept no liability for their loss or damage during the tour.' And, with a swift about-face, it headed off at pace. The crowd followed.

At the far side of the lobby, a spiral ramp descended. The Tell-2-U tour bot sped down the ramp. The crowd almost had to break into a jog to keep up. At the bottom of the ramp all was darkness.

'Valued customers, we are now entering the Flush Away Museum, created for Flush Away by the Creation Corporation.' The Tell-2-U tour bot paused and then, as if possessed, announced in an entirely different and clearly aspirational voice, '"We make the dream come true – just believe."'

'Valued customers, the Flush Away Museum has been designed for your edutainment and is presented by the Flush Away Corporation free of charge. It contains the most extensive collection of historic convenience artefacts in this sector,' added the Tell-2-U tour bot, returning to its original, accent-less voice.

There was a sudden burst of dramatic music and a spotlight shone upon a display case to reveal a mound of soil inside.

'In the beginning there was nothing but soil,' boomed a deep rumbling voice from the Creation Corporation's installation.

A hushed silence followed and, with the silence, the spotlight faded and all was again dark.

Again the music burst forth and again the spotlight shone upon the mound of soil.

'And behold, humankind used the soil for its convenience!' continued the deep rumbling voice. The spotlight focussed upon a small log-shaped shape on top of the mound of soil.

'Valued customers, the Flush Away Corporation is proud to set before your eyes the oldest know fossilised human excrement, neutron dated at over five million solar cycles!' interjected the Tell-2-U tour bot enthusiastically.

There were gasps of amazement from the crowd, although one voice was heard to say, 'Looks like a pile of crap to me!'

Billy Bob's jaw dropped. Cousin Jez had said that the masses needed to return themselves to the soil, and here was the earliest evidence of humankind doing so. Billy Bob felt he was on the edge of revelation. This was the very symbol of the Children Of The Soil's reason for being.

The music settled into a more melodic, gentle rhythm.

'Many hundreds of thousands of solar cycles passed and as humankind developed primitive tools, so it learnt to bury its excrement,' added the deep rumbling voice. Another spotlight shone upon another display case, this time showing a flattened patch of soil with a roughly hewn stick pushed into it.

The Tell-2-U tour bot moved forward and, in the distance, further display cases came to life, each like a stepping-stone on the path to sanitary enlightenment.

'As early civilisations developed so did their sanitation facilities. One of the first examples of a toilet, as we might recognise it, was found back on Ancient Earth on an island in the Mediterranean Lake inhabited by a proto-Hellenic tribe called the Minos,' elaborated the deep rumbling voice.

The crowd edged forward to peer into a display case containing a slab of rock with a hole in it.

'This toilet is many tens of thousands of solar cycles old. Of particular interest is that, underneath the seat, there was a sewerage system with running water, something that was not re-introduced until two thousand solar cycles later by that most important of Ancient Earth's early civilisations, the Roman tribe,' explained the deep rumbling voice.

'Of course, when the Roman tribe did re-introduce this sanitation technology the convenience became truly communal!' And, as the deep rumbling voice finished, the music built to a fanfare and there was a flash of light behind an enormous display case.

The Tell-2-U tour bot added, 'Valued customers, picture this, ten toilets side-by-side! Now that's what Flush Away wished every customer would buy!'

With this attempt at humour, by the Tell-2-U tour bot, elements of the crowd, who had been sniggering at the thought of ten toilets side-by-side, stopped doing so.

'Many consider this to be the zenith of humankind's sanitary endeavours because together with a fully-functioning sewerage system, the Roman tribe brought us the sponge on a stick.' As the deep rumbling voice spoke, a small display case descended from the ceiling containing a sponge attached to a wooden stick.

'Valued customers, after being buried in volcanic ash for thousands of solar cycles, this sponge on a stick was discovered back on Ancient Earth. It was found held in the very hand of its user. The Flush Away Corporation is proud to be the custodian of this valued treasure; a treasure that has been passed down through the generations.' The Tell-2-U tour bot appeared to vibrate with excitement.

Billy Bob was now totally engrossed in the tour. He pushed several small children aside and pressed his face up against the display case containing the Roman tribe's convenience.

With an upturn in the music's tempo, and further lighting effects, the deep rumbling voice moved on through the ages. Billy Bob found himself alone, his face still pressed to the display case. He pictured his brothers and sisters all sat in a row, sharing the joy of Roman tribal sanitation facilities, and shook his head. 'No way!'

When he eventually caught up with the tour party, they had travelled forward to Ancient Earth's late pre-industrial period. Towering above him was a castellated wall. At the very top what looked like a small wooden out-building protruded from the wall. As he looked closer he could see that there was a round hole in the underside of the out-building. The music quietened, and an all-too-familiar sound was followed by excrement plummeting from the hole.

'Valued customers, we at Flush Away believe this period in humankind's history to be when one of our most enduring expressions originated: "To be shat upon from a great height",' interposed the Tell-2-U tour bot. 'Only Ancient Earth's elite could afford castles and garderobes, and it was the unfortunate peasantry who ended up seeking shelter under their walls.'

The tour party looked on, relieved that in some respects times had changed.

'As we move on through the ages of Ancient Earth, we find that furniture often had multiple functions,' resumed the deep rumbling voice after the Tell-2-U tour bot's interjection. Ahead, a display case revealed a beautifully fabricated ornate wooden cabinet.

'This cabinet not only served to hold alcoholic drinks in glass bottles,' informed the deep rumbling voice, as the top and front of the wooden cabinet lifted to reveal a rack of bottles, 'but also chamber pots!' Doors at either end of the cabinet opened and two china chamber pots slid out.

The deep rumbling voice waited for the visitors to gather together. The music slowed and quietened as, one-by-one, the spotlights dimmed on the trail of display cases until all that could be seen was the tour party in one large spotlight. Then all became silent.

'We have now arrived at a pivotal point in the history of sanitation,' spoke the deep rumbling voice with great solemnity. 'There is one name that stands head and shoulders above all others. One name more than any other that is connected with the development of contemporary convenience technology. One name that has lent itself to the very word we most associate with the bodily function.'

The tour party, as one, drew breath, awaiting revelation. From the darkness a drum roll began. Suddenly spotlights flooded a yet unseen display case and then, as the drum roll reached a crescendo, there was the almost deafening sound of a chain being pulled and a toilet flushing.

'That one name is Thomas Crapper!' thundered the deep rumbling voice. 'The forefather of all contemporary conveniences, the male who gave the known universe the flushing toilet.'

Despite the best attempts of their parents, a few small children in the tour party giggled – 'crapper' is a hard word to hold in reverence, particularly when you are five.

'From his invention all contemporary sanitation facilities have evolved,' continued the deep rumbling voice, impervious to children's laughter. 'Whilst there is no effluent ejected from the irradiating sanitation units we now use, and it is true that many embellishments have been made, his original design is still at the heart of our contemporary technology.'

'Flush Away, together with the Creation Corporation is proud to present a fully restored, original Thomas Crapper flushing toilet.' The deep rumbling voice had reached a climax of enthusiasm, which left most of the tour party open-mouthed as they pushed and shoved to crowd around the ancient toilet in the display case.

From what Billy Bob could see it didn't look a whole lot different from the john back at the farmstead.

'Valued customers, Flush Away invites you to complete your journey to the present,' ushered the Tell-2-U tour bot.

And onwards Billy Bob's journey through the history of sanitation continued. It was a journey that took Billy Bob through time and across Ancient Earth's early tribal cultures; from the Gallic tribe's open-hole conveniences to the Oriental tribe's first attempts at contemporary technological marvels; from the Arabian tribe's convention of not shaking the left hand to the Hellenic tribe's convention of never flushing toilet paper.

It was a journey that explained so much. Billy Bob had seen the light. He now understood the true meaning of what Cousin Jez was saying: 'What came from the soil must be returned to the soil'.

And as the journey ended, with the Tell-2-U tour bot extolling the virtues of, and offering a discount on, the latest Flush Away Empress irradiating sanitation unit – with its Mould-It-To-Me technology, Billy Bob became even more certain of the righteousness of his cause.

[7] For The Good Of The Cause

Deputies D'Angelis and Gilbrae had spent their sunfall workshift sat in their unmarked law enforcement skyrider.

They had circled every grid, covered every skyway.

They had spoken to every lowlife snitch and walkway leaf dealer they could find.

And through the workshift, Deputy D'Angelis had given commentary to everything they had done. Deputy Gilbrae had just shrugged.

They couldn't even find the offworlder who'd jumped out of their skyrider earlier.

Deputy D'Angelis tapped on the steering control in search of an idea, as Deputy Gilbrae practised fast-drawing his hand-zapper.

The word on the walkway was nothing: no suspect, no leaf deals, nothing. Even Deputy Gilbrae's normally dependable, though blunt, interrogation technique had failed to give them a lead.

'Let's go through it one more time. We know the suspect arrived at the U-Tan-U Spaceport. We know the suspect was carrying. We know the suspect was dressed in a jump associate's white full-dress uniform. We know we lost the suspect, and we know nobody knows who, or where, the suspect is.' Having completed his commentary, on what they knew, Deputy D'Angelis paused, awaiting Deputy Gilbrae's response.

'Yep,' confirmed a surprisingly talkative Deputy Gilbrae.

But that was all they knew.

The trail had vaporised. There was only one thing for it, they would have to double back and return to the U-Tan-U Spaceport, from where this had all started, and try again. And so, in the half-light of an unusually dry sunrise, they took to the skies in their unmarked law enforcement skyrider.

Upon arrival at the Spaceport, Deputies D'Angelis and Gilbrae went straight to the incident-room of Operation Kicking Butt and viewed the previous rotation's surveillance recordings. Fortunately, Investigator Strait was off duty. Unfortunately, the rest of the Tactical Response Assault Patrol was on hand, polishing its weaponry and generally lazing around.

'I heard that D'Angelis managed to find his own butt the other rotation,' said a voice to no one in particular.

'Oh yeah! How'd he manage that?' asked another voice.

'Did he use both hands?' enquired a third.

'The rumour is, for one brief pulsar's pulse, he took his head out,' explained the first voice.

The other voices laughed.

Deputy D'Angelis ignored their comments. 'Do we know which starliner operator has its jump crew wear that particular white full-dress uniform?'

'Liberty Discount Star Line,' replied a chuckling voice.

'And how many of their starliners were in orbit at the time?' asked Deputy D'Angelis.

'Just one.' The chuckling voice stopped chuckling.

'And who interviewed the jump crew?' continued Deputy D'Angelis. There was silence.

'Don't tell me no one interviewed them.' Deputy D'Angelis bit his lower lip and shook his head. He turned to Deputy Gilbrae. 'You'd better holo the Liberty Discount Star Line and arrange to interview the jump crew.'

Deputy Gilbrae grunted, clearly in no mood for conversation.

'Perhaps I'd better holo the Liberty Discount Star Line and arrange to interview the jump crew,' reconsidered Deputy D'Angelis and picked up his holocom.

Deputy Gilbrae nodded.

And, carrying on his solo conversation, Deputy D'Angelis added, 'I hope the jump crew have stayed together onplanet, otherwise we'll be having to travel halfway across the Spiral Arm to find them. Oh, and I'd better ask the Liberty Discount Star Line to have the passenger record ready.'

*   *   *   *   *

The walkway had not proved to be as promising a fiscal proposition as Star Trooper Jonah Jones had hoped. The early flood of commuters had washed past, leaving a rather pathetic collection of discarded food wrappers and small change. These charitable donations would not even stretch to one carton of Drinkers' Delight.

And then the spitting drizzle turned to drifting rain.

With only time passing by, Jones began to wonder what had happened to Billy Bob. The young male's enthusiasm was only exceeded by his ideological naivety. Overthrowing corporate universisation! He had no idea. Did he really think that the system would be brought to an end by the disablement of sanitation facilities. Although the thought of bringing everyone down to his level, of having to use a spade to go to the toilet, did have its appeal – it even managed to raise a smile on Jones's face.

Across the way Jones noticed a figure hurriedly descending the steps that led from Flush Away's corporate headquarters. For a pulsar's pulse he thought it was Billy Bob, but no, the figure was wearing a military-style poncho, similar to the kind he wore in the Space Corps.

He shuddered as another flashback came.

He was in the driving rain of the Eden's World campaign…

50

They'd been pinned down for a whole lunar phase in that tropical jungle before relief arrived. He could hear the ear-splitting cacophony of the endlessly squawking chat-chat birds coming from the soaring parasol plants and the screams of his fellow star troopers as if it were only last rotation. Star troopers so desperate for sleep they'd literally fall to their knees and beg for silence, only to have their pleas perfectly mimicked by those relentlessly deafening chat-chat birds.

Oh, the noise...

With a blink of his eyes, and a shake of his head, Jones managed to re-sync with the cosmos, back to this rotation's reality. The figure was almost upon him. Instinctively Jones held up his sign, in anticipation of a charitable donation, but the figure was too intent on getting to wherever he was going. With well-practised timing, Jones lurched his wheelchair forward, but the figure, with equally well-practised timing, neatly sidestepped and proceeded at pace along the walkway. Not even his best move was going to work this rotation.

The figure seemed familiar. Jones tried to remember where he'd seen him before. Then it came to him: it was Billy Bob's target!

Where was Billy Bob? The figure was receding into the distance.

Then, with better-late-than-never timing, Billy Bob emerged from Flush Away's corporate headquarters. Jones waved his arms to attract Billy Bob's attention. Billy Bob peered over towards him, stopped, and waved back enthusiastically.

Jones shook his head. With frantic arm gesticulations he beckoned him over. Billy Bob waved harder. Eventually Jones resorted to cupping his hands around his mouth and shouting, 'Over here!'

Billy Bob stopped waving, looked around and pointed at himself.

Jones nodded and wondered whether natural selection had been busy doing something else the rotation Billy Bob had been born.

Panting, and wet from the drifting rain, Billy Bob arrived.

'It was him,' stated Jones.

'Who y'all talkin' about?' asked Billy Bob.

'Your target just walked past and went that way,' pointed Jones.

'Y'all sure?' gasped Billy Bob.

'I'm sure, and if we don't start after him we'll lose him,' replied Jones.

Billy Bob started in the direction Jones had indicated and then hesitated for a pulsar's pulse. 'Did y'all say "we"?'

'Yes,' replied Jones.

'Ya' mean y'all gonna' join the cause?' ventured an elated Billy Bob.

'Yes. You've got yourself a new volunteer,' committed Jones.

'I cain't believe it!' exclaimed Billy Bob and stretched out his hand to Jones.

Jones could scarcely believe it himself. Had he forgotten all that he had learnt from his many solar cycles in the Space Corps? The basic rule: never volunteer! Always, always, take a step back and let the other star trooper volunteer.

Although he knew, if he was honest with himself, begging for small change to keep him in Drinkers Delight was no life, and besides, the young male really needed help.

And so the union was formed. The Children Of The Soil had a new recruit – a recruit that wasn't related by blood.

Billy Bob beamed as he picked up his backpack and strode forth. Star Trooper Jonah Jones pushed along behind.

*   *   *   *   *

Johnson was also suffering from disbelief.

This rotation he had been certain that he would be looking for new employment, and now, well, he had just landed his big break: Nova Vega and the Creation Corporation, Flush Away's most important customer. Even if Chad was up to something, Johnson wasn't going to let this one leave his orbit.

Before his neurons had flickered into cognition, he'd reached the Sun Rise Cooperative Skybreaker. The express skyvator was waiting for him. It must be his providential rotation; normally the skyvator sulked on the top level and attempted to stop at every other level during its descent. With unnoticed efficiency the doors closed and Johnson was whisked up to the six hundred and sixty-fifth level.

In a photon's phase he'd returned to the skyvator and was on his way back down. Like all seasoned travellers he ensured he always had pre-packed luggage at the ready. So with luggage, the jump associate's white full-dress uniform and his newly acquired *lucky* poncho he headed for the spaceport.

By a stroke of providence a taxi-skyrider was waiting for him, its door already open. Johnson stepped inside, and the Easy-Does-It taxibot – a product from the Make-It-Easy Corporation – pulled away smoothly, guiding the taxi-skyrider up into the skyways, bound for the U-Tan-U Spaceport. He reclined in its Wipe-Me-Down-Easy seat, another product from the Make-It-Easy Corporation – the corporation that 'Makes it easy!'

Looking out of the window he could see the rare sight of Pacifica's sun breaking through the diminishing rain and cloud. Even the skyways' traffic control seemed to be in his favour; the taxi-skyrider didn't stop once: it was truly his providential rotation.

Arriving at the Spaceport, Johnson noticed that the rain had stopped. For a pulsar's pulse he thought he could hear birds singing and children laughing.

Johnson decided to plan what he was going to do, and what he was not going to do, next. He had to admit that this wasn't his usual approach. Normally life seemed to be one parsec ahead of him and he ended up tumbling along after it. This time he was going to think about what he was going to do before he did it.

Armed with his newfound approach to life, Johnson determined a plan. His plan was simple. Firstly he decided not to go to a beverage emporium, this had always been his undoing. Then he'd return the jump associate's full-dress uniform. After that he'd check in for his passage, sit down somewhere quiet and prepare for his business meeting with the Creation Corporation on Nova Vega.

He was definitely not going to a beverage emporium.

*   *   *   *   *

Chad Edger was pleased with himself, that's to say he was even more pleased with himself than usual. Chad was ever positive: when it came to all things Chad, he, and his self-belief, knew no limit. It was his universe and he wasn't about to let anyone forget it.

In his own words, Chad was 'Great Stuff'. He'd been Flush Away's best customer-relationship and promotions specialist for the last twenty solar cycles. He was always there when success was achieved, whether he'd been directly involved or not. Whilst facts and figures were one thing, Chad knew that what customers really remembered were the images and stories you put in their minds. No normal person recalled dry statistics. Chad always made sure he was seen in the images and included in the stories. If there were tales to be told he made sure he was in them, even if he had do the telling himself.

Chad based his success on three rules.

Chad's First Rule: it wasn't what he knew; it was who he knew.

Chad's Second Rule: it wasn't what he did; it was what others thought he did.

Chad's Third Rule: always leave them with a smile.

But to fully understand Chad was to know Chad's true love: credits. However, therein lay the source of his on-going frustration. He had mixed in all the right circles, consistently told everyone he was the best, and yet the Flush Away executive board had appointed *that female* to head up the customer-relationships and promotions team. Yes she knew all about facts and figures, but she was hardly charismatic. She just seemed to keep her antennae down and work all rotation, encouraging and instructing colleagues what to do and how to do it: that wasn't leadership! The job should have been his.

And, if the job had been his, he would have only been one parsec away from his ultimate goal: to be a member of Flush Away's executive board, a possessor of the fabled golden key to the executive toilet and all the riches and power that it bestowed.

Instead, he'd had to satisfy his fiscal desires by operating his own illicit sideline; a sideline that had started to bring reward, but had also started to become somewhat risky.

Ms D'Baliere sending Johnson to Nova Vega had been a great piece of timing. Whilst he worried what Johnson might do to his best account – an account it had taken him many solar cycles to develop – Johnson would prove to be the perfect decoy. An inspired accomplishment, even if Chad said so himself.

For some time he'd known that the law enforcement agencies would eventually get close. With Johnson as a decoy, he now had time to cover his vapour trail and reset his illicit sideline. And, with a little providence, the recent misplacement of his last leaf consignment might even lead to Johnson's incarceration.

Oh, what sweet joy that would be!

[8] By The Book

The jump crew had been looking forward to their time onplanet, and planned to relax and enjoy all that Pacifica had to offer. None had anticipated that this would include the delights of law enforcement interrogation.

They grumbled with discontent as they all stood in a row in some lost and forgotten corridor in the depths of the U-Tan-U Spaceport. One-by-one, they were invited into the interview-room.

Jump Engineer Olaf Gundersson sat across the table from Deputy D'Angelis whilst Deputy Gilbrae idly propped up the wall. Despite repeated questioning, Jump Engineer Olaf Gundersson said that he could barely remember the passage from Old MacDonald's World. In fact, at this point in the space-time continuum, he had trouble remembering his own name. He was nursing the forebear of all hangovers; the result of an unsuccessful sunfall spent losing at drinking games with a female jump associate, who he declined to name. He was sure she'd cheated.

Deputy D'Angelis tried one more time. 'Be clear this is a law enforcement interview, are you sure you don't remember anything out of the ordinary, anything at all?'

Gundersson's head throbbed. 'As I said, if I could remember anything I would tell you. The only time I left the control deck was when Rodger, one of the jump associates, called me out because all the toilets went down, and that's not out of the ordinary on that piece of space debris.'

A thought popped into Deputy D'Angelis's mind. 'Why did the toilets go down?'

'How should I know? I told Rodger that, once they shutdown, it's an in-dock-service job to repair them, a job for trained specialists. I told him he would just have to make other arrangements for the passengers and then I returned to the control deck,' grumbled Jump Engineer Olaf Gundersson.

'And what special arrangements did Rodger make?' continued Deputy D'Angelis.

Gundersson pondered for a while, trying to recall the previous rotation's events. 'Now you come to mention it, I'm not sure. When I got back to the control deck the system status showed all the sanitation facilities to be functioning properly, which was odd because they certainly weren't when I looked at them with Rodger. Anyway, I figured they must have started working again because no one came back to me. To be honest I didn't think anything of it.'

Deputy D'Angelis pulled the interview transcript from the Tell-It-All auto-transcriptor and passed it to Gundersson. 'Thank you, Jump Engineer Gundersson, now if you could read and touch the transcript in the places marked.'

When the door to the interview-room had slid shut, Deputy D'Angelis turned to Deputy Gilbrae and asked, 'What do you hide in toilets?'

Deputy Gilbrae furrowed his brow, but nothing came to him and, with what seemed like considerable effort, he answered, 'Dunno.'

'Leaf. It's the classic place to stash leaf. Generations have done it. I bet the leaf was stashed in the toilets and caused them not to work. I think it's about time we had a word with Rodger the jump associate.'

Deputy D'Angelis knew he was on to something.

*   *   *   *   *

Johnson had successfully accomplished the first phase of his plan, and had not gone to a beverage emporium. However, the second phase, handing in the jump associate's uniform, was proving to be a little more difficult.

He nested his head in his hands, with elbows firmly planted on the customer service counter of the Liberty Discount Star Line. The customer service associate he'd been speaking to had disappeared to seek advice from her supervisor. Returning uniforms did not appear to be covered within the vast annals of the star line's standard operating procedures.

Johnson sighed. He had long since become resigned to the fact that employee training, and the standardisation of working practices, resulted in perfectly capable employees becoming completely incapable of dealing with the simplest of circumstances. It was his opinion that the corporate universe had a lot to answer for.

He started tapping his fingers on the service counter.

After some time a door whooshed open and the customer service associate returned with a smile that suggested a solution was imminent.

'No problem, sir,' she beamed. 'When the jump crew become available I will personally ensure that you are able to return the uniform.'

Johnson stopped tapping. 'When the jump crew become available?'

'Ah, yes, sir, unfortunately they are all indisposed at this point in the space-time continuum,' answered the customer service associate.

'Indisposed?' repeated Johnson, who was starting to get that losing orbit feeling.

'Indisposed, sir, unavailable,' explained the customer service associate.

'Why are the jump crew unavailable?' asked Johnson.

'Because they are indisposed, sir,' concluded the customer service associate.

After taking a deep breath, Johnson persisted, 'May I ask why I can't just hand you the uniform?'

'Though the uniform is the property of the corporation, it is the employee who is responsible for its care, sir.' The customer service associate then recited what she'd clearly just been told to recite by her supervisor: '"The corporation can bear no liability for the use or misuse of items under an employee's care", as detailed in section forty-three, sub-clause c of an employee's standard contract, sir.'

Frustrated, Johnson decided to just leave the uniform on the service counter. He had better things to do than discuss the minutiae of employee contract law, but as he headed for his passage check-in the customer service associate called after him, 'Sir, I'm afraid you can't leave that here.'

'Well, just watch me.' Johnson continued to purposefully walk away.

'Sir, if you do not return and collect your belongings I will have to holo spaceport security,' announced the customer service associate loudly.

Johnson stopped. 'Pardon?'

'Sir, you should be fully aware that you cannot leave unattended items in this or any other spaceport. You are acting in contravention of *Spaceport Security & Trade Transit Statutory Regulations,* and it would be remiss of me in carrying out my duties not to warn you that such an offence can potentially carry a custodial sentence,' informed the customer service associate.

Johnson turned to face her. 'Let me comprehend the incomprehensible. I cannot return this uniform to you, even though it is your property, because it is not your responsibility. And if I just leave the uniform you will attempt to have me arrested.'

'Very succinctly put, sir.' The customer service associate smiled.

Johnson shook his head, returned to the service counter and muttered, 'Just excellent, thank you,' as he picked up the uniform.

It is always, and always will be, the simple things in life.

*   *   *   *   *

'Customers think it's all just glamour and the stellarlife, you know. I'll tell you, it's nothing like that. It's hard work. You barely have time to breathe with all of the checks and duties you have to perform. And the passengers! Let me tell you about the passengers. What is it with customers when they get on a starliner? They think they can just click their fingers and you'll drop everything and come running. Most of the time it's no better than being a slave. I'll tell you, customers show no consideration at all. And you should see the mess they leave behind, it's disgusting. How can they make such a mess?' asked Rodger, rhetorically.

Rodger had started to enjoy the interrogation. It wasn't often that he was able to unburden his frustrations, particularly with such good listeners. He felt he could say something about everything, and everything about something – although he wasn't going to mention a thing about his own complicity in leaf trafficking, obviously.

Deputy D'Angelis tried to regain control of the interrogation. 'Sir, whilst I appreciate that being a jump associate isn't the easiest vocation in the universe, we need to understand what exactly happened on the passage from Old MacDonald's World.'

'Now, as I was saying before you interrupted me,' replied the verbose Rodger. 'It was an ordinary passage full of the usual assortment of passengers and, as ever, things did not run smoothly. This time it was the toilets. Last time it was the food. Can you imagine five hundred meals consisting of one uncooked root vegetable and a smudge of no fat, no cholesterol spread? Slimmers' Surprise! Where do they get the caterers? I almost had a riot on my hands.'

'Sir, if we could return to the events surrounding your last passage from Old MacDonald's World,' interjected Deputy D'Angelis.

'OK, OK. You could be nicer you know. How would you like it if you were being interrogated by two intimidating law enforcement deputies who try to confuse you at every turn in order to extract a confession?' Rodger feigned hurt.

'Sir, I can assure you that we are not trying to confuse you or make you confess.' Deputy D'Angelis closed his eyes and breathed deeply and slowly. 'Patience, patience,' he told himself whilst clenching his fists in exasperation.

'Now, let me think. I was performing my duties as per normal, with a smile on my face, trying to bring a little happiness into the passengers' lives.' Rodger looked pointedly at Deputy D'Angelis. 'You'd be amazed what a difference a smile can make. In fact, if you ask me it makes all the difference in the universe.'

Deputy D'Angelis found himself trying to smile through gritted teeth.

'That's better, see a little smile isn't so hard is it?' Rodger seemed pleased and restarted telling his tale. 'Now where was I? Ah yes, bringing a little happiness into the passengers' lives. Anyway, I was talking to this absolutely charming male in row eighty-seven when I started to overhear a bit of a commotion. Being naturally attentive, I pardoned myself from the conversation and went to see what all the noise was about. A queue had formed near to one of the toilet blocks and the "Out Of Order" sign was flashing. "Oh dear", I thought. Then, when I looked around, all the toilet blocks appeared to be displaying the same message. "This is the last thing we need", I thought. Then the passengers started to get a bit irate and, I guess, desperate. I calmed them down and said I would go and talk to the jump engineer to get things sorted – although why I thought he would be of any use I do not know. He never is. Always it's the same answer: "In-dock-service". And then he returns to nursing his hangover.

Can you believe it? As ever, it's left to me to sort it out. Just then, in my time of need, this rather dishevelled-looking male introduced himself and asked if he could be of assistance. Who am I to refuse a cosmonaut in shining starlight, or, in this case, business attire that faded out of fashion some solar cycles ago – the things they wear, honestly! So I left the male to it and sought to reassure the passengers, some of who were clearly in need at this point. Anyway, the passengers and I waited outside the toilets. Then, in a photon's phase, he got them to work, although he did make a bit of a mess of the first one and I had to summon the cleaning bot. We tried to dry his attire out in the galley, but unfortunately it shrank due to an oversight in setting the oven's temperature control, so, after getting clearance from the principal jump associate, he was allowed to borrow a full-dress uniform.'

'And you wouldn't happen to have made a note of the passenger's name?' prompted Deputy D'Angelis, who marvelled at Rodger's ability to speak without breathing.

'Oh dear, I have no idea. I doubt I'd even recognise him if I saw him again. They all look the same, these business travellers: no style whatsoever,' replied Rodger.

'Is this the male?' asked Deputy D'Angelis, gesturing to the image of a male jump associate in full-dress uniform taken by the Eye Fly surveillance bot.

'Now, it might be, it might not be, I'm not certain,' lied Rodger.

Rodger was certain who it was. He could tell from the epaulets – epaulets he'd personally adjusted so that they stood higher on the shoulders to make his posture look that little more elegant, more officer than door attendant. But he wasn't about to tell the authorities. If they managed to apprehend the male and his uniform, they'd be sure to discover its contents and then he'd be for it.

Deputy D'Angelis sighed. He was getting nowhere with this jump associate.

'I think that'll be all,' concluded Deputy D'Angelis and passed the interview transcript across to be approved. 'Thank you, sir. If you could read and touch the transcript in the places marked please.'

After Rodger had left, Deputy D'Angelis turned to Deputy Gilbrae. 'We'll just have to go through the passenger record and eliminate them, one-by-one. Though I doubt our leaf trafficker would be travelling under his own identity'.

* * * * *

Johnson tried to contain his frustration with the Liberty Discount Star Line's customer service associate by counting to himself and pacing up and down. And then he happened to glance up. Look at the time! If he didn't put a rocket up it he'd miss the transit shuttle, and that certainly didn't fit in with his newfound approach of a planned business trip. He decided to leave the full-dress uniform in a compartment at the spaceport's left-luggage hall. He'd just have to hand it back in when he returned from Nova Vega.

In his haste Johnson almost wrenched the compartment door off its hinges. The space-time continuum was against him. He threw the uniform inside. It bounced back and came to rest on the very edge of the shelf. He stepped forward to push the uniform back in, but was just too late, it slipped through his fingers and tumbled to the ground.

Johnson cursed. He bent down to pick the uniform up and decided to save time by attempting to flick it back into the compartment with one easy movement of his hand. He missed and the uniform tumbled to the ground again. And again Johnson cursed, this time more loudly and, deciding that he'd get rid of the uniform once and for all, Johnson kicked it, sending it careering down the corridor, only to land at the tapping feet of a spaceport security associate.

The spaceport security associate picked up the uniform. 'Is sir aware that it is an offence, in accordance with *Spaceport Security & Trade Transit Statutory Regulation A/795/B/000786*, to leave items unattended in the spaceport?'

'Er, yes,' replied Johnson, who then managed to sequence his thoughts and added, 'I wasn't leaving it unattended, I discarded it.'

The spaceport security associate moved the uniform from one hand to the other. 'Is sir aware that it is an offence, in accordance with *Spaceport Security & Trade Transit Statutory Regulation A/775/K/010021*, to discard items in an inappropriate manner in the spaceport?'

'Er, no.' Johnson hung his head. 'I didn't so much discard it as kick it.'

The spaceport security associate stepped forward. 'Is sir aware that it is an offence, in accordance with *Spaceport Security & Trade Transit Statutory Regulation A/777/J/000003*, to play ball games or sports of any sort in the spaceport?'

Johnson began to feel the weight of offences accumulating against him and decided that contrition was probably his best form of defence. 'I can only apologise. You can be rest assured that it won't happen again.'

The spaceport security associate evaluated Johnson's response and nodded. 'Consider this to be a warning, sir, and make sure that it doesn't happen again.'

Johnson moved forward and held out his hand to retrieve the uniform. 'Thank you, I appreciate it.'

The spaceport security associate handed back the uniform, but added, 'Whilst there will be no formal charges, sir, I will, of course, have to note the incident and it will be brought into consideration if any further infractions occur.'

With a simple nod of his head Johnson indicated that he understood and returned to the compartment, this time managing to place the uniform inside without incident. He closed the compartment door, carefully and firmly, all under the watchful eye of the spaceport security associate.

Johnson refrained from returning the salute the spaceport security associate gave him as he exited the left-luggage hall. He knew it was late. Johnson ran the length of the concourse to find that his transit shuttle was... waiting there for him, ready to take off!

He'd made it. Had his new era of good luck returned following a momentary lapse over the full-dress uniform? How he longed for travel without incident, without stress. Somehow he doubted he would ever achieve such a state of nirvana, but there was no harm in hoping. He then proceeded to board the shuttle, cautiously.

After a short and uneventful trip the transit shuttle docked with the Freedom Of The Cosmos – a Liberty Discount starliner. Johnson embarked and found his All-Ways self-forming seat, whose memory control worked this time, and settled down to sleep across the universe, planetbound for Nova Vega.

It seemed only a pulsar's pulse later when a voice nudged him to say that the starliner had arrived and it was time to disembark to the waiting transit shuttle. He could hardly believe it: he'd slept for the whole passage. The Gods certainly were smiling on him as a new rotation came to pass in his life.

Johnson made his way to the transit shuttle. Once aboard, he sat by a porthole. He had been told that the descent to historic Nova Vega offered spectacular views. He was not disappointed. As the shuttle dropped through the atmosphere, a vast, barren landscape of red sand, seemingly devoid of water and vegetation, opened out before him; an empty desert whose total human habitation was huddled into one mountain-encircled conurbation. And there it was, emblazoned with countless lights and crowded skyways, the conurbation itself: Nova Vega, with its cathedrals of entertainment; the casinos, classically styled in neon – tradition ran deep on Nova Vega.

Johnson recalled that on Nova Vega a sizeable proportion of the population were old, drawn to live there by the nostalgia of a bygone age, the constant warmth of the climate, and the longevity it promised. Nova Vega was also a vacation destination. These factors led to a higher than average use of sanitation facilities. And with credits free flowing, investors were not afraid to spend on infrastructure. In short, Nova Vega represented the business opportunity of all business opportunities for a sanitation products sales representative.

Johnson allowed himself a smile as he exited the transit shuttle. At last he was transacting in the corporates. He now had a chance to shine.

Behind him, two figures were trying not to draw attention to themselves as they exited the shuttle: a young male of similar build to Johnson but awkward, dressed in ill-fitting best attire and carrying an overstuffed backpack; and a somewhat dishevelled, older male in a wheelchair.

[9] How It Was

Meanwhile, back on Pacifica, Chad sat back and relaxed. He was swirling his drink in the executive lounge of the Silver Service Star Line – U-Tan-U Spaceport's premium executive lounge. He was waiting, planetbound for Old MacDonald's World.

The lounge echoed to every sound made. The faux art cube-o seating was unoccupied, save for a small number of tired-looking, grey-attired executives busying away at their holocoms, or vainly trying to catch up on missed sleep.

Chad clicked his fingers and a rather attractive hostess sashayed across to ask him how she could be of service. She leaned forward with the broadest of smiles. He could see that her name was Lucinda, from her strategically placed name-badge. He returned the smile and, with the slightest of hand movements, indicated to his empty plastiglass tumbler.

'Certainly sir, and would sir like anything else?' cooed Lucinda.

'No thank you,' smarmed Chad and added, with a wink, 'not at this point in the space-time continuum.'

'My pleasure.' And the rather attractive Lucinda refilled his tumbler from a carton of genuine pre-aged Skotch – fresh as the rotation it was vacu-sealed. She served it from the ubiquitous silver tray she carried, the very symbol of the Silver Service Star Line. It was corporate policy on the Silver Service Star Line that everything was to be served from a silver tray.

Whilst this was a rather obvious merchandising gimmick, it had been something of a legal coup when the Silver Service Star Line's merchandising department had managed, against all expectation, to trademark the term 'Silver Service'.

Many, both inside and outside commerce, were surprised that this could have happened. And whilst some competitors, such as the Liberty Discount Star Line, rather sourly voiced their suspicions that the legal system had been corrupted, many saw this as a business opportunity. And so began a period of frantic commercialisation, of what had previously been freely available common words and phrases.

This period of commercialisation was remembered fondly in the annals of legal history as the 'Golden Age Of Valued Speech', though perhaps it was more aptly described as the '*Gold Rush* Of Valued Speech' by the more sardonic observers of the time. However, it was a golden age that, like so many fashions in history, all-too-abruptly came to an end. This appeared, quite coincidentally, to be around the time a number of the key, influential justices decided to retire quietly to their private terraformed planetoids, on their private space-yachts, after their short but lucrative callings to judicial service.

Ironically the period of revision and reversal that followed was remembered with equal fondness in the annals of legal history. It was known as the 'Golden Age Of Freed Speech'. Unsurprisingly those sardonic observers of the time described it as '*Gold Rush 2*'. But again, like so many of the fashions in history before, it all-too-abruptly came to an end when there became a lack of caseload capacity in the legal system. This occurred when a number of the key, influential advocates decided to retire quietly to their private terraformed planetoids, on their private space-yachts, after their short but lucrative legal careers.

So, when all was cross-examined and summed up, most words and phrases, previously trademarked during the Golden Age Of Valued Speech, were reversed during this, the Golden Age Of Freed Speech. However, some phrases remained steadfastly legally bound. And, much to the delight of the Silver Service Star Line's merchandising department, one of these legally bound phrases was 'Silver Service'.

Chad continued drinking, although this was more to do with the rather attractive Lucinda than the carton of Skotch she bore on her silver tray. And thus, with little conscious effort, Chad drank himself to somewhere on the happy side of mild inebriation.

Old MacDonald's World was not high up on the list of *must go* places for Pacifica's executives. And when the time came, only a few executive passengers in the lounge were called. This was accomplished on schedule, as might be expected on the Silver Service Star Line, by a hostess bearing a card on a silver tray. Each card had the passenger's name and seat number written on it by hand.

Chad arose from his firmly cushioned faux art cube-o seat and made his way the short distance to the executive transit shuttle, ably guided by a string of politely smiling hostesses. Chad chose to wink at each one as he passed. He knew how much they wanted him. Unfortunately they'd have to live with their disappointment, he had a starliner to catch – maybe next time females!

The executive transit shuttle was a smart, sleek affair, bedecked in faux art cube-o allusions. Chad felt it more than comfortably accommodated the taller passenger.

Whilst it was Flush Away's clearly stated corporate policy that all employees were to travel economy, unless contractually obligated not to: such a thought sent a shiver down Chad's spine. He had always managed – through his own able negotiation, the persistence of his enquiry, or sometimes just a lucky upgrade – to get transferred to an executive passage, even when the ever-diligent Miranda, despite his persuasive suggestions, inadvertently followed corporate procedure. Although, occasionally, he did have to pay – though he'd never admit it.

On an executive transit shuttle there was no need to strap yourself in, or return the seat to an upright position. In the event of an emergency, the highly advanced Save-Your-Soul passenger seat would do it all for you. And if the emergency turned into a disaster, it would act as an escape capsule come survival pod.

But most significantly of all, due to these highly advanced safety features, which were only available in a Save-Your-Soul passenger seat, the single most important development in a thousand solar cycles of passenger travel had been made: the executive passenger was now spared the requirement to watch, read or listen to the endless repetition of pre-passage safety briefings, safety literature and safety information screenings.

Almost imperceptibly the executive transit shuttle lifted off.

Chad looked to the porthole and could see the vista of Pacifica fall away far below – an increasingly small island of densely packed skybreakers in a seemingly endless sea. And then it was gone. The transit shuttle had entered the cloud cover.

The horizon darkened as the shuttle passed into the upper atmosphere and, as if in a flash, the stars appeared. The transit shuttle had broken into orbit and immediately began to re-orientate itself towards a distant dot. Below, Pacifica appeared a perfect sphere of mottled blue and grey.

The distant dot grew bigger until Chad began to see the distinctive hemispherical outline of a Smith Starship Company starliner.

The Silver Service Star Line proudly operated Smith Starship Company starliners. And the Smith Starship Company prided itself that its starliners were operated by the Silver Service Star Line.

A further source of pride for the Smith Starship Company was its history. Having always been owned by the Smith family, it had resisted corporate advances and had been passed down from generation to generation. It was able to trace its lineage back through to Ancient Earth and to the first pioneering times of space travel. It proudly boasted that its starliners, like the Smith family, were the result of generations of selective breeding.

The company had always fabricated solid, robust starliners: starliners to last. The technologies it used had become enshrined in the company's very being since their conception by the Smith family's forebears' forebears. You could be sure that the Smith family weren't about to change something, which had become tried and tested over the generations, merely because of the fad of short-term profit.

Their phased gravity enhancement system enabled passengers to experience the sensation of gravity without the nausea that often accompanied the competing cost effective, but disorientating, Hold-Me-Down gravity-simulation system favoured by some other starliner fabricators.

Their fail-safe pulse dark-energy drive, though more expensive than the alternative, enabled their starliners to jump from star system to star system without exhibiting the occasional explosive instability that the competing Gigastar matter-anti-matter propulsion system did.

But whilst the Smith Starship Company's starliners had these admirable traits, it was gradually becoming apparent that they suffered from one terminal flaw: nobody wanted to buy one; they cost too much to operate.

For as long as anyone could remember, the Silver Service Star Line had operated Smith Starship Company starliners, but there were now unsubstantiated reports, just whispers, that the Silver Service Star Line may change to the lower-priced offering from the Jetsui Corporation. Such a change would have a fatal impact on the Smith Starship Company for, as long as anyone could remember, it only had one customer: the Silver Service Star Line.

Chad's executive transit shuttle drew close to its rendezvous. Then in a single, synchronised manoeuvre, it docked with the umbilical tunnel that extended from the looming side of the starliner. The tunnel had transparent top and sides so that those embarking could visualise the full grandeur of the starliner, elementally named the 'Iridium'.

Chad and his fellow passengers were ushered from their seats. As they passed into the umbilical tunnel most felt relief; there was a clear sense of up. The phased gravity enhancement ensured that all passengers felt their feet were firmly attached to the walkway. Above, the curved hemispherical side of the Iridium was stacked like a layer cake, deck upon deck, each delineated by rows of portholes, with the lower decks painted darkly and the upper decks in a radiant white.

Even the most seasoned business traveller couldn't help but be aghast at the sheer majesty of the Iridium. The starliner, that had once been the flagship of the Silver Service Star Line fleet, still managed to retain its dignity; even though it was now consigned to regional star jumps rather than the grand inter-sector passages it had originally been commissioned for. In its time there wasn't a spaceport in the Spiral Arm that had not welcomed this resplendent starliner.

As the passengers filed from transit shuttle to starliner, a myriad of multicoloured ice particles floated past them as the drive was being readied, all adding to the sense of occasion.

Chad, like all the other passengers, was met with a smart salute from a young well-presented line officer stood at the head of a line of well-presented crew. He welcomed each embarking passenger and offered the help of his crew, if needed.

Chad followed the passageway to the centre of the Iridium, passing through a number of solid, heavily engineered bulkheads – all set to reassure those travelling that this was a safe, sturdy vessel. This impression was rather over-engineered by the preponderance of visible bolt heads. This was particularly so, given that the last time a bolt was used in spaceship hull construction was over two thousand solar cycles ago.

The passageway opened out into an enormous arched atrium that formed the central axis of the starliner. Around its circumference, plastiglass skyvators carried passengers to the travel lounge, sited some ten decks above. These plastiglass skyvators were a pleasure to travel in, tribologically smooth, not a hint of a judder.

The atrium had a magnificence all of its own. A vast, open space reflecting the opulence of a former age, adorned with decorative features styled to emphasise the glorious beauty of the starliner.

Chad loved it. This was how starliners should be: big, bold and brash with just a hint of elegance.

The Iridium now prepared to begin its journey. With stately grace it idled away from the mottled grey and blue ball of Pacifica until it was at a sufficiently safe distance to jump. The fail-safe pulse dark-energy drive was ignited. Then, to the human eye, the Iridium simply vanished with the smallest of twinkling flashes, leaving nothing more than the empty space it had once occupied.

[10] Would You Believe It?

Deputy D'Angelis sat down and prepared to sift through the passenger record to see if he could identify their suspect. It was a prospect that failed to fill him with joy. It would be dull, it would be tedious, it would take time and, more than likely, it would be resultless.

'This passenger record, shall I start at "A" and work through to "Z"?' asked Deputy D'Angelis, knowing that a structured approach would be more likely to stand up in the justice hall or, if things didn't quite go as well as he hoped, in any subsequent internal law enforcement investigation.

Deputy Gilbrae shrugged his shoulders indifferently; administration wasn't his thing. He was more of a *hands on* law enforcement deputy.

And so time passed. One passenger looked pretty much like another passenger, and each face just merged into the next as Deputy D'Angelis worked his way through the alphabet – an alphabet that seemed to have a lot more letters in it than he remembered.

Sunfall came, and Deputy D'Angelis grew increasingly concerned that the leaf trafficker was slipping away. And, perhaps most worryingly of all, if they didn't get a break soon they'd be made to answer questions themselves.

Then, unnoticed, sunrise arrived. Deputy D'Angelis was snoring face down on the workhub.

Deputy Gilbrae was waiting, motionless, as he had been since sunfall.

Deputy D'Angelis yawned, sat up and stretched his arms. He had been awoken by a shaft of light streaming in through the room's solitary window. As the room drew into focus he could see that the shaft of light had fallen upon the holoplay, illuminating an image.

'Would you believe it, right in front of my eyes, it's our suspect!' Deputy D'Angelis read the name aloud, 'Johnson.'

*　*　*　*　*

Deputies D'Angelis and Gilbrae again stood before Investigator Strait's workhub as he slowly switched his gaze between the two.

Investigator Strait leant back in his chair. 'Good news I hope, deputies.'

'The suspect, we know who he his, where he lives and where he works,' replied an excited Deputy D'Angelis, and passed the details across to the Investigator.

'Indeed, and you wouldn't happen to know where he is now, by any glimmer of providence would you, so that we might perhaps apprehend him?' asked Investigator Strait.

'Nova Vega,' beamed Deputy D'Angelis.

'Nova Vega, are you sure?' repeated Investigator Strait.

'Yes Investigator, he's planetbound to Nova Vega. I just holoed his employer a few photon phases ago and they said he's gone to a meeting at the Creation Corporation's headquarters,' replied Deputy D'Angelis, who was clearly very pleased with himself.

Investigator William B. Strait sighed. Of all the planets the leaf trafficker could choose it would have to be Nova Vega. The words of the chief of law enforcement seemed to be etched indelibly in his mind as he remembered the unfortunate incident concerning the visiting goodwill ambassador from Nova Vega. Whilst he might hope that all would be forgotten somehow Investigator Strait doubted it. In fact, he distinctly remembered being told that the planet and its system, together with its inhabitants, inhabitants' relatives, inhabitants' friends and any other associates of the inhabitants, were strictly off limits to him and, should he be found in contact with said associates, friends, relatives, inhabitants, planet or system, there would be repercussions. Though the exact nature of the repercussions had not been written in the stars for him, he suspected that they would be career limiting and, knowing the kind of bosses his superiors were, unnecessarily unpleasant.

It was with these thoughts that Investigator Strait entered a trance-like state. Nothing moved. Nothing was spoken.

Time passed.

Then, opening one eye followed by the other, Investigator Strait re-fixed his gaze on his deputies. 'Right then, you two, we're going to Nova Vega to catch this leaf trafficker, but it will have to be a covert, undercover operation. No one is to know: not even the rest of the squad, and particularly not the chief or the First Citizen, understood? This will be our opportunity to redeem our reputation after what happened to that goodwill ambassador. So go and pack as if you're going on vacation, and I'll meet you at the spaceport. We'll catch the next passage to Nova Vega. And remember not a word to anyone.'

'Yes Investigator.' Deputy D'Angelis glanced at the immobile Gilbrae, prodded him. They then about-faced smartly and left the room.

Investigator Strait knew he was taking an enormous risk. If it all went wrong he'd be in deep trouble, but he also knew that if all went well then perhaps past transgressions would be forgotten and that elusive next career opportunity could be his.

*   *   *   *   *

Investigator Strait, dressed inconspicuously in light-coloured vacational attire, spotted Deputies D'Angelis and Gilbrae from some distance as they approached along the concourse at Pacifica's U-Tan-U Spaceport. With resigned fortitude, he knew that he would not be alone in being able to spot them. Their Neo-Holo attire flashed images of sun-drenched beaches and barely clad females, making it clear for all to see what was on their minds. It was an ensemble that was topped off with matching straw hats and particularly colourful Follow-You floating luggage; semi-intelligent luggage that you don't have to carry and is guaranteed to follow you everywhere or your credits back. The deputies truly were a sight that was hard to ignore amid the sea of corporate grey that filled the concourse.

'Do the words "covert" or "undercover" mean anything to you?' asked Investigator Strait, as Deputies D'Angelis and Gilbrae elbow-locked each other and then went to try and repeat this quaint ritual with him.

'Hey Investigator, we're in disguise. Ain't no one gonna' think we're law enforcement deputies; they're gonna' think we're just ya' normal, average males on tour looking for some action and a good time,' announced Deputy D'Angelis.

'That I can believe, but it's hardly discrete and undercover. If this operation is to be covert no one is supposed to notice us. Have you got any other attire?' asked Investigator Strait, more in hope than expectation.

'Ah, nope,' replied a somewhat more subdued Deputy D'Angelis.

'Right then, let's get going. If we don't put a rocket up it, our suspect's trail will evaporate into the ether. Follow me,' commanded Investigator Strait.

Dutifully Deputies D'Angelis and Gilbrae fell in line and followed Investigator Strait as he negotiated his way through the bustling concourse.

*   *   *   *   *

By contrast the spaceport on Nova Vega was surprisingly austere. Johnson had expected barrier-to-barrier gaming machines, omnipresent holoverts in splendid Vibraround, and a profusion of Go-To-Show novelty bots – all with that most important of aims: to entice the prospective customer to spend, spend, spend. But instead, he was met by blank walls, clear corridors and empty open spaces.

Unknown to Johnson, the reason for this was not because of some local civic plan to present an image of clean austerity. No certainly not, far from it. The reason for the blank walls, clear corridors and empty open spaces lay, or perhaps more correctly was being presided over, in the local justice halls.

The planet of Nova Vega had now completed several orbits of its star since proceedings over the spaceport's sponsorship rights had started. The Lose-It-All Corporation, with its highly successful range of weight loss supplements, believed it had scored something of a coup when the spaceport's owners agreed to what would have been a very lucrative sponsorship deal. With the large numbers of tourists visiting the planet for relatively sedentary vacations, which generally involved over indulgence of one form or another, the demographics for the promotion of weight loss supplements were amongst the best this side of the Spiral Arm. However, the local chamber of commerce, which mostly comprised of gaming and associated industries, was mortified at the prospect of Nova Vega's spaceport becoming known as the Lose-It-All Spaceport! And so battle, in the purely legal sense, had ensued.

Johnson, after being reunited with his luggage, strolled into the arrivals hall. He followed the directions for the taxi-skyriders, which led him to stand next to a sign and an activation icon. He operated the icon and a taxi-skyrider seemed to just materialise in front of his eyes. Amazing! And no queuing either. The taxi-skyrider hovered silently, and then the passenger door slid open. Johnson stepped inside.

'Destination,' requested the synthetic voice of the Ever-On taxibot inside.

'The Golden Towers with all possible haste,' replied Johnson. The Golden Towers were the headquarters of the Creation Corporation, and Johnson did not want to be late for his appointment.

'Please confirm, the Golden Towers,' echoed the Ever-On taxibot.

'Confirmed,' confirmed Johnson. The passenger door slid shut and Johnson settled back to enjoy the ride.

Without warning, the taxi-skyrider tipped back and ascended vertically to emerge from the sterile tranquillity of the spaceport's taxi rank to the mayhem of a multi-strand, multidirectional super skyway. Everywhere there were skyriders travelling at speed, all changing direction in apparent random motion and all against a backdrop of a garishly lit urban sprawl. It was a sight that evoked the memory of ancient traditions. In fact, many deemed Nova Vega worthy of Galactic Heritage status.

Johnson closed his eyes as the taxi-skyrider rolled, and then dived into another stream of traffic.

'Destination imminent,' informed the Ever-On taxibot.

Johnson opened his eyes just as a produce-skyrider crossed directly in front. He braced himself for impact, but, by less than the blink of an eye, the impact didn't happen. Traffic seemed to be drawn to his taxi-skyrider by some unknown force, only to be inexplicably repulsed at the last possible pulsar's pulse.

Johnson began to visualise the drink he was going to have that sunfall, and the one after it and the one after that. In fact he'd quite like that drink now.

Ahead, through the traffic, there appeared a forest of immensely tall skybreakers emerging on the horizon: skybreakers bedecked in lights and holographic images – too many to count; skybreakers so tall he had to crane his neck to see their apices; skybreakers drawing closer at an alarming rate. And at their centre stood five golden towers, even taller than the rest, more elegant, more imposing. Towers that arched together to form a single pinnacle pointing towards an enormous, rotating 'CC': the Creation Corporation's trademarked logo.

*   *   *   *   *

Billy Bob and Star Trooper Jonah Jones stood and sat in the arrivals hall of Nova Vega's austere spaceport. They had lost their target.

Billy Bob shuffled his feet uncertainly. There was just the tiniest element of confusion about Cousin Jez's mission in his mind. While he pretty much understood the meaning of most of the mission's words individually, when he put them together understanding them became a struggle.

Billy Bob stopped shuffling his feet. He decided that now was not the time to be unsure. He re-found his inner resolve and, to reinforce this re-found inner resolve, Billy Bob stood tall, turned to Jones and announced, 'Cousin Jez says that: "At all times we must seize any opportunity to spread the organic word and bring about the collapse of the unorganic corporations that infest the universe with their attempts to enslave the very masses they are meant to serve in themedom". Y'all have to excuse me, I need to go 'n continue my mission, but I shall return. Y'all just wait here.'

'OK,' replied Jones as he looked quizzically at Billy Bob stride towards the nearest toilet. He was sure Billy Bob was a few meteors short of a shower, and, at best, the mission they were on was pointless, but hey, what else did he have to do?

It was as Jones watched the local newscast, on a holoplay, that the commotion started. Whilst enthralling as the debate on the ever-pertinent issue of walkway cleanliness was, Jones found himself distracted by the sound of shouting coming from the nearest toilet. He turned to see a seemingly pregnant Billy Bob walking towards him, innocently.

'Hide these,' commanded Billy Bob as he opened his attire. Cartridges of toilet Paperette tumbled out. 'We got us many more 'a these here toilets to disable.'

Jones allowed himself a little shake of his head as he stowed the cartridges under his wheelchair.

'What about our target?' asked Jones, less than impressed with his new role of keeper of toilet Paperette.

'Trail's done 'n evaporated in the ether, we'll have to try 'n pick it up later. Anyways we've got us work to do in this here spaceport. Let's go find us the next convenience to inconvenience,' Billy Bob chuckled to himself.

Jones wondered quite what they'd do with all the toilet Paperette.

*   *   *   *   *

Johnson stood in the shadow of the five golden towers, luggage in hand, mouth wide-open. There were impressive skybreakers, and there were impressive skybreakers, but this skybreaker was simply awe-inspiring. The enormous towers were perfectly smooth, organic; no window or door nor mark or blemish was visible. To enter, visitors seemed to just pass through the walls at the base of each tower. Johnson had heard of light-screen doorways before, but had never seen one.

Johnson walked to the base of the southern tower and paused for a pulsar's pulse. All he could see was his own reflection in the golden surface. To his right a hand emerged, quickly followed by its arm, torso, head, legs and trailing arm. Johnson stepped forward and found that he was standing in a foyer. He looked behind to see the world outside as clear as if there was no light-screen doorway at all. He was tempted to step back and stand half-in, half-out. No, no, no. He needed to act professionally. He made his way across the marble foyer to the tower's reception.

'Welcome to the Creation Corporation. How may we be of service?' asked the professionally pleasant greetings associate.

'My name is Johnson,' Johnson stated. 'I have an appointment with your resources department, sanitation section, a Ms Carlsson.'

The greetings associate smiled. 'Please be seated. Ms Carlsson will be with you momentarily.'

Johnson turned and went to find somewhere to sit. He scoured the foyer; there were no seats. He returned to reception.

'Welcome to the Creation Corporation. How may we be of service?' repeated the greetings associate, with precisely the same demeanour.

'Um, you asked me to take a seat, but I don't seem to be able to find one,' said Johnson, feeling vaguely stupid.

'If sir would care to be seated, I think he will find that there is no shortage of seats.'

'But where are the seats?' asked Johnson.

'Anywhere sir would care to sit.'

Johnson was confused. 'Well, I can't see one.'

'If sir would care to sit, he will find that there will be a seat underneath him,' explained the greetings associate, with well-practised patience.

'Sit?' worried Johnson.

'Yes sir, sit,' instructed the greetings associate.

Tentatively Johnson did as he was told and, as he reached the point of balance, he felt something supporting him. He looked down and there was a chair, a simple golden-coloured chair; arched, smooth and organic

73

in form. He sat. He then rose and, as he went past the point of balance, he could no longer feel the chair. He looked down. It was gone. He went to sit again, this time looking as he sat, and, just at the same point of balance, the chair appeared.

Bemused Johnson stared at the chair and then across at the professionally pleasant greetings associate, and asked, 'How?'

'Welcome to the Creation Corporation,' replied the greetings associate. 'We make the dream come true – just believe.'

[11] We Do What We Do

In a corner of a field, on Old MacDonald's World, Jez pulled up his working attire. He refilled the hole he'd just used and leant on his spade. He always felt a sense of satisfaction when all had been returned to the soil from whence it came: Nature was put back in balance. His thoughts turned to Cousin Billy Bob, and he wondered how his cousin was progressing with the mission.

Jez had *volunteered* Billy Bob because Billy Bob was loyal. However, he knew for the Children Of The Soil's newest member it was going to be an initiation. Jez trusted that Billy Bob would follow instruction and not get carried away. After all, he knew Billy Bob would not want to let his kinfolk down.

Jez had explained the mission as simply as he could, root and branch: Billy Bob was to track Johnson, the Flush Away Corporation's representative. He was to cause maximum disruption, by leaving a trail of inconvenienced conveniences in his wake. Billy Bob was *not to get distracted*; he was to *observe* how Johnson reacted and was then to *report back* so that the Children Of The Soil could learn from this initial foray into interstellar positive action.

Jez was confident that this insurgency into the universe of irradiating sanitation would help Johnson see his trajectory miscalculation. It could make Johnson consider turning against the Flush Away Corporation, and even make him want to join the Children Of The Soil. Then there would be one more believer, and not just any believer, but someone who could help them overturn the system from the inside.

*   *   *   *   *

Meanwhile, in Nova Vega's austere spaceport, Star Trooper Jonah Jones had finally managed to convince Billy Bob to stop inconveniencing the conveniences, when the pile of toilet Paperette cartridges under, in and around his wheelchair started to attract undue attention. A small crowd had gathered in the spaceport's arrivals hall to see if there was some entertainment to be derived from the situation. Perhaps the male in the wheelchair and his oddly dressed associate were some kind of experimental performance arts ensemble, employed to enliven an otherwise dreary spaceport.

Jones knew it wouldn't take a countdown before someone would start to pose questions to the authorities.

'We need to reacquire our target, Billy Bob. Come on, let's roll,' urged Jones, tugging at Billy Bob's over-large sleeve.

'OK, OK,' replied Billy Bob.

To a polite, but less than rapturous round of confused applause, Jones and Billy Bob made their exit, and headed for the mass-transit terminus. Jones had suggested to Billy Bob that they should go to the very centre of Nova Vega, where all paths crossed, and see if they could pick up Johnson's trail from there.

At the mass-transit terminus the doors of the maglev transit glided open, and Jones rolled his wheelchair on board.

Billy Bob followed, remarking, 'Never bin' on no maglev transit before.'

'Nothing to be concerned about,' assured Jones. 'Take a seat and it'll soon get going.'

Billy Bob sat, and the doors glided shut. All was silent. Billy Bob and Jones were the only two passengers in the compartment.

The buildings through the windows started to move, other than that there was no sense of motion, no noise.

'It don't seem like we's goin' at all,' commented Billy Bob. But through the windows the movement of the buildings became faster and faster. The buildings began to blur.

Billy Bob then realised what was happening and exclaimed, 'Wow-wee, we sure is goin' fast!'

Whilst Billy Bob was distracted by the passing panorama, Jones started to offload some of the toilet Paperette cartridges from his wheelchair, hiding them under the nearest seats.

Gradually the blur resolved back into buildings, and the maglev transit drew to a halt. A pre-programmed voice announced that the transit had arrived in Nova Vega and could all passengers please remember to take their luggage with them.

Billy Bob and Jones rolled off the transit and followed the 'Walkway Exit' signs until, with one final 'whoosh', the last set of sliding doors led them out into the experience that was Nova Vega.

All senses were addressed in a bid to win custom. No opportunity to promote what Nova Vega had to offer was missed: holoverts, lights, holoplays and Go-To-Show novelty bots all proffered those indulgences and temptations that are so hard to resist.

Billy Bob stood rooted to the spot; something that Jones only realised when he'd rolled a good distance along the walkway.

'Billy Bob, come on!' echoed Jones, through cupped hands.

As a reformed addict lapses, so Star Trooper Jonah Jones inhaled the all-too-familiar sensations of Nova Vega. He breathed in the air for all he was worth. This was where he belonged. He couldn't think why he'd left to go to Pacifica. How could he have deserted the lights, the excitement, the thrill and the stellar gambling of Nova Vega for a planet where, other than work, rain and its various derivative forms of precipitation seemed to be the singular focus of interest in the inhabitants' lives?

*　*　*　*　*

Inside the foyer of the Creation Corporation's headquarters, Johnson watched Ms Carlsson approach. She was young, attractive and smartly dressed in fashionably-cut business attire. Her golden skin glowed with a somewhat unnatural aura; it positively effervesced. She was clearly a devotee of U-Tan-U's personal colour enhancement products. Johnson tried not to stare as he stood to press her hand. With holocards and pleasantries exchanged, he followed her.

Their polite conversation continued in the skyvator and, as the doors opened at the resources department level, Johnson began to half-hope that his life was starting a new phase; a normal, successful phase.

He was led to a perfectly normal meeting-room and, this time, asked to take a perfectly normal seat. Ms Carlsson's holocom buzzed. She looked, and briefly apologised for having to step out of the room.

Johnson smiled his best smile. 'No problem.'

Sit back, relax, he told himself, be calm. But before he achieved that rarely attained inner serenity, the face of an anxious young male appeared at the door and looked around furtively.

'Like where's Chad, man?' asked the anxious young male.

A little taken aback, Johnson replied, 'Um, I have come to do a, er, deal in Chad's place.'

'Oh right, man. Like, have you got it?' The anxious young male continued to look around.

'Pardon?' asked Johnson, confused.

'Have you got it?' insisted the anxious young male, whispering as loudly as he dared, but careful not to raise his voice.

'Er, got what?' queried Johnson, perplexed.

'You know, man, *it*, like any *leaf*, man?' The anxious young male kept searching around, on the lookout for something, or someone.

'Sorry, I don't quite understand what you mean.' Johnson shrugged his shoulders.

'Man, you gotta' know what I mean, like *it*, *leaf*, you know, the s**t, man! Like Chad always says his little rhyme, it's like his calling card: "When it comes to s**t there's no need to plead, I've always got all the s**t you need". So like have you got the s**t, man?' pressed the anxious young male.

Johnson was doubly confused. Firstly, Flush Away employees were normally asked for the means to remove the 's**t' not to provide it. Secondly, it had been engrained in all Flush Away employees, from the first pulsar's pulse they strode up those corporate steps, that the use of the 's' word was against corporate policy. This was fully documented in a tomely and indigestible volume, succinctly called *The Flush Away Way*, to which all employees had to put their name. The use of the 's' word, in any context, was a disciplinary offence. The Flush Away Corporation dealt with waste by-products not 's**t'. Surely Chad wouldn't have used the 's' word, would he?

But before Johnson could resolve his confusion and reply, the anxious young male said, 'Look catch you like later, man,' and disappeared.

Ms Carlsson re-entered the room. Johnson decided to say nothing about the anxious young male – he was clearly a few asteroids short of a belt.

The meeting started. Ms Carlsson outlined her requirements and Johnson nodded and agreed, ensuring he was friendly, positive and excited: as all good sales personnel need to be; whilst not being too subservient, or sycophantic, of course: an easy trap to fall into – a trap that Johnson had admittedly flung himself into on a number of desperately unfortunate occasions.

But not this rotation! For once Johnson felt he was firing on all thrusters, and, at the appropriate point, mentioning the magic words, 'Let me demonstrate', pulled out his Show-It-All holostrator and placed it on the ground. A complete, full-size image of an irradiating sanitation unit appeared.

'If you would care to observe, our mid-range Dante irradiating sanitation unit not only has the feature packed functionality that customers expect, but also that attractive design edge that makes it one of our best sellers.' Johnson had decided to initially pitch mid-range, to allow himself some space to re-orientate in the negotiations if needed.

Johnson proceeded to demonstrate the sanitation unit's features, ending with a flourish as he described its Warm-It-For-Me posterior temperature sensing technology – technology that enabled the toilet seat to automatically match its temperature to that of the user, prior to being sat on, thus providing the prospective client with a pleasurable experience on contact without that uncomfortable thermal shock.

Ms Carlsson appeared intrigued and asked, 'What if we up-speced? What would we get for our credits?'

Johnson felt the shudder of delight a sales representative gets when the customer starts asking about the top of the range, highest margin, and, of course, highest commission product. It was as if all his devotions to the God Of Selling were at last being answered after many solar cycles of being ignored.

Johnson selected the Empress irradiating sanitation unit – a product that both did and was fit for! He was particularly proud of this feature crammed product. In addition to the Warm-It-For-Me posterior temperature sensing technology of the Dante, it also had a Mould-It-To-Me seat that, not only formed itself to the shape of the descending posterior, but also massaged those tense and aching gluteus maximus muscles on contact!

'Ah, that is interesting,' commented Ms Carlsson. 'As we discussed, the Creation Corporation operates a number of themed resort complexes. What can Flush Away do to further help us enhance our customers' experience?'

Had Johnson hooked his customer? Sensing a sale, he explained that any of the products in the Flush Away range could be themed to a client's particular needs. And with an imperceptible movement, Johnson selected various themed guises for the Empress irradiating sanitation unit. Key periods from humankind's past were represented in faux overmouldings, together with replicated scents and sounds, all to give an *impressive* sensory experience worthy of the sanitation unit's name. And beyond the history and cultures were the more specialist themes: particular animals, cartoon characters, celebrities and fashionable genres.

'Whatever you can imagine we can deliver,' exclaimed Johnson. And, as every Flush Away employee had been trained to do, he ended his product demonstration with the obligatory catchphrase, '"Smile and Flush Away".'

Although, in the case of irradiating sanitation units, the 'flush' was more of a 'flash in the pan' followed by a brief suck. Irradiating sanitation units utterly irradiated any deposit, ensuring that all living organisms were no longer, and then vaporised what was left, leaving no trace. Though, of course, any number of simulated flushing sounds were available to give customers the full, authentic experience should they wish.

'Let's talk,' suggested Ms Carlsson.

'Excellent,' replied Johnson.

* * * * *

Chad stood in the arrivals hall of Old MacDonald's World's Insem-A-Sow Spaceport. Its elegant, contemporary lines suggested offworld design. This was particularly evident when he compared it to the landscape of tumbledown buildings he could see through the hall's panoramic windows.

It certainly looked like nothing much had changed since he had last been on Old MacDonald's World. He remembered that visit clearly.

He had been asked to undertake a fact-finding assignment. Flush Away's executive board had wanted an assessment of the market demographic so that the potential for exploitation could be determined. His boss had made it very clear to him that this was an executive board directive and, as such, needed to be executed with haste, and to the best of his ability, and oh, by the way, strictly commercial-in-confidence. He'd been expressly told not to identify himself by his real name, or mention Flush Away in any context whatsoever. The cover he'd been given was that of George Tree, a representative of Pacifica's Organic Farming Interest Lobby, which he'd guessed was a non-existent organisation because, as far as he knew, there were no farmsteads on Pacifica.

Whilst he'd thought it a little odd that the assignment hadn't been given to a member of the merchandising department, he hadn't been about to let the opportunity go. It was a chance to gain further recognition from the executive board, a chance to climb another level on that career skyvator.

He'd put what he'd been doing in stasis and had caught the first starliner he could. He had been instructed to visit the Usherman Farmstead, a typical family smallholding. Whilst there, he was to study the family, their sanitation behaviour and needs, and report back on all he saw, and make sure he took many images.

It was whilst he had been carrying out his instructed tasks that it came to him, his little idea for a sideline. Jez, the young male who had shown him around the farmstead, had enthused about the organic agricultural practices he'd put in place, but had said that it was hard to scratch a living. Chad had enquired whether Jez had considered diversification.

And that had been when Chad mentioned the 'leaf' word in a half-joking manner, in case Jez understood the illegality of what he'd suggested. But Jez had seemed un-phased by the thought of growing leaf and had asked what Chad would pay for it. Chad had tried it on and gave a price a tenth of the market value. Jez's eyes had lit up and a deal was done. In good faith Chad had given Jez the first payment in advance, and told him where and when to leave each consignment.

Until this last *lost* shipment, Chad's sideline had worked with positronic precision. Jez had left a regular consignment in the same compartment, at the Insem-A-Sow Spaceport, a rotation before the starliner departed for Pacifica. This was exchanged for an envelope of credits by Rodger, the jump associate, who then couriered the consignment to another compartment at the U-Tan-U Spaceport on Pacifica, where he exchanged it for another larger envelope of credits.

Unfortunately this sweet little operation was going to have to come to an end. The law enforcement agencies had got too close. Chad was going to have to see Jez and change the supply route, but first he had a meeting at the headquarters of Old MacDonald's Wholesale General Stores to follow up on Johnson's pitiful attempt to sell product.

[12] Taking The Credit

As Nova Vega's intense yellow sun reached its zenith in the brilliant pink sky, Star Trooper Jonah Jones rolled up in front of the Black Hole Casino. The pull was simply irresistible, that call of chance, that opportunity to risk it all. Easy credits beckoned. The possibility of personal redemption stood before him. It had been a lifetime ago in this very place that he'd lost everything. He had to be lucky this time; it was, after all, the law of averages.

The Black Hole Casino was as he remembered: an impressive sight, very large and very black, its spherical form standing out from the plainer, more rectangular buildings that nestled alongside. Waves of crackling blue ionic discharge emanated from the massive floating 'Black Hole' sign that bobbed above the entrance; ionic discharge that washed out, racing over the casino's clean black surface.

'Let's look for our target in here,' suggested Jones.

Billy Bob seemed a little reluctant, but he knew that the mission came first and replied, 'OK.'

Once across the threshold, Jones was drawn through the crowds into the ever-darkening interior, past row upon row of shimmering holographic gaming machines, past the garish themed beverage emporiums and eateries, past the bright Event Horizon Show Stage – which promised that belief would be suspended in the name of entertainment, and into the Black Hole's heart. There, before him, were the gaming tables, each subtly lighted in the darkness like stars in the heavens.

'Have you got any credits, Billy Bob?' asked Jones.

Billy Bob took his Keep-It-All credit holder from his attire and looked inside. 'Yep, I got me some.'

Saying nothing, Jones outstretched his arm with his hand palm-up, and, with the slightest of movements, gestured with the tips of his fingers.

Billy Bob slowly, and somewhat reluctantly, lifted one note out of his credit holder and placed it into the palm of Jones's hand.

The fingers gestured again and another note followed.

And again.

And again.

And finally, when the credit holder had just one left, again.

'What y'all gonna' do?' asked Billy Bob.

*   *   *   *   *

From under the shadow of the Creation Corporation's Golden Towers, Johnson emerged into the light and threw his poncho high up into the pink sky, much to the surprise of passing onlookers – for who wore a poncho on Nova Vega?

What a glorious rotation! The biggest deal of his career was agreed. Ms Carlsson had loved what he had to offer.

He couldn't wait to see the team's faces back at headquarters, together with the applause he'd be given, as he strode triumphant through the workplace. And he couldn't wait for the smile of congratulation he would receive from Ms D'Baliere when he delivered the transacted deal. But most of all, he couldn't wait to see the look on Chad's face, the forced smile that Chad 'the team player' would have to wear, a smile that would mask the ire Chad would surely feel because he, Johnson, had completed Chad's deal. Johnson was already savouring the scene.

Although, there was something about it all that still nagged at the back of his mind. Why had Chad let him take on the account so easily at Ms D'Baliere's request? It just wasn't like Chad to let something go for nothing.

Enough worrying. He was sure it was his constant uncertainty, his insecurity that had held him back all these solar cycles. For once he was going to have the confidence to enjoy himself. For one sunfall he was going to live the life of a stellar gamblestar here on Nova Vega, after all, now that he was earning big credits he had to get used to spending big credits.

As he stood contemplating his bright future, a gleaming black spherical taxi-skyrider drew up. He could see the fleeting reflection of a successful sales representative staring back, smiling, but then vanishing as the door slid open. He stepped inside.

'Destination,' requested the Ever-On taxibot.

Johnson thought for a pulsar's pulse and then declared, 'A good time!'

'A good time, please confirm,' responded the Ever-On taxibot.

Johnson repeated his request, 'A good time!'

With Johnson inside, the door slid shut and the black spherical taxi-skyrider followed its programming and headed for its default location, the location of its sponsor.

* * * * *

Outside the Insem-A-Sow Spaceport, on Old MacDonald's World, Jez waited, as he always did, checking that no one was following, no one was watching. Only when he was sure that all was as it should be did he make his way inside to the left-luggage hall to the usual compartment. He opened it. But instead of a credit-stuffed envelope, Jez found a note simply stating, 'Will collect in person'. Thoughtful, Jez took the note and left.

He read the note again, turning it over to check he had not missed anything. He decided he had better get going and collected his archaic, but organic, ute from the skyrider park. It was a long way back to the farmstead.

The ute coughed and spluttered as it lifted from the ground, and continued doing so as it sped over the patchwork farmsteads. Jez pondered what this change in routine might mean.

The credits had become essential to the cause; they were currently funding Billy Bob's mission. If the Children Of The Soil were to mount any more missions they would need more credits; revolutions required funding. Throughout history this had always been the case and always would be. Jez had no qualms; he would stop at nothing to end the unorganic corporate universisation that permeated the cosmos. The ends justified the means. And anyway, what he was doing was entirely in keeping with the movement's principles, after all this was *organic* leaf!

* * * * *

Star Trooper Jonah Jones sat in his wheelchair and could just see over the long gaming table. He was the centre of attention.

Jones snapped his fingers and another drink appeared, served with a smile by an attractive waitress dressed in very little. It was his fifth drink, or so Billy Bob had determined. Counting was not one of Billy Bob's strengths, but Billy Bob knew that Jones had certainly drunk more than one or two.

Jones was rolling dice, and each time he rolled, the crowd gathered around the table would cheer, and the smartly dressed male, who stood at the end of the table, would give Jones some more gaming markers.

Billy Bob had tried to warn Jones about his trajectory miscalculation. But Jones ignored him and seemed intent on continuing his reckless, sinful behaviour; totally absorbed in trying to increase the size of the piles of gaming markers stacked up in front of him. He even reached over to Billy Bob and offered him some. 'Here, go enjoy yourself, the Prophet Of Providence sure is proving to be profitable this sunfall!'

Billy Bob looked in fear at the gaming markers.

'Go on, have a good time,' urged Jones, and nudged Billy Bob in the direction of the beverage emporium and a row of alluring females who sat quietly minding their drinks – whilst hoping to catch a glancing eye. 'Or, why don't you try the tables, or some of the gaming machines?'

Billy Bob felt more than unnerved by the thought of approaching females, particularly ones he didn't know. He had been raised to treat females with reverence and respect, a message that been reinforced repeatedly with many sharp slaps around the back of his head. And whilst he was aware of a certain urge, he was also aware of the consequences of misbehaving. He knew that any female he might meet, and wanted to know better, he would have to take back to Ma so she could make sure the female was of a suitable upbringing and disposition.

And as for gambling, he shuddered as he remembered the sermons that had made it clear, in no uncertain terms, that gambling was high among the many deadly sins he was in mortal danger of committing. Sins that would lead him unto the path of temptation, sins that would lead him unto eternal fire and damnation in the Evil One's dominion. He trembled as he recalled the thunder and the passion of Preacher Jedidiah Grimthorpe's voice reverberating in his head.

Visibly shaking, Billy Bob backed away from Jones. 'If I was to be so foolish as to gamble, or frequent with females not 'a my acquaintance, then I surely would burn in the Evil One's dominion. Y'all should consider savin' ya's soul and repentin' y'alls sinful ways.'

Jones just smiled and replied, 'Sure, by the stars, I'll give that some consideration, right after I've won us enough credits so we can eat and have a roof over our heads!'

[13] A Picture Of You

After an uneventful landing on Nova Vega, Investigator Strait, in his light-coloured vacational attire, and his undercover deputies, together with their Neo-Holo attire, matching straw hats and garish Follow-You luggage, checked into the Second Chance Hotel; an inconspicuous, value-for-credits establishment – stylised by cost effective construction and favoured by the less-than-lucky many, together with those on accountable expenses.

After freshening up, Investigator Strait and his undercover deputies sat at a small table in a quiet corner of the Second Chance Hotel's lobby. Over the table Investigator Strait had projected a holoview of Nova Vega with the locations of their hotel, the spaceport and the headquarters of the Creation Corporation flashing in radon-red. Projected above the holoview was an image of Johnson, in business attire frowning a corporate smile; a blurred image of a jump associate in full-dress uniform passing through customs on Pacifica and, most recently of all, an image of Johnson in his workplace, sporting a military-style poncho and a somewhat bewildered look.

'Our suspect is a male of many disguises,' began Investigator Strait.

'Many disguises?' queried Deputy D'Angelis, who had swiftly counted the three images projected over the table.

'Many disguises,' retorted Investigator Strait. 'I think we can safely assume that an interstellar leaf trafficker, with our suspect's guile, will have many disguises and will stop at nothing to achieve his villainous aims.'

'You told us not to *assume* anything after what happened when we arrested those other citizens who were in disguise,' countered Deputy D'Angelis.

'Ah, if I remember rightly, you must be referring to those citizens who were in fancy dress?' responded Investigator Strait.

'That's right.' Deputy D'Angelis folded his arms. 'The citizens who were in disguise and wearing masks.'

'The citizens in fancy dress and wearing masks who were going to the First Citizen's New Solar Cycle Masked Ball,' clarified Investigator Strait.

'We only found that out after we interrogated them,' defended Deputy D'Angelis. 'Ain't that right Deputy Gilbrae?'

Deputy Gilbrae nodded – once.

'How could I forget? Interrogations whose subtleties those citizens were only too keen to share with the First Citizen who, in turn, shared them with the chief of law enforcement who, in turn, shared them with me!' With a long, wistful sigh Investigator Strait considered his distinguished career, and wondered what might have been if he hadn't been surrounded by deputies for whom the word 'arrested' only ever seemed to be used in conjunction with the word 'development'.

'Our suspect is a male of many disguises,' repeated Investigator Strait, pausing to see if there was going to be any further argument. There wasn't. 'We believe that he is currently assuming the alias of one "Johnson..." Do we have any more on the name?'

'No. His employer said that was the entire name they had on record,' replied Deputy D'Angelis.

Investigator Strait continued, 'Our suspect is assuming the alias of one "Johnson", who is employed by the Flush Away Corporation as a customer-relationship and promotions specialist, or, to you and me, a sales representative.'

'Did you say customer-relationship and promotions specialist?' asked Deputy D'Angelis sniggering.

Investigator Strait wondered what was so funny. 'OK, out with it,' he ordered. 'Let's all share the joke.'

'Don't you get it? Johnson's a C R A P specialist!' Deputy D'Angelis was now outwardly chuckling.

'On my, what merriment they must make in those corporations!' said Investigator Strait who, finally, and unfortunately, got the joke. 'Right then, enough, we need to execute this covert operation very carefully if we're goin' to catch our suspect. So listen, here's the plan.'

* * * * *

Johnson's gleaming black spherical taxi-skyrider pulled up outside the Black Hole Casino.

'A good time,' repeated the Ever-On taxibot.

Johnson looked out at the casino and decided that this was as good a place as any to have a good time. He exited the taxi-skyrider.

As he stood beneath the massive 'Black Hole' sign, Johnson particularly liked the waves of crackling blue discharge that ionised the casino's exterior. The Black Hole Casino certainly was something out of this world.

Johnson strode inside, head held high. Through the crowds he could see countless luminous holographic gaming machines fading into the distance.

He decided he would check in first, drop off his luggage and spruce himself up before spending the sunfall becoming the stellar gamblestar he now aspired to be.

Circling unnoticed high above, large black spherical Hi-2-U greetings bots scoured the crowd for customers to assist. Identifying that Johnson was carrying luggage and had stood still for more than its pre-programmed time limit, one of the Hi-2-U greetings bots swooped down in front of Johnson and dropped an arrow-headed sign that displayed the word 'Reception' in crackling blue ionic discharge.

'Beep – Respects, sir – beep,' intoned the Hi-2-U greetings bot, in an over-exaggerated nasal voice. There was a pause. 'Beep – On behalf of the management and associates of the Black Hole Casino please accept our most heartfelt welcome – beep.' Another pause followed. 'Beep – We would be only too delighted to offer rooms and any other services sir may wish for – beep.' A further pause. 'Beep – Please follow the sign – beep.'

Johnson waited to see if the Hi-2-U greetings bot was going to say anything else, and then mumbled, 'Um, OK.'

'Beep – Would sir like me to carry his luggage? – beep,' asked the Hi-2-U greetings bot.

'Er… yes, um, thank you,' hesitated Johnson, who was more used to the budget 'carry-your-own-luggage' hotel – on the rare occasion that Flush Away would bear the expense.

Underneath the black spherical Hi-2-U greetings bot a pair of small bomb-bay style doors opened and a tethered hook glided out, circled around the handle of Johnson's luggage and locked itself back onto its tether. With the faintest of whirrs, the Hi-2-U greetings bot lifted the luggage off the ground.

'Beep – If sir would care to follow me please – beep,' instructed the Hi-2-U greetings bot. Then, at a pace it judged to be appropriate – based on the estimated age of its customer – it set off into the heart of the casino.

And, within the flicker of a falling star, Johnson had lost sight of the casino's entrance and had stepped into a bedazzling and fortuitous world of glittering promises. As he passed the holographic gaming machines, they would each float different images of their potential prizes in front of him. His vision became a swirl of tumbling credits, luxury dwellings, sun-drenched beaches and exotic females. In fact females seemed to figure in most of the images: young, extremely attractive females clad in attire that only seemed to enhance their attractiveness – the type of females that Johnson had never met.

As if sensing Johnson's growing interest, the black spherical Hi-2-U greetings bot drew to a halt. 'Beep – If sir would care to play, I would be only too happy to wait – beep.'

Johnson certainly felt the temptation, but decided, in the spirit of the new, successful Johnson, he would stick to his plan and check in first. 'No, let's go. Is it far to reception?'

'Beep – Two hundred and sixteen of your paces – beep,' informed the Hi-2-U greetings bot and set off again with Johnson's luggage in tow.

Several turnings, corridors and stairs later, and past what seemed to be an endless succession of gambling opportunities, Johnson was delivered to the casino's reception.

The Hi-2-U greetings bot deftly unhooked itself from the luggage, bade Johnson a fond farewell – expressing the hope that Johnson thoroughly enjoyed his stay – and, with a final 'beep', departed.

*　*　*　*　*

Elsewhere in the Black Hole Casino, Star Trooper Jonah Jones rolled his last marker, glumly, from one hand to the other. The Prophet Of Providence, together with the admiring crowd, had deserted him. He was sat across the table from a pious Billy Bob, who stared down on him with folded arms.

'Darn 'n damnation! Now that y'all's gone 'n lost all my credits, we'd better find a way outta' here,' said Billy Bob.

Jones continued to roll the marker from one hand to the other. He sighed the long, resigned sigh of a male destiny had fated to always lose.

Billy Bob stood, and Jones reversed his wheelchair from under the table. With no signage to indicate which way was out, Billy Bob headed left, a dejected Jones followed.

Rank upon rank of holographic gaming machines loomed oppressively in the darkness. Billy Bob strode forward, but Jones remained rooted to the spot. Noticing the lack of companionship, Billy Bob stopped and looked back to see the sad, pathetic figure of his comrade, slumped in his wheelchair holding on to that last marker.

'Just one more chance,' muttered Jones to himself and wheeled over towards the nearest machine. A machine that promised so much, but so often delivered so little. He inserted the marker and grabbed the machine's operating lever with both hands. He pulled, hard.

The images danced before his eyes, each blurring and morphing, cycling through hundreds of different objects. All that needed to happen to win was that each of the images formed into the same object. The first image formed, a black sphere, then the second, another black sphere, and finally, the third, yet another black sphere! Three perfectly formed black spheres.

Silence. And then the machine began to hum; a hum that gradually started to build, turning into a crescendo and then into a fanfare. Silver and gold stars fluttered down from the ceiling, glittering in the fountains of up-light.

Star Trooper Jonah Jones was a winner.

Billy Bob looked on, shaking his head.

Jones bathed in a wave of joy as his gambler's desire to take a chance paid off, his arms raised aloft in triumph.

And after the stars had stopped raining down, and the fanfare had died away, the up-lights dimmed. Star Trooper Jonah Jones began to wonder what was going to happen next. What had he won?

*   *   *   *   *

'The plan is simple. You two will go undercover, posing as tourists. You'll befriend our suspect and suggest an interest in leaf, at an appropriate point. When he produces leaf you'll reveal yourselves to be law enforcement deputies and apprehend him and the evidence. Remember, we need the evidence; no evidence no case.' Investigator Strait sat back. 'Any questions?'

Deputy D'Angelis raised his arm. 'I have a question. Can we wear our Neo-Holo attire?'

'Yes, you can wear your Neo-Holo attire,' Investigator Strait agreed.

'What about the straw hats, can we wear the straw hats?' continued Deputy D'Angelis.

'And the straw hats.' Investigator Strait began to wonder whether this was an undercover operation or a fashion parade. 'Right then, is there anything else?'

'What about the credits?' asked Deputy D'Angelis.

'What credits?' replied Investigator Strait.

Deputy D'Angelis leant forward. 'The credits we're gonna' need to buy the evidence.'

Investigator Strait recognised that Deputy D'Angelis had a point. For an operation like this he would normally requisition credits from the central law enforcement store, but given he had no official sanction that wasn't going to be an option. He could see no other way, he was going to have to fund the deal with his own credits. 'Don't worry about the credits; I've got that covered. What we need to do now is search for, locate and apprehend our suspect, one Johnson.'

*   *   *   *   *

Johnson had asked the casino's reception to reserve him a table for dinner at their best, full-service eatery. And now he sat in Les Temps Perdu. There was a real white cloth on the table. The eating utensils appeared to be fabricated from real metal. The glasses appeared to be fabricated from real glass. There was a real white cloth napkin in a real metal ring, a real flower in a vase, all set in the ambience of real candlelight.

Childishly, Johnson held his hand over the candle's flame to confirm its reality. Having then had his fingers burnt, he turned his attention to the menu, a menu written in exquisite handwriting on real paper. There were no prices on the menu. There were no numbers next to the dishes. The choices were in a language he could not read.

A real waiter drew up, stood before him and offered greetings.

'Would sir care for an aperitif?' he asked in a very well-spoken voice.

'Yes, thank you.' Johnson felt that there was no reason not to have a celebratory drink now that the deal was done.

The waiter clicked his fingers and another real, but younger, waiter emerged, with a white cloth draped over his arm, holding aloft a small tray that bore a small glass. With a semi-pirouette the younger waiter lowered the tray, and, in one graceful movement, placed the aperitif in front of Johnson. The younger waiter bowed slightly and then disappeared back into the eatery.

'And has sir chosen from the menu?' asked the well-spoken waiter.

'Um,' Johnson stuttered. 'Not fish.' Johnson reviled all things fish and fish related.

'Perhaps I might recommend the chef's seasonal special. We have a light, harvested starter, picked from the bounty of the forest, followed by freshly zapped plunder from the field, garnished with sprigs of the pastures, and, to finish, a mélange of seasonal hedgerow offerings.' The waiter smiled.

'Er, OK, that sound's fine.' Johnson wasn't entirely sure what he'd ordered; the chef's special made less sense than the menu, but so long as it wasn't fish.

'Wine, sir?' enquired the well-spoken waiter.

'Um, sure, why not.' Johnson had now decided that a *few* celebratory drinks wouldn't hurt.

'Perhaps I might recommend a lightly fragrant wine, with the merest hint of citrus, to compliment the meal, sir?' added the well-spoken waiter.

'Er, OK.' Johnson was more used to Wine-O-Mate – a popular wine-flavoured alcoholic drink whose fabricators, Scoff Enterprises, claimed self-adjusted its flavour to suit any foodstuff it came into contact with.

'And will that be all, sir?' asked the well-spoken waiter.

'Um, yes, thank you.' Johnson smiled weakly.

'Thank you, sir,' concluded the well-spoken waiter, who then bowed slightly and withdrew from the table.

Johnson needed a drink and downed the aperitif in one. Being served by real waiters was a lot more stressful than getting food from a dispensing machine, or even having Made-4-U serving bots deliver it. He felt he was being judged on every answer to every question.

In a pulsar's pulse, two more waiters arrived at his table, one carrying an antiquarian metallic ice-bucket, and the other a real glass bottle of wine, which was held ceremoniously in front of him. Both waiters appeared to be waiting for something. Johnson looked at them blankly.

'Sir's wine?' prompted the taller of the waiters.

'Um, yes?' For Johnson it was if he was in a play, but he didn't know his lines.

The taller waiter opened the wine, poured a little into Johnson's glass and, with the slightest of gestures, indicated that Johnson should taste the wine.

Johnson drank the wine. The two waiters waited. Johnson looked from one to the other and back. He felt he was being urged to do something, but what that something was eluded him.

After an uncomfortable few pulsar's pulses, the taller waiter asked quietly, 'Is the wine to sir's taste?'

'Um, very tasty, thank you.' At which point everyone seemed to breathe a sigh of relief. The taller waiter filled Johnson's glass and placed the bottle in the antiquarian ice-bucket. Both waiters then bowed, turned and left.

Johnson drank the glass of wine in one. He needed another drink. He went to reach for the bottle, but before his hand made contact a waiter appeared from nowhere, picked up the bottle and refilled his glass.

'This sure is the life. Just sit back, relax and let it all happen,' said Johnson to himself.

*   *   *   *   *

As Old MacDonald's World's sun rolled across an otherwise clear sky, Amy Mae – niece to Joshua Jeremiah Legrand, the proprietor of Old MacDonald's Wholesale General Stores – waited, dreaming away the time, happy in her own thoughts of what might be.

Amy Mae was the only daughter of Emmy Lou and Henry James Legrand, and was just of age. For Amy Mae reality and imagination, regarded by many as two separate states, often became merged, interchangeable and indistinguishable.

At last she saw the smartly dressed, if somewhat tall, sales representative arrive outside her uncle's warehouse – or, as he liked to call it, his 'headquarters'. She had been waiting in hiding since sunrise, ready to take the sales representative's image and send it to Jez.

The things she did for love. Jez sure did have his funny ideas, but he was way brighter than any of the other young males she knew – and he hadn't tried to get his hands all over her, neither. He was true and honest, and she truly and deeply admired him.

Amy Mae almost forgot to image the sales representative, as her mind took her off on an imagined tour of future possibilities. How she dreamed of that wedding in the chapel and Preacher Grimthorpe residing over the service, making it clear and plain to everyone that this wedding was gonna' be to death us do part and anyone tryin' to tear them asunder would be feelin' the wraith of a mighty vengeful Holy One.

She could see it all now. Her lookin' so beautiful in that pearl-white flowin' dress, she'd seen in her holozine, with flowers in her hair. Jez dressed smart in timeless tradition. Judy Ann, her best friend from school, bein' her chief bridesmaid and all, dressed up in carrot-orange, and the rest of the bridesmaids dressed in each of the colours of the rainbow. It sure would be beautiful. She wondered who Jez would choose as his best male.

Something brought her back to the present, and then she remembered to send the image to Jez, ending her message, 'Amy Mae xxx'.

How she longed for him to return her messaged kisses for real.

* * * * *

Paolo 'Two Fingers' Cigstano, general manager of the Black Hole Casino, stood next to Star Trooper Jonah Jones with the traditional winner's credit certificate stretched between them, and smiled his big broad beaming bright smile whilst the Eye See holodisplay bot took the obligatory winner's image.

The All Seeing Corporation, who fabricate the Eye See holodisplay bot, along with many other ocular products, describe themselves, unsurprisingly, as a corporation that is, 'All seeing'.

The crowd, which had gathered like mirzamic blue moths to a glow globe, clapped and cheered. Billy Bob frowned his displeasure, but this was unnoticed by a jubilant Jones.

Paolo 'Two Fingers' Cigstano was so-called because he always held his hands like a child makes a hand-zapper: with two fingers forming the focusing lens, and the rest, together with his thumb, tucked into the palm of his hand. When he greeted you, he would point his two-fingered hands at you in rapid succession. When he bade farewell, he would raise a two-fingered hand to his forehead and then, smartly, snap off a salute. And he always did these gestures with a big broad beaming bright smile. In fact his big broad beaming bright smile hardly ever left his face, but when it did it was time to worry.

There were various theories, among the casino's associates, as to why he used this two-fingered gesture. The more generous associates thought it was because he liked to pretend he was a zapper-toting lawbreaker – although most suspected he didn't need to pretend. The less generous believed him to be some kind of idiot, employed on a purely nepotistic basis, and that the 'two fingers' indicated the limit of his arithmetic development. However, no one was quite so stupid as to voice that opinion.

The Eye See holodisplay bot rose above the crowd and started to spread the news that the Black Hole Casino had yet another winner. It floated along projecting images of the winning fanfare, the shower of silver and gold stars, and a beaming casino manager presenting that credit certificate, with a lot of numbers on it, to an equally beaming Star Trooper Jonah Jones. And, as it drifted through the gaming halls, it re-projected these images repeatedly, interspersing them with the casino's own catchy slogan, 'Everyone's a winner!'

When the crowd had eventually dissipated, one of the smartly dressed members of Mr Cigstano's entourage approached Star Trooper Jonah Jones. He said that the casino would be only too delighted for Jones to use the penthouse suite for the duration of his stay, in fact it insisted. And, of course, for as long as he frequented the casino, he was free to eat and drink in whichever eatery or beverage emporium he so chose, all at the casino's expense. He also explained to Jones that the traditional credit certificate was purely for show, his winnings were redeemable from any of the casino's own credit dispensers. Oh, and he also rather strongly emphasised that the casino would be only too happy if he were to spend his winnings *here* in the Black Hole Casino.

'Enjoy, my friend, enjoy.' Paolo 'Two Fingers' Cigstano patted Jones on the back heartily and, as he bade him farewell, he raised a two-fingered hand to his forehead and snapped off a salute.

'I will, Mr Cigstano, I certainly will,' replied an extremely grateful Jones.

Billy Bob stood by as Jones span round and round in his wheelchair whooping with glee. Eventually a somewhat dizzy Jones stopped spinning and looked up at his comrade-in-arms.

The Children Of The Soil, and its mission, seemed to have become a distant memory in Jones's mind. He had returned to the casino where he'd previously lost everything: his 'severance' pay from the Space Corps, his artificial legs, the very attire from his body, and his self-respect. Now he was a winner! It was as if he'd regained his life.

'Y'all ain't gonna' forget about the mission we're on?' reminded Billy Bob. 'We came here lookin' for our target 'n all y'all's gone 'n done so far is the Evil One's work.'

[14] A Deal's A Deal

With his image now projected throughout the Black Hole Casino to the sound of 'Everyone's a winner!' Star Trooper Jonah Jones's anonymity was clearly forsaken; though he thought this was a small price to pay for being a winner. And as he and Billy Bob arrived at the casino's premier eatery, Les Temps Perdu, the maître de seemed only to happy to welcome them, announcing their arrival to the diners, who responded with a muted but polite round of applause.

The maître de signalled to a waiter, and the waiter ushered them to a table. Other waiters gathered round, chairs were moved, napkins were laid upon their laps, and menus were passed to them. To approving smiles and praising nods from their waiters they ordered, although, if truth be known, Jones and Billy Bob had no idea what they'd ordered.

'This sure is the life. Just sit back, relax and let it all happen,' said Jones to himself.

Billy Bob prodded Jones. 'There ya' go, y'all were right.'

'Uh?' said Jones.

'He's here, over by the wall,' whispered Billy Bob.

'Who's here?' Jones hadn't quite picked up on the conversation yet.

'Our target, we're back on trajectory. The mission's all systems go!' Billy Bob was ready to leap out of his chair and tackle their target there and then, but Jones held him back.

Meanwhile, their target, who was oblivious to their intentions, began his first course.

Jones leaned forward. 'Remind me again about our mission.'

Billy Bob drew breath and, looking skywards, started to recite the mantra, 'Cousin Jez says: "We are ideologically dedicated to organic principles and the overthrow of corporate universisation. Our mission is to spread the organic word and bring about the collapse of the unorganic corporations that infest the universe with their attempts to enslave the very masses they are meant to serve in themedom."'

Jones thought for a pulsar's pulse. 'And that has what to do with our target?'

Billy Bob looked skywards again and, drawing deep from within his mind, continued, 'Cousin Jez says: "Our target is the embodiment of corporate universisation. He is an agent of one of the most unorganic corporations – a corporation that infests our universe with irradiating sanitation facilities. He tried to enslave our world by attempting to sell those very sanitation facilities to Amy Mae's uncle."'

'OK, so what do we have to do precisely?' asked Jones.

It was as if another voice was speaking through Billy Bob. 'Cousin

Jez says: "We are to make him see the miscalculation of his trajectory, turn him against his corporation, and make him become one of us so we can overturn the system from the inside". Also, "We are to continue our acts of random sabotage". Cousin Jez says: "It is only through our relentless pressure that the system will collapse. Every small act is a step closer towards our goal.'"

Jones was impressed by Billy Bob's ability to remember, though Billy Bob did look tired from the mental strain of reciting Cousin Jez's words.

'Your cousin sure has a lot to say,' commented Jones. 'So what would your Cousin Jez advise us to do now?'

At this Billy Bob looked confused. Thinking for himself had never been one of his stronger attributes. After a considerable amount of reflection, but without much conviction, Billy Bob ventured, 'Commit a small act of sabotage?'

Jones shook his head. Whilst he admired this 'child of the soil' for his commitment and dedication to the cause, it was clear that Billy Bob simply had no idea about how to achieve his aims.

'These small acts of sabotage are just going to irritate everyone. It's a message that will be lost on them. They'll just think that it's things going wrong and breaking down in an ordinary sort of way.' Jones looked directly at Billy Bob. 'What you need to do is to make a statement that they'll take notice of.'

Billy Bob looked at Jones. 'Like what?'

And then it happened. A star of an idea burst forth lighting the usually alcohol-soaked mind of Jones. 'I have an idea.'

Billy Bob waited to hear.

Jones sat back in his wheelchair, rubbed his hands together, and then leant forward, opening his arms and ushering Billy Bob to draw near.

Billy Bob drew close, eager to hear.

Jones beamed a broad smile, exercising muscles that had rarely been troubled over these last few solar cycles.

Billy Bob started to wonder whether he was missing something.

Jones seemed to be transfixed and remained motionless, staring into some bright, distant future all of his own imagining.

Billy Bob decided to prompt Jones. 'And?'

This simple word managed to pull Jones back from his envisioned future. He looked straight at Billy Bob. 'We're gonna' kidnap our target and hold him for ransom.'

Billy Bob opened his mouth and, after he remembered to start breathing, uttered, 'What?'

'I said we're gonna' kidnap him and hold him for ransom,' repeated a now resolute Jones.

In Billy Bob's mind the extraordinary occurred, several thoughts came into being at once and scrambled to be spoken. It was an unnerving sensation, something that Billy Bob had not experienced before. The first thought to be spoken was, 'Y'all's just havin' one 'a them there jokes at my expense, right?'

Given the absence of a response, Billy Bob's next thought was, 'When we've gone 'n bin' caught, 'n the trial's all done, they'll send that holokey so far into orbit it won't ever be comin' back!'

Jones sat in silence, with an air of confidence, further unnerving Billy Bob.

And then Billy Bob spoke his last thought. 'Even if I'm dumb enough to go along with this here chicken-brained plan 'a y'alls, I cain't see how y'all, in that chair 'n all, and me is gonna' do it.'

Jones decided he needed to reassure his clearly nervous co-conspirator. 'By the cosmos, let me put you at ease, this isn't gonna' be any ordinary kidnapping, so you needn't worry, because we're not gonna' kidnap him.'

'We're not gonna' kidnap him?' Billy Bob shook his head, and whilst he tried to hang on to these last few words, he was now lost. And the confusion that had dogged his mind throughout his childhood returned. The memories of bewilderment, when questions were asked and he tried to understand and answer, and the pain of the subsequent classroom ridicule just came right back. He attempted to rally his thoughts. 'So let me get this right. Y'all's sayin' we're gonna' kidnap him 'n hold him for ransom, but then y'all's sayin' we ain't gonna' kidnap him?'

'That's right, you got it in one.' Jones was pleased that Billy Bob seemed to understand.

'It don't make no sense to me,' concluded Billy Bob.

Jones decided he'd have to spell things out. 'We're gonna' tell his employers at the Flush Away Corporation that their employee is with us, which they'll misinterpret as him being kidnapped, but as far as Johnson's concerned, he isn't gonna' know that they think he's been kidnapped; he'll just think he's spending some time with us.'

Realisation glimmered feebly in Billy Bob's mind, and he tried to further clarify what Jones had told him by saying, 'Uh?'

'What we're gonna' do is keep him fully occupied, but out of everyone's sight. He'll think he's just having a good time. We will then say to his employers that he is with us and requests organic restitution; we won't use the word 'ransom'. It can't fail. Are you in?' Jones couldn't spell it out any clearer than that.

'In where?' Billy Bob was at least a sentence behind in the conversation.

With a mental count, Jones answered. 'In on the plan.'

Billy Bob thought for a while. 'No kidnappin'?'

'No kidnapping,' confirmed Jones.

'And no ransom, just requestin'?'

'Just requestin',' echoed Jones.

And as the galaxies continued to separate from each other in their inexorable journey from the birth of the universe, so Billy Bob took his time to consider what had been said. And then, somewhere in the cortex of his brain, a neuron fired.

'Y'all can count me in, after all no kidnappin' 'n just requestin' ain't against no law,' reasoned Billy Bob, though in the back of his mind he vaguely remembered Cousin Jez saying he was '*not to get distracted*', just to '*observe*' and to '*report back*'.

*   *   *   *   *

Investigator Strait and Deputies D'Angelis and Gilbrae stepped outside of the unadorned, square-set structure that was the Second Chance Hotel. Each deputy wore a big straw hat, with frayed edges, and sported garish Neo-Holo attire, which currently displayed cards being dealt and gaming markers being piled higher and higher.

It had been agreed that, from this point on, they would separate. Deputies D'Angelis and Gilbrae would go deep undercover and assume their new identities, as tourists, whilst Investigator Strait would pick up on Johnson's trail. Once he had found Johnson, Investigator Strait would let D'Angelis and Gilbrae know of his location and the undercover deputies would establish contact themselves.

Investigator Strait had withdrawn his own credits from one of the many floating Hole-In-The-Sky credit dispensers to be found on Nova Vega – credit dispensers that located you rather than you having to locate them. On Nova Vega, inhabitants and visitors alike much preferred the untraceable flexibility of credits rather than the traditional, but traceable, holocom payment transactions.

With clear instruction, and a certain reluctance, Investigator Strait handed the credits over to his deputies. 'Remember when you apprehend the suspect we need the evidence on his person. Oh, and by the way, bear in mind these are *my* credits, so I'll be wanting to count them all back in.' He then added, looking at the gambling activities displayed on their Neo-Holo attire, 'So don't even think about gambling.' At which point the Neo-Holo attire images abruptly changed to scenes of a pastoral nature.

Deputies D'Angelis and Gilbrae crossed the walkway and mingled with passers by, soon disappearing from Investigator Strait's view. Investigator Strait pulled his holocom from his attire. The holocom started to 'ping'. A reassuring 'ping' that meant that the credit sized tracking device, he had placed in with his credits, was working. When it was your credits you could never be too sure.

Investigator Strait then hailed a taxi-skyrider and set off for Johnson's last known location; the headquarters of the Creation Corporation. His holocom switched to silent mode as he placed it back in his attire, where he could feel its comforting vibrations against his chest like a second heartbeat.

Traffic in the skyways was heavy and the taxi-skyrider ambled along. Through the window, Investigator Strait admired the clean regularity of the conurbation. However, immediately to his left, casinos lined up like some giant oversize identity parade, their signs flashing hypnotically trying to entice all who looked upon them to come and play. Each was themed to appeal to their prospective customers' imaginations. Their names were designed to evoke the emotion of times past and desires yet to be fulfilled. Next to the iconic Elvis Regency, shaped as an enormous statue of the fully posed singer from antiquity, came the Tumbling Dice, formed as huge interlinked dice frozen mid-throw. The Raging Bull was all too lifelike, snorting great clouds of steam from its flared nostrils, and then there was the Winning Hand, shaped as a towering house of cards. And on and on the casino parade continued.

Investigator Strait knew the seemingly endless flood of credits, that passed through those casinos, attracted every lowlife and lawbreaker on the make, this side of the Spiral Arm. Citizens always wanted what they weren't allowed and, as was tradition here on Nova Vega, there would be someone ready to satisfy that illicit need – for a price, of course. It had always been thus, and Investigator Strait suspected that even with his best efforts, it would probably always be thus; such was the way of the universe. However, that wasn't going to stop him trying to apprehend the lawbreakers.

The taxi-skyrider began to move faster, passing through the forest of skybreakers that constituted the very heart of Nova Vega. Each trying to out reach the other, all emblazoned with holoverts and signage to catch the passing eye. But ahead, at their centre, stood the tallest of their number; the five golden towers, all inwardly arched together, pointing at an enormous, rotating 'CC'. This could only be the Creation Corporation's headquarters.

On arrival, the taxi-skyrider descended. Investigator Strait stepped out and stood awestruck beneath the southern tower, watching visitors pass through the light-screen doorways. He walked forward and followed them through onto a vast marble expanse of foyer.

'Welcome to the Creation Corporation. How may we be of service?' asked the professionally pleasant greetings associate.

Investigator Strait smiled and projected his law enforcement identification in front of the greetings associate. Whilst he was technically out of his jurisdiction, he found that citizens tended to just see the words 'Law Enforcement' and not pay much attention to the detail.

'I'm looking for this male.' Investigator Strait then projected three images of Johnson from his holocom. 'I believe he had an appointment with one of your employees, a Ms Carlsson.'

The professionally pleasant greetings associate nodded and, breaking from her usual corporate platitudes, spoke, 'Oh him! I remember him, Johnson, and his poncho. I ask you who carries a poncho around with them on Nova Vega?' Then, conspiratorially, she leant forward. 'He had difficulty sitting down, you know. That's to say he hadn't experienced our Just Believe chairs before.' She allowed herself a chuckling smile then leant back, regained her professional demeanour, and asked, 'I can see if Ms Carlsson's available if you like?'

'Thank you, but I just need to see the security recordings of Johnson arriving and leaving,' continued Investigator Strait.

'Of course, sir, I'll just get security.' The professionally pleasant greetings associate operated a radon-red icon on her workhub and almost immediately a large cobalt-blue Ever-On security bot, of robust blaster-proof construction, arrived.

'Compute, Security Bot 996 reporting. Compute, what is the problem?' boomed the Ever-On security bot, which, somewhat disconcertingly, raised and rotated its armoured head through three hundred and sixty degrees to survey the potential incident scene.

'No problem,' explained the professionally pleasant greetings associate. 'The Investigator would like to see the security recordings of this visitor arriving and leaving.' She pointed to the images of Johnson.

'Compute, uploading.' Security Bot 996 uploaded the images from Investigator Strait's holocom. 'Compute, projecting.' It then holographically projected recordings of Johnson's arrival and departure.

Investigator Strait's holocom noted the time of departure and the details of the black spherical taxi-skyrider that Johnson had left in.

'Thank you, you have been most helpful.'

'Compute, to obey is to serve,' responded Security Bot 996, which again raised and rotated its head through three hundred and sixty degrees.

As Investigator Strait turned to leave, he was sure the professionally pleasant greetings associate winked at him in a way that was not part of the customary corporate farewell. Whilst a little flattered, he knew he had to press on if he was going to follow Johnson's trail. Given the somewhat delicate legality of his covert undercover operation it was best to keep as low a profile as possible. Regretfully, he just smiled and said goodbye.

Outside he waited for a black spherical taxi-skyrider, just like the one Johnson had departed in.

*　*　*　*　*

Having taken a taxi-skyrider from Old MacDonald's World's Insem-A-

Sow Spaceport, Chad had been dropped off outside a large, dilapidated geodesic dome he supposed was the headquarters of Old MacDonald's Wholesale General Stores. He strolled up to the front door and, even after figuring out it was manual entry, had something of a struggle to pull it open.

Inside, the warehouse was piled high with containers of all shapes and sizes. Chad stood at the empty, unmanned counter and waited. Clearly he'd arrived at a less than busy time. He was about to call out when he found a buzzer half-hidden under an out-of-date hololouge. What a dump. And then, as if to confirm his initial impression, the universe's oldest Ever-On forklift bot whirred and clattered its way into view.

The Ever-On forklift bot juddered to a halt. 'Forklift Bot TE... um, something, er... something, reporting, sir!'

'I am Mr Edger and I have an appointment with Mr Legrand,' stated Chad.

There was a pause. The Ever-On forklift bot whirred. 'Forklift Bot TE... um, something, er... something, awaiting your orders, sir!'

Chad repeated his appointment details and the Ever-On forklift bot continued to await orders.

Chad was not a patient male, and trying to communicate with a pile of junk, long overdue for dematerialisation, did little to improve his disposition. He rang the buzzer again, hoping that something or someone more capable of intelligent conversation might turn up: talking to this stack of mechanical debris was clearly a waste of time and he did not have time to waste.

At last, he could hear the sound of footsteps, or more specifically the stomp of boots. A male with the shortest and squarest of haircuts emerged, dressed head to foot in military fatigues.

Seeing that it was not one of his regular customers, and thus must be his offworld visitor, Joshua Jeremiah Legrand introduced himself with a full salute, 'The name's Legrand, Joshua Jeremiah, 'n I'm in command 'a this here operation y'all see around ya'.' After dropping his salute Joshua Jeremiah Legrand continued at ease, 'Wonderful mornin' we got ourselves here. Hope y'all had a good trip 'n found my lil' ol' headquarters OK.'

Chad smoothed into sales mode, passed his holocard to Mr Legrand and, chameleon-like, mirrored the salute. 'Yes sir, no problem, kind of you to ask. Just admiring your facility here, great stuff. It sure is some set up.'

'Put it all together myself. Used all my life savings 'n my severance pay from the Space Corps 'n bought me this here beauty.' Mr Legrand beamed as he patted the wall of the dome. 'Yeah this ol' dome's sure seen some action in her time, but she's stood by me good 'n strong over the solar cycles. Got me that ex-Space Corps Ever-On forklift bot thrown in for nothin' too.'

'I can see,' said Chad, gazing at the Ever-On forklift bot that looked as though it had made one planet drop too many – the last having evidently been completed without the aid of an atmospheric-descent retarder.

'Over the solar cycles I've bin' able to build up this here business through hard work 'n military discipline, 'n, with the support of the good folks 'a these here parts, it's become what y'all can see,' Mr Legrand boasted proudly.

Chad looked and smiled, his face displaying no indication of his true thoughts.

'I got me everythin' y'all could ever need, 'n I say to my customers: "If I ain't got it, it ain't worth havin",' continued Mr Legrand.

Chad could see rack upon rack, burdened with every conceivable shape and type of container, stretching off into the distance.

Mr Legrand looked directly at Chad and said, 'I was expectin' that other fella, the one who came last time.'

'He was regrettably called away I'm afraid, but I'll think you'll find that I can more than satisfy your requirements, sir,' Chad replied with the utmost of confidence. 'Has there been any interest in the domestic irradiating sanitation units we left with you?'

'I cain't hardly believe it, but them ten units have just flown outta' here, sold the last one last rotation. It seems that a lot 'a folks just ain't satisfied with a piece 'a ground 'n a spade no more, they wanna' do things the contemporary way! I must say I'm a might surprised, folks round here tend to be fixed in their ways ya' know, but who am I to stand in the way 'a progress, particularly when progress means business.' And at that thought Mr Legrand rubbed his hands together.

'Great stuff, that is good news, sir. Perhaps we could discuss what Flush Away might be able to do for you in the future?' asked Chad.

'I'm a might busy, but if y'all make if brief,' replied Mr Legrand.

And Chad was in.

He holographically displayed the range of irradiating sanitation units Flush Away had to offer and worked through their features, careful to vary his pitch to match his customer's apparent level of interest.

He concluded with a short demonstration of what he knew would be too aspirational a product for Old MacDonald's World at this time, though he saw no harm in setting sights early. The themeable Empress irradiating sanitation unit, with its Mould-It-To-Me seat – with posterior massaging capability – was always impressive! And, as all Flush Away employees had been trained to do from their very induction, he ended the demonstration with the line, 'Smile and Flush Away', adding his own actions.

Mr Legrand was literally bowled over. Never had sanitation products caught his imagination so. He could see his customers queuing, desperate for them.

Chad just smiled. He never tired of demonstrating his wares, particularly to those who were new to the universe of irradiating sanitation products and all it had to offer. He never tired of seeing those sceptical faces change to ones of delight and admiration. How he loved the thrill of the sale. What could be better in life than the sweet, sweet taste of commission?

Closure was now key, and Chad wrapped his arm around Mr Legrand, whilst explaining the various retail options and terms he was able to offer. This included, of course, his 'one-time only special introductory deal', although he wasn't sure it was still available, he would have to check.

Mr Legrand asked, if he agreed now, would Chad be able to commit to the 'one-time only special introductory deal'. And Chad, who made sure he took an agonisingly long time to think about it, said that, although he was taking it to the outer rim, just this once he'd make sure, no matter what, that the 'one-time only special introductory deal' would go through even if he had to personally go down on one knee and beg in front of his boss to make it happen.

And, with two approvals and a press of hands, a contract for ten thousand units, with future options, was agreed. Chad had no doubt who Flush Away's best customer-relationship and promotions specialist was. Great stuff!

*   *   *   *   *

Wearing their Neo-Holo attire, together with matching big straw hats, Deputies D'Angelis and Gilbrae were being carried along the main pedestrian walkway, taking in the traditional local atmosphere, but not doing what tourists generally did on Nova Vega: gamble. They were waiting for Investigator Strait to direct them to Johnson.

They managed to be carried past the classic, iconic Elvis Regency, the Tumbling Dice and the Raging Bull Casinos without succumbing to their allures, but by the time they reached the Winning Hand Casino their primitive urges had become too great.

They stepped off the walkway and looked up. The Winning Hand Casino was shaped as a towering house of playing cards. Its entrance was a fanned hand of five massive cards, which lifted individually as customers walked through.

Deputy D'Angelis nudged Deputy Gilbrae, and they too passed underneath one of the giant entrance cards. No sooner were they across the threshold than they were approached by one of the many Happy-Ho-Ho meet and greet bots that circled the entrance hall. The bot was a product from the seemingly inexhaustible range of Happy Bot products fabricated by Lightweight Industries, the corporation that 'Likes to make light of your work'.

'Howdy partners, how'd ya' like to play?' enquired the Happy-Ho-Ho meet and greet bot, which consisted of two large, almost human sized playing cards leant together, pyramid-style, floating above the ground. It had four gesticulating arms and two small articulated crowned heads.

'Play?' replied Deputy D'Angelis, trying to work out which side of the Happy-Ho-Ho meet and greet bot he was talking to.

The Happy-Ho-Ho meet and greet bot rotated in the air, tilted to one side and then, with outstretched arms, chimed in stereo from both of its heads, 'Name your game and we'll show you the way to play!'

Deputy D'Angelis saw that one side was the jack of hearts and the other was the jack of spades, and that both heads spoke. He and Deputy Gilbrae regularly played cards at shift-end, or on long stakeouts when there was nothing better to do. They always played seriously and always played for credits.

The gyrating Happy-Ho-Ho meet and greet bot gently gestured with its gloved hands, trying to elicit an answer.

Surprisingly, it was Deputy Gilbrae who spoke first. 'Poker.'

The bot bounced up and down for joy and chimed, 'Follow me to play the game your way!' At which it set off through the entrance hall towards a downward slope.

The deputies followed the Happy-Ho-Ho meet and greet bot cautiously, as it descended the slope into a vast open arena. The arena was lit by hundreds of small shafts of light shining down upon card table after card table. The bot deftly navigated between the tables.

Soon Deputies D'Angelis and Gilbrae had lost sight of the entrance. They were led to an empty card table operated by a Deal-2-U croupier bot. And within a pulsar's pulse the deputies found themselves sat with drinks and hands of dealt cards in front of them. When they looked around, the Happy-Ho-Ho meet and greet bot had just slipped away.

'Dot dot – Cards players? – dot dot,' asked the Deal-2-U croupier bot from behind its over-exaggerated visor. Both deputies looked at their hands of cards and sent back three cards each. The Deal-2-U croupier bot dealt replacement cards without appearing to need to look at what it was doing.

Both Deputies D'Angelis and Gilbrae declined to continue and folded.

The Deal-2-U croupier bot's outstretched arm whisked the spent cards from the table and returned them to the bottom of the deck in one fluid motion. More cards were dealt, forming the exact same pattern in the exact same place as they had in the last hand.

Deputies D'Angelis and Gilbrae settled down to play cards.

[15] Easy Meet

Johnson had enjoyed the 'freshly zapped plunder from the field, garnished with sprigs of the pastures'. Meat that had had a natural life was a rare delicacy.

For dessert it transpired that a 'mélange of seasonal hedgerow offerings' was a wild berry mousse. Johnson devoured it.

He had finished the bottle of real wine, savoured the real brandy – two glasses – but passed on the real coffee. He decided not to ruin the sunfall by looking at the bill and, after crediting the debit with his holocom, upped and went in search of some action. Being a stellar gamblestar really was fun, he was surprised he hadn't tried it sooner.

Across the corridor from Les Temps Perdu Eatery, the Inner Horizon Beverage Emporium appeared to be an attractive and convenient next stop on Johnson's stellar sunfall.

Inside, Johnson hoisted himself onto a stool and asked the beverage associate for a drink, which he would leave to the beverage associate's discretion to select.

The beverage associate, whose name was Peter, placed a coaster and an empty plastiglass tumbler in front of Johnson. He then searched under the counter and found a dust-covered carton from which he poured a liberal amount.

Johnson looked in the tumbler and held it to his nose. 'What's this?'

'Good for you,' replied Peter.

'Well, here's to you,' toasted Johnson and downed the drink in one. Almost immediately the tumbler slipped from his clasp and he grasped his throat with both hands.

Peter picked up the tumbler, cleaned its rim with his cloth, and asked, 'Another?'

Johnson, who had just started to breathe again, wiped the tears from his eyes and gasped, 'What in the cosmos was that?'

'Oh, that was a drink from my homeworld, a drink for the serious connoisseur. We call it moonblaze.' Peter smiled and picked up another plastiglass tumbler to clean with his cloth.

'I think I'll pass. Do you have something a little smoother, something less prone to asphyxiating your clientele?' rasped Johnson.

Peter, with an air of disappointment, lifted a new tumbler to one of the drink dispensers behind the counter and filled it. 'Try this.'

This time Johnson gently sipped what turned out to be the all-too-familiar taste of Old Redeye, the 'more affordable drinker's drink' fabricated by Scoff Enterprises.

'Excellent. This sunfall, Peter, if I may call you Peter,' said Johnson, reading Peter's name tag, 'this sunfall I am looking for a good time. What would you recommend?'

This was a question that Peter was posed on a regular basis. Luckily for Peter he was reimbursed to provide an answer.

Peter bent forward and looked around slowly, ensuring that no one else in the empty beverage emporium was listening. Johnson was drawn in and leant close to listen. 'The best game in Nova Vega is the Singularity. It's a high risk game and it's played right here at the centre of this casino, you can't miss it just keep on goin' the way you're goin' and you'll find yourself there in a photon's phase.'

'Excellent, one more drink I think, thank you,' responded Johnson. He knocked it back in one, left a generous tip and made for the exit. He turned and waved to his newfound friend who smiled and pointed out the way to the Singularity. Johnson nodded and took some rather unsteady steps towards his next stop on having a good time.

Behind him Peter shook his head and repeated to himself his most often used phrase; 'There's one born every pulsar's pulse.'

* * * * *

Outside the Creation Corporation's Golden Towers, Investigator Strait clambered inside the black spherical taxi-skyrider.

'Destination,' requested the Ever-On taxibot.

'Your control centre,' replied Investigator Strait.

'Black Hole Casino Taxibot Control Centre, please confirm,' responded the Ever-On taxibot.

'Confirmed,' said Investigator Strait.

'Destination imminent,' informed the taxibot and, with a jolt, the taxi-skyrider ascended vertically into the fast moving stream of traffic.

Investigator Strait looked through his passenger window out across the classic skyline of Nova Vega to the surrounding mountain peaks that dwarfed the conurbation below; mountains fabricated by the terraforming forces that had created this planet; mountains that had never been eroded by water or ice, mountains with sharp peaks.

Below, the valley basin was entirely covered with grid bound human habitation. The hydroponic polytunnels, in which food was grown, circled the conurbation's edge – a conurbation that became denser towards its core, and whose buildings became taller, morphing into the skybreakers of the central business district. And between all of these were oases of colour and irregular form, the unmistakable shapes of the casinos and entertainment complexes – traditional sights that evoked a simpler, happier time in a long-lost past.

Behind, right at the conurbation's core, looming above everything else stood five golden towers and the enormous, rotating 'CC' logo of the Creation Corporation. Investigator Strait couldn't help but think that the Creation Corporation really did lie at the centre of things here on Nova Vega, and not just geographically.

And, as always seemed to be the way, the taxi-skyrider dropped away without warning, leaving Investigator Strait's stomach to continue with the skyway traffic. A few photon phases later and the taxi-skyrider juddered to a halt at the rear of the Black Hole Casino. An erratically flashing sign fizzed 'Taxibot Control Centre' in ionic blue above rank upon rank of dormant black spherical taxi-skyriders in various states of disrepair.

Investigator Strait walked to the control centre's door. It whooshed open. Inside all was dark and buzzed with the intermittent crackle of communication and tracking devices. Behind the counter a dishevelled old male in a carbon-black uniform busied himself at the holoplay. The badge on his chest said his name was Bud.

Bud didn't look up on hearing the door open, he just asked gruffly, 'What do ya' want, cain't you see I'm busy right now?' At which point he coughed and spat, missing his intended target, the spittoon by the door. Bud had clearly managed to avoid any form of customer service training for at least a generation, which probably accounted for his less than meteoric rise up the corporate career skyvator; a rise that had, to date, culminated in his current position of maintenance operative.

Investigator Strait walked across to where Bud was sat and projected his law enforcement identification over the counter.

Bud looked up and, recognising the words 'Law Enforcement', muttered, 'Oh.' Again he coughed and spat, and again he missed the spittoon.

'I'm looking for this male.' Investigator Strait projected the three images of Johnson for Bud to see. 'I have reason to believe he took a ride in one of your taxi-skyriders.' Investigator Strait's holocom recited the taxi's designation and the recorded time of the journey.

'Can you tell me what his destination was?' And by way of a somewhat half-hearted afterthought Investigator Strait added, 'Sir.'

Bud deliberated for a while.

'I might be able to, Investigator, but my memory ain't what it used to be. This here holoplay system done and got itself one of them passwords and I just gone and plumb forgot it. Bein' old ain't easy ya' know, it just gets harder and harder to... what was it now?' Bud paused for effect. 'Harder to remember, that's it, harder to remember.' He then coughed and spat, as was his way. This time he managed to accidentally hit the side of the spittoon.

Investigator Strait sighed. He was being led down that same skyway he had been led down a thousand times. If there was one thing that could be relied upon it was the predictability of human nature.

'Is there anything I can do to help you remember?' asked Investigator Strait.

'Come to think of it there may very well be. What was it now?' ruminated Bud, who concluded his thoughts with a further cough and then, returning to his usual accuracy, spat well wide of the spittoon.

'Perhaps something to help ease that cough of yours?' suggested Investigator Strait.

'That might be it.' As ever Bud coughed and again spat some way off from the spittoon.

'Perhaps you could buy yourself something, something medicinal.' Investigator Strait produced some credits and placed them on the counter.

Bud smiled as he placed his hand over the credits.

'Let's see, ah, it's all comin' back to me in one of them there flashes.' And, with the obligatory cough and badly aimed discharge, he interacted with his holoplay.

After a few attempts with the password, the occasional cuss, cough and badly aimed spit, Bud looked up.

'Got it. Your male landed at this here casino, and I ain't got no record of him takin' no other taxis since. I reckon he's still here, probably gamblin' away his credits like the rest 'a them there fools.'

Investigator Strait's holocom noted and highlighted the words 'Black Hole Casino'. He then looked Bud directly in the eye.

'I'm sure you'll forget our conversation Bud, ain't that right?'

Bud considered Investigator Strait's words carefully.

'What conversation?'

*　*　*　*　*

As Old MacDonald's World's sun shone down on him, Jez pondered. He considered Amy Mae to be by far the ablest member of the Children Of The Soil. Even given her young age, she was always attentive when he spoke; she seemed to hang onto his every word. This made a pleasant change from the others who, dare he say, seemed to have both the attention span and the intellectual capacity of an oh-oh fish; an increasingly rare fish that, when facing one of its numerous and plentiful predators, opens its mouth wide and rolls on its back pretending to be dead; a defence mechanism which sadly fails to take account of the fact that its predators are as happy to eat a dead oh-oh fish as a live one.

So when Amy Mae had sent him the image he asked for, of her uncle's latest visitor from the Flush Away Corporation, he was more than a little surprised. There, imaged entering the wholesale general stores, was none other than George Tree, Pacifica's Organic Farming Representative and buyer of much leaf, as tall as ever and dressed in smart business attire. She must have got the wrong male.

Jez sent her a message by return, 'Are you sure you got the right male?'

Amy Mae was sure and replied with a message, 'Sure. After he'd bin' 'n gone I went inside to pick up a bail 'a twine. Uncle JJ was all smiles. He said he'd just done a deal with a Mr Edger, the male from Flush Away, 'n was now the sole planetary distributor of their irradiating sanitation products.' After some thought Amy Mae had decided to end the message with 'Amy Mae XXX', making the kisses bigger this time in the hope that Jez would notice, but as ever he didn't.

'Are you sure it was a Mr Edger?' requested Jez.

'Yes, "Chad Edger, customer-relationship and promotions specialist, sanitation products, Flush Away Corporation", that's what was projected from the fancy business holocard Uncle JJ showed me.' Amy Mae was so busy spelling out the holocard's details that she almost forgot to add the kisses, 'XXX.'

Much to Amy Mae's disappointment, Jez ended their dialogue with a kiss-less, 'Thank you. Jez.'

*   *   *   *   *

In the Winning Hand Casino – which was proving not to be – Deputy D'Angelis turned to Deputy Gilbrae. 'That was Investigator Strait. Our suspect is in a place called the Black Hole Casino. He says we're to go there and locate the suspect. We're then to await further instruction.'

'Right,' replied a distracted Deputy Gilbrae, engrossed in a card game. He tossed out two cards. The Deal-2-U croupier bot nimbly dispensed two replacements.

'We'd better be goin',' remarked Deputy D'Angelis.

'Right,' acknowledged Deputy Gilbrae and glanced at his new cards. He looked up at the Deal-2-U croupier bot and pushed a pile of coloured gaming markers forward. The bot mirrored his action, adding more markers to the pile. And so the stakes were raised, each adding more and more gaming markers until, finally, the hand was called.

Deputy Gilbrae was not pleased at the outcome and, somewhat unusually, vocalised his feelings, 'Damn bot ain't gonna' beat me. Deal again.'

Deputy D'Angelis stood and tapped his colleague on the shoulder. 'I said we'd better be goin'. You can beat the bot later.'

'Right,' replied Deputy Gilbrae and stood begrudgingly, rather less weighed down with credits than he'd been when he'd started playing cards.

'How do we get out of here?' wondered Deputy D'Angelis.

Deputy Gilbrae shrugged.

Deputy D'Angelis thought and then announced, 'Right, we'll go this way.'

And being males of action, the two deputies set off.

Some time later, Deputies D'Angelis and Gilbrae realised that they were back where they had started. It was at this point that Deputy Gilbrae decided to grab the attention of a passing Happy-Ho-Ho meet and greet bot.

'Way out?' Deputy Gilbrae asked bluntly.

The Happy-Ho-Ho meet and greet bot, a lowly pair – the two of clubs and the two of hearts – span in the air and then pointed with its four outstretched arms in all four directions of the compass at the same time. Its two small crowned and articulated heads sang, 'Howdy partners, every way is a way to play, how'd ya' like to stay?'

'Way out?' repeated Deputy Gilbrae with a discernibly menacing edge to his voice as he grabbed hold of one of the bot's arms.

The bot tried to shake itself free whilst its heads continued to sing, 'Name your game and we'll show you how to play!'

Deputy Gilbrae pulled the bot close and pressed his face directly against one of the articulated heads. 'Way out?'

The bot managed to free its arm, shrank back and chimed, 'Follow me for your way!' At which it set off at pace in one particular direction.

Deputies D'Angelis and Gilbrae followed, half-running. Soon they ascended an inclined slope and stood, catching their breath in the entrance hall.

The Happy-Ho-Ho meet and greet bot bobbed up and down, span round, and with a bleep and a whirr reset itself. With renewed vigour it asked, 'How about a game, partners, a game that you can name?'

As the deputies left the Winning Hand Casino, D'Angelis asked Gilbrae whether tying the bot's arms in a knot, and inserting its crowns into its mouths, had really served a useful purpose.

Deputy Gilbrae simply replied, 'Yep.'

'Fair enough,' commented Deputy D'Angelis.

* * * * *

An inebriated and unsteady Johnson had stumbled past the rows of shimmering holographic gaming machines, past more garish themed beverage emporiums and eateries, past the bright Event Horizon Show Stage and eventually into the Black Hole Casino's heart.

There, before him, were gaming tables. As he faltered past these, he noticed a dark space in the middle of the gaming hall. On closer inspection he found that a giant black dome occupied the space. No light shone through nor emanated from the dome. He meandered up to it. Remembering the Creation Corporation's light-screen doorways, and fortified with the courage that only alcohol can bring, Johnson stepped forward, decisively.

There was darkness and then, little by little, there was light, matched by a gradual growing, throbbing pain. Johnson began to make out a pair of amiable elderly faces.

'I wonder what happened to him?'

'Drunk too much if you ask me.'

'Is he all right?'

'That's the trouble with this generation, they can't hold their drink.'

'Ah, he's coming to.'

'When I was young we learnt to drink from an early age.'

'Are you all right, dear?'

'If you couldn't hold it you weren't to drink it, that's what we used to say.'

'If I were you, dear, I'd go and lie down, sleep it off.'

'I don't know, what is the universe coming to?'

Johnson sat up and rubbed his head. His newly gained admirers ambled off and he found himself sat all alone except for his pounding headache. It was then that he caught sight of the titanium-yellow rope cordon wrapped around his feet, and the tumbled golden posts that encircled the black dome. He had tripped.

Eventually, by using one of the upright posts that had contributed to his downfall, he managed to pull himself up. He decided a mere trip was not going to halt his quest for the Singularity and he continued on his circumnavigation of the dome, this time with the aid of the cordon.

It was as he reached the other side that he spotted the Singularity's entrance. He let go of the stabilising rope, straightened himself up, and tottered purposefully towards it.

'Sir,' acknowledged the Ever-On entrance bot. With a practised salute, it lifted the cordon to allow Johnson to pass.

'Thank you,' said Johnson and walked through as steadily as he could, past a small plaque embossed with the 'CC' logo.

Inside, all light was cast upon a giant black gaming wheel. All eyes were transfixed upon its movement. And as it slowed, and the blur gradually came into focus, Johnson could hear the intakes of breath held in anticipation of the outcome. Silence. And then, in realisation, shouts of joy followed by clapping and cheering. Johnson drew closer to the wheel to try and work out what was going on.

'Will those who wish to risk all in the Singularity step forward and take your seats. Everyone else please stand back,' announced a booming voice.

The giant black gaming wheel had seats, incorporated in its outer rim, which faced towards its centre. As each player sat an overhead restraint bar descended, leaving the player with just enough room to place bets on the gaming surface. When all had finished placing their bets, the wheel started to spin, slowly at first and then faster and faster, until it became a black blur. With this the lights dimmed until all was darkness in the dome. Then, without warning, there was a searing flash. The light level gradually returned, the black wheel slowed and stopped. And then silence. And then, in realisation, there were shouts of joy followed by clapping and cheering.

Johnson noticed that one of the seats was empty.

'Will those who wish to risk all in the Singularity step forward and take your seats. Everyone else please stand back,' repeated the booming voice.

At this, a smartly attired male stepped forward and sat in the empty seat. Bets were placed and the giant black gaming wheel span up again. Darkness, a flash, light returning, silence and then shouts of joy, clapping and cheering.

Again Johnson noticed there was another empty seat where there had not been one before – it was where a female had sat. He looked around in the crowd, but could not see her. Where had she gone?

'Will those who wish to risk all in the Singularity step forward and take your seats. Everyone else please stand back,' repeated the booming voice.

Again another thrill-seeker stepped forward, bets were placed, the wheel span: darkness, a flash, light, silence, but this time there were no shouts of joy, no clapping, no cheering and no empty seats.

'Will those who wish to risk all in the Singularity step forward and take your seats. Everyone else please stand back,' repeated the booming voice.

Two customers, who Johnson assumed to be newly-weds from their attire, though rather older than most, dismounted from the Singularity and made for the exit. More fearless thrill-seekers stepped forward to replace them and the cycle began again.

With alcohol still left circulating in his blood stream, an unsteady Johnson followed the couple. Outside, he congratulated them on their marriage and asked, 'I can't help but notice that not everyone who gets on seems to get off. What happens to them?'

The couple smiled happily and the bride said, 'Oh, you mean the losers. They don't come back.'

'They don't come back?' repeated Johnson.

'Nope. All gone,' replied the bride.

'Where do they go?' asked Johnson.

'Who cares? They're losers!' laughed the couple. And arm in arm, buoyed with their winnings, the newly-weds sauntered away.

* * * * *

Billy Bob and Star Trooper Jonah Jones had followed their target with stealth. They had tracked Johnson from Les Temps Perdu Eatery to the Inner Horizon Beverage Emporium, and from the Inner Horizon past the rows of shimmering holographic gaming machines, past the other garish themed beverage emporiums and eateries, past the bright Event Horizon Show Stage and into the Black Hole's heart, the Singularity – all without being noticed, although this was probably due more to Johnson's inebriated state than their tracking skills.

Jones sat in his wheelchair admiring the Singularity. It was singularly the best game in Nova Vega, a game where those who had the courage could take on the ultimate challenge and chance all. You could win big or you could lose big. He ached to play and for once he had the credits to do it.

They watched Johnson in conversation with a newly wed couple and wondered what he would do next.

Jones then span his wheelchair round and caught Billy Bob on the shin.

'Ow! What'd y'all do that for?' asked Billy Bob, hurt.

'Just trying to see if you're awake and on the case. Right, time to start putting our plan into action,' replied Jones, who had decided that he needed to do something to take his mind off gambling or, as sure as the universe was expanding, he would find himself offering devotion to the Prophet Of Providence again. 'Firstly we engage the target.'

Billy Bob, whilst not entirely sure what Jones meant, nodded in agreement.

A few photon phases passed.

'By the heavens, come on, let's engage the target,' instructed Jones. 'Push, push.'

Billy Bob responded and pushed Jones directly towards Johnson.

'Faster, faster,' urged Jones.

As Billy Bob accelerated, Jones braced himself for impact. And then the impact came.

An entangled Johnson began to wonder whether he was fated to be unlucky in life or was it just an innate ability he had?

After all had disentangled themselves, Jones could only apologize for Billy Bob's incompetence and insisted that he bought Johnson a drink. It was the least he could do for the inconvenience that had been caused.

Johnson tried to refuse politely. His body was telling him that alcohol was the cause of his problems not its cure.

'A caff-o perhaps?' continued Jones.

'A caff-o?' echoed a somewhat disorientated Johnson.

'A caff-o it is. William Robert,' commanded Jones and elbowed Billy Bob, who was wondering quite who 'William Robert' was. Billy Bob, as instructed, then rolled Jones on towards the quietly lit Last Bean Caff-O House.

'Let us introduce ourselves. This is William Robert, my somewhat, shall we say, hapless aide,' said Jones, 'and I am Mr Jones, at your service, Mr...?'

'Um, Johnson,' responded Johnson extending his hand. 'Pleased to meet you.'

Something flickered in the back of Johnson's mind.

'William Robert and I are here enjoying all that this casino has to offer. For you see fortune has favoured us and we have been lucky enough to win a not inconsiderable sum. A sum presented to us by Mr Cigstano, the casino manager, only this rotation.' Jones smiled cheerfully.

Johnson now knew where all his luck had gone: to Mr Jones. 'You must be a lucky male.'

'By the stars, I wouldn't go as far as to say that. William Robert and I have our own trials and tribulations,' replied Jones looking down at where his legs would have been, had he still had them.

*   *   *   *   *

Deputies D'Angelis and Gilbrae arrived at the very large, and very black, Black Hole Casino. The chase was on. Without stopping to admire the eye-catching display of crackling blue ionic discharge, which washed over the casino's surface, they made for the entrance. They had been tasked to find Johnson.

Once inside, they systematically reconnoitred the casino, following their law enforcement agency training. They built a mental holoview of the interior whilst always being observant, searching for Johnson. They looked along the rows of shimmering holographic gaming machines; in the garish themed beverage emporiums and eateries; and in the bright Event Horizon Show Stage. They reached the main gaming hall and instigated a search pattern, circling round, gradually spiralling in towards its centre.

Deputy D'Angelis nudged Deputy Gilbrae, and indicated towards a caff-o house – the Last Bean Caff-O House. He had spotted Johnson, and Johnson was not alone. He was sat with two males: one was in a wheelchair, and seemed to be doing all the talking, whilst Johnson drank from a cup of caff-o; the second, younger than the others, was dressed in somewhat ill-fitting attire.

As Deputy D'Angelis observed the two males more closely, he recognised the second, younger male. He was the male they had marshalled into the back of their skyrider, back on Pacifica. He was the offworld scratcher they had failed to notice escaping, the male they had omitted to tell Investigator Strait about. Perhaps the offworld scratcher wasn't a scratcher after all.

Deputy D'Angelis checked around to make sure no one was listening. He then raised his holocom to his face and spoke, 'Investigator, we've tracked down Johnson. He's with two other males and, as instructed, we're just observing.'

Deputy D'Angelis then listened to Investigator Strait tell him to carry on and do nothing, just observe.

'OK, Investigator, and by the way, I think I recognise one of the two males with Johnson,' added Deputy D'Angelis.

There was a pause whilst Investigator Strait spoke.

'I recognise him from Pacifica,' replied Deputy D'Angelis.

Another pause.

'When we started to tail Johnson,' answered Deputy D'Angelis.

A long, rather more subdued, pause followed.

'We picked him up. He was in the back of our skyrider, but he escaped,' responded Deputy D'Angelis.

In anticipation of Investigator Strait's rebuke, Deputy D'Angelis pulled his holocom well away from his ear.

Investigator Strait started shouting, and continued to shout for some time.

'We thought he was just some offworld scratcher, so we didn't think it was important,' Deputy D'Angelis managed to interject.

More shouting.

'No, Investigator, I understand, thinking is something we'll refrain from doing in the future,' replied a contrite Deputy D'Angelis.

Slightly less shouting.

'Yes, Investigator, it won't happen again,' apologised Deputy D'Angelis.

There was another a pause.

'Yes, Investigator,' replied Deputy D'Angelis as he cautiously moved his holocom back towards his ear.

A final pause.

'Right, Investigator, we'll observe and see what we can find out about the two males... Yes, Investigator, I'll stream you a hololink so you can take a look and see if you can identify them... Right, Investigator, we won't intervene until you tell us... Over and out, Investigator.' The conversation ended, much to the relief of Deputy D'Angelis.

'I'm telling you he isn't happy, he sure isn't happy. There again I can't remember a time when he was ever happy,' remarked Deputy D'Angelis.

Deputy Gilbrae grunted.

As instructed, Deputy D'Angelis selected hololink mode and pointed his holocom at Johnson and his two acquaintances. It gathered their images and transmitted them to Investigator Strait.

In the distance, an Eye See holodisplay bot circled the gaming hall blaring out 'Everyone's a winner' and, with a fanfare, projected images of winners for all to see and all to aspire to.

'Some sure are lucky,' commented Deputy Gilbrae, recalling his recent gambling experience.

'Lucky, yes,' responded Deputy D'Angelis, who was surprised to have been engaged in conversation. 'Wait a pulsar's pulse, isn't that?'

And there, amid the projected shower of silver and gold stars, was a male in a wheelchair, who looked a whole lot like the male in the wheelchair with Johnson. He was being presented with the traditional credit certificate – a credit certificate with a lot of numbers on it.

'I'll be, he's a winner. I guess I'd better let the Investigator know.' And Deputy D'Angelis reluctantly checked in with Investigator Strait again.

At the other end of the conversation Investigator Strait digested the news. Here they were on Nova Vega with Johnson, who in his mind was undoubtedly a leaf trafficker. And Johnson happened to be talking with a rich male, and this male happened to be with some offworld scratcher, a scratcher who his deputies had narrowly missed apprehending back on Pacifica. Coincidence? In his experience coincidence happened to others. He told Deputy D'Angelis to hold on, he was coming over.

'The Investigator says we're to hold on, he's coming over,' relayed Deputy D'Angelis, who felt obliged to keep Deputy Gilbrae abreast of the situation, although he suspected that Deputy Gilbrae was generally less than interested until it came to the hand-to-hand combat part.

A disinterested stare encapsulated Deputy Gilbrae's singularly predictable response.

* * * * *

Johnson listened and Mr Jones talked. Well, he half-listened; his head really did ache. He wasn't certain whether it was the alcohol, or the rather regrettable fall he'd had, that caused his head to throb, but throb it did. Sipping caff-o was only serving to clear his mind and make the headache more apparent – so much for being sober!

'I'll tell you what, why don't you join William Robert and I for the rest of the sunfall. We'll experience the best this casino has to offer, on me. We could do with some company couldn't we William Robert?' suggested Jones

'Huh… yep.' Billy Bob was struggling to come to grips with his new persona of William Robert, aide to Mr Jones. He'd never been an aide before and wasn't quite sure what one did. Come to think of it, he'd never been a William Robert before either. He thought it was best to say as little as possible and not to ask any questions.

'William Robert's up for it, what d'ya' say?' persisted Jones.

Johnson toyed with the idea. The *old* Johnson surely would have gone to his room by now and would be watching the best of whatever programming the holoplay had to offer. But as far as the *new* Johnson was concerned, Johnson the stellar gamblestar, the party hadn't started.

'Excellent, sounds good to me,' said Johnson as enthusiastically as he could.

'Then, by the cosmos, let's go.' Jones smiled.

And as the three left the Last Bean Caff-O House to continue their sunfall, Jones turned to Billy Bob and whispered, 'Just make sure he's always got a drink. Apart from that keep quiet and follow my lead.'

At the dice table, Johnson thought his luck might change, but all-too-quickly the mountain of gaming markers Mr Jones had passed to him had become eroded by the winds of chance to become a small foothill, which then turned into a desolate plain.

Next came the card table. Johnson proved to be nothing if not consistent, and the latest pile of gaming markers managed to simply vanish; there one photon's phase, gone the next! However, Mr Jones kept feeding him gaming markers, so Johnson had no reason to stop playing. One thing that didn't seem to vanish was his drink. Every time he thought he'd finished, he found his plastiglass tumbler to be full.

It was after Johnson had the disappointment of a particularly poor sequence of improbable card combinations that Mr Jones suggested they play the Singularity.

Johnson was more than happy to play something else; dice and cards were clearly not his thing. In fact Johnson was more than happy, as long as he had that ever-full tumbler in his hand. Which reminded him, now where had it gone? 'Thank you William Robert.' What was that phrase he often said to himself? 'Ah yes, "Drink to forget, but don't forget to drink."' It was a credo that so seemed to fit his life.

[16] Revolutionary Thinking

Jez sat and thought. He sat on a handmade organic wooden bench at the edge of an organic orchard overlooking a field of grazing organic altairian sheep. The blue, cloudless sky was positively radiant, glowing from the light of Old MacDonald's World's deep orange sun. Just above the horizon, the planet's solitary ring circled from edge to edge. And, high up in the stratosphere, the deep blue sky was streaked with zigzag ribbons of green; a phenomenon peculiar to Old MacDonald's World that no one, as yet, has been able to explain.

Jez took the zigzag ribbons of green as the very symbol of his planet's organic status. He truly believed that after the 'Organic Revolution' had brought about the demise of the unorganic corporations he, as leader of the Children Of The Soil, would raise a flag of zigzag green ribbons over this and many other planets.

But at this juncture in the space-time continuum, it seemed to be the corporations that were winning. Flush Away had established a foothold on his beloved homeworld, and he could only imagine the thousands of irradiating sanitation units that were on their way to undermine the very essence of his movement. They had to be stopped.

*   *   *   *   *

Upon his arrival at the Black Hole Casino, Investigator Strait marshalled his team into a small, secluded booth near the gaming hall's only access way. Here they could have a quiet discussion without being overheard, and would be able to see if any of the suspects left.

'These three are up to something and we're going to find out what it is. There are too many coincidences goin' on,' explained Investigator Strait.

Investigator Strait's holocom buzzed. It had completed its holobase match for the identities of the other two males who were with Johnson. He read the results out aloud in the ponderous, methodical way all members of law enforcement agencies have learnt to do, 'The male in the wheelchair, a Mr Jonah Jones, is an ex-star trooper, an offworlder who arrived on Pacifica some time ago. He is a vagrant who has become well-known for his persistent begging and drunkenness.'

'And the other male, Investigator? Do you know his identity?' prompted Deputy D'Angelis.

'Unfortunately the other male is unknown to the law enforcement holobase on Pacifica, Deputy D'Angelis,' announced Investigator Strait solemnly, but then added with a sly smile, 'however, his face has been matched, on our Operation Kicking Butt surveillance sub-file, to that of a starliner passenger, a Mr Billy Bob Brown. He is another offworlder who arrived on Pacifica a few rotations ago, a citizen of the agricultural planet of Old MacDonald's World. Other than that we know nothing else about him. Right then, I wonder: why are these two now on Nova Vega, and what could they have to do with Johnson?'

'Looks like they're having a good time to me,' replied Deputy D'Angelis.

'Yep, who wouldn't be having a good time with all the credits they've won,' added an unusually talkative, though bitter, Deputy Gilbrae.

His colleagues looked at each other. It was rare that they were graced with a whole sentence from Deputy Gilbrae.

Armed with more questions than answers Investigator Strait leant back, closed his eyes and assumed his *concentrated cognitive thought* position with his hands behind the back of his head and his mouth wide-open.

Deputies D'Angelis and Gilbrae knew better than to interrupt the Investigator when he went into this position. They had long since learnt that interrupting the Investigator, when he was in this state, would lead to a tirade of abuse and, generally, some kind of punitive duty. Whereas, leaving him often led to the Investigator entering *concentrated deep sleep* and peace and quiet for all!

As he leant back Investigator Strait could only hypothesise. A sales representative, a vagrant and an offworld scratcher all at a casino. Somehow it must be tied up with the leaf trafficking, but how?

Investigator Strait held the view, based on more solar cycles of law enforcement than he would care to remember, that everyone was guilty of something and law enforcement was just a matter of proving it. This meant that, based on his laws of probability, what seemed most obvious was often most true. If asked, he would always say to go with your gut instinct, after all that was what had enabled him to rise to the rank of Investigator after a lifetime of dedicated service, and that was what was going to help him rise further, even if it took another lifetime.

Then, as if by revelation, it came to him. Jones is from the walkway. He lives on the walkway, he knows the walkway, and he even sits close to the walkway. He had to be the walkway dealer selling the leaf to those pathetic, pitiful addicts. And what a masterful disguise, everyone would know him, but the authorities would just see him as a drunken vagrant begging for loose change. It even explained why he hauled himself around in that ridiculous wheelchair: what better place to hide the leaf?

Brown is an offworlder from an agricultural planet. You didn't need to be able to derive the theory of relativity to work out: a farmer, an agricultural planet, and what do farmers do? They grow things, or more specifically in this case: leaf!

Johnson is a sales representative, travelling back and forth, doing the deals.

They must have all gathered together here on Nova Vega to launder their ill-gotten gains. Where better to suddenly acquire wealth? No one would think twice about large amounts of credits changing hands here.

So that left the finance and organisation behind the leaf trafficking.

Ah ha! That was the easy part. It was so obvious, it was in front of everyone's eyes, floating past: the Eye See holodisplay bot was projecting it for all to see! Amid the winning fanfare, and the shower of silver and gold stars, there he was: the beaming casino manager presenting a credit certificate to an equally beaming Jones.

Never had credit laundering been so blatant. 'Everyone's a winner!' indeed. Not this time, he'd soon wipe those smiles off their beaming faces.

Investigator Strait could see it all now. He and his Tactical Response Assault Patrol, through their tenacious, hard and diligent work, were about to bring Operation Kicking Butt to a successful conclusion. The whole leaf-trafficking ring was going to be brought down. This would surely mean promotion.

He left *concentrated cognitive thought* and sat forward. He opened his eyes and addressed his team. Both D'Angelis and Gilbrae nodded and agreed at the appropriate points as he explained it all to them.

'What do we do now, Investigator?' asked Deputy D'Angelis.

Investigator Strait thought and thought.

'We need what we've always needed: evidence.'

'We've still got your credits, in case you'd forgotten. Why don't Gilbrae and me follow through on our original plan and go and buy some leaf from Johnson? If he produces it, we'll grab him and the leaf. If not, we'll just walk away,' suggested Deputy D'Angelis, with an uncharacteristic display of determined clear thinking.

'You're right, but we must be careful, we don't want another diplomatic incident do we? If in doubt, leave it, we can try again another rotation,' cautioned Investigator Strait.

And so Deputies D'Angelis and Gilbrae set off in search of their suspects, leaving Investigator Strait as backup, waiting near the gaming hall's only access way.

It was at the Singularity that they found them. There, inside the black dome: Johnson, Jones and Brown were stood facing the giant black gaming wheel, in awe.

'They're queuing to play the Singularity. Shall we join them?' whispered Deputy D'Angelis into his holocom.

Deputy D'Angelis waited for Investigator Strait to pass on his instructions.

119

'OK, we'll wait for them to finish and then we'll talk to Johnson,' he confirmed.

*   *   *   *   *

'Will those who wish to risk all in the Singularity step forward and take your seats. Everyone else please stand back,' announced a booming voice.

As providence would have it, Jones counted three empty seats – just what they needed. He invited the others to play. In the giant black gaming wheel each seat was sequentially numbered, alternating in black and red up to thirty-six.

Billy Bob lifted Jones from his wheelchair and placed him in one of the empty seats. He then sat next to Johnson.

Johnson saw he was in *unlucky* black thirteen, William Robert was sat next to him in red twelve and Mr Jones had managed to end up in *lucky* black seven.

The overhead restraint bars descended.

Each of them had a large pile of gaming markers and a certain amount of anxiety. For Jones this was the pinnacle of his gambling career, the highest stake game of all. He could feel the adrenalin pumping. Johnson, given his seat number, wondered what might go wrong. And Billy Bob started to feel nauseous with guilt as he began to recall the sermons of Preacher Jedidiah Grimthorpe.

A soft, sensual voice then spoke in their ears, 'Players, please place your bets.'

Billy Bob saw Jones push all of his gaming markers onto twenty-one black and, as instructed, followed his lead, placing all his gaming markers on twenty-one black also.

Johnson looked in front of him. Within arms length there was an individual circle segmented into thirty-six parts with all the odd-numbers black and all the even-numbers red. Beyond that was a segmented circular track, which started with a green zero and then alternated in black and red from one to thirty-six. At the very centre of the Singularity Johnson could see a large silver ball spinning on its axis in free space. He decided he would play safe and not place a bet this time around. He'd wait and see what happened first.

The soft, sensual voice spoke again, 'Sir, please place your bet. The game cannot begin until all bets have been placed. If you do not wish to place a bet, please leave the game.'

Johnson saw that the rest of the players were looking at him. Clearly he had to play and decided to place some of his gaming markers on – he could feel the eyes of the other players bearing down on him with increasing intensity the longer he was indecisive – on *lucky* number seven.

The soft sensual voice spoke, 'Players, all bets have been placed. Let's play the Singularity!'

Unexpectedly there was no sensation of movement. It was the universe outside the Singularity that started to spin, faster and faster, until it became a blur; a blur that darkened until it became black. Then there was a searing flash and the spinning silver ball was released. It rapidly spiralled out to race round and round the inner circular track. The ball bounced and ricocheted, randomly leaping from one numbered segment to another.

And, as it lost its energy, so the light of the outside universe began to return.

And, as the ball slowed, so the Singularity slowed until both came to rest in silence.

And then there were shouts of joy followed by clapping and cheering.

* * * * *

Sat under Old MacDonald's World's deep orange sun, Jez considered the fact that the male he was doing business with, George Tree – Pacifica's Organic Farming Representative and buyer of much leaf – was also Chad Edger – one of Flush Away's customer-relationship and promotions specialists, and seller of irradiating sanitation products. Such a male was clearly duplicitous.

However, Jez realised that this revelation presented a whole new scope of opportunity for the Children Of The Soil. If a trusted employee of the Flush Away Corporation was exposed as a leaf trafficker, well that would look bad for the corporation's much-valued image of social responsibility. This knowledge could be a great deal of use in their struggle.

And what if it is more than one employee? What if leaf trafficking and the like were endemic throughout their entire rotten corporate culture? When revealed that would surely bring about the demise of Flush Away.

Flush Away would be flushed away!

And, if one corporation was behaving this way, what about the rest? It would be the end for all of them.

Jez stood with clenched fists and proclaimed with fundamentalist fervour to the field of disinterested organic altairian sheep grazing before him, 'The Children Of The Soil will soon harvest what they have grown!'

* * * * *

In the Singularity the silver ball had come to rest on number twenty-one. Johnson had lost again. However, he could see that Mr Jones was beside himself with delight, though William Robert seemed strangely afraid of the gaming markers that appeared before him.

'Will those who wish to risk all in the Singularity step forward and take your seats. Everyone else please stand back,' announced a booming voice.

Johnson looked around and saw two vacated seats, but these were quickly filled. Everyone wanted to play the Singularity.

The soft, sensual voice then spoke, 'Players, please place your bets.'

Johnson watched as Mr Jones pushed his tottering tower of gaming markers onto twenty-one black again and, as instructed, William Robert followed his lead. There were gasps from the other players.

'What were the chances of twenty-one black coming up again? Better than any number he might pick,' thought Johnson. And so Johnson decided to follow Mr Jones's lead and pushed all of his remaining gaming markers onto twenty-one black.

Johnson stared intently at the large silver ball spinning at the very centre of the Singularity. He found himself willing the ball to land on his chosen number.

The soft sensual voice spoke, 'Players, all bets have been placed. Let's play the Singularity!'

Without sensation the universe outside started to spin faster and faster until it blurred to black. In a searing flash the silver ball was released. It spiralled out, racing around the circular track. It bounced and ricocheted, leaping from one numbered segment to another. As it lost its energy so the light from the outside universe began to return. And, as the ball slowed, so the Singularity slowed, until both came to rest in silence.

Red twelve.

And that was all Johnson saw before the universe around him blanked out. He felt a stomach churning sensation and, released from the embrace of the overhead restraint bar and the support of the seat below, he fell into the darkness.

[17] True To Nature

Once every lunar cycle Flush Away's executive board gathered together behind closed ancient oak-panelled doors. Only board members were invited, and only board members attended. For it was at this meeting that the executive board ran through its defined agenda to ensure that they were performing the correct and proper governance of the corporation.

The executive board was there to enhance the corporation's value and return for its shareholders, whilst ensuring the promotion of, and adherence to, a full programme of corporate social responsibility. This was documented and was clear for all to see in the minutes of their meeting.

But what is written and what happens behind closed ancient oak-panelled doors can often differ. Sometimes it's what's not written that needs to be read.

This time, like every time before, Flush Away's executive board members greeted each other as long-lost friends, whilst jostling for the upper hand with smiles and pleasant small talk seeded with jokes they would only tell in their own company.

A casual observer would consider this to be nothing more than normal group behaviour and interaction, but to a more experienced eye much had already been done and said. Alliances had been forged and broken, deals offered, insults traded, innuendos made and all with a single purpose: self-interest.

To be a member of Flush Away's executive board the single most important survival trait was the ability to be self-serving. Ironically, this was the one trait that was never included in the leadership evolution sessions, the team enhancement events, or the capability enrichment processes that pervaded every aspect of a Flush Away corporate career.

Not one documented annotation was to be found among the endless pages that detailed the evaluation and assessment of the numerous capabilities and potential of Flush Away's employees. Which was most odd because without the ability to be self-serving an employee's career in the Flush Away Corporation was going nowhere.

To be able to display this key trait, the single essential question that had to be asked over every word, action or proposal was simply, 'What's in it for me?' So as far as those gathered around the ancient oak table were concerned the Flush Away Corporation solely existed as a vehicle to enhance their own self-interest.

Not all of Flush Away's executive board members showed the same level of adeptness at being self-serving. However, all knew that there were no friends in the room. Each would gladly sacrifice the other to the God Of Self-Interest, and often did.

Chief Executive & President Joseph Firtop, a male of indeterminate age, sat at the head of the table. Outwardly charming, amiable but with a clear focussed intent, he presided over, or more often than not refereed, the executive board. He was a male who considered every interaction a deal. In fact to many he gave a superficial first impression of being a pre-utilised bot sales representative. A male who rarely trusted himself never mind others.

Ably assisting the chief executive and president, and sat at his right-hand side was Chief Fiscal Officer Tobe Milton, a male whose small physical stature was totally eclipsed by his calculating, clinical logicality. He could deconstruct all to numerical form, rapidly determine a percentage, and impassively act without being hampered by those unnecessary human traits of compassion, empathy or sentimentality.

Fulfilling the role of vice-president of conception and evolution, and sat at Joseph Firtop's left-hand side, Aron Grace physically towered over the rest of the board. He was a male of remarkable innovative intellectual ability who could bedazzle all with his limitless technical jargon to a devastatingly soporific effect. He had an unerring talent to cause offence without intent in the most pleasant of ways. But perhaps his most notable aptitude was his ability to marshal and direct every resource available in search of the latest holy grail of sanitation product design without ever running the risk of finding it.

It is said that a sales representative, a true sales representative, is born and not made. If this were the case then Vice-President Of Customer-Relationships & Promotions Francis Stein was sewn together from what body parts were lying around in the mortuary at the time, and was shocked into life on the slab with lightning from a passing solar storm. His approach was based on relentless positiveness and a dogged drive to never let go, achieving not so much a win-win as a pyrrhic outcome. And, much against everyone's better judgement, he had only one true love: himself.

Vice-President Of Merchandising Luton Touch was a clever male who had managed, despite his apparent handicap of being bereft of any personality, to rise to the lofty heights of executive board membership. His ability to de-empower those around him, by imposing his central command and control management style, was legendary. What was more miraculous was that he did this without ever making a decision himself. Never did an employee work so hard and diligently on his own career development, a career in which he actually achieved nothing. A master of presentations, meetings, networking and one-to-one sessions he managed to ensure none outshone him.

And, never too far away, sat Vice-President Of Fabrication Tim Moontide who was responsible for product fabrication in the Flush Away Corporation. A lesser mortal would view this as a lose-lose position, given the impossible complexity of the task. It was a statistical certainty that at any one time something, somewhere, somehow would go wrong. But to counteract this unfortunate statistical situation, Tim Moontide had developed an unambiguous and transparent blame culture in which those responsible could be readily identified. This had the double benefit of suppressing any risk taking or free thought, and provided Tim Moontide with an excellent tool to eliminate those who he deemed to be a threat to his tenure.

Though to focus solely on the members of the executive board of the Flush Away Corporation is to do a disservice to the thousands of humans, bots and other quasi-sentient machines that toiled rotation in, rotation out to make Flush Away what it is. Employees and machines whose leadership had engendered such affection that they poetically referred to the Flush Away Corporation as 'Sweet Flush Away' or, perhaps more often, simply, 'Sweet F. A.' This term of endearment seemed to embody the whole spirit of the Flush Away Corporation and capture both the achievements of the executive board and what the realistic outcome of the workforce's aspirations would more than likely be.

As Chief Executive & President Joseph Firtop sat at the very ancient oak table it was evident that he was not particularly concerned about the executive board meeting or the details of the minutes. He left it to others to perform the drudgery of noting actions. For him the real actions were determined and agreed outside the meeting. A word here, a suggestion there, a prompt or reminder, a casual remark, a comment, and all, most importantly, off the record.

Other executive boards would have used a trusted employee, such as a personal associate, to be more effective in minute taking. However, in the Flush Away Corporation, because a *trusted* employee was a misnomer, this was not done.

Not unsurprisingly among the board members there was no shortage of volunteers for minute taking. All perceived taking the minutes as a way to ensure that their cosmic perspective was clearly documented. A simple word change here, a grammatical alteration there, and, all of a sudden, the way a sentence was written was as it should be: your way.

Joseph Firtop always left it to the melee of petty intercourse between the other board members to select the minute taker. If, as was more than often the case, the debate became irreconcilable he would normally chose the most vociferous person, believing them to be the most needy and thus the most grateful when selected.

Unusually, this time, Vice-President Of Merchandising Luton Touch had risen to the top of the heap and assumed the burden of minute taking, which he started doing immediately, despite the fact that no one had said or agreed anything yet.

'Aren't we being a little premature with our minutes, Luton,' commented ever-vigilant Chief Fiscal Officer Tobe Milton.

'Busy, busy, busy. No harm in being ahead of the game,' replied Luton Touch, playing the productivity card. He then added, 'You don't want to slow the meeting down by having to wait for minute taking to be finished, do you?'

Un-distracted, Joseph Firtop stood.

'Greetings. Let me first welcome you all to this the five thousand, seven hundred and thirty-eighth consecutive meeting of the executive board of the Flush Away Corporation, a record of meetings we are all very proud of. As is tradition, I am sure you will all join me in toasting the memory of the founder of this fine corporation.'

To a male – and without even a token female – the executive board stood and raised their plastiglass tumblers to a rather dusty holographic image on the wall.

'To Sam Carthopper!' resounded Joseph Firtop.

And the rest of the board joined in. 'To Sam Carthopper.'

'May he be remembered every time a Flush Away sanitation unit is flushed, wherever that may be.' Joseph Firtop smiled.

'Wherever that may be,' agreed the rest of the executive board.

'A OK. So, tradition aside, shall we get down to business? What's first on the agenda?' Joseph Firtop rubbed his hands with anticipation as he and the rest of the board sat.

The vice-president of merchandising, who had resumed interacting with the holoplay, stopped for a brief pulsar's pulse and pointed at the hundred or so numbered lines of densely packed writing projected above the middle of the ancient oak table for all to see. 'Actions from the last meeting.'

He then continued with this meeting's minutes.

There was a collective sigh from the rest of the board. This part of the agenda invariably threw the rest of the agenda adrift on a sea of minutiae, intractable points, and irresolvable issues.

* * * * *

Out across the vast, open agricultural expanse of Old MacDonald's World, Chad Edger – who had now assumed the character of George Tree for the purposes of his visit – descended towards the ramshackle buildings that comprised the Usherman Farmstead. He stepped from the taxi-skyrider and looked around. It was as run down as he remembered; rusting machinery and lean-to timber constructions all gently decaying in the post meridian sun.

He walked up to the whitewashed main house and, from the veranda, tapped on the traditional wooden front door. In the yard the odd Go-To-It utility bot scurried past, fetching and carrying. Beyond the picket fence, the farmstead was surrounded by field after field of crops stretching to the horizon.

He waited. On top of the swing seat, at the end of the veranda, a large lazing regulian cat stretched out on the cushion and watched him, carefully.

He waited. The regulian cat lost interest and rolled onto its back. He could hear footsteps. The front door opened and Ms Mary Usherman, Jez's mother, stood before him.

'Why, Mr Tree, what a pleasant surprise!'

'Respects, mam,' greeted a jovial Chad.

Mary Usherman looked a little confused. 'Jez did not mention that you were going to pay us another visit.'

'Oh, I happened to be planetside and dropped him a note. Thought I'd see how you were getting on. He probably hasn't had a chance to tell you yet.' Chad carried on beaming his customer-relationship and promotions specialist's smile.

'Do not stand out there; come on in. I believe Jez is just out back. He is very excited about that new crop variant you introduced us to. He says it will be an excellent credit crop for us.' Jez's mother smiled and indicated to a chair in the living-room. 'And it is not as if we do not need the credits. Take a seat and I will go and get him.'

'Great Stuff!' Chad sat back and cast his eye around the room. It had that faded but loved quality. Most everything seemed to be fabricated from wood. It was a room whose contents would not be out of place in a museum.

There was a wood-burning stove in a brick fireplace, with a basket of logs and some archaic-looking implements to hand, a bookcase with real books, a wooden table with a white tablecloth, and a real glass vase full of saffron-yellow flowers. Real paintings hung on the walls. There was an antiquarian piano with family images on it: Jez, Jez's mother, Jez and his mother, extended family, older couples, but no obvious image of a father.

The door opened and Jez came through. Chad stood and they pressed hands.

Jez spoke first.

'Good to see you, Mr Tree. Got your note. Shall we go outside? I will show how that new crop is coming on if you like.'

Chad nodded in agreement.

'Mother, we are just going outside to look at the new crop,' shouted Jez, as they left the room.

There was a muffled reply.

'Right, this way,' indicated Jez.

'Before we go, I need to use the washroom,' stated Chad.

'Certainly. It is just out back,' replied Jez.

'Out back?' Chad seemed a little uncomfortable about the prospect.

'Yes. We are totally organic. You will not find any of those unorganic irradiating sanitation units here. On this land what comes from the soil is returned to the soil,' answered Jez, rather pointedly.

'Oh right, yes, good idea,' agreed Chad, trying to remember to be George Tree.

'This way.' Jez showed Chad around to the back of the house.

Before them, in the middle of the backyard, stood a solitary wooden shack that looked just large enough to hold one person, uncomfortably.

'It is something special, it is called a dunny,' announced Jez proudly. 'It is of primitive Ancient Earth design, primarily developed for very dry climates where water is at a premium. It was later adopted by the organic movement and has been further improved to what you see before you.'

Chad thought, 'He can't be serious!' He then, rather hesitantly, asked, 'Improved?'

'Yes. This contemporary incarnation offers a new level of comfort and sophistication. Here let me show you.' Jez walked to the dunny.

Chad had been in the business, so to speak, for many solar cycles, but this was something of a universe-expander. Reluctantly, very reluctantly, a combination of Nature's call and human curiosity drew him closer.

Jez pulled open the door.

'Is it not wonderful, the aroma of Mother Nature at work? Here recycling all our human waste into compost from which the food we eat will grow, and thus restarting the organic cycle again.'

Chad tried not to retch. 'Great stuff!'

'For comfort I have added a contoured wooden seat, the traditional dunny had a couple of nailed-together planks with a hole in the middle,' continued Jez.

Chad looked at the roughly hewn slice of timber, with its centre knocked out, and thought of splinters.

'Organically, a further enhancement is the availability of large plant leaves for personal hygiene.' Jez pointed to a sharpened wooden stick upon which rough-looking green leaves were impaled.

Chad needed to go.

'If you look up you will see a modified gas lamp which runs entirely off the natural gas generated. Before...' Jez was interrupted whilst in full flow.

'You'll have to excuse me.' And, with singular intent, Chad pushed past and closed the dunny door behind him, turned, dropped his attire and sat with one rapid motion. Having become numb to the smell, the joy of relief was almost satisfying. However, the discomfort of the rough leaf wipe was not. He sensed a strange tickling sensation between his legs.

Chad could hear a muffled voice from outside.

'What I was going to say was that it is important to lift and check around the seat prior to use. Numerous organisms find these dunnys key to their organic lifecycle. Many of Mother Nature's smaller creatures have come to rely upon them, and for some it provides their entire ecosystem.'

Chad froze attentively to the seat, keenly focussed on the strange sensation between his legs. Almost without breathing he managed to brave the word, 'Creatures?'

'Yes. Most of these creatures are harmless, but there is one we need to be particularly careful of,' informed Jez.

'And that would be?' asked Chad.

'The weedle worm,' answered Jez.

'The weedle worm?' ventured Chad, ever aware of the strange sensation between his legs, but not daring to move.

'Yes, it is indigenous to Old MacDonald's World. It evolved shortly after the planet was terraformed, one of those unpredicted mutations that proved to be quite successful,' replied Jez.

Rigid and with gritted teeth, Chad found himself asking the question he didn't want to ask, 'And why do *we* need to be particularly careful of the weedle worm?'

'The weedle worm exists solely on faeces: animal, human, it is not particular. But that is not what makes the weedle worm so unique. It is the weedle worm's preferred choice of habitat.' Jez was rather enjoying having someone to talk to who had such an enquiring mind.

'Habitat?' Chad fully expected to not want to know the answer to his question.

'Yes, for you see the weedle worm prefers to feed at source,' Jez explained.

'Source?' Chad had closed his eyes, subconsciously hoping, like we all do, that this would make anything bad go away.

'It typically enters the body of a host during defecation, whereupon it makes its way into the alimentary canal and thrives, eating and reproducing until the host dies,' concluded Jez.

There was silence from inside the dunny.

Jez became a little concerned. 'Mr Tree, are you alright?'

Chad felt like the bottom had dropped out of his world, although, in fact, it was the worry that the reverse may have happened which had caused him to feel this way.

Jez knocked on the door. 'Are you alright in there?'

There was an ultimate irony to the situation that Chad found himself in. He was a male who had lived by the toilet, only to find that he was now about to die by the toilet. He never thought it would end this way.

Without hearing a response, Jez decided to take matters into his own hands. He yanked open the door to find a somewhat startled, but still breathing, Chad sat enthroned. 'Are you alright?'

Chad, fatalistically aware of the strange tickling sensation between his legs, shook his head and mumbled, 'I think it's a weedle worm.'

'Shall we have a look then,' urged Jez. 'Come on get up.'

With all modesty brushed aside, Chad stood and hobbled forward, attire around his ankles. And, as he stood, the strange tickling sensation suddenly stopped.

Jez looked past Chad into the dunny. 'Did you feel a strange tickling sensation when you were sat on the dunny?'

'Yes,' replied a terminally resigned Chad.

'And has that sensation now gone?' asked Jez.

'Yes,' answered Chad, now certain of his own demise.

'Take a look.' Jez gestured to Chad to turn and look in the dunny. There, in plain view poking up from the hole in the middle of the seat, was the stalk of a leaf: a leaf that Chad had used for his own personal hygiene, a leaf that remained stuck in the hole.

'There is your weedle worm, Mr Tree.' Jez tamped down the leaf and shovelled in some wood shavings.

'Great stuff,' replied an emotionally exhausted, but relieved Chad.

Chad just managed to regain his composure and, still trembling, pulled up his attire. He barely remembered to assume the character of George Tree and, with little conviction, suggested, 'Let's see how this crop of yours is doing.'

'We will need some transport,' replied Jez.

Leaving the fateful dunny behind, Jez led Chad to the stable block.

'In here. I have got something special to show you.'

Chad wasn't sure whether he wished to see 'something special', after the dunny experience, but as ever, the lure of profit drew him on.

Jez pulled open the rickety wooden doors. 'My mother says this is where I was born.'

'Great Stuff!' Chad looked at the mainly disused and neglected stables on either side of the stable block. Their only occupants, a large capellan cart-horse and a rather sad, solitary centaurian donkey, watched them with interest.

Much to Chad's relief, Jez indicated past the animals to a ute; an aging ex-Space Corps utility skyrider, parked at the back of the stable block. 'We will take the ute, Mr Tree.'

The craft listed ominously to one side and made a persistent hum. Under the scars of many solar cycles of hard use, and accidental damage, it was painted in what appeared to be its original striking pink and purple camouflage – clearly conceived to blend in with some kind of vegetation, although not the vegetation of this planet.

With a simple straddle jump, Jez landed in the ute's driving seat and indicated to Chad to join him. Chad pulled on the passenger door lever, and then pulled a little harder. The ute listed further towards him, but the door wouldn't budge. On closer inspection, Chad could see that the door had been welded shut. Given no other option Chad leapt and, in one mighty bound, found himself in the passenger seat, though this did cause the ute to ground out.

'All safely in?' asked Jez, and, without waiting for an answer, he pushed the control stick forward, the pitch of the ute's hum got higher until suddenly the ute juddered forward. Chad grasped for something to hold onto. Jez released the control stick and the tone of the ute's hum dropped. Chad found himself being flung forward as the ute came to a dead stop outside the stables.

'Space Corps surplus you know,' said Jez conversationally. 'Bought her off Old JJ over at the wholesale general stores. He did me this great deal and she has run sweet and true ever since. What do you think?'

'Great stuff,' was all an unconvinced Chad could say.

'Shall we go, Mr Tree?' Jez pulled back on the control stick, the hum became a rattle, and the ute began to shake. Searching in vain for some kind of safety harness, Chad began to think that the equine alternative might have been the safer option.

Bang! And in a plume of billowing earth-brown smoke the ute ascended skywards, banked over the farmstead's once new but now rusting water tower and headed out across the fields. Then, disarmingly, the thunderous rattle suddenly stopped and, in the silence, the ute went into freefall, just enough for Chad to feel as though his stomach was in his mouth. Then the ute's drive restarted.

It was during the next heart-stopping silence that Jez turned to Chad, who was still desperately trying to find some kind of safety restraint, and said, 'You may not have noticed, but I have converted the ute to run on organic matter.'

The thunderous rattle restarted and Chad just nodded.

Chad had hardly taken another breath and the rattle stopped again. Jez continued, 'This means that not only can I travel using organic power but also…'

The rattle restarted and Chad wondered whether an atmospheric-descent retarder might be of more use than a safety harness.

The rattle stopped. Jez further explained, 'I am able to fertilise the crops with the by-products of the energy generation process.'

Chad looked back at the cloud of earth-brown smoke spreading over the ground. Reassuringly the rattle restarted, but again, a few photon phases later, it stopped.

'It will not be long now, Mr Tree,' said Jez. 'Relax, enjoy the view.'

Chad closed his eyes. It wasn't that he disliked the view; it was that he and the view might become acquainted too closely. He wondered how many deaths he might die between now and when they eventually landed.

Relief, the rattle restarted.

Clearly happy at the helm of his ute, Jez had stopped being conversational and had started to sing one of his favourite holy tunes: 'To grow for thee is to know for thee, Oh Holy One, Let me toil the soil for thee...'

For Chad, hearing excerpts from a holy tune every time the propulsion system stopped only served to add emphasis to the near death experience he felt he was having. And Chad wondered how long 'not long' might be. So far, at least one lifetime seemed to have passed.

And then Jez nudged Chad and pointed at a field beneath them. 'We are here, Mr Tree.'

The thunderous rattle did not restart and to Chad's ears the silence grew louder and louder. He could sense the ute descending and more worryingly the ground ascending, but dared not open his eyes.

The next thing he knew, Jez was asking him if he had fallen asleep. Chad opened his eyes and found that by some miracle they appeared to have landed. He clambered out, fell to his knees, but just managed to restrain himself from kissing the ground.

[18] Profit And Loss

Still on his knees, a rattled Chad had re-gathered his thoughts and, with what felt like his last breath, turned to Jez.

'How are things going with the leaf crop?'

'Mr Tree, as you can see, we have an abundant crop and there is plenty of dried leaf in storage.' Jez pointed to a large wooden shed across the way from where the ute was parked.

'Great stuff!' was all Chad managed, and, after standing, he walked across towards the shed. Jez followed.

Chad turned and looked Jez in the eye.

'I need ten times more leaf shipped than you're currently producing.'

'No problem, Mr Tree,' replied Jez.

'Great stuff! I've arranged for an alternative shipment method. Every lunar phase, or so, I'm expecting a consignment of returnable packaging to leave the wholesale general stores bound for Pacifica. I need you to arrange for the leaf to be hidden inside that consignment.'

Jez thought and then said, 'I shall ask Old JJ. I am sure he will do it for me.'

'Perhaps best to leave Mr Legrand out of it. He's a busy male with too much to do to be bothered with this,' suggested Chad.

Jez thought again. 'There is Amy Mae; she is the niece of Old JJ. She works part-time over at the stores, I am sure she will do it for me if I ask.'

'Great Stuff! That's job done. As for the credits, here's next shipment's payment in advance.' Chad handed Jez a thick bundle of credits.

Jez, holding more credits than he'd ever seen, imagined what they could do to further the cause.

'I expect to be back again before the lunar cycle is out,' added Chad, 'so if the leaf supply is good I'll have some more credits for you. Oh, and as I know you are aware, we need to keep this just between ourselves.'

Jez flipped through the credits, thoughtfully.

'No problem, not a word to anyone, Mr Tree.' Although Jez said to himself, 'Not a word until the time is right, Mr Edger! And then we, the Children Of The Soil, will reveal the truth about your corrupt corporate culture. And our heaven sent words will rain down on you and your kind. And the abomination that is the Flush Away Corporation will be no more. And so will perish all, as is the organic way. The Children Of The Soil will reap what they have sown!'

* * * * *

'And so, after due and full consideration by the executive board, and consultation with the workforce and their appropriate representative bodies, together with the requisite planetary administrative and advisory organisations, it has been agreed that employees may whistle while they work, so long as the whistling cannot be heard by their fellow colleagues, or by themselves, as this may cause distraction leading to a potential incident and, as a consequence, the corporation may be shown to be negligent in the execution of its responsibility of duty of care towards the workforce.' Vice-President Of Merchandising Luton Touch finished rereading the minutes.

'A OK. That should satisfy everyone, shouldn't it, Tim?' added Chief Executive & President Joseph Firtop.

Vice-President Of Fabrication Tim Moontide looked around the ancient oak table at a gallery of disinterested faces. He had long since learned to keep his antennae down and not to rock the spaceship. 'Always be seen to be positronic and in agreement' was an axiom that had stood him in good stead. Whilst he knew that all parties would in fact be less than satisfied, he also knew that pushing the point would be less than advantageous from the perspective of his career. He nodded his head with resigned agreement. 'Thanks, Joe, I'm sure all parties will be equally satisfied with our deliberations on the matter.'

'A OK. If that's the actions from the last meeting concluded, let us move on to the next agenda item; profit and loss. Over to you, Tobe,' directed Joseph Firtop.

Attention regained, all eyes turned to the chief fiscal officer. This was why they were gathered here: profit. Profit meant bonuses, and what could be more important than bonuses?

With a wave of his hand, the space above the centre of the ancient oak table became alive with numbers and graphs and charts. As ever confusion reigned in their interpretation – such was the complexity of the numbers' derivation. But to be seen not to understand would not be good for one's livelihood, so all showed rapt interest and comprehension as the chief fiscal officer communicated in his native tongue of fiscal doublespeak.

Time passed and Tobe Milton's fiscal verbage was ever less understandable. It was becoming clear to the rest of the executive board that a definitive profit number was not going to be forthcoming from their chief fiscal officer.

Never afraid to step into the particle accelerator, the self-proclaimed towering intellect of the board, Vice-President Of Conception & Evolution Aron Grace astutely interjected, in his naturally patronising tone, 'So, if I understand correctly, what you're saying is the corporation has made both a loss and a profit in the last lunar cycle.'

'Correct,' replied the chief fiscal officer, relieved that at least one of his colleagues had been able to understand what he'd taken such care to simplify. Although a quick glance at the others made it clear that the credit hadn't completely dropped everywhere, so Tobe Milton confirmed what Aron Grace had said. 'Yes both a loss and a profit.'

Always keen to be seen articulating the positive, Vice-President Of Customer-Relationships & Promotions Francis Stein ventured, 'So that must be good news.' Although the silence that followed caused him to add, 'Mustn't it?'

'A is not OK,' responded Joseph Firtop. 'For the vice-president of customer-relationships and promotions, and the rest of you, it is not good news. Were the results the other way around, and we had made a profit and a loss, then this would be a much happier occasion.'

For the Chief Executive & President the credit had dropped, and dropped some time ago. You didn't get to the top of the corporate skyvator without having at least a modicum of fiscal knowledge; and, in Joseph Firtop's case, he had more than a modicum – though it never paid to let on how much he knew. 'Always be one parsec ahead' and 'always keep them precognicating' were two key principles in his management approach – principles that had kept him at the top all these solar cycles.

Tobe Milton was thus forced to commit the worst of executive transgressions and bring bad news to the table. 'It is my duty to report that, for the first time in my tenure as chief fiscal officer, under our management-fiscal reporting framework we are on trajectory to make a nett fiscal loss, thus jeopardising our bonuses.'

There was silence – a silence that, if left undisturbed, would have consumed the entire universe.

With bravery and fortitude, seldom displayed by any member of Flush Away's executive board, Chief Fiscal Officer Tobe Milton continued, 'And, somewhat unfortunately, the issue is compounded by the fact that, under the latest set of planetary taxation-reporting regulations and guidelines, we will, at the same time, have to declare a nett profit to the authorities, thus extending the weakness of our fiscal position.'

He could now see that the credit had dropped as, one-by-one, the rest of the executive board members slowly and reluctantly digested the consequence: no bonus.

At times of crisis it is the role of the leader to lead. Chief Executive & President Joseph Firtop stood and loomed over those gathered around that ancient oak table. Ensuring he had their full and undivided attention, he spoke.

'I want to know who is to blame!'

*　　*　　*　　*　　*

Chad's return to the Usherman Farmstead was no less terrifying than the outbound trip had been. The knowledge that the ute's propulsion system worked in an intermittent manner served only to intensify the gut wrenching sensation that he felt as the craft flew along. A sensation that was further worsened by Jez's incessant holy tune singing, this time with a rendition of *Oh Holy One, I Give Thanks To You, For Your Wondrous Holy View* though, ironically, Chad also found himself offering thanks to the Holy One when they did eventually land.

As Jez and his mother bade him farewell from the veranda, Chad gratefully got into the waiting taxi-skyrider and vowed never to travel in a craft powered by organic propulsion again, particularly if it was piloted by someone with a predilection for holy tune recital.

At least Chad was able to console himself with his new leaf supply route. And, not to forget, he'd sealed the 'one-time only special introductory deal' for ten thousand irradiating sanitation units with Old JJ Legrand.

He looked forward to a civilised return passage aboard the Iridium Silver Service starliner, and being able to bask in its radiant glory and wallow in its magnificent opulence.

He looked forward to salivating over the menu and to being served by the lovely hostesses, particularly the luscious Lucinda. He was sure her star twinkled for him.

He looked forward to picking up their conversation from where he'd left off. He could picture her now, leaning over, asking how she may be of service, her name-badge nestling in clear view.

He looked forward to returning to Pacifica and being welcomed as the male who, finally, achieved real market penetration on Old MacDonald's World.

He looked forward to hearing Johnson's tales of law enforcement harassment and seeing Johnson's face as he, Chad, told of his success.

And he looked forward to the credits that his not so little sideline was about to generate.

He almost had it all. All he needed now was the golden key to the executive toilet and Chad would be a satisfied male, and then he would be able to announce to the universe that he truly was 'Great Stuff!'

[19] Lost And Found

Sat in the Singularity, at the very epicentre of Nova Vega's Black Hole Casino, Billy Bob felt guilty. He had sinned, all in the name of the organic cause. Would he, could he, ever be forgiven? All of his gaming markers were gone, Star Trooper Jonah Jones was gone and their mission's target, Johnson, was gone. All he could see was the silver ball shimmering in front of him, occupying segment red twelve.

As his overhead restraint bar rose, a soft voice spoke, 'Sir, please exit the Singularity. You have lost everything, but you can be thankful that the luck of the ball has saved you from the loser's ultimate fate.'

Billy Bob got up.

Although the machine had said he'd been saved, he worried for his mortal soul. A little shaken, he made his way from the Singularity. He stood by Jones's empty wheelchair. Where had he gone? Jones couldn't have got far without his wheelchair. And where was Johnson?

It was a mystery. Perhaps the Holy One had taken them for their sins. This was a salutary lesson in the perils of gambling. He should not have let Jones talk him into it. Never again would he allow himself to be led unto the path of temptation and transgress the Holy One's commandments.

Then, much to the surprise of the casino's clientele, Billy Bob dropped to his knees, head lowered. And, in a loud voice and with the sign of the star, he thanked the Holy One for delivering him from temptation and the path that led to eternal fire and damnation in the Evil One's dominion. He thanked the Holy One for giving him a second chance and promised that he, Billy Bob Brown, would never let himself be led astray again for as long as he should live.

As in a vision, Billy Bob could see Preacher Jedidiah Grimthorpe shaking his head slowly and expressing his disappointment by just simply turning away. How Billy Bob begged for forgiveness. Billy Bob closed his eyes and hung his head in shame. In devotion he began to recite the many holy verses he'd learnt as a child. Billy Bob was in search of redemption.

Initially intrigued, and wondering what he might do next, the crowd that had gathered around Billy Bob gradually dissipated, muttering such phrases as 'It takes all sorts' and 'That's one poor gambler who's found salvation' and 'I'm bored, let's get a drink' and, perhaps most poignantly of all, 'What a loser'.

Billy Bob continued to offer devotion.

*   *   *   *   *

Deputy D'Angelis looked at Deputy Gilbrae, and Deputy Gilbrae looked at Deputy D'Angelis. Then, in turn, they both looked at Investigator Strait who stood shaking his head.

Realising that two of their suspects had literally vanished in front of their eyes was bad enough. Not being able to understand how it happened was worse. But watching the third suspect fall to his knees, beg forgiveness and give praise to the Holy One for being given a second chance just about eclipsed it.

Had Johnson and Jones known they were being watched and made their escape?

Had they left that poor offworld scratcher, Brown, to carry the canister?

Or had the casino manager tried to dispose of them all in some leaf-trafficking feud?

Investigator Strait felt he and his Tactical Response Assault Patrol were now two parsecs behind instead of being one parsec in front, and he didn't like it. He had vowed to bring Operation Kicking Butt to a successful conclusion. This leaf-trafficking ring was going down one way or another!

They needed to act fast. The more Investigator Strait thought about it the more he believed that the casino manager was the key. He was the one with the connections and this was his corner of the cosmos. He was the one they should now put under surveillance. He would lead them to Johnson and Jones, and if they proved to be corpses then that would be a matter for the local law enforcement agency to deal with.

'We've lost the suspects, Investigator. What do we do now?' asked Deputy D'Angelis.

'I can see that we've lost the suspects, thank you, D'Angelis,' retorted Investigator Strait who, realising he was on the verge of losing it himself, counted to ten and several numbers beyond.

Deputy D'Angelis was about to unwisely speak again when Investigator Strait spoke first, 'I think the key to this particular situation lies with our casino manager. Let's find out what he's up to and perhaps he'll lead us to the others. Come on you two, follow me.'

Investigator Strait turned to leave the Singularity.

'What about him?' Deputy D'Angelis pointed towards the penitent Billy Bob Brown.

'By the state of him I don't think it's worth blowing our cover to see if he knows anything. He seems to be as much a victim of this vile leaf trade as everyone else,' replied Investigator Strait. 'No, it's the casino manager we want. The closer we get to him, the closer we'll get to the truth and the closer we'll get to Johnson. Let's go see what he's up to, he shouldn't be too hard to find.'

So, with new direction, Investigator Strait and his law enforcement deputies left the Singularity.

*   *   *   *   *

Johnson looked at Jones, and Jones looked at Johnson. They sat in silence, in darkness. Was this the end? Had they passed to the other side?

Johnson did think it a little odd that, if this was the afterlife, Mr Jones should accompany him. But there again, if they'd gone at the same time, then why not?

It certainly seemed like they were at the end of a long, dark tunnel. And what was that in the distance? A light? So it was true. Johnson felt himself being drawn towards the light. His heart raced. And the light drew closer, the light flashed. The light shouldn't flash. The light was a shrouded sodium-yellow. The light shouldn't be sodium-yellow it should be white.

Johnson began to hear clattering and could start to make out the outline of a Take-It-Easy refuse bot sweeping as it approached in a cloud of dust. His heartbeat slowed. Unless angels took the guise of refuse bots he had clearly not passed through to the other side.

'I wonder where we are?' Johnson mused, trying to see beyond the Take-It-Easy refuse bot and its billowing plumes of white dust.

'Out with the rest of the trash,' coughed Jones. 'Always the same. When you've got credits they treat you like stellar celebrities. When you're broke, you're garbage.'

'Excellent. Ah well, winning isn't everything, we've still got the rest of our lives to look forward to,' remarked Johnson, trying, unsuccessfully, to dust himself off. He was relieved at not having to deal with an afterlife when he had barely come to terms with his current life.

Jones said nothing, mostly because he didn't want a lung full of dust. He sat with what he always knew would be the inevitable outcome of his gambling: disappointment.

For Johnson the sunfall had come to an all-too-predictable unpredictable end. It was no surprise. He never expected much of a positive nature to happen and he was rarely disappointed. He coughed and wondered how he would ever clean the dust off his best business attire.

For Jones his unceremonious ejection from the Singularity only made him more determined to be a winner. He had tasted both gambling's highs and gambling's lows, and he knew which tasted best.

As the Take-It-Easy refuse bot and its attendant dust storm disappeared into the distance, Johnson's eyes became accustomed to the darkness. He could see that they'd been deposited near to the end of a long service-tunnel. Well, there was nothing for it but to get up and make their way out.

'Let's make a move,' he said and stood.

'And how do you propose I do that?' Jones pointed to the absence of

139

his wheelchair.

'Um, yes.' Johnson thought for a while. 'I'll tell you what. You wait here and I'll go and get William Robert to bring the wheelchair back. How about that?'

Jones nodded reluctantly and Johnson set off up the tunnel, trudging in the tracks of the Take-It-Easy refuse bot.

Eventually Johnson emerged from the darkness to find himself among rank upon rank of black spherical taxi-skyriders in diverse levels of dysfunction. Across the way a flashing sign, in ionic blue, read 'Taxibot Control Centre'.

Johnson walked to the door and it dutifully whooshed open. The smell of Free-N-Easy synthetic lubricant pervaded the air. Photonic equipment chattered, and behind the counter a male in a carbon-black uniform interacted with a holoplay. As Johnson approached he read the name 'Bud' on the male's lapel badge.

Without looking up Bud said curtly, 'I'm busy, go away. If you're another one of them there Singularity losers we don't do free taxi rides, so you'd better start walkin' now.' He then followed this simple message by spitting out whatever his hacking cough had just regurgitated in the general direction of a spittoon by the door.

Undeterred, Johnson drew near. Such greetings were normal fare for a sales representative – particularly a customer-relationship and promotions specialist in the cutthroat universe of irradiating sanitation products. No one ever welcomed a sales representative. And with his many solar cycles of experience Johnson was hardly going to be rebuffed by an 'I'm busy, go away', even if it was accompanied by the discharged contents of the speaker's throat.

'Are ya' deaf or what?' Bud continued, sensing that the customer had not gone away. He spat again and then looked up to see a male dressed in business attire covered in dust. He looked a little more closely. There was something familiar about the male's face.

Bud generally became cautious when it was a face he thought he recognised. His prior encounters with customers generally resulted in unfavourable outcomes. For some reason customers tended to remember him in a bad light. Just to be on the safe side he decided to put on his best customer caring persona. Again he cleared his throat.

'What do ya' want?'

Johnson, with the ease of a well-practiced sales representative, looked directly at Bud. Always look them in the eye, they'll soon back down, but make sure you smile, you don't want to appear to be too aggressive otherwise they might take fright.

Johnson smiled and Bud looked worried.

'Now there, mister, I don't want no trouble.' Bud's voice was noticeably shaky and whatever he had just coughed up he'd visibly swallowed. Bud recognised Johnson from the image that the Investigator had shown him, and he was sure Johnson was here to extract revenge for informing on him.

It appeared to Johnson that he'd overdone using his direct approach. He tried to calm the old male down. 'I just want to ask you one question.'

There was an anxious pause that was just too much for Bud to take.

'I confess: it was me that tol' that Investigator, but he made me,' Bud sputtered and sank back further into his chair. 'He's a real nasty one, that one. He threatened me, he did, me an old male.'

This was not quite what Johnson had been expecting. He'd come in to ask for directions back to the casino's entrance, but instead he'd somehow managed to extract a confession, about what Johnson had no idea.

Johnson just looked at Bud. Bud withered.

'All right, all right, I tol' him where ya' was. He showed me your image. I had no choice.' Bud again coughed and swallowed.

This was making no sense to Johnson. 'What Investigator? What image? What are you talking about?'

Bud realised that he'd said too much. He should have kept his mouth shut. Why was it that he couldn't keep his mouth shut? This customer didn't know the authorities were after him. Bud decided on a new tactic and pretended he hadn't said anything.

'The Investigator, the image?' asked Johnson again.

'What Investigator?' replied Bud.

'The Investigator you just talked about. The one who threatened you,' pressed Johnson.

'Ain't no Investigator threatened me, mister,' responded Bud, truthfully.

'You just said that an Investigator threatened you and you told him where I was.' Johnson was beginning to doubt his own memory. Anyway what Bud said made no sense. Why would law enforcement be following him?

'Oh that, just joshin' about. Bit of banter make's it more entertainin' for the customers. Anyways, what can I do for ya?' asked a strangely rejuvenated Bud.

Johnson decided that the old male was a few stars short of a constellation. 'I'm looking for directions back to the Black Hole's entrance.'

'Ah, no problem, mister, just follow the service walkway round and y'all soon find yourself at the front of the casino.' A relieved Bud coughed.

'OK, just out the door and follow the service walkway round?' confirmed Johnson.

'Yep, just follow that walkway round and y'all get there in a photon's phase.' Bud coughed again, this time with newfound confidence.

'OK, thank you.' Johnson decided to take his leave and exited.

'No problem.' Bud relaxed and after he was sure that Johnson had well and truly gone, added, with a customary discharge, 'Good riddance.'

* * * * *

Investigator Strait led his team back to the casino's foyer where they stood next to a wall that bore a holographic image of the casino's manager, simply titled 'Mr Paolo Cigstano – Casino Manager'. Underneath this larger-than-life portrait was a whole gallery of associates and bots whose images appeared to be sized in proportion to the relative importance of their jobs. And next to these images was a ground plan of the casino.

Deputies D'Angelis and Gilbrae looked at the wall with disinterest.

Investigator Strait touched one of the images whereupon a dot lighted up on the ground plan. 'Now that's customer service for you.'

'I'll be, it shows where everyone is, Investigator,' commented Deputy D'Angelis as he stepped forward and pressed an image himself. Another dot appeared on the ground plan. 'If only all law enforcement could be as easy as this. Imagine, if we had one of these back on Pacifica, we'd never lose a suspect.'

Investigator Strait sighed and then pressed the casino manager's image. 'Let's see where Mr Paolo Cigstano is.'

No dot appeared and a voice simply stated, 'Mr Paolo Cigstano is unavailable. For assistance please try another associate.'

'He doesn't appear to be in,' concluded Deputy D'Angelis.

Investigator Strait was too lost in his own thoughts to take notice of D'Angelis. So had Mr Paolo Cigstano gone to ground? The trail had vaporised and, for Investigator Strait, tiredness and frustration were starting to set in. He decided that he and his team should return to the Second Chance Hotel and rest up.

With their sights set on sleep perhaps Investigator Strait and his law enforcement deputies weren't as alert as they might have normally been as they left the casino. Perhaps their eyes were too distracted by the waves of crackling blue ionic discharge that emanated from the massive 'Black Hole' sign floating above the entrance. Whatever it was that held their attention they failed to notice Johnson as he re-entered the building, even though he was covered in white dust from head to toe. A quick turn of the head, or a glance over the shoulder, would have successfully concluded their covert undercover operation there and then. But these actions were not taken and, unknowingly, Johnson passed by undetected.

[20] The Seeds Of Love

Romance.

Amy Mae could think of no other word that could better describe what was about to happen as she sat on the edge of her sleep-cot. She cradled her faux-jewel bedecked holocom. Jez had just sent her a message asking to meet. He wanted to rendezvous outside Old MacDonald's Wholesale General Stores after she finished her workshift this sunfall.

She closed her eyes and fell back into the comfort of her sleep-cot. In her mind it would be a chance touch, a word, a glance and their eyes would lock. She would fold into his arms, lost in love's deep embrace, trembling with desire for love's first kiss…

'Earthling, I am but one of many.'

She opened her eyes and found herself eye to ocular appendage with her favourite childhood toy; the giant green space monster, Mo Mo. She pushed it to one side. 'Oh, Mo Mo, you surely know how to ruin the occasion.'

'Earthling, bow down and worship me,' continued Mo Mo.

'Mo Mo, not now.' Amy Mae sat back up.

'Earthling, dare you speak my name,' announced Mo Mo.

She turned and gave an order to her favourite childhood toy; 'Mo Mo, shut up!'

Mo Mo whirred and closed his oral cavity leaving his three giant flesh-eating fangs protruding. Amy Mae felt a hint of sadness as Mo Mo lay there on her sleep-cot. He had that coy 'please come play with me' look which had made him so endearing when she was a child.

What to wear? She stood. She pulled out drawers. She opened storage units. She paced her room. She stared at herself in her Fairest-Of-Them-All holomirror, her head-to-toe image rotating before her. She paced some more.

In the end, amid the half-empty drawers and their room-strewn contents, Amy Mae finally decided, and admired herself in the holomirror.

'What do y'all think, Mo Mo?' she asked.

Mo Mo whirred back to life and opened his oral cavity. 'Earthling, I want to devour you.'

'Do y'all? Am I really that delicious?' asked a rather flattered Amy Mae.

'Earthling, you are at my mercy,' continued Mo Mo.

Amy Mae nodded. 'I know. What will I do if he makes advances towards me?'

'Earthling, you must surrender,' instructed Mo Mo.

'Do y'all think so? Surrender to his charms? Will I be caught in the clutches of his tender embrace, his lips pressin' close to mine?' Amy Mae closed her eyes in anticipation.

'Earthling, do not doubt me,' persisted Mo Mo.

'Oh, how he has stolen my heart.' Amy Mae sighed and looked directly at Mo Mo. 'Oh, Mo Mo, what is a female to do?'

'Earthling, resistance is futile,' answered Mo Mo.

'I know, I know, y'all's so right,' Amy Mae agreed.

'Earthling, be afraid,' warned Mo Mo.

'I am, just a little, but it makes it that much more excitin',' mused Amy Mae.

'Earthling, you cannot escape,' concluded Mo Mo.

Amy Mae just smiled and said wistfully, as she left her room, 'I know.'

And with the door shut and no sensory trace of a person to amuse Mo Mo whirred, closed his oral cavity and shut down.

Amy Mae's mother, Emmy Lou Legrand, heard the sound of footsteps thundering down the corridor. 'Amy Mae?'

The footsteps stopped. 'Yes, mother, what is it?' asked Amy Mae.

'Can y'all ask ya' uncle to tell ya' father, whichever creek he may be up, that, as much as I appreciate the peace 'n quiet of him goin' fishin', I expect him to come back by sunrise. There's chores to be done. OK?' From the tone of her voice it was clear that Amy Mae's mother was not as happy as she could be with her father.

'Yes, mother,' replied Amy Mae.

'And can y'all tell ya' uncle to tell ya' father I don't want no more fish neither. The food storage units are overflowin' with the things. If I see another fish I shall really go where no one's gone before!' added Amy Mae's mother.

'Yes, mother,' sighed Amy Mae.

'And another thin', y'all can tell ya' uncle to tell ya' father that if he thinks I'm gonna' wash his attire he's got another thin' comin'. I ain't goin' anywhere near those stinkin' fish smellin' rags 'a his 'n he'd better not wear 'em inside neither,' continued Emmy Lou Legrand, much to her daughter's annoyance.

'Yes, mother.' Amy Mae had reached the end of the corridor. 'See ya' later.'

'And don't y'all be late neither,' warned Emmy Lou Legrand.

'No, mother,' replied Amy Mae.

The stocky frame of Mrs Legrand emerged into the corridor just as the outside door began to close.

'And why are ya' wearin'...' But the door had shut and Amy Mae was gone.

Mrs Legrand went to look outside, but all she could see was the dust trail of Amy Mae's skimmer. Why was Amy Mae all dressed up? She shook her head. Who knows what goes on in the minds of the young? And so with shoulders hunched, from the resignation born of many solar cycles of unappreciated domestic servitude, Mrs Legrand returned to what she knew best: chores.

*   *   *   *   *

Amy Mae slid to a halt in a plume of dust outside the wholesale general stores. She stepped off her skimmer and, with one twist of her foot, flipped it up into her hands. She then rested the skimmer, which was adorned with the timeless symbolism of youth, against the store's dented skin.

What a dump.

She turned and pulled the door handle and then, carefully, lifted the door. It opened. Once inside she could hear the whirr and clatter of TE, the senile Ever-On forklift bot, rattling down some distant aisle. And so her workshift started. She rang the buzzer twice then three times to let her uncle know she'd arrived. She then lifted the counter top and sat on her stool, awaiting that rush of customers that never came. It was so boring.

Amy Mae picked up the well-worn bridal holozine that she'd already read twice.

The clattering got louder and TE emerged from the forest of racking. 'Forklift Bot TE... um, something, er... something, reporting, sir!'

Amy Mae turned. 'How y'all doin' TE? Found anythin' useful back there in this here museum for the terminally useless?'

There was a pause. The Ever-On forklift bot whirred. 'Forklift Bot TE... um, something, er... something, awaiting your orders, sir!'

To pass away the time Amy Mae had devised a game she'd called 'Fetch'. She would pick a random stock code number and ask TE to retrieve whatever it happened to be. 'Retrieve A – C – 0113 7194 – M – 0703 – X.'

Suddenly alert, as indicated by the dim glow of a yellow light on its upper surface, TE trundled into action. 'Retrieving A – C – 0113 7194 – M – 0703 – X, sir!'

Amy Mae could barely wait and returned to her holozine.

Time passed.

Slowly.

Clattering and beeping, TE returned. 'Mission accomplished, retrieved A – C – 0113 7194 – M – 0703 – X, sir!'

Amy Mae lowered her holozine and looked. TE had retrieved a Near-N-Far slurry tank syphon bowl. 'Take it back, return A – C – 0113 7194 – M – 0703 – X.'

Again, as if re-energised, and as indicated by the dim glow of a yellow light on its upper surface, TE trundled back into action. 'Returning A – C

– 0113 7194 – M – 0703 – X, sir!'

More time passed.

More slowly.

TE reappeared. 'Mission accomplished, returned A – C – 0113 7194 – M – 0703 – X, sir!'

The dim yellow light then went out.

Amy Mae wasn't sure she could be bothered with playing 'Fetch' anymore, but TE looked even more bored than she felt. 'Retrieve K – X – 7517 3779 – Z – 1244 – D.'

TE's yellow light came on again and the Ever-On forklift bot set off once more. 'Retrieving K – X – 7517 3779 – Z – 1244 – D, sir!'

Even more time passed.

Even more slowly.

TE returned. 'Mission accomplished, retrieved K – X – 7517 3779 – Z – 1244 – D, sir!'

The yellow light went out.

Amy Mae lowered her holozine and looked. TE had found a small Sim-O-Board box, which, according to its fabricators – Imitation Industries – is the cardboard substitute you don't have to biodegrade. Amy Mae opened the box. Inside, hidden among the packaging, was a small, round copper washer. Amy Mae took the washer, held it up to the light and then tried it on the small finger of her left hand. It fitted perfectly. She sat back, hand outstretched, and admired it. She laughed. 'Good job, TE, just what I've always wanted. I guess this means we're wed!'

There was a bang and a shake. Amy Mae looked to the door. Someone was trying to come in. That door had a sentience all of its own, but with further persuasion it finally shuddered open.

'When's ya' uncle gonna' fix the door, Amy Mae?' asked Drue Ann Brown. 'I've come thro' that darn door a hundred times, 'n a hundred times it's jammed on me. I'm surprised he gets any custom at all. Anyways, how y'all doin'?'

'Happy as can be, thanks for askin', Drue Ann,' replied Amy Mae. 'And y'all?'

'Not so bad, not so bad. We're all missin' Billy Bob since he's gone on his trip. He wasn't too clear what it was all about. Mind you, Billy Bob never has bin' too gifted in the speakin' department,' concluded Drue Ann.

'And the rest 'a the family?' Amy Mae asked; she had all sunfall.

'Ma 'n Pa are busy as ever, 'n I don't see Bart Bob from sunrise to sunfall. He 'n Pa are puttin' in drainage ditches out past the Collins's place. Philippa Sue says John Peter's about to say his first words – let's hope he'll be a might more talkative than Billy Bob. Oh 'n, for some reason best known to himself, Jimmy Bob's taken to howlin' like a wolf every time he sees a good-lookin' female, which is a might off puttin'.

146

The triplets is behavin' well for a change, 'n Johnny Bob is tryin' to teach Simple to be some kinda' huntin' dog, but Simple, bein' simple, just rolls over on his back every time. And Bella Sue, she just gets more 'n more pretty by the rotation.' Drue Ann paused to glance at Amy Mae's holozine and then added, 'Judy Ann says ya' father's gone fishin'.'

Amy Mae nodded. 'Yep, father's gone fishin' all right 'n mother's none too pleased. She says we've done got more fish than there's in the sea 'n it's about time he did somethin' useful around the farmstead.'

Drue Ann looked at Amy Mae's hand and then back at the holozine. 'Why, Amy Mae, is there somethin' y'all ain't tellin' me?'

Amy Mae looked puzzled.

'The ring, Amy Mae, the ring,' prompted Drue Ann.

Embarrassed, Amy Mae withdrew her hand under the counter and slipped the copper washer off.

'Who's the lucky young male? Anyone I know?' asked a delighted Drue Ann. 'My this is news. I hope y'all's told ya' mother 'n father. Y'all ain't expectin'?'

'Drue Ann stop.' Amy Mae regained her composure. 'Course I ain't gettin' wed. I was just playin' around. Ain't no harm in messin' about ya' know.'

'That depends, Amy Mae. Who is he?' enquired Drue Ann.

Amy Mae tried to stall the question. 'Who's who?'

But Drue Ann was having none of it. 'The young male.'

'What young male?' said Amy Mae, trying to avoid answering.

'The young male y'all's got ya' eye on, Amy Mae. The one who y'all want to put that ring on ya' finger.' Drue Ann had drawn up close to Amy Mae and was now looking for truths to be told.

'Drue Ann, I'm tellin' y'all there ain't no young male,' lied an indignant Amy Mae. 'Now I assume y'all came in for somethin' 'n not just to pass the time 'a rotation.'

'I'm sorry, Amy Mae, just pullin' ya' finger,' chuckled Drue Ann. 'Is ya' uncle around?'

'I ain't seen him this sunfall, but I'll bet he's in his command-bunker as usual, commandin' operations. Try pressin' the buzzer 'n he might come out.' Amy Mae waved in its general direction.

Drue Ann leant on the buzzer and waited. Amy Mae busied herself by moving things around. Eventually the unmistakable sound of Space Corps boots could be heard marching towards the counter from the depths of the stores. And then a voice followed, muttering, 'Now who is ringin' that there buzzer? A male cain't get his work done with that there buzzer ringin' all the time. Where's that young female I employ?'

As JJ Legrand turned the corner, he spied Drue Ann.

'So it's Drue Ann. How y'all doin'?'

147

'I'm doin' good, Mr Legrand. And y'all?' Drue Ann smiled.

'Cain't complain, cain't complain. Now what can I do for ya'?' asked JJ, easily swayed by a young female's smile.

'Pa says he's havin' trouble with that seedin' bot, ya' know, the one we bought last fallow season – the ex-Space Corps assault bot y'all converted. Instead of firin' seeds into the ground that bot's dun bin' firin' them at anythin' that moves. Pa 'n Jimmy Bob had a pitched battle with the darn thin'. It was only 'coz it ran outta' seed that they managed to disable the thin' by throwin' a sack over it, though it's still flying up and down the field like crazy. Anyways, Pa says y'all'd better come over right away 'n fix it before the thin' does any more damage.' Drue Ann thought and then added for good measure, 'I think that's what Pa said, there might 'a bin' a few words he shouldn't 'a said as well now I come to think about it, but I ain't gonna' repeat them.'

JJ sighed; this last batch of ex-Space Corps bots was proving to be troublesome. They were probably too battle hardened. The incessant combat they'd experienced had become so imbedded in their systems' architecture that, even with extensive reprogramming, it would only take a simple event and they would revert back to their original routines.

'I'll follow ya' over, Drue Ann. Got all my tools in the back 'a the ute. Amy Mae, y'all mind the store now 'til I get back, OK?'

'But uncle I've gotta'…' Amy Mae stopped mid-sentence. With Drue Ann there she daren't say she was going to meet Jez.

'Gotta' what, Amy Mae?' asked JJ.

'Gotta' do my schoolwork. But I guess that can wait 'til sunrise. See ya' later uncle 'n ya' too Drue Ann, see ya' soon. Hope that seedin' bot gets fixed. Bye now.'

Amy Mae waited for the door to be closed before cussin' to herself. Typical, her big date and it was all going to be ruined because of some halfwitted bot. She banged her fist on the counter in frustration.

She'd just have to let Jez know she was going to be late for their rendezvous.

[21] The Key To What We Want

Amy Mae watched the time and, every time she watched the time, no time seemed to have passed at all. Since Drue Ann had spirited Uncle JJ away not a soul had tried to battle the door to gain entrance to the wholesale general stores. Not that she was surprised. It was hardly the retail experience to end all retail experiences. You had to be in definite need to choose to come here.

The silence of her vigil was only punctuated by the occasional crash as TE, the errant Ever-On forklift bot, wondered the gangways of the stores. TE was relocating stock as instructed by commands from the warehouse holoplay in its futile attempt to optimise inventory availability.

She'd now read her bridal holozine so often that she could recite it word-for-word, and even playing 'Fetch' with TE had lost its appeal. Thoughtfully, Uncle JJ had holoed her to say he was going to be some time, but it was OK as he'd let her mother know, and so she needn't worry about getting back late.

Amy Mae realised that if she was going to make her rendezvous with Jez she was going to have to delegate the responsibility for minding the store to someone else. Unfortunately anyone she knew would want to know what she was up to, and that she did not want to tell.

There was only one thing for it: she'd have to get TE to mind the store. Given the level of trade this sunfall it shouldn't be a problem. In fact given the level of trade a small rock could do the job.

Amy Mae overrode the warehouse holoplay, and dutifully TE laboured its way to the front counter.

There was a pause and then the Ever-On forklift bot whirred. 'Forklift Bot TE... um, something, er... something, awaiting your orders, sir!'

'TE, y'all listen very carefully. I need to step out for a while 'n I want y'all to mind the store. If anyone should come in 'n ask for somethin' y'all's to holo me. Understand?' said Amy Mae, rather more in hope than expectation.

There was a further pause and then TE replied, 'Forklift Bot TE... um, something, er... something, awaiting your orders, sir!'

What a useless heap of junk. Amy Mae decided to try a new vector. 'Attention!'

'Sir!' The Ever-On forklift bot rattled and appeared to draw itself together. A bright green light came on. Amy Mae had never seen TE display a bright green light before. The best Amy Mae had ever achieved was to get the dim yellow one to flash.

'I order ya'...' announced Amy Mae. She searched her mind for Space-Corps-like commands that TE would understand. 'I order ya' to be on sentry duty!' There she had it.

'Yes, sir!' And the bright green light flashed. 'Establishing perimeter, sir!' Unprompted, TE rotated and moved along the counter towards the far wall, at which point it about-faced and returned, only to about-face again at the near wall. Thus it established its perimeter, which it now patrolled diligently.

'Good job there, TE, good job.' Amy Mae was impressed. 'Y'all keep doin' what y'all's doin' 'n if anyone turns up, or anythin' happens, y'all just gotta' holo me.'

TE continued patrolling its perimeter, but Amy Mae was still a little unsure as to whether TE understood about holoing her. She needed to think of that Space-Corps-like way of saying what she wanted. Then, after some consideration, she tried, 'I order ya' to identify 'n communicate any target to me.'

'Yes, sir!' A red light came on; that appeared to have done it.

It was time for her rendezvous. She skipped to the washroom, and made sure everything was as it should be. Her heart pounded.

And with a 'TE, see y'all later, 'n be sure to be good!' Amy Mae left the building.

Amy Mae emerged into the warm sunfall air. She could see Jez silhouetted, leaning against her uncle's sign.

He stood up straight. 'Hello, Amy Mae. Glad you could make it. Hope this is not too inconvenient for you.'

'Huh? No, not at all, glad to see y'all too.' Amy Mae closed her eyes as she fumbled for words. He sure was wonderful, always thinking about her. She needed to pull herself together.

'Perhaps we could go somewhere quiet so we can talk. That is if you do not mind.' Jez stepped forward and indicated across the way to his striking, if a little battered, pink and purple ute. 'Your transport awaits.'

Amy Mae smiled brightly, trying not to betray the nervousness she felt inside. The first date; she needed to be calm. She walked slowly, and with trepidation, towards his ute.

Amy Mae pulled on the passenger door lever. It seemed stuck. 'Jez?'

'Ah yes, I had to make a little modification to strengthen the ute up, so you will have to climb over to get in. Here, let me help you.' Jez walked around and, with a gracious outstretched arm, helped Amy Mae clamber inside.

'Why thank y'all, kind sir,' she said.

'No problem, Amy Mae.' Jez smiled and returned to the driver's side. He could see her struggling to find the safety harness. He reached across and retrieved it from behind the passenger seat. 'Here, let me help.'

As Jez fitted the safety harness, Amy Mae could feel the heat of his body, the brush of his arms. Oh, how she longed for that body to press close to hers, those arms to embrace her.

He struggled to engage the central clip and leaned closer.

Could this be it? Amy Mae tipped her head back, closed her eyes and moistened her pouting lips. The expectation of love's first kiss was almost too much to bear. She'd tumbled into an eternity of anticipation, waiting for the world to shudder, waiting for angels to sing love's sweet tune.

But then Amy Mae found herself suddenly flung back into her seat as the ute jolted upwards with a thunderous bang. She opened one eye and then the other. Jez had the control stick clasped between his hands and was singing, 'All praise be to the pastures of the Holy One…' above the ute's stuttering roar.

It wasn't quite what she'd hoped for. Momentarily, love's flame flickered, but then it re-ignited as she came to see that her gallant escort had taken her aboard his carriage and was carrying her off into the double shadow of Old MacDonald's World's twin moons, Ei and EiO.

With its cruising altitude achieved the ute levelled out, though given the intermittent nature of its propulsion it was more of the roller coaster kind of level rather than the flat kind of level. But Amy Mae was oblivious to all; she was inextricably drawn to Jez.

Oh, how his eyes sparkled in the reflected light of Ei and EiO. He had such intensity, such energy about him, not like those other young males. She looked across at his sparse grown beard, as his long hair tangled in the wind. Though she couldn't help thinking that his beard would have to go and the hair really did need to be trimmed.

The ute continued on its undulating course, skimming above the endless fields, outlined in the brilliant darkness of the star filled sky. It traced past a backdrop of Ei and EiO, glowing orange and red, and the immense scatter of stars that shaped the Spiral Arm, its path guided by the shining Northern Star. For Amy Mae this was true love's course, for she had fallen hopelessly into its all-consuming desire.

And, just above the rush of the air and the ute's rumbling drive, Jez had started to intone another holy tune, 'Harvest ye, Harvest ye, Thanks be…' Amy Mae felt she could fly forever and closed her eyes.

And so, as she flew along, time passed as in a dream she hoped never to be awoken from.

'Huh.' She'd been nudged and, a little disorientated, she looked around.

Jez pointed to some lights flickering below. 'Apologies, I did not mean to startle you, but I thought that you should not miss this.'

'What?' Amy Mae asked, awakening gradually.

'There!' Jez pointed again.

Amy Mae looked, but could not see what Jez was pointing at. 'Where?'

'There, it is where we are going. I tried to wake you earlier, but you had fallen asleep so I thought it best to leave you until now. You simply cannot miss this view.' Jez smiled and Amy Mae melted.

Below, against a sheer cliff edge, a waterfall cascaded down, its torrent unbroken. It dropped through a canopy of trees up-lighted by a series of bright lights embedded in the river far below. And wrapped around the waterfall, some halfway up the cliff, a semicircular wooden building appeared to be suspended in the air.

'It is the Neither Up Nor Down Eatery. I find it to be a place of organic inspiration.' Jez gently bumped his ute into one of the many empty docking bays.

The timber-inspired organic theme continued inside. Roughly hewn benches and tables followed the semicircle of the building round, all focussed on the cascading waterfall. The concertina screen of doors, which normally stood between diners and water, had been pulled back and the eatery resounded to the rolling roar of the waters. The air was filled with an all pervading mist. Jez indicated to a bench for Amy Mae to sit at. He then took a place opposite her.

For a time Amy Mae just stared at the falling water, entranced. Her eyes then turned to the vista of flowers and butterflies that intermingled with the surrounding tree canopy. She smiled. 'Sure is mighty pretty, Jez,' and then added, 'it's so romantic.'

'I think you are right; young star-crossed lovers often frequent this eatery. It should serve as the perfect cover for us. Would you like something to eat or drink?' Jez asked politely.

As if on cue a waitress, dressed in oversize tree technician's attire, came to the table. She introduced herself as Millie Sue, a fact confirmed by her leaf-shaped badge, and asked if she could take their order.

'Groundnut brew, Amy Mae?' Jez prompted.

Amy Mae did not hear; she was lost in romance.

Jez turned to Millie Sue. 'We will take two groundnut brews. Is groundnut brew alright for you, Amy Mae?'

'Oh yes, thanks,' replied Amy Mae dreamily. 'What did y'all say, Jez?'

'I asked whether you would like a groundnut brew,' clarified Jez.

'Oh yeah, sure. Sorry, it's so beautiful 'n fine here, Jez, I do so love it, thank ya'.' Amy Mae's smile brightened the whole eatery. She was in her dream.

'Two groundnut brews comin' right up.' And Millie Sue, recognizing at least one star-crossed lover, turned to get the order.

Jez looked around the eatery. Surprisingly there were few diners in this sunfall, and those that were appeared to be lost in conversation, or caught in a trance by the waterfall.

As quickly as she had left, Millie Sue returned bearing their drinks aloft on a wooden platter, which she placed on the table with well-practised ease.

It was when they were alone that Jez looked directly at Amy Mae and said, 'Amy Mae.'

Amy Mae put the menu down and looked into his eyes. Nervously she replied, 'Jez.'

'Amy Mae,' repeated Jez.

'Jez,' sighed Amy Mae.

'Amy Mae, I have something to ask you,' continued Jez.

Amy Mae went to open her mouth to speak, but Jez raised his hand to quieten her.

'Before you say anything, Amy Mae, you need to understand that what passes between us has to remain a secret.' Jez looked furtively from side to side.

'Secret? A secret? A secret romance? What could be more... more romantic,' thought Amy Mae.

'Yes, a secret until the time is right for us to tell the universe.' Jez looked directly into her eyes. She could have swooned.

Amy Mae's heart pounded. A secret romance, then when the time was right, they'd announce their engagement to the universe. It was all too good to be true. She could barely speak. She just nodded in agreement. 'Our secret.'

Jez leant forward. 'Amy Mae, I have asked you here because I need you.'

'Oh, Jez, y'all need me?' interrupted an impassioned Amy Mae.

'Yes, Amy Mae, I need you,' repeated Jez.

'Oh, Jez.' Amy Mae could hardly breathe for the excitement of it all.

'I need you to do something for me, something for the cause,' confided Jez.

Silence.

The cause? Amy Mae felt the conversation hadn't quite gone the way she'd anticipated.

'The Children Of The Soil need you. I need you. Our mission, to spread the organic word, needs you. You do believe, Amy Mae, do you not?' asked Jez.

And reality broke into her dream – as it tends to have an unfortunate habit of doing. She should have known. Jez was too caught up with his organic movement to even notice her feelings for him.

She managed to hold back the tears and, with maturity beyond her age, put her disappointment behind her. She realised she'd just have to be patient. Her time would come. Meanwhile, she'd be there for him.

Amy Mae took a deep breath and, with her heavy heart hidden, said, 'Of course I believe, Jez, y'all know I do.'

'Good, I knew we could count on you, Amy Mae, you are simply the best.' Jez smiled, pleased.

It wasn't quite the 'love of my life, I can't live without you' line Amy Mae had hoped for, but it would have to do for now.

Jez looked about, in case of unintended ears, and then detailed his plans. 'Every lunar phase your uncle will ship a consignment of returnable packaging bound for Pacifica. I need you to pack some important organic material into those consignments. Can you do that?'

'Of course I can, Jez, no problem.' Amy Mae stretched across the table to clasp his hand and looked deeply into his eyes, but all she could see was the reflection of the organic surroundings he'd brought her to.

* * * * *

For Chad, the return passage on the Iridium to Pacifica proved to be as delightful as the outbound trip. Silver Service really was silver service on the Silver Service Star Line. The luscious Lucinda appeared to be only too pleased to be at his disposal and nothing seemed to be too much trouble for her. She was the female of his dreams and would be his in a pulsar's pulse, if it weren't for the fact that he was already spoken for.

As the Iridium jumped, Chad's thoughts turned to what was important: himself. With Johnson otherwise occupied, and his little sideline in leaf re-established, it was time to focus on his career development and, more specifically, his promotion up the corporate skyvator.

Ms D'Baliere had to be removed, of that there was no doubt, but he needed to develop a plan. Now, if she could be implicated in Johnson's nefarious activities then the path to promotion would be clear. He'd wanted to get the vice-president of customer-relationships and promotions on side, but so far Mr Stein had not been particularly supportive of his career development. In fact it had been Mr Stein who had appointed *that female* above him in the first place.

Perhaps he should set his sights higher. If he could get rid of both D'Baliere and Stein then there would be nothing to stop him gaining his ultimate prize: a seat on the Flush Away board and, with it, his coveted golden key to the executive toilet. However, to make that happen he would need the patronage of other members of the board and perhaps even Chief Executive & President Joseph Firtop.

Chad needed to think it over.

Through the viewing window Chad could see the executive transit shuttle docking with the Iridium's extended umbilical tunnel and, in the distance, against the carpet of stars, his destination, the ever-clouded grey with a hope of blue ball that was Pacifica.

After being called by one of the hostesses, bearing a card on a silver tray, Chad made his way to the docked shuttle. He settled comfortably into his designated Save-Your-Soul passenger seat and prepared for the descent. It was only when he saw the shadow of Pacifica, looming large through the porthole, that he realised the descent had begun. It was flawless, with the gentlest of landings. In fact the only discomfort Chad felt was the effort of trying to extract his rather tall frame from his seat against the pull of Pacifica's gravity.

*   *   *   *   *

On Nova Vega, Johnson stood in the foyer of the Black Hole Casino trying to dust himself off, but no sooner had he taken a step to return to its centre than a black spherical Hi-2-U greetings bot descended in front of him.

'Beep – Respects, sir – beep.' There was a pause. 'Beep – On behalf of the management and associates, please let me welcome you back to the casino, and please accept our most heartfelt commiserations on your recent loss on the Singularity – beep.' Another pause followed. 'Beep – Be assured that the management and associates are here to offer you every assistance in making your stay with us both pleasurable and memorable, for as long as your credit rating remains positive – beep.'

Johnson muttered.

The Hi-2-U greetings bot continued, 'Beep – If we can be of further service please don't hesitate to ask – beep.'

It waited a few photon phases and then left.

Johnson made his way through the crowds into the casino's interior, to the dark space at the centre of the gaming hall that was occupied by the Singularity.

'Sir,' acknowledged the Ever-On entrance bot, as it admitted Johnson.

And there, kneeling by the giant black gaming wheel was William Robert, his head lowered; hands apart in devotion. Johnson walked across to the repentant figure and shook him by the shoulder.

'William Robert, it's me, Johnson.'

Hesitantly, the devotion stopped. One eye opened and then the other, and William Robert looked up, but fear ran across his face and he began to tremble. 'Ya' terrible ghost, y'all's bin' sent back to haunt me, ain't ya!'

This took Johnson somewhat by surprise and he found himself wanting for words. He finally managed to utter, 'No.'

'Don't y'all lie to me ya' gruesome spectre!' exclaimed a terrified Billy Bob.

Johnson became aware of the attentive gaze of onlookers and leant forward to speak to Billy Bob.

'Be gone foul apparition!' howled Billy Bob, tears streaming down his face. 'My soul is in torment enough without y'all standin' over me.'

Johnson decided to speak calmly. 'William Robert, it's me, Johnson. I'm no ghost, I'm real.'

'So you say!' replied a disbelieving Billy Bob.

Johnson thought and then slapped Billy Bob across the face. 'Feel that? See I'm real.'

Billy Bob felt the sting and looked Johnson in the eye. 'Y'all's real?'

'Real as the rotation is long,' replied Johnson.

'Really real?' questioned Billy Bob.

'Really real,' confirmed Johnson.

'But y'all look like a ghost,' said Billy Bob.

Johnson looked at himself and brushed some of the dust off.

'It's just dust,' he explained.

Billy Bob rose with a smile as wide as an asteroid belt and grabbed Johnson by his arms. 'Why it's a miracle! Y'all's alive, glory be! Praise be to the Holy One. I knew, if I set myself to it, the Holy One would answer my devotions. Is Mr Jones alive too?'

Johnson nodded. 'Yes, he's alive too. Come on, I'll take you to him. You'll need to bring the wheelchair.'

Billy Bob was full of questions about what had happened.

Johnson explained that they'd been taken to a place of darkness, but they too had seen the light.

'Praise be to the Holy One,' incanted a reborn Billy Bob.

'Yes, er, praise be to the Holy One,' agreed Johnson, not wishing to get drawn into further debate.

So Johnson and Billy Bob made their way to find Mr Jones and, after retrieving him from the service-tunnel, Johnson tried desperately to bid farewell to his two fellow revellers, but Mr Jones would have none of it and absolutely insisted that Johnson join them for a drink in his penthouse suite.

Johnson agreed reluctantly, though once there he had to admit the view was impressive.

From the panoramic Vis-U-All window, with its 'The more you look, the more you see' technology, he could observe the entire historic Nova Vega skyline. Beyond the surrounding casinos, and their classic all-too-real themes, he could focus on Nova Vega's tall skybreakers, centring on the five arched golden towers upon which the enormous 'CC' logo of the Creation Corporation rotated. In between, above and below, streams of traffic banded across the dark sky, feeding those monuments to humankind's achievements.

It was a magnificent sight, so much more vibrant and colourful than the overcast cold grey of Pacifica. There seemed to be so much more space somehow, even with the darkness of sunfall the sky here was larger, broader, more open.

Beyond the mountains, and the barren desert escarpments that formed the horizon, Johnson glimpsed an occasional blinding, star-like luminance streak across the sky up to the heavens as transit shuttles lifted off from the spaceport to make their rendezvous with the starliners that orbited above.

His sunfall, as a stellar gamblestar, had been nothing if not eventful, but Johnson knew that in his heart it was not a life for him. No, it was time to return to being a sales representative. It was a life, not everybody's kind of life, but it was his life and no matter how much he felt frustrated, disappointed, let down or just plain bored, he knew it would always bring him the comfort of knowing where he belonged in the universe. And so he yawned.

'Another drink,' encouraged an enlivened Mr Jones, who had decided to sample each and every one of the drinks that resided on the shelf behind the penthouse suite's beverage counter.

'No, thank you,' replied Johnson. 'I have a transit shuttle to catch at sunrise.'

Not taking 'no' for an answer, Jones turned to Billy Bob, who had been reluctantly cast in the role of beverage associate – after the Happy-Chappy butler bot had been dismissed for the sunfall. 'William Robert, make one last drink to toast our new found friendship.'

'One last drink, Mr Jones?' repeated Johnson.

'Yes, one last drink.' Jones smiled. 'You won't refuse *one last drink* will you, Johnson?'

'No, I guess not, but then you must excuse me, I really do need some sleep.' Johnson yawned again.

Billy Bob brought three drinks and handed one to Johnson, another to Jones and held the last tumbler himself.

Jones raised his tumbler. 'To new friends and new adventures.'

'New friends and new adventures,' replied Johnson and downed the contents of his tumbler in one. Jones and Billy Bob looked on, tumblers still in hand.

Johnson put his tumbler down and put his hand out to press goodbye. 'Well, it's been, um, er, excellent, truly excellent. I wouldn't have missed it for all the stars in the Spiral Arm. I wish you all the best, farewell, stay in touch...' And then he crumpled, very slowly.

Johnson had fallen backwards into a chair. His eyes were closed. Sleep had come to him.

Jones and Billy Bob waited to see if Johnson would re-awaken, but from the snoring it was clear that Johnson had well and truly drifted off.

'He just can't hold his drink,' remarked Jones, placing his untouched tumbler on the table in front of Billy Bob. 'You'd better dispose of this.'

Billy Bob took the remaining tumblers, returned them to the beverage counter and emptied their contents away.

Jones rubbed his hands together. 'At last, we have our male! And now, by the stars, it's time for action, time to put our plan into place. You'll need to retrieve his belongings from his room. I'll get his holocom and reconfigure it for you to use.'

Johnson's snoring persisted loudly and uninterrupted as Jones searched Johnson's attire. Then, in something akin to a wrestling match, Jones managed to lift an eyelid and use Johnson's sleeping iris to unlock the holocom.

When Billy Bob returned, he and Jones pushed the chair bound Johnson in front of a blank wall. They sat him up, put his hands behind his head, lifted up his eyelids and tried to make his face smile.

'One Johnson ready to have his image taken,' concluded Jones.

Whilst a little nervous, mostly because he wasn't quite sure he fully understood what was going on, Billy Bob was in no doubt that he was being faithful to his mission. To fully reassure himself he recanted Jez's mantra: '"To spread the organic word and bring about the collapse of the unorganic corporations that infest the universe with their attempts to enslave the very masses they are meant to serve in themedom."'

Under Jones's direction, Billy Bob took an image of Johnson using Johnson's holocom. Jones and Billy Bob then returned Johnson to his pre-image position, by the beverage counter, and, finally, let Johnson's head drape over the chair's arm.

'Billy Bob, if you put our guest's belongings in one of the rooms, I'll compose an appropriate message to send to his employers,' instructed Jones.

And the message simply read,

FLUSH AWAY
YOUR EMPLOYEE IS WITH US
REQUESTS ORGANIC RESTITUTION
YOU HAVE THE TIME OF CREATION
THE CHILDREN OF THE SOIL

[22] Beep Beep Beep

Sunrise over Nova Vega and Johnson slept.

Star Trooper Jonah Jones looked at Billy Bob. 'Try not to talk to anyone. Be inconspicuous.'

An uncomfortable Billy Bob had put Johnson's business attire on over his own, giving him the appearance of someone who'd dined out on corporate expenses once too often. However, with a quick restyling of his hair, and the ever-present poncho draped over his arm, Billy Bob bore a passing resemblance to Johnson.

'By the heavens, I can hardly believe it; you could be twins,' remarked Jones. 'Not identical twins, but twins none the less.' Although, not wishing to sap Billy Bob's fragile confidence further, he added mentally, 'To a blind male, at a thousand paces, under a moonless sunfall sky.'

Billy Bob's task was straightforward, although Jones had come to realise that the words 'Billy Bob' and 'straightforward' were a dangerous combination if used in the same sentence.

Billy Bob was to impersonate Johnson. He was to lay a false trail of Johnson's movements before sending the message to the Flush Away Corporation. There needed to be as much distance between where Flush Away, and presumably Pacifica's law enforcement agency, thought Johnson was last seen and where he actually was.

Billy Bob, as Johnson, was to check out of the Black Hole Casino, catch a taxi-skyrider to the spaceport and then embark on the Liberty Discount starliner back to Pacifica. It was while he was on the starliner that Billy Bob was to send the message. However, Billy Bob was not going to complete the passage to Pacifica. He was going to disembark secretly from the starliner and stowaway on the return transit shuttle to Nova Vega, leaving Johnson's trail lost in space.

Jones made Billy Bob recite the various stages of the plan until he was sure that it had taken root fully. He then wished Billy Bob the best of providence and reminded him why they were doing what they were doing. 'It's for the good of the cause. Cousin Jez will be proud of what we're about to achieve. This one act will do more to spread the organic word, and help overthrown corporate universisation, than anything else you've done before.'

With a slightly more reassured, 'See y'all later,' a smarter – although purely in the fashion sense – Billy Bob made his way to the Black Hole Casino's reception with Johnson's luggage.

Whilst checking out proved to be relatively easy, finding the exit to the casino was not. Billy Bob walked and walked, and walked and walked, taking many turnings, traversing corridors and stairs, passing through an endless expanse of gaming halls only to find that he'd returned to the very reception he'd just checked out from.

Conscious of Jones's instructions, to try and not talk to anyone and to be inconspicuous – whatever that meant – Billy Bob had a flash of inspiration. He'd wait for the next guest to check out and follow them to the exit. Billy Bob found a potted parasol plant to hide behind and waited, much to the amusement of the casino's reception associates.

After several false starts, Billy Bob struck lucky: at last, a guest with luggage to follow. Maintaining a consistent ten pace gap, even when the elderly guest began to speed up to a heart-attack-inducing jog, Billy Bob arrived in the foyer of the Black Hole Casino. The guest, who had collapsed into a chair and was gasping for breath, stared at him with a mixture of fear and confusion as he walked past her.

Billy Bob was sure that Jones would be pleased with his progress. As he made his way across the foyer he looked outside. He stopped in surprise. He could see that the weather was doing something it was not supposed to do on Nova Vega: it was raining, in fact there was an absolute flood falling from the sky.

Everyone was running for cover, their attire pulled up over their heads in a futile attempt to stay dry. Those inside looked on in amazement, it never rained on Nova Vega, not according to the tourist literature anyway.

Who'd of thought that Johnson's poncho would come in useful? Billy Bob placed the luggage on the ground and started to pull the poncho over his head only to become desperately entangled. Unfamiliar with this type of attire, he'd somehow managed to end up standing on the hood with an arm and a leg stuck where he thought his head should be.

Noticing that Billy Bob had luggage and had stood still for more than its pre-programmed time limit, a large black spherical Hi-2-U greetings bot swooped down and dropped an arrow-headed sign that displayed the word 'Reception' in crackling blue ionic discharge.

'Beep – Respects, sir – beep.' There was a pause. 'Beep – On behalf of the management and associates of the Black Hole Casino please accept our most heartfelt welcome – beep.' Another pause followed. 'Beep – For rooms and any other services, that you may require, please follow the sign – beep.'

Billy Bob managed finally to wrestle the poncho over his head, with appropriate limbs protruding from appropriate holes, although it was the wrong way round. He looked blankly at the Hi-2-U greetings bot.

'Beep – Would sir like me to carry his luggage? – Beep,' asked the Hi-2-U greetings bot.

'Why that'd be mighty kind, but I ain't stayin',' replied Billy Bob.

Oblivious to the last part of Billy Bob's response, the Hi-2-U greetings bot dropped its tethered hook onto the handle of his luggage and lifted it off the ground.

'Beep – If sir would care to follow me please – beep,' instructed the Hi-2-U greetings bot. It then set off towards the heart of the casino.

Billy Bob was caught by surprise and was trying to rotate the poncho to be the right way round. 'Hey, what are y'all doin'?' He then belatedly dived after the Hi-2-U greetings bot, managing to get a hand to the luggage. The bot pitched down, but continued as Billy Bob's hand failed to gain purchase and slipped off. An unbalanced Billy Bob tumbled to the ground amidst the throng of casino customers.

Billy Bob scrambled to his feet and set off in pursuit of Johnson's luggage, his poncho flapping about him. The Hi-2-U greetings bot, together with the luggage, continued apace and climbed up above head height to avoid colliding with the gathering crowd.

'Y'all give me back that there luggage or y'all be in more trouble than a five legged castorian stallion come geldin' time,' threatened Billy Bob as he pushed through the crowd. He jumped in the air and just missed the luggage. The intrigued onlookers cheered as Billy Bob rose, and sighed as Billy Bob fell.

'Give it back now ya' no good hunk 'a junk!' Again Billy Bob leapt, again the crowd cheered, and again Billy Bob missed, much to their amusement.

The whole foyer, having lost interest in the rain, now appeared to be engrossed in this comic chase, human versus bot, all for the prize of a piece of luggage. And being of a gambling nature, a number of the spectators were starting to offer odds and exchange bets on the pursuit's outcome. The current consensus appeared to be that the Hi-2-U greetings bot was the 'odds on' favourite.

Billy Bob collected himself to make a more concerted effort. He allowed the Hi-2-U greetings bot to pull away so that he could have more of a run at it. The expectant crowd hushed and drew back. Those who could see the look of concentration on Billy Bob's face placed bets on the human, the odds shortened, and Billy Bob began his run, head down, focussed.

All was silent as Billy Bob sprinted towards the Hi-2-U greetings bot and, with one giant bound, he grasped the luggage between his hands. There was a cheer from all around as Billy Bob swung underneath the bot, which was pulling hard towards the ceiling. Billy Bob jerked his arms firmly, but this failed to release the luggage, and the Hi-2-U greetings bot continued to climb.

'I'll kick your sorry tin butt from here to eternity if ya' don't release the luggage,' yelled Billy Bob. The Hi-2-U greetings bot stopped. The crowd became silent. Those directly beneath parted. Billy Bob could feel his fingers starting to slide down the luggage.

The Hi-2-U greetings bot whirred. 'Beep – Certainly, sir – beep.' And the tethered hook undid.

Billy Bob suddenly became aware of his predicament and, like all those who faced similar predicaments before him, closed his eyes. The multitude below had their eyes wide-open and, to them, his impending impact was going to be all-too-real.

The crowd gasped as Billy Bob separated from the Hi-2-U greetings bot. But as he plummeted the poncho ballooned out like an atmospheric-descent retarder, slowing his fall. He floated down, landing on the hard marble foyer. Winded, Billy Bob groaned and then began to move. Those around strained to see. Billy Bob shook himself a little and with one rather jerky effort, stood, luggage in hand.

The crowd, or at least the part that had put credits on Billy Bob, burst into applause, shouting and cheering. Billy Bob felt somehow elated and responded to those around him by taking a bow.

It was a little later, as Billy Bob remembered Jones's words, that he realised he'd probably not handled this part of his task as well as he might. Amid the applause Billy Bob decided to slip away quietly to catch a taxi-skyrider to the spaceport.

*   *   *   *   *

Following a restless sleep, where sunrise came all-too-slowly, Investigator Strait collected Deputies D'Angelis and Gilbrae, and together they returned to the gallery of associate images in the foyer of the Black Hole Casino.

'Ready?' asked Investigator Strait.

'Ready, Investigator,' replied Deputy D'Angelis.

Deputy Gilbrae nodded.

Investigator Strait raised his arm and touched the casino manager's image. However, to Investigator Strait's disappointment, the voice said, 'Mr Cigstano is unavailable. For assistance please try another associate.'

'He doesn't appear to be here,' commented Deputy D'Angelis, always ready and able to articulate the obvious.

Investigator Strait ignored D'Angelis. He was not going to be put off for a second time. Cigstano, Johnson and Jones had to be somewhere, but where?

It was all the commotion that first distracted Deputy Gilbrae. As compensation for being a male of few words – if compensation were needed – Deputy Gilbrae could hear what others could not, though he didn't always chose to listen. His highly tuned ear was almost a sixth sense and was unerring in its ability to detect the abnormal. The cheering that filled the foyer certainly wasn't normal. He drifted off from the other two, who were staring fixedly at the images on the wall, each lost in their own thoughts.

'Sometimes he was just plain lucky,' he thought to himself, for there, floating above the crowd, was a male wearing a military-style poncho, grasping hold of some luggage, whilst being held up by one of the casino's Hi-2-U greetings bots. And, if he wasn't mistaken, that male was Johnson. He turned to his colleagues and shouted, 'Look!'

His colleagues ignored him. They were in heated discussion.

Deputy Gilbrae stepped back and shook Deputy D'Angelis by the shoulder. 'Look!'

'What is it? The Investigator and me were just debating what to do next,' replied a distracted Deputy D'Angelis.

Insistent, Deputy Gilbrae grabbed D'Angelis's arm and tugged him towards the now hushed crowd.

'What is it?' repeated Deputy D'Angelis.

Deputy Gilbrae pointed above the crowd.

'What?' Deputy D'Angelis was looking, but could not see.

Deputy Gilbrae pointed, harder.

Deputy D'Angelis looked to the atrium of the foyer, but all he saw was a black spherical Hi-2-U greetings bot hovering.

Suddenly there was cheering then a tumultuous round of applause. You could bet your planetoid that something was going on. The deputies pressed forward, firmly pushing bystanders aside, and there he was: Johnson!

Deputy D'Angelis ran across to the Investigator. 'We've seen him, Investigator; we've seen Johnson. He's just leavin' the building!'

Investigator Strait turned and stared directly into Deputy D'Angelis's eyes. 'You're certain?'

'Yeah, sure. He is wearing that poncho in the image we have, and he's sure in a hurry,' replied D'Angelis.

A smile drew across Investigator Strait's face; Operation Kicking Butt was back on. 'Let's go!'

* * * * *

Billy Bob – as Johnson – stepped into the taxi-skyrider and stated his destination, but nothing happened.

'Please repeat,' requested the Ever-On taxibot.

Billy Bob leant forward and yelled at the screen, 'Spaceport!'

'Please be aware the use of abusive language, or language spoken in a threatening manner or with an offensive tone, is not acceptable,' responded the Ever-On taxibot. 'Restate your destination, or exit this skyrider.'

Billy Bob was about to hit the screen, but thought better of it. Perhaps it was the noise of the rain that was confusing the taxibot. He decided to speak as slowly and clearly as he could, 'Spa–ce–por–t.'

For a pulsar's pulse the Ever-On taxibot processed his response. 'It is standard procedure for the passenger door to remain open until the destination is confirmed. Restate your destination, or exit this skyrider.'

Billy Bob deliberated and then he deliberated some more. This leaving a false trail was proving to be a lot more difficult than he thought. Then, at last, he had an idea. He would spell out his destination, he managed, 'S–P–A–C, ah, P–O–R–T.'

There was a short pause. Then the Ever-On taxibot began buzzing in an alarming manner and, in an entirely different, expressionless voice, replied, 'Special Priority Activation Code A: "P–O–R–T" accepted, countdown to self-detonation commencing. Ten, nine, eight, seven, six...'

A somewhat startled Billy Bob panicked and decided to take the agricultural approach; he hammered on the screen with his fist.

For a pulsar's pulse the screen blanked out and the taxibot stopped counting. Then, after some strained whirring, its original synthetic voice returned. 'Destination?'

Billy Bob drew breath slowly and stated as clearly as he could, 'Spaceport.'

'Please confirm, spaceport,' responded the Ever-On taxibot.

'Confirmed.' The passenger door slid shut and a relieved Billy Bob sat back.

There was a sudden bang on the door and Billy Bob caught sight of two hands slipping down the rain soaked window as the taxi-skyrider ascended. 'Folks in these parts sure are always in a hurry; they'd do anything to catch a taxi-skyrider,' he thought.

The taxi-skyrider lifted to join the multi-strand, multidirectional super skyway that fed Nova Vega's spaceport. Billy Bob brushed the window with his hand, but the rain obscured the view. Only the brightest lights and tallest skybreakers in the conurbation's sprawl emerged through the downpour.

'Destination imminent,' informed the Ever-On taxibot.

Ahead, to the horizon, Billy Bob could just make out the krypton-white glow of transit shuttles lifting off from the spaceport, en route to planetary orbit. The taxi-skyrider pressed on, heading towards them.

*　*　*　*　*

Investigator Strait, who had led the chase to the taxi-skyrider, fell to his knees, his arms outstretched as Billy Bob literally slipped through his hands. He cursed.

Deputies D'Angelis and Gilbrae pulled up alongside, their matching straw hats wilted over their heads. Their Neo-Holo attire was soaked to their bodies and displaying images of despondent athletes who had just failed to win their events.

'Missed him then, Investigator?' remarked Deputy D'Angelis.

Investigator Strait said nothing. He just turned and glared.

The rain fell. Investigator Strait did not move.

After a while Deputy D'Angelis managed to build up enough courage to venture, 'I wonder where he's gone?'

Investigator Strait did not respond.

'You all right, Investigator? We should be going, it's still raining you know, we're getting a bit wet.'

It was only when the maelstrom of frustration had finally blown through Investigator Strait's mind, sufficiently for him to stand and speak, that he said, 'He had his luggage with him. My guess is that he's gone to the spaceport to catch the next starliner back to Pacifica. I will go to the spaceport. D'Angelis, you and Gilbrae go back to the Second Chance Hotel, collect our luggage and check us out. Meet me at the spaceport, at the departure point for the Pacifica passage, and be hyper-phased about it, that's an order.'

'Right you are, Investigator,' replied D'Angelis. 'Spaceport, departure point, Pacifica passage. Got it.'

Investigator Strait tried to will the taxi-skyrider he'd caught to go faster, but he knew it made no difference. He'd had Johnson within his grasp. He'd even seen his face through the window just an arm's length away. If only he could have reached inside, then Operation Kicking Butt would have netted its first major success.

Investigator Strait glimpsed the distant glow of transit shuttles tracing through the pink sky. His quarry was just ahead of him. He needed to focus. When the taxi-skyrider landed he would go straight to the shuttle departure point for the Pacifica passages. He had the advantage: he knew Johnson, but Johnson didn't know him. In fact, as far as Investigator Strait knew, Johnson was unaware that he was under suspicion.

His spirits lifted. His Ever-On taxibot gave him the expected time of arrival. Not long now. Investigator Strait counted down the time. At last! The taxi-skyrider descended. He could see the outline of the spaceport buildings. Frustratingly the taxi-skyrider slowed as it descended.

Touch down! Investigator Strait almost wrenched the passenger door off as it slid open. He sprinted down the taxi rank, heading for departures. Where was the sign? There it was. Turn to the left, follow the green arrows and the upward-facing transit shuttle symbol. Luckily, in a spaceport, travellers didn't think anything of someone running. He was starting to get out of breath. Slow down, slow down; he needed to even out his pace if he was going to get there. No sign of Johnson though.

Best to walk now. Observe. Look at the faces, look out for that poncho. No sign of it at this juncture in the space-time continuum. Was that him up ahead? No just a traveller in a brand new chromium-green waterproof.

He arrived at the departure point and finally there was Johnson! His back was turned, but the poncho was unmistakable.

Investigator Strait about-faced and walked across to the Liberty Discount Star Line check-in. As he did so he holoed D'Angelis. He told him that he was going to try and get them on the Pacifica passage. D'Angelis said that he and Gilbrae had just left the Second Chance Hotel with the luggage. Closing down his holocom, Investigator Strait greeted the check-in associate.

'I'd like three one-way passages to Pacifica,' announced Investigator Strait.

'And when would sir like to travel?' requested the check-in associate, interacting with her holoplay.

'Now,' answered Investigator Strait.

'Ah.' The check-in associate stopped interacting with her holoplay.

'Ah?' quizzed Investigator Strait.

'Yes, I'm afraid so, sir. I can no longer accept passengers for this rotation's passage. Boarding commences momentarily.' The check-in associate smiled, as all Liberty Discount Star Line's associates had been trained to do when bearing bad news to passengers.

Investigator Strait leant forward and projected his law enforcement identification over the counter. 'I am an undercover investigator and your passage has my suspect about to board it. Me and my deputies need to be on that passage.'

'This is most irregular, sir,' responded the check-in associate. 'I will have to defer to my supervisor. If you wouldn't mind waiting.' The check-in associate turned to her older colleague. There was much hushed debate, nodding, then shaking, then nodding, then shaking and then, finally, nodding of heads.

Investigator Strait waited.

The check-in associate returned. 'Sir, I have consulted with my supervisor and he has agreed that we can sell you three one-way passages on two provisos.'

'Which are?' asked Investigator Strait and pulled out a roll of credits ready to pay.

'Firstly, your luggage will have to follow on later, we do not have time to scan and load it,' said the check-in associate.

'No problem,' replied Investigator Strait.

'And, secondly, your fellow travellers must be here soon or we will not be able to process their details,' continued the check-in associate.

'Right then.' Investigator Strait turned and pulled his holocom to his ear. 'D'Angelis where are you? You need to be at the Liberty Discount Star Line check-in now... No, I'm not joking... You'll just have to run... Indeed, you will just have to run faster... Don't disappoint... End of discussion.'

Investigator Strait turned back to the check-in associate and said, with a half-smile, 'No problem.'

'Fine, sir. Shall we begin by processing you?' responded the check-in associate.

Investigator Strait started to watch the time as he answered the check-in associate's questions and provided the appropriate verification.

Time passed.

The check-in associate waited.

Investigator Strait waited, muttering to himself. And so as more time passed, his tension increased. The check-in associate appeared impassive.

Investigator Strait's holocom broke the silence, and he lifted it to his ear. 'You're here at the spaceport... Indeed... No both of you... What do you mean twisted his ankle...? I don't care... Carry him if you have to... What...? Right then, you can tell him from me to stop complaining and to get moving... Get here now!'

'Sir, will your colleagues be arriving soon?' enquired the check-in associate. 'We cannot hold the shuttle up for much longer.'

'Absolutely.' Investigator Strait began to count down time under his breath.

Ten. The check-in associate asked if Investigator Strait wished to proceed with his passage, unaccompanied. Investigator Strait hushed her and peered down the concourse. There, in the distance, he was able to make out a shape that appeared to be closing faster than the other shapes heading his way. Was that them?

Nine. The shape grew larger.

Eight. The shape grew larger still.

Seven. Investigator Strait was able to discern detail in the form.

Six. The shape had a head, too many arms and no legs.

Five. No, the shape had two heads.

Four. And three arms, one waving and two outstretched.

Three. The shape had wheels and a tail.

Two. Deputy Gilbrae was sat in a trolley, arms akimbo with a leg pointing directly forward. Deputy D'Angelis stood, chariot-style, at the rear, trailed by their Follow-You luggage, which was clearly struggling to keep up.

One. The trolley continued to accelerate. Deputy D'Angelis was yelling something.

Zero. Deputy Gilbrae managed a wry salute as Deputy D'Angelis's pallid face tried to mask the fear of an impending collision.

Investigator Strait turned to the check-in associate and smiled a smile of confidence.

'My colleagues…' CRASH! Investigator Strait paused and then, unphased, concluded his sentence, 'and our luggage have arrived.'

* * * * *

Seat upright and safely strapped in, Billy Bob now considered himself to be a seasoned star-voyager. And, as he had done before, Billy Bob watched the safety instructions intently. His neighbouring passengers politely tried to ignore him as he repeated every word, every phrase, every sentence, loudly.

And so began the sequence of events that made up the short trip to the Freedom Of The Heavens, as his awaiting starliner was named: the cycle of activity that crew and passengers shared as the transit shuttle lifted off, left the atmosphere, orbited and then docked.

First came the slight judder, as the shuttle rotated in preparation for take off. He loved the big number countdown displayed on the holoplays. He too liked counting along.

'Five, four, three, two, one, lift-off!'

He felt the gentle, irresistible push the transit shuttle gave as it separated from its launch pad and climbed through the sky. Then came the transient weightlessness and the consequent nausea as the shuttle broke into orbit. But what he liked most of all was the sense of wonder and insignificance he felt for that brief pulsar's pulse, as the planet fell away beneath him, and all were stars pitched in the darkness.

'Sure is pretty out there,' Billy Bob said to no one in particular and then added, 'and sure is pretty in here!'

His attention was now captivated by the jump associate, who'd introduced herself on embarkation as Aurora. She was truly the prettiest thing he'd ever seen. He locked on and tracked her every move.

Aurora was checking on the condition of the passengers, occasionally using her Go Suck portable suction pack to capture the unfortunate consequences of weightlessness. And, a few rows back from Billy Bob, one such hapless victim of this condition was Deputy D'Angelis. He'd managed initially to hold back and re-digest, that which weightlessness had brought forth, only to then gag and regurgitate again, spewing his stomach's contents all around. To add further to Deputy D'Angelis's woes his colleagues, sat on either side, expressed their displeasure by subjecting him to a stream of colourful language and sharp elbows.

It was then that the holoplays announced that docking was to commence. The transit shuttle's drives began to hum and the transit shuttle started to rotate front end up. It was now anyone's estimation as to where

Deputy D'Angelis's free-floating vomit might land.

Billy Bob sat, unaware of the events thrown up behind him, unaware of Investigator Strait and the two law enforcement deputies following him.

The transit shuttle manoeuvred and then docked with the starliner with only the faintest of bumps. Billy Bob released his safety harness, stood and made his way with the rest of the passengers to the transit shuttle's airlock, a little unsteady in the starliner's artificial gravity.

Aurora smiled and hoped he'd had a pleasant trip. Billy Bob smiled back.

At a distance, Investigator Strait and his two deputies looked on. Investigator Strait, dressed in his light-coloured vacational attire, was a little be-speckled by the residue of recent events, but still managed to blend easily into the crowd. However, the visceral hunting scenes displayed by his deputies' Neo-Holo attire made them somewhat more conspicuous. A state of affairs not helped by the fact that Deputy Gilbrae was hitting Deputy D'Angelis over the head with his wilted straw hat.

Fortunately, Billy Bob did not turn around. Billy Bob was standing, rooted to the spot, transfixed, smiling at Aurora until the following passenger nudged him rather forcefully in the back to get him moving.

Billy Bob re-gathered his thoughts and, with regret, overcame the distraction of Aurora. He needed to complete his mission and he knew he had little time to act.

Once aboard the Freedom Of The Heavens, Billy Bob scoured the starliner's passenger deck, headed straight for the nearest toilet and started to set up Johnson's holocom ready to send the message.

Barely a few paces behind, Investigator Strait surveyed the curving, windowless passenger deck in search of Johnson. They'd momentarily lost sight of him when they'd filed through the airlock.

He indicated to Deputies D'Angelis and Gilbrae to walk counter-turnwise around the passenger deck whilst he set off turnwise. It didn't take a countdown before they met again on the other side of the deck, each having completed one half of the circumnavigation. No Johnson.

Many embarking passengers had now found their seats and the jump associates were beginning to usher those left standing to sit. In a few photon phases the starliner would start to manoeuvre, ready to pull away from the historic delights of Nova Vega.

Investigator Strait gestured to his deputies to spread out and continue their search. Johnson had to be somewhere.

After a frustrating fumble of one-fingered interaction, Billy Bob finally managed to set up the message on Johnson's holocom. It was ready to go. Once the send icon was enabled, the message, together with the attached image of Johnson, would be on its way via Galactic Union, the interstellar relay service, to the Flush Away Corporation.

But Billy Bob wasn't going to send the message just yet. He needed to be long gone before it went. Instead he was going to rely upon the next person to use the toilet to send it for him. He'd wrapped Johnson's holocom in toilet Paperette and wedged it under the toilet seat cover. When the cover was next lifted, the holocom's send icon would be enabled, the message sent and the Paperette wrapped holocom would drop into the bowl. There, if seen at all, it would be mistaken for an un-flushed deposit left by the previous occupant. And then, when operated, the irradiating sanitation unit would destroy and vaporise Johnson's holocom completely, leaving no trace.

Jones had told Billy Bob that he felt a certain pride in devising this part of the plan. He felt it was only fitting that the Flush Away Corporation's very product should play such an instrumental role in aiding the Children Of The Soil's cause. Billy Bob remembered what Jones had said, 'There is pure poetry in turning the enemies tools against itself!'

But no time for that now, he had to put a rocket up it. Billy Bob quickly disrobed, rolled up Johnson's business attire and put it, together with the poncho, into a foldout bag. He ruffled his hair and looked in the holomirror. Welcome back Billy Bob! Time to make his escape. He opened the toilet door and stepped out onto the passenger deck. Most passengers appeared to be settling into their seats.

Without a second glance Billy Bob strode across the passenger deck and quietly joined the end of the queue of passengers boarding the transit shuttle ready for its return transfer to Nova Vega.

As he stepped through the airlock, Aurora, the jump associate, smiled and hoped he'd have a pleasant trip. She thought she recognised this last passenger but couldn't place where she'd seen him. Mind you the job was often like that, you saw so many passengers.

Back on the Freedom Of The Heavens, the time for the jump was drawing near. All passengers were requested to take their seats.

Investigator Strait decided to take the opportunity to go to the toilet, and, as he stood relieving himself, he marshalled some of his favourite expletives into a sentence. He promised, aloud, that he wasn't about to let that 'beep beep beep' Johnson escape this time.

Which was odd for, as he uttered those very words, he was sure he heard something go 'beep beep beep'. No matter, his mind moved on and he exited the toilet.

The jump associates were checking that all of the passengers were safely seated.

Investigator Strait, the last passenger standing, had to be coaxed to sit down. He was frustrated. Where was Johnson? He had to be here somewhere. He couldn't simply vanish, could he? Investigator Strait sighed and finally sat down.

With all passengers secure, the starliner began to rumble, and the whole passenger deck started to shake. The manoeuvring thrusters were slowly pushing the starliner away from the pull of Nova Vega's gravity and towards the jump point.

The thrusters stopped thrusting and the jump countdown commenced. With it came a faint buzzing sensation, as the jump drive was prepared. Some passengers claimed that during the jump they felt something. Investigator Strait never did. All that ever happened for him was that the buzzing sensation went away.

As soon as they had jumped, and were back in the Pacifica System, he would be able to holo the rest of his team. He'd put them on alert, ready for their arrival. With deputies planetside and deputies in space, there was no way that Johnson would be able to evade capture.

And then the starliner jumped.

To anyone watching from space, the starliner simply vanished, with the faintest of twinkles, gone as if it had never been there.

* * * * *

Billy Bob was glad to be back planetside. Whilst the view from space sure was spectacular, nothing felt quite as good as when your feet were onplanet, and a sky was above you, particularly if the sun was shining.

He stood outside Nova Vega's spaceport and took in the air.

The rain, that had marked his recent departure, had gone, no trace was left under the red, fading-to-pink sky, it had all evaporated.

Billy Bob began to reminisce. His thoughts shifted to his homeworld and the harvest, and all the hard work that came with it, and the time he spent on the land; a happy time spent with Pa, Jimmy Bob and Bart Bob – who'd even leave his beloved almaakian cattle to help out in the fields.

He missed his family. He could picture Ma in the cooking-room, and Philippa Sue lookin' after the young un's: Jamie Bob and Hew Bob, and, of course, John Peter. He bet the older ones: Judy Ann, Bella Sue and Johnny Bob would be up to all those school tricks he used to get up to and then some. And Drue Ann – she'd always been a might too serious for games – she'd have her head stuck in the numbers, tellin' Pa what and when to buy and sell. Billy Bob had long since figured that she'd been blessed with more than her fair share of brains, and he'd been the one who'd been left short at the trough.

Billy Bob realised that he'd been so busy doing what he'd been doing that he'd not thought about his family for rotations. He realised that he hadn't even thought about Simple, his flea-bitten mutt of a procyon hound dog.

Billy Bob wanted to go back to Old MacDonald's World.

171

However, he'd promised Cousin Jez he'd complete the mission. He couldn't let his kinfolk down. So even though he didn't really understand half of what Cousin Jez had said to him – about being 'ideologically dedicated to organic principles' or 'the overthrow of corporate universisation' – Billy Bob knew he had to see it through.

He stepped into a taxi-skyrider and headed for the Black Hole Casino. And, whilst he remained bedazzled by the adventure, and the lights and the sounds of Nova Vega's historic urban sprawl, in truth he really missed the fields of Old MacDonald's World.

[23] Missing

Flush Away's greetings associate, the ever-conscientious Miranda, scanned the incoming coms, as she did at the start of every workshift. And, as ever, her holoplay flowed with endless messages. Although sometimes interspersed with final demand notices, blind merchandising communications and the odd misdirected delivery, most of the messages were customer complaints. These ranged from the polite, and helpfully suggestive, to the frankly abusive and inappropriately forthright.

It had taken many solar cycles of strategic thinking, debate and initiatives within Flush Away's corporate organisation to finally decide that the post of greetings associate was best positioned to handle the task of dealing with this torrent of customer communication.

It was absolutely clear to all, in the conception and evolution department, that its precious resources needed to be focussed on the problems of the future, not embroiled with the mistakes of the past.

Of course it went without saying that the merchandising department was fully supportive of the organisation's strategic, customer-centric initiatives. To this end it had extensively evaluated, reported on and sought full market indicators, which it regularly reflected in its coms, trend analyses and sector potential studies. What more could it do?

And the customer-relationships and promotions department, well it was there to sell, sell, sell! Nothing could be allowed to distract it from its primary task, for without sales where would the organisation be?

And the fabrication department would most certainly act in an unambiguous and transparent way upon any customer issues raised that could be clearly attributable to its activities. You could depend upon fabrication to ensure that those responsible would be held to account and dealt with appropriately. But given that the fabrication department needed to focus on producing the product, and that it had no direct customer contact, it hardly seemed appropriate for customer issues to be handled within its structure.

And thus, through logical debate, those thorny customer issues landed with Flush Away's greetings associate. The ever-reliable Miranda didn't mind. Being at the lower reaches of the corporate hierarchy she understood that her role was to do as she was told. After all somebody had to do it.

So, over time, she had developed her own system of customer complaint categorisation and response.

For the frankly abusive and inappropriately forthright complaints, the response was straightforward and easy: a simple counter-threat of litigation, unlimited fines, custodial sentencing or worse, all dressed up in the latest verbage from Flush Away's always-busy litigation team.

For the polite and helpfully suggestive customers, complaining for the first time, she always responded with a thankful apology, appreciative of the efforts that the customer had gone to, and a non-specific reassurance that the whole of the Flush Away organisation was focussed on improving what it did for its customers.

For customers who were complaining for a second time, she always added that she simply couldn't understand how their concern had been misplaced, and that the customer could be rest-assured that they were being dealt with immediately.

Customers complaining for a third time typically got a profuse apology, without any admission of liability of course, and the comforting news that the person who had been dealing with their concern was no longer with the organisation.

Persistent customers could often prove to be a little more problematic. However, the ever-capable Miranda had evolved a number of techniques that she was able to apply.

There was always the option of asking the customer to complete Flush Away's own exhaustive, and some would say incomprehensible, complaint questionnaire; required for *further clarification*. This often proved to be just enough of a bureaucratic hurdle to sap the customer's will.

Alternatively, the promise of a visit by one of Flush Away's customer-relationship and promotions specialists often resulted in the customer reviewing whether it really was worthwhile proceeding, given the unwelcome prospect of a sales representative turning up at their airlock.

Totality in totality, it was because of the ever-industrious Miranda that the many key – as they all perceived themselves to be – functional departments of the Flush Away Corporation could proceed with their important work, unimpeded by the vagaries of the customer.

So it was a pleasant surprise for the ever-dedicated Miranda when she received a message from Johnson, her favourite customer-relationship and promotions specialist, particularly as it was a message he'd taken the time and expense to send offplanet via Galactic Union. He was her cosmonaut in shining starlight, who regularly saved her from the clutches of the obnoxious Chad – the thought of whom would send an involuntary shudder through her body accompanied by a sensation of mild nausea. Unfortunately the pleasant feeling of surprise turned to puzzlement upon reading the message.

FLUSH AWAY

YOUR EMPLOYEE IS WITH US

REQUESTS ORGANIC RESTITUTION

YOU HAVE THE TIME OF CREATION

THE CHILDREN OF THE SOIL

The ever-thoughtful Miranda wondered whether this might be one of

Johnson's rather feeble attempts at humour, although she struggled to see the joke.

It didn't make sense. Soon worry began to permeate her thoughts. She read the message again, and this time she noticed there was an attached image, which she opened. It was of Johnson leant back in a chair.

It couldn't be?

It couldn't be, could it?

No, it couldn't.

Could this be a ransom demand?

In disbelief the ever-prepared Miranda re-read the message. She didn't fully understand it. What did 'organic restitution' mean and who were the Children Of The Soil?

Could Johnson really have been kidnapped?

And then the darkest thought of all came to her mind. Her whole being became racked with guilt. Could it be that one of her many disgruntled customers had finally reached the end of their parabola and, in a desperate bid to gain satisfaction, kidnapped Johnson?

*   *   *   *   *

Johnson had a headache. It was not the first headache he'd had, nor, he suspected, would it be the last. But it certainly was one starburst of a headache.

He eased one eye open, to be sure as not to let in too much light. He had a shock. With eyes now wide-open, he wondered quite where he was.

The sleep-cot, the room, the door were all unfamiliar. He had a thought, his heart raced. He tentatively reached his arm out behind him, across the other side of the sleep-cot, dreading that it might make contact. No one there. He rolled over and looked across. The adjoining head cushion appeared to be untouched. He breathed a sigh of relief and relaxed. Then his head started to throb with all-too-much clarity, throbbing with his every heartbeat.

He sat up. And that brought the pain sharply into focus. This was one forebear of a hangover. Perhaps there was something he could take. He needed a drink of water.

At least he'd removed his attire. His thought pattern stopped. He didn't remember taking his attire off. He looked around the room. His attire wasn't anywhere to be seen. He wondered where it was.

He needed relief. He headed for the adjacent washroom and watched as the lid lifted on what looked like a fairly low-grade utilitarian sanitation unit. And, as relief came, he recognised the sanitation unit as a Rear Admiral, a low-cost commercial chemical sanitation unit fabricated by one of Flush Away's bitterest rivals, the Poseidon Corporation.

175

After sticking his head under the faucet, and drinking copious amounts of water, Johnson walked back into the room. It was very smartly furnished, not the grade of room he was used to on Flush Away expenses. Although the décor was somewhat dark, majoring on the black, he quite liked it.

As Johnson stared, realisation came to pass, well in part anyway: a sunfall of drink and food, and drink and gambling, and drink and loss and drink.

And, oh no! Did it really happen? That fateful phrase *'one last drink'* after which he remembered nothing – probably because it wasn't *'one last drink'*.

Johnson groaned.

He wondered what lay beyond the door and opened it.

'Greetings, Johnson.' A decidedly clear-headed Mr Jones smiled. 'Sleep well? One too many drinks perhaps? Would you like a little something to help?'

Jones gestured to the eager Happy-Chappy butler bot that bobbed up and down behind the beverage counter at the far side of the room.

'Er, no. No, thank you,' concluded Johnson after giving the matter some thought.

'Nonsense, it'll do you good,' persisted Jones, deftly swivelling his wheelchair across to the beverage counter to personally get a drink for Johnson. 'You'll find it'll make all the difference, bring you down slowly, gently, rather than the crash landing you're feeling at this point in the space-time continuum.'

Jones set the drink down in front of Johnson.

Well, Johnson couldn't argue that he felt like he'd been in a crash. He took the drink, sipped, and then drank the remainder in one gulp.

'Perhaps another?' suggested Jones.

'No,' affirmed Johnson quickly. 'Thank you.'

Johnson looked around the room; very smart, although the décor was, again, a little too black for his taste. However, it was Nova Vega's intense yellow sun that caught his eye; it was in the wrong place. And Johnson, unfortunately, knew he'd worked out the answer before he asked the question, 'What time is it?'

'Sometime after mid-rotation,' replied Jones without checking.

'Oh no! I've missed my passage back to Pacifica.' Johnson was decidedly unamused. Why hadn't his holocom woken him up?

* * * * *

The ever-resourceful Miranda knocked on Ms D'Baliere's door. A brief and clearly busy silence was followed by a curt but professional 'Enter.'

Ms D'Baliere was focussing studiously on her holoplay. Her workhub was covered in reports sorted neatly into piles.

The ever-aware Miranda had never known Ms D'Baliere not to be working. In fact the ever-attentive Miranda had never known Ms D'Baliere not to be at work. Always there at shift-start, working when the ever-willing Miranda arrived, and always there at shift-end, when the ever-dependable Miranda left.

The ever-dutiful Miranda wondered whether Ms D'Baliere ever left, or even if she had somewhere to go. She must go somewhere, for each and every workshift she was dressed in different, equally smart business attire with not a hair out of place.

Ms D'Baliere stopped looking at her holoplay. 'How may I help you, Miranda?'

The ever-composed Miranda wasn't quite sure how to raise the topic of Johnson's apparent kidnap, and lowered her head.

'Is everything all right?' asked Ms D'Baliere.

'Ah,' mumbled the ever-calm Miranda, uncharacteristically.

Ms D'Baliere wondered what the reason for Miranda's incoherence was. Miranda was normally one of Flush Away's most talkative employees. She was often to be found in conversation about a wide variety of topics with a wide number of co-workers, although Ms D'Baliere had not generally found these conversations to be work related.

Ms D'Baliere gestured to her solitary visitors' chair. 'Why not sit down and start at the beginning, Miranda?'

The ever-resolute Miranda sat and began to sequence her thoughts. 'I came to work like I normally do. In fact, this workshift, I was early. I like being early; it means I can get on with things before everyone else gets in. You know, sometimes it gets so busy that I just seem to have a stream of visitors, and everyone wants something, and before I know it the shift has past and I haven't even managed to do what I wanted to do. Anyway, this workshift I sat at my workhub and started to scan the coms, as usual.'

The ever-kind Miranda stopped and looked at the ground.

'And?' prompted Ms D'Baliere, sensing that all was not well.

The ever-giving Miranda lifted her head slightly. Her eyes began to moisten. She was welling up. Ms D'Baliere was not used to tears.

'There was a message.' The ever-smiling Miranda started to sob.

'A message?' asked Ms D'Baliere.

The ever-accomplished Miranda managed to speak between sobs, 'A message in the coms.'

Ms D'Baliere patiently drew breath. 'And the message said?'

The ever-engaging Miranda could hardly bring herself to continue. But then, stealing all the courage she could muster, she blurted out, 'They've taken him!'

Sobs and tears gushed forth. It wasn't quite what Ms D'Baliere was expecting. 'Pardon?'

Sobs and tears turned to crying. The ever-poised Miranda was distraught. 'They've kidnapped him!'

Ms D'Baliere wasn't sure she'd heard what Miranda had said. 'Kidnapped?'

'I've gone and upset one customer too many, and they've gone and kidnapped Johnson. The Children Of The Soil have kidnapped Johnson!' There, at last, she'd said it. Somehow relieved, the ever-considerate Miranda began to calm herself and wiped the tears from her face with the back of her hand.

Ms D'Baliere got up and walked around to the front of her workhub. She stood before the ever-happy Miranda and looked directly into her red-stained eyes. 'Let me be sure I've got this right. You're telling me that Johnson, that is Johnson the customer-relationship and promotions specialist, has been kidnapped by one of our customers, an organisation called the Children Of The Soil.'

'Yes,' confirmed the ever-thorough Miranda.

A steady-eyed Ms D'Baliere continued to look into the ever-upbeat Miranda's tear-drained eyes. 'This isn't some kind of set-up is it, Miranda? A workplace in-joke to be played out at my expense?'

'No.' The ever-efficient Miranda shook her head and projected a copy of the message and attached image for Ms D'Baliere to see. 'See for yourself.'

Ms D'Baliere read the message and looked at the image. She then calmly sat back down at her workhub, closed her eyes, and against *The Flush Away Way* – Flush Away's employee code of conduct, by which all employees are contractually obliged to behave – she uttered the four-letter word that was never to be said, the 's' word.

The ever-professional Miranda was quite taken aback.

* * * * *

Having jumped into the Pacifica System, Investigator Strait was able at last to communicate with the other members of Operation Kicking Butt. He placed the team on full alert and sent the latest details and images he had of Johnson. He emphasised that Johnson was a 'master of disguise' so extreme vigilance was necessary. As soon as planetfall was made, Johnson was to be apprehended by any means. Then, remembering some of the previous, less successful operations he'd participated in, Investigator Strait added the word 'alive' to his instructions.

He sent Deputy Gilbrae to be the first in the transit shuttle queue, so each passenger could be checked as they boarded. Deputy D'Angelis was to wait where he was and observe the passengers as they lined up. Investigator Strait would be the last to embark, to ensure that Johnson didn't try and board disguised as a jump associate – a little trick he'd used before.

As Investigator Strait gave his deputies their instructions, he emphasised that they were not to approach Johnson, merely observe, follow and report. They were to let the planetside team arrest him. They were to remain undercover. Investigator Strait hoped that Johnson would be the first of many arrests, and he didn't want his team's cover blown. But most importantly, no matter what the circumstance, they were not to lose Johnson.

Back on Pacifica, in a forgotten corner of the U-Tan-U Spaceport, the rest of the Tactical Response Assault Patrol were happily passing their time away in Operation Kicking Butt's incident-room when the incoming instructions arrived. They were a little surprised. As far as the team were concerned, Investigator Strait and Deputies D'Angelis and Gilbrae had gone on vacation and weren't expected back for several more rotations. Senior Deputy, or, as he had described himself since their absence, *Acting-Investigator* Aloysius O'Herd dropped his hand of cards and swung into action.

There was going to be an arrest! Amid tumbling chairs and overturned tables the team hastily donned their combat fatigues and strapped on their body armour. Lovingly they checked that their assault blasters were fully charged and their combat knives were affixed, sharpened and ready for action, just in case they were needed of course, purely precautionary.

The results of their latest sweepstake were brushed aside from the incident holoplay, and *Acting-Investigator* O'Herd sketched his arrest plan on a backlit diagram of the spaceport arrival terminal.

There were to be no covert Sniff-A-Whiff sensors or Eye Fly surveillance bots. No, this time they were going to confront the leaf trafficker face-to-face, mano-a-mano, and this time there would be no doubt about who was going to come out on top. Positions were set, crossfire coverage considered, medical evac facilities notified.

And so the trap was set.

*   *   *   *   *

'I hope you don't mind, but I took the liberty of asking William Robert to fetch your luggage from your room as you seem to have lost your attire,' said Mr Jones. 'Perhaps you might like to freshen up. The guest-room is completely at your disposal.'

'Er, thank you,' replied Johnson, and took his luggage into the guest-room. He tried not to think about what might have happened last sunfall.

179

Yes, best to put the past behind him and make a fresh start, and no more stellar gamblestar.

Johnson returned, dressed. Having missed this rotation's starliner all he could do was reserve a passage on the next one bound for Pacifica. He reached for his holocom. He then remembered it was in the attire he was wearing last sunfall.

Johnson sat and thought. He'd lost his holocom, his attire, his credits, but worst of all he didn't even know whether he'd had a good time doing it.

Well, upon reflection, at least he'd sealed the deal with Ms Carlsson at the Creation Corporation, although it was the euphoria of that particular achievement that had led to his current predicament.

Johnson rested his head in his hands.

'You appear troubled, my friend,' commented Jones.

Johnson explained.

'No need to worry; William Robert can reserve you a passage on the next starliner to Pacifica. No credits is no problem, you can bunk in with us. We have plenty of room, don't we, William Robert?'

Billy Bob nodded.

'No, I couldn't, really,' replied a dejected Johnson.

'I won't hear of it,' insisted Jones, adding, a little more truthfully than he might care to admit, 'after all, we feel partly responsible, don't we, William Robert?'

Billy Bob nodded.

'Well, I don't know. You're too kind,' stated Johnson.

Jones rolled over to Johnson and gave him a hearty pat on the back. 'Come on, what is it they used to say in the Space Corps? Ah, yes. "Visor up", and what else was it? "Worse things happen in the Magellanic Cloud."'

Johnson couldn't quite figure out how lifting up his visor, if he had one, might help. However, he was glad he wasn't lost in the Magellanic Cloud, it must have been an awful place to be with a hangover: he felt sick enough as it was.

*   *   *   *   *

Ms D'Baliere drew a deep breath. It wasn't as if she didn't have enough problems to deal with, what with Flush Away's sales literally going down the toilet. She really needed to clinch that deal on Nova Vega. It should have been a certainty. She couldn't have made it any plainer to Johnson. 'No mistakes', she'd said. But oh no, instead that fool Johnson had to go and get himself kidnapped by some irate customer – called the Children Of The Soil of all things! And now they're requesting 'organic restitution', whatever that means: probably some compensation payment or other – everybody wants compensation.

Calm. Ms D'Baliere breathed in, slowly, and then breathed out again. She'd been pacing. She knew that, as she now found herself standing at the other end of her workspace, away from her workhub. She had a habit of involuntary pacing when she was stressed.

Calm. Ms D'Baliere spoke to herself.

'Remember we are a team: what are we? A team.'

Calm. Think. She closed her eyes to clear her mind, and then opened them.

'Right!'

The ever-helpful Miranda, who had continued sobbing quietly to herself, stopped and looked up.

'Here's what we need to do,' a resurgent Ms D'Baliere instructed. 'Firstly, we shouldn't say anything to the team about this until we are as certain as we can be that it's not a hoax. Let's see if we can confirm that this message is genuine before I refer it to Mr Stein. I'll send Johnson an unrelated message asking him to update me on the Creation Corporation deal. If you could holo Johnson's cooperative to see if he's there. I think he's supposed to be arriving back this rotation. You'd better just check that his starliner has arrived from Nova Vega.'

A few photon phases later, the ever-meticulous Miranda returned to Ms D'Baliere's workspace. She'd had no response from Johnson's co-op. The Key-4-U concierge bot at the Sun Rise Cooperative Skybreaker did confirm, with something of a stutter, that Johnson was due back this rotation. And the Liberty Discount Star Line, whilst being unable to comment on individual passengers, was able to confirm that the starliner from Nova Vega was in system and due to orbit shortly.

Ms D'Baliere had had the response, 'Unavailable', to her message asking Johnson to update her on the Creation Corporation deal. If Johnson were aboard that starliner he should've picked up and responded.

All was inconclusive. She decided to refer it to Mr Stein anyway. Ms D'Baliere opened the hololink to Mr Stein's personal associate, Mrs Shelley, and asked to see him. 'It was most urgent… No, she couldn't discuss the matter over the hololink… Yes, now… Right, they'd be straight up.'

Ms D'Baliere, together with the ever-positive Miranda, marched to the plastiglass skyvator and ascended to the top level. In front of them was a wide concourse of doors. It was a concourse of silence and plastiglass and silverillium, interspersed with the odd plant, chair and product imagery – traditional and corporate. All suggesting that, unless you knew where you were going, you shouldn't be there: all to intimidate.

Ms D'Baliere knew where she was going and saw no reason to feel intimidated, after all this was where she planned to be in the none-too-distant future. The ever-able Miranda followed, having to almost run to keep pace with the determined stride of Ms D'Baliere.

The door slid open. Inside, the anti-chamber to Mr Stein's inner workspace stretched out before them. And at the end sat Mrs Shelley, busy.

Ms D'Baliere strode up to her. 'Respects Mrs Shelley, we're here to see Mr Stein.'

Mrs Shelley continued being busy.

The ever-hopeful Miranda edged her way around from behind Ms D'Baliere, whom she'd been using as a kind of human shield, to take a peek at the infamous Mrs Shelley, a female known by reputation rather than by sight.

Mrs Shelley was smartly attired in a fashionless, timeless kind of way. Her slate-grey hair was swept back in a utilitarian cut. Mrs Shelley looked up. The ever-polite Miranda quickly withdrew.

'Please sit,' she replied, with a tone that made the ever approachable Miranda wish she were somewhere else. 'I will see if Mr Stein is available.'

They sat. They sat in silence and waited whilst Mrs Shelley opened her hololink to Mr Stein. Mrs Shelley then turned to the visitors and said, 'You may go in now,' in a way that made it distinctly clear who was in charge.

'Thank you.' Ms D'Baliere and the ever-devoted Miranda rose.

Mr Francis Stein's workspace showed little sign that any work was done there. The furniture looked comfortable, but though it belonged in a hotel rather than in the workspace. The workhub was bare except for some personal images that, on closer inspection, were all of Francis Stein performing various feats. Further images adorned the walls: Francis Stein with his arm around Chief Executive & President Joseph Firtop; Francis Stein handing a large credit certificate to the First Citizen Of Pacifica; Francis Stein with Pacifica's chief of law enforcement; Francis Stein spinning a ball with 'Hands Down' Hirokawa, the spinball player. And so the gallery of Francis Stein continued.

Francis Stein always gave visitors time to admire these images of himself before engaging with them in dialogue.

Ms D'Baliere thought one Mr Stein was more than enough and pressed to the nucleus.

'Mr Stein...'

'Call me Francis; you know you should call me Francis, Lucretia. We're all part of one big, happy Flush Away team. Isn't that right Miranda? It is Miranda isn't it? The lovely Miranda from reception.'

'Yes, Mr Stein,' stammered the ever-pleasant Miranda, feigning a smile – though she began to realise there was something about him that made her epidermis itch.

'Francis,' continued Ms D'Baliere.

'Yes, my dear Lucretia,' replied a self-satisfied Francis Stein. 'Come, let us make ourselves more comfortable, please take a seat.' And he gestured to the two opposing antiquarian ottomans that occupied the centre of his workspace, either side of a large plastiglass table.

The ever-interested Miranda had never heard anyone address Ms D'Baliere as 'Lucretia' before. They all knew it was her name, but no one dared use it – that is not to her face anyway. But it was the 'my dear' that made her wince.

Ms D'Baliere was un-phased and sat on one of the ottomans. The ever-sociable Miranda made sure she sat next to Ms D'Baliere, she positively recoiled at the thought of having to sit next to Francis Stein.

Ms D'Baliere started again. 'Francis, the team has a situation.'

'A situation?' repeated Francis Stein calmly.

'A situation. Three rotations ago I sent Johnson to Nova Vega to conclude a deal with the Creation Corporation,' continued Ms D'Baliere.

'Isn't that Chad's baby?' enquired Francis Stein.

'Yes, normally Chad manages the Creation Corporation account, but to further teamwork I decided to let Johnson complete the deal, whilst Chad went to Old MacDonald's World to help improve our market penetration there,' explained Ms D'Baliere.

'Ah,' replied Francis Stein.

Ms D'Baliere returned to the point she was trying to make. 'At shift-start Miranda had this message and image come through.' The ever-proficient Miranda projected the message and image across the plastiglass table.

'And what exactly do you believe Johnson's *situation* to be?' asked Francis Stein, apparently un-phased by what had been presented to him.

'Whilst the information we have is limited, and does not completely confirm that Johnson has been kidnapped, at this juncture in the space-time continuum I suspect this may be the *situation*. We have holoed his cooperative, but he is not there, though the Key-4-U concierge bot confirmed he is due back this rotation. He should be in system now, on a starliner from Nova Vega, so I have sent him a message requesting an urgent response, but I have had no reply to date,' answered Ms D'Baliere.

Vice-President Of Customer-Relationships & Promotions Francis Stein sat back on the ottoman and flipped his attention between message and image, image and message. 'Do we happen to know who or what the Children Of The Soil are?'

Ms D'Baliere paused before responding. 'We thought it could be an irate customer calling themselves the Children Of The Soil, but we've found no specific reference or record of the name in our holobases.'

'Ah. I wonder what "organic restitution" means?' Francis Stein asked rhetorically. 'Leave this with me. Let me know immediately if you hear from Johnson. Does anyone else know about this *situation*?'

Ms D'Baliere and the ever-responsive Miranda shook their heads.

'Fine, keep it to yourselves. And on your way out, Lucretia, could you ask Mrs Shelley to step in,' instructed Francis Stein. He then stood and the meeting was over.

*   *   *   *   *

As The Freedom Of The Heavens entered orbit around Pacifica, Deputy Gilbrae waited in line. More precisely, he waited at the front of the line – a solitary position he had maintained for some considerable time. It was part of a law enforcement deputy's work to be patient, and Deputy Gilbrae was good at his work. In his mind he could switch off, just leave himself running on stand by. Most of his fellow deputies were amazed by his capacity for being able to do nothing for long periods of time. But the fact was that he'd spent most of his life on stand by.

In the lottery of Investigator Strait's orders, Deputy D'Angelis had been a little luckier. He was sat across the way from Gilbrae, observing the passengers covertly – not that there had been anything to observe, other than the remarkable motionlessness of Deputy Gilbrae.

But time had passed, and a queue of passengers was now forming in anticipation of the transit shuttle's arrival. Quite why a queue should form bemused Deputy D'Angelis. What was there to queue for? Was one seat better than another? Was there time to be saved in the race of life?

Deputy D'Angelis cast his eye, and his holocom, over the queuing passengers. He was sharing their images with Investigator Strait, who was sat at the far end of the passenger deck. So far not one looked promising.

At last the passengers were called and the queue grew. And, as the passengers vacated their seats, a busy swarm of small, hemispherical Happy-Scrubby cleaning bots floated through the passenger deck, announcing that cleaning was in progress and warning that surfaces could be slippery.

Investigator Strait sank further down into his seat, reviewing the images of the passengers. But as he processed them through the face recognition holobase, no match was found. With little expectation of a positive response he messaged Deputy D'Angelis, 'Johnson?' and Deputy D'Angelis messaged back, 'No.' All he could do was wait. He'd leave disembarking until the last possible pulsar's pulse. He knew Johnson had to be somewhere, but where?

The transit shuttle docked. Finally, the cordon was lifted and the disembarking passengers walked to the airlock led by Deputy Gilbrae.

Once through, Deputy Gilbrae sat and positioned himself so he could see each passing face. He asked himself, 'Johnson?' and invariably the answer was, 'No'.

Deputy D'Angelis joined the end of the queue. As far as he could figure either Johnson was the absolute 'master of disguise' or he simply hadn't boarded the transit shuttle yet. Once through the airlock he sat next to Deputy Gilbrae who shook his head.

And after Deputy D'Angelis came some of the jump crew, smiling and laughing, clearly looking forward to planetfall, but none bore any resemblance to Johnson.

Finally, neither smiling nor laughing, Investigator Strait followed. He made a brief apology for being late to board. Deputy Gilbrae looked up, as did Deputy D'Angelis, but with a sigh Investigator Strait shook his head and joined his colleagues: no Johnson.

[24] What To Do?

Johnson sat with his hangover, looking forlornly at Nova Vega's skyline and all it promised. Billy Bob had returned and said he'd managed to reserve Johnson a passage back to Pacifica. Unfortunately, it wasn't going to be until the rotation after next: for some reason next rotation's starliners were full.

Johnson was going to be in trouble, not that that was anything unusual. He had hoped this business trip would be the lift-off his career so desperately needed. But as ever, something had gone wrong and now he was going to return late from Nova Vega. Well, looking on the star-lit side, at least it would be the inflection point on his declining sales graph.

'Given we've got the rest of this rotation and all of next before you leave, I suggest we get positronic and make the most of it. How about it?' asked Mr Jones, sensing that Johnson was a little deflated.

Johnson did not reply, his mind had fast-forwarded to the future and, more specifically, to his debrief with Ms D'Baliere. He hoped that his deal with the Creation Corporation would save his somewhat lamentable career. Well, there was nothing he could do about it now. It would have to wait until the rotation after next. 'Sorry, what did you say?'

'I suggested we should make the most of your time with us,' repeated Jones. 'After all this is Nova Vega!'

Johnson and his hangover looked unconvinced. It was participating in what historic Nova Vega had to offer that had disrobed him into his current predicament.

Jones started to suggest, 'How about we…?'

But before he could finish, Johnson responded, 'No gambling.'

'OK, how about we…?'

Again Johnson interrupted. 'No drinking.'

'Or we could…?'

'No females,' stated Johnson.

Clearly Johnson could read his mind. Jones was running short on ideas. In fact he'd exhausted them all. Beyond the three pursuits he'd suggested, Jones struggled to think of anything else to do in life that was worthwhile.

There was silence in the room.

'We all could go on one 'a them there tourist trips,' suggested Billy Bob.

'Tourist trips, William Robert?' asked Jones.

'Yeah, I seen 'em in holoverts. I ain't ever bin' on no tourist trip before,' enthused Billy Bob.

'How about it, Johnson? Fancy a trip with the rest of the tourists?'

186

asked Jones.

Johnson pondered. He had nothing better to do, and if it took his mind off his hangover, and so long as it avoided gambling, drinking and females, what harm could it do? So he replied, 'OK.'

'By the stars, that's settled then.' Jones picked up the hotel suite's holocom and browsed tourist trips for all to see. 'How about a trip to Ererador, Nova Vega's only moon, to visit the old mining complex in the Southern Mountains? "Strike it lucky! Marvel at the depths you can sink to in search of gold! Spend a rotation living and working as those miners did all those solar cycles ago, breathing apparatus provided", and what's that in the small print, "not suitable for acrophobics, claustrophobics, climacophobics, hadephobics and scotophobics". Hm… perhaps not.'

'What about this one?' continued Jones. '"Thrill-seekers wanted! Can you spend a rotation in the desolation of Nova Vega's rugged Ghost Hills? Be dropped in the middle of this barren wasteland and see if you can crawl out alive armed with nothing but your wits to survive on."'

Jones looked over at Billy Bob and Johnson to gauge their enthusiasm. 'Perhaps another time.'

He continued to scour the seemingly endless list of less than promising trips, most of which were aimed at the old, or the young, or the recklessly insane.

'Here you go, Johnson, this trip meets all your criteria. "Dream of a simpler life? Of a life without temptation? Of a life closer to the Holy One? Then why not come and spend some time with us and be at one with the universe? Come, join us in peace and love, and see how life should be lived. Visit the Simucalc Monastery, residence of the Order Of The New Desert Brethren, an oasis in the Red Sand Sea, an oasis in the insanity of contemporary society, a registered not-for-profit organisation. Glory be to the Holy One! Strictly no gambling, no alcohol and no females". What do ya' say Johnson?'

'No gambling, no alcohol and no females?' queried Johnson.

'That's what it says,' confirmed Jones.

Johnson thought and, sick of feeling sick, decided then and there. 'I'm in. What about you, William Robert?'

William Robert nodded, and so the trip was set.

* * * * *

Chad arrived at Pacifica's U-Tan-U Spaceport in good time. He'd been surprised when Mrs Shelley had opened the hololink and said that Mr Stein wished to see him. And when Francis, as Mr Stein had insisted on being called, asked him to personally do a little job, what could he say? He just said 'no problem' and smiled – Chad's third rule: always leave them with a smile.

As Chad's tall frame towered over the impatient passengers crowding through the spaceport, unanswered questions buzzed around in his head.

Clearly something was up, but what?

Why had he been asked to go meet Johnson at the spaceport and accompany him directly back to Mr Stein?

Why had he been expressly told not to discuss the matter with anyone, other than Mr Stein, and to make sure that Johnson did likewise?

And why was Ms D'Baliere not there?

Questions aside, Chad looked forward to hearing Johnson's tales of woe and gloating over the deal that he, Chad, had landed on Old MacDonald's World.

As Chad reached the vast arrivals hall, with its vaulted ceiling and deluge of holoverts for personal colour enhancement products, he noticed that he was not the only one waiting for someone to land. A team of law enforcement deputies jogged into view two by two, assault blasters at the ready, combat knives glinting, dressed in combat fatigues and body armour.

Someone's going to have a reception they won't forget. Had the authorities finally put matter and antimatter together and come up with Johnson? How sweet that would be. Chad decided to stand back and let the entertainment begin.

The law enforcement deputies pulled up to a halt with a well-practised crescendo of boots. Orders were barked and the team split to either side of the arrivals channel. The gathered crowd was encouraged to retire to a safe distance by gentle prodding with outstretched assault blasters.

All was silent.

Chad watched the holoplay flow through the arrival details of the Pacifica-bound starliners. The Freedom Of The Heavens, the Liberty Discount starliner from Nova Vega, was in orbit and its transit shuttle had landed. It would only be a few photon phases before Johnson came down that arrivals channel. He could hardly wait to see Johnson's face.

The first passengers appeared and looked a little confused over the law enforcement reception. More passengers arrived and were ushered through. No Johnson yet.

Chad looked on with growing impatience. That must be most of the passengers by now – so typical of Johnson to be last.

And then a male in light-coloured vacational attire came through shaking his head and sweeping his arms. He was followed by two more thickset males wearing straw hats and dressed in Neo-Holo attire displaying images of empty fishing nets. They appeared to be arguing. The first male turned and shouted at the other two. They stopped arguing, their heads dropped in contrition. The law enforcement cordon stepped forward, lowering its assault blasters. And then they all began talking and gesticulating expressively to each other. Finally, they all walked off down the concourse.

Chad was left standing, Johnson-less. All he could do was report back to Mr Stein, and this he did.

Chad admired Mr Stein's workspace. He admired the tasteful furniture. He admired the images on the wall. Perhaps 'admired' wasn't quite the right word. He *desired* Mr Stein's workspace, his furniture, and his 'I've made it, look at who I know' images. However, what he really desired, what he really craved, were the two little tied words that Mr Stein was entitled to use on his business holocard, 'Vice-President'.

'And?' questioned Francis Stein.

'And that was it. No Johnson, just law enforcement deputies.' Chad shrugged.

'OK, Chad. Thanks for doing that for me, I appreciate it.' Mr Stein patted Chad on the back and, with the slightest of pressure, indicated that the conversation was over.

'Great stuff, no problem, anytime Francis.' Chad smiled and walked to the door.

As the door to Mr Stein's workspace began to close behind him, Chad heard Mr Stein say, 'And remember my portal is always open.' At which point the 'portal' shut.

Inside, Francis Stein sat at his workhub and tapped his fingers on the plastiglass top. He'd have to let Joseph Firtop know. It appeared that one of his customer-relationship and promotions specialists might have actually been kidnapped.

Francis Stein activated Joseph Firtop's image on the hololink and waited to be linked. 'Joe, yeah it's me, Francis.'

'How ya' doin', Francis?' asked Chief Executive & President Joseph Firtop.

'Couldn't be better,' replied Francis Stein, with true belief. 'And you?'

'A OK.' Joseph Firtop was always 'a OK'.

Francis Stein decided to be direct. 'I'll get right down to it. One of our customer-relationship and promotions specialists, Johnson, may have been kidnapped.'

'Was he any good?' responded Joseph Firtop.

'Any good?' asked Francis Stein, slightly thrown by Joseph Firtop's question.

'Yeah, any good as a customer-relationship and promotions specialist?' clarified Joseph Firtop.

Francis Stein thought for a pulsar's pulse. 'Not particularly. In fact he was one of our poorest performers, now I come to think of it.'

'I'm sure you'll do what's best, Francis. And remember, if there's anything I can do to help, you know, you've only got to ask and I will be there for you.' Joseph Firtop maintained his smile and then the hololink terminated.

Francis Stein had expected little from his boss and, as ever, he wasn't disappointed. If Joseph Firtop saw nothing in it for himself then he was not interested, it had been how he'd risen to the top of the corporate skybreaker. And, of course, Francis Stein would have done the same himself. But at least he'd let Joseph know, so he couldn't try and deny all knowledge and say he hadn't been consulted if things went awry later.

* * * * *

Billy Bob had never seen so much sand. It rolled from horizon to horizon, undulating in massive, crested, windblown dunes, shimmering under Nova Vega's dry, red, fading-to-pink sky. As far as he could make out, as they skimmed along, nothing lived down there. And it sure did look hot. The red sand dunes seemed to warp and twist in the heat haze, almost melting under the intense yellow sun.

Jones thought. He thought that things were going well. Whilst he'd lost most of the credits he'd won at the Black Hole Casino, he knew that it was easy materialise, easy dematerialise. But most of all, he had a new found sense of belonging. Admittedly the Children Of The Soil were a bit off the light barrier, and their fundamentalist organic beliefs were hard to compost, but Billy Bob was proving to be a solid and honest companion – not the brightest star in the sky, but well-meaning.

Jones thought the mission, 'To spread the organic word', was progressing well. They'd managed to *kidnap* Johnson, without kidnapping him, and Johnson didn't even know! Yes, totality in totality, things were going well. He looked across at Johnson.

Johnson and his hangover slept, head back, mouth open. The monotonous, barely-audible hum of the dirigible's solar-powered ionic drives seemed to have had a soporific effect on him.

Billy Bob squinted at what he thought was something glinting away in the distance. It glinted again. The dirigible began to bank gently and turn in that direction. 'Hey, Mr Jones, can y'all see what I can see?'

'Oh, to see through another human's eyes,' sighed Jones to himself. And then he spoke to Billy Bob, 'See what?'

'Over yonder, somethin's flashin',' pointed out Billy Bob.

Jones leant over and peered out across the dunes, but all he could see was sand, sand and more sand. 'I can see sand.'

And then it glinted again.

'There, it flashed ag'in,' said Billy Bob.

'I saw,' replied Jones.

Billy Bob looked at Jones. 'I wonder what it is? The dirigible's turned towards it.'

'It's probably the monastery,' speculated a less than interested Jones.

'I guess we'll find out when we all get there,' concluded Billy Bob.

'I'm sure we will,' agreed Jones and relaxed back into his seat. 'You just keep on looking.'

At least the emptiness of the Red Sand Sea was sufficiently engrossing to keep Billy Bob occupied, otherwise he'd have his family images out and be talking endlessly about them and life on the farmstead. For Jones there was only so much wholesome rural reminiscing a male could digest. He decided to follow Johnson's lead and leant back, eyes closed. And against the hum of the dirigible's ionic drives he too drifted off to sleep.

His mind flashed back to the past.

He shuddered as he remembered the buffeting on that long, long descent through Wonderland's clear, cloudless atmosphere. The rasping screech of the assault crafts' drives on full thrust. And then the jump – the assault craft couldn't land on the planet's ice-thin crust for fear of falling through. And, as he tumbled down to land, all was silent, eerily silent, no wind, no noise just the breath he took and the beat of his heart. Then he remembered slipping and sliding on the planet's mirror-smooth surface, being unable to stand, seemingly performing some kind of un-choreographed dance amid the multicoloured trace of blaster fire. And, breaking the eerie silence, his compatriots turned and pointed, laughing as he involuntarily gained momentum and pirouetted headlong towards the enemy's emplacement. If only he'd remembered to attach his crampons.

Oh, the terror...

Jones awoke suddenly, shivering in a cold sweat. A voice had broken the silence.

'Valued passengers, we will soon be arriving at our destination, the Simucalc Monastery. On behalf of Starshine Tours, the corporation that "puts the shine in your star tours", I'd like to thank you for travelling with us and hope to see you again on one of our many specialist tours for the discerning adventurer. We wish you an enlightening visit and remind you that alcohol, gambling and females are strictly forbidden. And as we like to say, "Have a nice stay!"'

The dirigible's passengers gathered their belongings.

Jones noticed that all his fellow passengers, with the exception of Billy Bob and Johnson, had rather more facial hair than was fashionable, and wore ragged attire that flowed to the ground, attire with deep hoods that, when drawn up, hid faces.

'I can see it!' announced Billy Bob and gestured to Jones to come and look.

Below, the monastery played out in complex form. Constructed from reconstituted white marble and sandstone, its roughly angular lines resembled a dismembered, stepped chessboard. The outlying buildings interconnected to a vast, domed citadel contained within irregular towers at the five points of the star. And at the centre, high above, almost touching the heavens, a golden five-pointed star bedazzled all; the glinting star that had guided them.

With an intake of breath Billy Bob added, 'Wow-wee, now that's a mighty impressive buildin'!'

Jones looked on, transfixed. He could only agree. He nudged Johnson. 'We're here.'

*　　*　　*　　*　　*

The Tactical Response Assault Patrol returned to Operation Kicking Butt's incident-room, Johnson-less. Disappointment hung heavy, stifling the wit and banter that normally pervaded the air. It wasn't as if the team hadn't tasted disappointment before. They had. Indeed, they'd faced nothing but disappointment for the last six lunar cycles, since the very inception of the operation. They needed success. They needed inspiration. And, like any pack, they needed the adrenaline rush of the chase, the capture and the kill – figuratively speaking, of course. Though Investigator Strait had his suspicions that there were those among his ranks for whom 'the kill' was not simply a metaphoric expression.

Investigator Strait began his debrief by thanking everyone involved for the professional job they had done.

Silence…

He said that he was proud to be their leader and he knew that their time would come; they just had to be patient.

Silence…

Investigator Strait reminded them of what they had achieved. 'We've become a smooth-running, organised and structured unit. We've put in place a surveillance operation that is the best in the sector and, most importantly, we've identified several suspects, not least of which is Johnson. Yes it is disappointing that Johnson, a "master of disguise", has eluded us so far. Believe me, no one is more frustrated than I am. But there will be a next time and, if necessary, a next time again and a next time after that. We will not rest until the leaf-trafficking ring is broken and the perpetrators are incarcerated.'

In his mind there was a rousing cheer, as his team rose as one, clapping their hands and stamping their boots.

In reality, silence…

Senior Deputy Aloysius O'Herd looked on with a hidden smile. If Investigator Strait didn't get results soon, it wouldn't just be the support of the team he'd lose, it would be his job. Of course, Investigator Strait would still have a role to play – a role in the archiving department, the graveyard for those law enforcement deputies whose stars had collapsed and were facing extinction, law enforcement deputies who weren't quite up to the job. And then he would step into Investigator Strait's recently vacated position, newly promoted, *Investigator* Aloysius O'Herd. How good that title sounded!

Investigator Strait reviewed the room. They needed a providential break. Johnson had to be somewhere; he couldn't just vanish.

'D'Angelis, Gilbrae and O'Herd, I need a word. The rest of you at ease.'

Silence turned to murmured discussion, the loosening of body armour, the removal of boots and the reluctant sheathing of combat knives.

D'Angelis, Gilbrae and O'Herd gathered round.

Investigator Strait spoke one simple command: 'Think.'

He could see that his deputies were clearly uncomfortable with this command by the nature of the returned looks they gave him, which ranged from blankness, to confusion, to blind panic.

Deputy D'Angelis was the first to stutter, 'Think?'

'Yes, think. I need you to think. Between us we need to outwit this leaf-trafficking ring, and the only way we're going to do it is by being one parsec ahead of them, instead of the two parsecs behind we've been so far.' Investigator Strait gauged the faces gathered round. His request was clearly taking them into uncharted space.

Time ticked.

In the absence of any kind of response, Investigator Strait prompted, 'What are we missing?'

Time ticked slowly.

'We're missing a suspect?' suggested Deputy D'Angelis somewhat tentatively.

Investigator Strait shook his head. 'We have a suspect, several in fact.'

'We have a suspect? Where?' asked Senior Deputy O'Herd innocently, choosing not to miss an opportunity to aggravate Investigator Strait.

Investigator Strait glared at O'Herd and then turned to D'Angelis to try and clarify the situation. 'We have suspects, but none, as such, in custody.'

'So we *are* missing a suspect then?' repeated Deputy D'Angelis beginning to get a little lost in the conversation.

For Investigator Strait this conversation was stuck in geostationary orbit. 'We have suspects, everyone clear?'

There was a pause followed by a muted 'Yes', a 'Yes, Investigator!' and a nod of the head from the ever-silent Deputy Gilbrae.

'It's just that our main suspect, a certain Johnson, is missing,' continued Investigator Strait, immediately regretting his choice of words.

'So we are missing a suspect?' rounded Senior Deputy O'Herd.

Sensing that this argument could go on for eternity, and with little to be gained over the semantics of the word 'missing', Investigator Strait decided to concede. 'OK, so we are missing a suspect, but we know who he is. What else are we missing?'

'Our luggage?' ventured a slightly more confident Deputy D'Angelis, now that his case for a missing suspect had been proved.

Deputy Gilbrae nodded in agreement.

Investigator Strait opened and then closed his mouth. Others may have thought this to be a facetious response from Deputy D'Angelis, but if Investigator Strait knew anything, he knew his team, and he should have predicted that something like this would come from Deputy D'Angelis's mouth. 'Yes, we're missing our luggage, but it should turn up next rotation on the next starliner in from Nova Vega. So apart from the suspect, who we know, the luggage, which will turn up next rotation, what else are we missing?'

Time ticked.

'Evidence.' Everyone turned and looked at Deputy Gilbrae. Simple but correct, Investigator Strait was delighted. It didn't happen often, but occasionally one of his team would exhibit that all-too-rare of conditions: intelligence. They had chased suspects from one star system to another and back to where they'd started. In all that time the one thing they had not come close to finding was evidence.

'Good point, Deputy Gilbrae. The fact is we have no evidence. We have no leaf. Investigator Strait looked at each of the deputies in turn. 'When we've caught Johnson we'll need to produce evidence, and my guess is he won't have it on him. So we should now look to the source. Where is the leaf being produced?'

Senior Deputy O'Herd shrugged. Deputy D'Angelis thought hard, but to no avail. However, Deputy Gilbrae answered, 'Old MacDonald's World.'

Investigator Strait looked quizzically at Deputy Gilbrae. There was something about him that he couldn't quite put his sensor on. 'You got it. It's where Johnson's passage had embarked from, when we detected the leaf on him at the spaceport. It's where that character Billy Bob Brown is from.'

'Are we gonna' take another vacation then, Investigator?' asked Deputy D'Angelis.

'It wasn't a vacation! Be clear, it was a self-initiated undercover surveillance operation.' Investigator Strait was sure he could feel his blood pressure rise. He paused to calm down. 'This time we're gonna' do things by the sub-routines, no shortcuts, which means we won't have the flexibility we had. I'm gonna' have to see the chief about this, and I'll bet he'll have to get the First Citizen to do some kind of inter-system agreement before we can set this next operation in place.'

'What should we do in the meantime?' asked Deputy D'Angelis.

'Senior Deputy O'Herd needs to redouble surveillance here at the spaceport. We now have a number of potential suspects we need to keep a scanner out for. Any one of them could return.' Investigator Strait then turned to Deputies D'Angelis and Gilbrae. 'And you, Deputy D'Angelis, should go with Deputy Gilbrae and stakeout Johnson's co-op. OK? Right then, everyone clear about what they're to do?'

'Yes,' replied Senior Deputy O'Herd.

'Yes, Investigator!' saluted Deputy D'Angelis.

And Deputy Gilbrae nodded his head.

After his deputies had departed to set about their duties, Investigator Strait said to himself, 'This time I'm gonna' get the full backing and support of the chief, the First Citizen and every other civic dignitary this side of the Spiral Arm, if that's what it takes.'

* * * * *

Francis Stein sat at his workhub and admired his favourite image. The one in the antiquarian silver frame that took pride of place, the one he had created through the wonders of image manipulation, the one where he was congratulating and pressing hands with himself.

A possible ransom note, a missing employee, his boss consulted. Francis Stein decided now was the time to speak with his friend, Hank Garett, the chief of law enforcement. He activated Mrs Shelley's image on his hololink. 'Mrs Shelley can you link me to Hank Garett.'

He relaxed back in his chair and cast his eyes over the images on his wall, searching for the image of Hank taken at last solar cycle's Law Enforcement Benefit Ball. There it was, both of them smiling as he handed Hank a sizeable, tax-deductible credit certificate on behalf of the Flush Away Corporation. He always ensured that Flush Away supported the *right* causes. And, to make it that little bit more memorable, he'd got the merchandising department to put up – what proved to be the star item in the charity auction – an Empress irradiating sanitation unit installed and themed to choice, also tax-deductible, of course.

His hololink flashed. 'Law Enforcement Chief Garett for you, Mr Stein.'

'You know you can call me Francis, Mrs Shelley,' replied Francis Stein.

'Yes, Mr Stein,' replied the formal Mrs Shelley.

Francis Stein activated the image of Law Enforcement Chief Garett on his hololink, pulling up the chief's personal details at the same time. 'Hank, how are you? And how's Wilma that beautiful wife of yours? You know my offer still stands if you ever need the credits!'

'We're all good. How are you, Francis?' asked Chief Garett.

'Couldn't be better,' replied Francis Stein. 'And Jo-Jo and Ricki, how are they getting on at school?'

'Very well, thank you for asking. What can I do for you, Francis?' asked the busy chief of law enforcement.

'Hank, to come right to the nucleus, it appears that one of our employees may have been kidnapped,' explained Francis Stein.

All went quiet at the other end of the link. This wasn't quite the 'Look the other way...' or the 'I've got a friend who...' or the 'It was an accident...' that Chief Garett usually expected from these 'close, personal friend of mine' conversations. 'Kidnapped?'

'So it would seem. Anyway, Hank, I thought it best to holo you to ask for your advice about what to do. You know, work out the best course of action before everything becomes official. Should we or shouldn't we pay? Should we just ignore it? You know, that type of advice,' ventured Francis Stein.

Before answering, Chief Garett asked, 'Let me pose a couple of questions to you first.'

'OK, Hank, no problem, blast away,' responded Francis Stein.

'Have you checked, to the best of your ability, that your employee is really missing?' asked Chief Garett.

'Yes,' replied Francis Stein.

'Have the kidnappers been in contact?' continued Chief Garett.

'Yes,' answered Francis Stein.

Chief Garett paused and then spoke quietly, 'Right. Now I'm going to ask my last and most important question: to what extent would you go to get your employee back?'

Francis Stein thought for a photon's phase. 'As a fair, caring and compassionate organisation we treat our employees as valued individuals. Obviously each employee is different and thus our response for each individual would have to be handled in a way that's appropriate to that individual on a case by case basis.'

Chief Garett was still in deep space over Francis Stein's answer. 'And for this particular individual?'

'Tell me, Hank, in your experience as law enforcement chief what are the typical outcomes in such cases?' asked Francis Stein.

'Typically, in the cases where the kidnappers' demands are met, the outcome for the individuals concerned is generally positive, although the kidnappers themselves often avoid capture,' replied the law enforcement chief. 'Of course, in my official capacity as chief of law enforcement, I would always council against this particular course of action as it tends to lead to a lower arrest rate and only encourages future lawbreaking.'

'And the typical outcome where the kidnappers' demands are not met?' continued Flush Away's vice-president of customer-relationships and promotions.

'The outcome in these circumstances tends to be less positive for the individuals concerned. However, I'm proud to say that the arrest rate is much higher and the community as a whole is much stronger,' concluded Chief Garett. 'We would always council taking this course of action. Does that answer your question, Francis?'

'Certainly, thank you, Hank,' responded Flush Away's vice-president of customer-relationships and promotions. 'And I can reassure you that the Flush Away Corporation, as an upstanding constituent of the metropolis and a net contributor to the fabric of Pacifica's society, would always seek to follow law enforcement council in full.'

The chief of law enforcement was pleased. 'I'm glad to hear that, Francis. I'll send over some of my most experienced team to initiate the law enforcement operation. We will do our utmost to apprehend these kidnappers and bring them to justice, making Pacifica a safer and stronger metropolis for all, and ensuring that corporations, like yours, can go about their business unimpeded by the actions of such lawbreakers.'

'Thank you, Hank. Look forward to seeing you at the next Law Enforcement Benefit Ball.'

And so the conversation ended.

[25] All Brothers Under The Sun

The dented brushed-metal hull of the dirigible scraped alongside one of the monastery's towers, its droning ionic drives working hard to maintain stability whilst its passengers disembarked.

For those who had them, hoods shielded eyes from the blinding reflected sunlight. Jones was beginning to see the appeal of a hood.

Johnson simply had his hand over his eyes. He was disorientated and, despite sleeping on the journey, he still had his hangover. Bright sunlight was the last thing he needed. What had he drunk last sunfall? Oh Holy One, he felt awful. And where was he? And then he remembered. Well, perhaps he was in the right place if he was going to start talking to the Holy One about how he felt, although he suspected the conversation might be somewhat one-sided.

Billy Bob was excited. At last, on this planet of temptation, he would have the chance to redeem himself. He was sure that Preacher Grimthorpe would approve of what Billy Bob had come to see as his pilgrimage to this monastery.

When the last of the visitors had disembarked, the solar-powered dirigible slipped away, unnoticed, leaving them standing on top of a sandstone tower, baking in the heat of the desert sun.

What little conversation there had been died away until all stood in silence; a silence muffled by a heat-soaked breeze that barely had the energy to blow. The relentless sun scorched all before it, even the red sand folded under its haze.

Time slowed. Each pulsar's pulse could be counted, marked and remembered as it rolled into the next. Each pulsar's pulse presented time to think and reflect, time to contemplate, time to see something far larger than eyes can see.

Johnson began to sway. His ever-present hangover, combined with the oppressive heat, started to make his universe rather unsteady. He sat down. He still felt like he was falling. He rolled backwards and, with outstretched arms and legs, lay spread-eagled on the tower roof – a position from which he could surely fall no further. But his body was sending his mind a different message: he was in freefall, tumbling downward, his stomach churning endlessly. Overcome with nausea, he started to incant the words, 'Oh Holy One, oh Holy One,' over and over.

Jones looked across to see Johnson horizontal on the tower's roof. He wheeled his way to him and nudged the prostrate Johnson. 'Hey, Johnson, are you OK?'

Johnson just continued to groan, 'Oh Holy One, oh Holy One.'

Jones nudged harder. 'Johnson, come on get up.' But the groaning only continued.

Jones was about to enlist Billy Bob's help when, as if appearing out of the ether, a hooded monk stood before them. The hooded monk had his arms crossed and was dressed in flowing white robes with a gold five-pointed star hung on a chain around his neck.

'Brothers, welcome.' The hooded monk's voice was deep and reassuring.

All the visitors, with the exception of the recumbent Johnson, turned to the hooded monk's voice.

'Welcome to the Simucalc Monastery, the physical abode of the Order Of The New Desert Brethren.' The hooded monk then added, reluctantly, 'A registered not-for-profit organisation.'

The hooded monk paused, opened his arms and then continued, 'Brothers, all you see is but a mere construction of stone. The true abode of the Order Of The New Desert Brethren, a registered not-for-profit organisation, does not lie within its walls, nor does it lie amidst the desert sands that surround us, or the sky that shields us.'

The hooded monk looked at each and every one of the visitors who stood on that tower, and then dramatically drew his hands to his body. 'Brothers, it lies in here. It lies in the pure spirituality of the soul. It lies in the love we have. For, in the words of one of the truly devotional verses passed down to us by our forefathers' forefathers, "Love is all."'

Some of those gathered replied, 'So be it.'

The hooded monk continued, 'Brothers, we hope in your brief time with us you can all start to find pure love, whether through our words or through the privations of the desert and the self-discipline it brings, so that you, too, may be allowed to follow the Holy One's call.'

The odd 'Praise be' was now added to the response of 'So be it's. The hooded monk turned to Johnson. 'Brothers, it seems that spirituality may have come to some of us sooner than others. Praise be, brother, praise be.'

Johnson continued groaning, 'Oh Holy One, oh Holy One.'

The hooded monk raised his arms aloft. 'Brothers, glory be to the Holy One! For he has seen fit to bring his love into this brother's soul.'

'Glory be's now joined the crescendo of 'Praise be's and 'So be it's.

The hooded monk cast his arms down towards Johnson. 'Brothers, come join me in devotion. Holy One, we thank you for the miracle of spirituality you have set before us...' At which, with unfortunate timing, Johnson rolled onto his side and vomited the contents of his stomach over the monk's sandalled feet.

There was silence, a heavy silence only broken when Jones came forward. 'I think my friend's communion with the Holy One, and his contemplation of spirituality, is more to do with the spirit found in a drink carton than the spirit found in the soul.'

'Brother, I offer devotion so that your friend may find salvation from his sins and redemption for his soul.' The hooded monk's reply was cold. He looked unflinchingly at Jones.

'Brothers, and I say this to you all, take heed: this is no place for the sins of mortal humans. The Holy One's heaven-sent retribution can be swift and,' as the hooded monk paused, no breath was drawn by those on that tower, 'absolute.'

The hooded monk then beckoned to the rest of his visitors. 'Brothers, follow me please. Your induction awaits.'

*   *   *   *   *

Investigator Strait said nothing when he returned to Operation Kicking Butt's incident-room. Those inside the incident-room turned to see the door slide open and a manifestation of pure, un-distilled anger stand before them. His face was as stone, but his eyes, oh how his eyes burned with rage.

The chief of law enforcement had just cancelled Operation Kicking Butt, or as he'd so eloquently put it, 'After six lunar cycles of sitting on its butt going nowhere, it was time to kick Operation Kicking Butt's butt into touch'.

And, in answer to Investigator Strait's initially restrained question, 'Why?', the chief of law enforcement had said, 'No evidence, no beeping evidence', an answer that almost caused meltdown in Investigator Strait's brain; it was this very lack of evidence that had been Investigator Strait's reason to come and ask the chief of law enforcement for an extension to the remit of Operation Kicking Butt in the first place!

But the chief of law enforcement had shown no further interest in Investigator Strait's appeal to reason, nor his subsequent expressive pleading, nor even in Investigator Strait's consequent, and somewhat ill-advised, all-encompassing and prolonged rant.

And when, finally, Investigator Strait was emotionally spent, Chief Garett simply asked if that was all. Clearly it was. Investigator Strait was speechless.

Then, to add to Investigator Strait's miseries, Chief Garett had gone on about a new priority: the reported kidnap of some nobody or other.

The biggest leaf trafficking operation of contemporary times, his operation, involving a ring of ruthless interstellar lawbreakers, had been brought to a premature end because some fool of a nobody had probably gone and got themselves lost.

In his mind Investigator Strait was about to bring about the demise of a whole leaf-trafficking ring, a ring that had brought the misery and social shame of leaf smoking to incalculable numbers of citizens' lives. Where was the sense of perspective? Where was the justice?

But what really made his particles collide was when he was dismissed with a nonchalant 'I don't want to hear it' flick of the wrist by the chief of law enforcement.

Investigator Strait was incandescent with rage.

*　　*　　*　　*　　*

An inquisitive Chad strolled across to the ever-lovely Miranda's workhub. He wanted to know what was up. More specifically he wanted to know what was up with Johnson, who was due back from Nova Vega this rotation; the very Johnson who he'd been sent to pick up from the spaceport by Mr Stein, no less; the Johnson who appeared to have had a reception committee of every law enforcement deputy on Pacifica waiting for him.

The ever-charming Miranda tried to hide under her workhub, but to no avail. When she eventually looked up, Chad was still there.

'Miranda, my sweet, how are you?' oozed Chad.

'Busy,' replied the ever-amiable Miranda, but she knew that this attempted brush-off wouldn't work on Chad.

'I guess you heard about my little success?' Chad beamed.

'We all heard,' sighed the ever-empathetic Miranda.

'One of my greatest successes, if I don't mind saying so myself,' continued the relentless Chad. 'You know, not everyone could have pulled that deal off on Old MacDonald's World. Look how Johnson tried, and what did he get? Ten units, ten miserable units on approval. Do you know how many I achieved?'

The ever-patient Miranda shook her head, though not just in response to the question.

'Ten thousand units. Let me say that again, ten *thousand* units; entered, coded and transacted on contract. Great stuff! I'm not Flush Away's best customer-relationship and promotions specialist for nothing you know.' Chad ballooned with pride.

How she hoped that hololink would flash. Please someone, anyone, I'll do anything, save me! But her wish remained un-granted.

'I went to pick Johnson up from the spaceport this rotation. Thought he might appreciate it after his long, arduous Nova Vega trip. But do you know what?' asked Chad, and he looked directly down at the ever-pleasing Miranda.

She couldn't avoid responding. 'What?'

'He wasn't there. He wasn't on the starliner. I waited and waited for him. Most odd.' Chad did not take his eyes off of the ever-entrancing Miranda. He was looking for a telltale sign, but she was determined not to give the game away.

'Really. Were you waiting long? Perhaps you missed him,' she suggested.

'I was there from the time the transit shuttle landed until the last of the jump crew came through, and there was no Johnson on that transfer.' Chad paused, and then asked, 'Have you heard from him at all?'

'Not since he left.' Which is true, she told herself, if Chad meant had she heard from Johnson *directly*.

'I hear that Mr Stein, or should I say, Francis – to those of us who know him – is looking for Johnson. Did he happen to mention anything to you about Johnson at all?' persisted Chad.

'No.' The ever-informative Miranda began to feel uncomfortable as she distorted the truth a little further. Mr Stein had not *mentioned* anything about Johnson to her, he'd *instructed* her about Johnson.

Chad released his gaze from the ever-understanding Miranda and returned to idle conversation. 'You know, Miranda, if the current Mrs Edger hadn't thrown herself at my feet and begged me to marry her, you could have had that chance. Never mind, better luck next time!' And with a wink Chad turned and walked off – always leave them with a smile, Chad's third rule.

The ever-sensible Miranda pondered what she might have done had she a blaster, but then thought it wouldn't be worth the effort of having to recharge it afterwards.

* * * * *

A partially re-hydrated and recovering Johnson struggled with Billy Bob to carry Jones's wheelchair, together with Jones, down the narrowing spiral stairs. They were trying to keep up with the other visitors who were, in turn, following the hooded monk as he descended from the tower roof. Words were clearly not to be spoken as all passed single file into the darkness.

Gradually their sunlight-accustomed eyes became adjusted to the faint glow globes that marked their downward course. And down and down they went.

Johnson and Billy Bob had to stop more and more frequently as fatigue set in. And the more they stopped the further the others got ahead. Firstly they could no longer see them, and then they could no longer hear their footfalls on the stone stairs.

'We've lost them,' panted Johnson.

'By the stars, how can we have lost them? There's only one way to go. Come on, hurry up,' urged Jones.

They reached the bottom of the spiral stairs. Before them a wide arched passageway opened out offering a simple choice: left or right.

Jones, relieved to be in control of his own movement again, turned right and rolled off down the corridor. Billy Bob shrugged and followed. After recovering his breath, Johnson looked up and set after Billy Bob.

Jones's wheelchair glided effortlessly over the smooth flagstones. From either side of the wide arched passageway glow globes illuminated and dimmed as he passed. The passageway terminated at a T-junction, he had another left or right choice. Right again.

To try and keep up, Billy Bob hastened and lengthened his stride, but Jones was drawing away leaving an increasingly long trail of glow globes dimming to darkness. And much against the sentiments of his body, Johnson also picked up his pace.

At last Jones could make out a figure in the distance. He speeded up to close, and saw that the hooded figure was wearing a coarse brown robe. It looked like one of the visitors they'd arrived with. The figure turned left into another corridor. Jones rounded the corner to follow, and was met with a blank recessed wall and a stone water-fountain. He stopped, confused. Where had the visitor in the brown robe gone? Jones rotated round in his wheelchair. He could see no passageways, no doors. He was sure the figure had turned left. He looked to the right, and the corridor continued. He looked back behind him, and someway down the passageway he could see Billy Bob following.

Perhaps it was a trick of the light. There was only one way to go, so he followed the corridor to the right. Ah, there, up ahead, someone coming towards him.

Jones rolled to a halt. The tall figure was dressed in a hooded white flowing robe. This was not the same person he'd been following.

The tall monk walked up to Jones. 'Brother, welcome. You appear to be lost.'

'Ah... no, I was just following the rest of the visitors,' replied Jones, uncertainly.

'Brother, I believe you are mistaken. No visitors would have come this way. You must have taken the wrong turn at the bottom of the tower stairs.' The tall monk's voice was steady, reassured. 'Brother, let me show you the way.'

With a sweep of his arms the tall monk shepherded Jones back in the direction he had just come from, collecting Billy Bob and an out of breath Johnson on the way.

The tall monk guided them past the tower stairs they'd descended from, and along a maze of passageways, turning left and right in no particular order to a vaulted hall. Piercing shafts of sunlight struck the flagstones from high-set slit windows. In the centre of the vaulted hall, suspended from the ceiling, a gold five-pointed star hung motionless and, in front of them, there were long trestle tables at which their fellow visitors sat.

Without a word the tall monk turned and departed.

'Brothers, welcome.' The hooded monk, who'd greeted them on their arrival, looked briefly in their direction. He then returned to address the whole group. 'You are sat in the visitors' refectory, which is an exact, stone-by-stone replica of the refectory of the novices; a place where our initiates gather each rotation to draw strength during their induction, prior to abandoning the mortal trappings of this universe and following the Holy One's call. For some this process takes but a lunar phase, for others many solar cycles may pass, but all seek divine enlightenment.'

The hooded monk paused to allow his words to dissipate. 'Brothers, we now offer you a chance to experience a little of this path. Some of you may even chose to follow this journey further, but we hope that all of you will at least be able to take away something to help you on your voyage through life.'

There was a polite smattering of 'So be it's. The hooded monk continued, 'Brothers, after you have finished your repast you will be shown to your cells, where you will remain until sunrise. You will find robes to wear and a receptacle to place all of your worldly belongings into. Once changed, we will remove your belongings for the duration of your stay, and leave you to contemplate and offer devotion if you should wish, for it is said, "Sit in thy cell and thy cell will teach thee all."'

And so the monastic visitors ate that which was in front of them. After this hooded monks in grey robes, wearing gold five-pointed stars on chains around their necks, appeared and ushered the gathered group of visitors to their cells.

Johnson looked forward to the peace and quiet, a chance to get his head down and try and finally clear his hangover; a chance to sleep.

Billy Bob felt that he was taking a step on the path to salvation, a chance to atone for his sins.

Jones wondered. He wondered whether the hooded figure in the brown robe was a figment of his imagination or not.

[26] Fact Or Fiction?

A new rotation, and what had been half a solar cycle in the making barely took a workshift to dismantle. Investigator Strait and his Tactical Response Assault Patrol, the very nucleus of Operation Kicking Butt, emptied the incident-room they had occupied, and departed Pacifica's U-Tan-U Spaceport almost unnoticed.

They returned to The Black, as Pacifica's law enforcement headquarters was less than affectionately known. It was a skybreaker that descended as many levels below ground as it ascended above. Subtly constructed of black-faced, foamed armour salvaged from a decommissioned Space Corps dreadnought. A practical, if inelegant, building that had the added benefit of being impervious to all but the most substantial of spaceborne weaponry. Unfortunately many of Pacifica's citizens, particularly those in the architectural community, felt this singular benefit to be something of a detriment – as it would only be through the use of such spaceborne weaponry that this notorious eyesore could be demolished.

Investigator Strait stood by his old workhub. A workhub he had not occupied since the commencement of Operation Kicking Butt. He calmly placed his things upon it and sat back in his favoured, worn chair. His Tactical Response Assault Patrol had been reassigned to their original units and was now dispersed to the eight corners of The Black.

He sat, waiting patiently, in the large open workplace among colleagues of many solar cycles standing, for he knew it was coming: the wit. It wouldn't be open and it wouldn't all come at once. It would be the odd hidden remark here, the odd comment there, unobtrusive, almost undetectable. Who would be first to try?

Senior Deputy Sol Moon, wisest of the wise, and certainly oldest of the old, looked up from his workhub, chisel-faced. He gazed around. He was a male for whom change was what you got when you paid for something. He was still wearing the same undercover attire he'd been wearing when Investigator Strait had started in law enforcement, all those solar cycles ago. Sol Moon just grinned as he stood and strolled away, document in hand.

Deputy Ossman, a male for whom administration had become the solitary reason for his existence, carried numbered boxes back and forth, his mind clearly adrift in a sea of filing.

But it turned out to be none of these firm favourites who made the first move. It was a young deputy named Hildale. 'Enjoy your vacation, sir.'

'Pardon?' replied Investigator Strait.

'Vacation, sir. Did you enjoy it?' repeated Deputy Hildale as she walked past.

Investigator Strait beckoned her over. 'Deputy, come here.'

Deputy Hildale, who was slightly taken aback, stopped and shuffled towards Investigator Strait's workhub.

And then Investigator Strait continued in a controlled, monotonous tone just loud enough for all to hear, 'Right then, for the record, I have not been on vacation, I was deep undercover.'

'Oh, I'm so sorry, sir,' replied Deputy Hildale with just the faintest hint of sarcasm. She wasn't about to be intimidated by some over-the-event-horizon Investigator, and added, as she walked away, 'You know, I was sure that the others said you'd been on vacation.'

Investigator Strait looked out across the workplace to see if he could catch a guilty eye, or a half-hidden smirk, but all the familiar faces just happened to be turned away.

And then it started. Just a pulsar's pulse after his exchange with Deputy Hildale a conversation began to which he was not a party to...

'So, if he wasn't on vacation, what was he doing?'

'The rumour is that he was in pursuit of a suspect who just happened to be going to Nova Vega.'

'That well-know vacation destination?'

'The very one.'

'What happened to the suspect?'

'That's the mystery.'

'Apparently he managed to lose the suspect on a starliner deep in the middle of interstellar space.'

'Never!'

'It's true.'

'But how's that possible?'

'Perhaps the suspect opened one airlock too many?'

'I heard the suspect vanished in a puff of smoke.'

'What, leaf smoke?'

There was a deliberate pause.

'Anyway, all's well that ends well.'

'Oh?'

'I'm told that, when he did finally return, the full resources and intellect of his Tactical Response Assault Patrol were deployed to greet him at the spaceport. They were so pleased to see him that they even fixed combat knives.'

'That's nice. At least they managed to find each other.'

There was another pause.

'There's something else.'

'What?'

'If I tell you, you're not to tell anyone else now. Do you promise?'

'We promise.'

'I'm told that Operation Kicking Butt's been terminated.'

'Scandalous!'

'Not a word of a lie. Operation Kicking Butt's just got kicked in the butt.'

The conversation stopped as all considered this momentous news.

'But Operation Kicking Butt is Investigator Strait's pride and joy. It's his baby.'

'That's what my sources tell me.'

'You mean all his hard work has just gone and got stubbed out?'

'You got it.'

'But why?'

'You're not to repeat this to anyone.'

'We won't.'

A hushed silence descended on the group.

'I'm told, and this is in the strictest confidence from on high, I'm told that Investigator Strait couldn't even catch a cold!'

Laughter broke out.

And there it was, one of the oldest jokes in the history of law enforcement, laid at his feet. He just looked and shook his head as those all-too-familiar faces laughed and then, one-by-one, stood and walked across to greet him.

'Nice to have you back, Investigator.'

'At least you've found your old workhub.'

'Onwards and upwards, eh, Investigator?'

*   *   *   *   *

As the tumbling rain fell, the law enforcement skyrider ascended. The rain shrouded the lights and holoplays of the metropolis to make all appear as a merging monotone. It was persistent rain; rain that drummed on the skyrider's roof; grey rain from a grey sky against a backdrop of skybreaker after skybreaker. It was how it was: normal.

Investigator Strait was teamed with Senior Deputy Sol Moon, and his timeless undercover attire. They were en route to the headquarters of the Flush Away Corporation, a name that seemed familiar to Investigator Strait, but he just couldn't quite place it.

Chief Garett had given them few details about the reported kidnapping. And anyway, more than likely, it would be a simple missing person case. After all, who would want to kidnap your average corporate employee? No one.

Investigator Strait could guess what this would turn out to be: an employee who's extra-marital affair just got that little too complicated, or perhaps the expenses claimed didn't quite match the receipts received, or maybe it was the traditional 'it all got too much', and the employee just decided to up and go. Whatever it was he doubted that it would be a kidnapping.

The one thing Investigator Strait had gathered was that the Mr Francis Stein, they were to meet, was a 'close and personal' friend of the law enforcement chief, so it was going to have to be best behaviour, mind you when wasn't it best behaviour? No doubt all they did or didn't do, say or didn't say would go straight back to the chief.

Their skyrider dropped out of the traffic stream and juddered to a halt, implicitly reminding its occupants that all that stood between them and certain death, a few hundred levels below, was the diligence of the skyrider's maintenance crew back at The Black. Much to their relief, the skyrider descended slowly and smoothly, passing Flush Away's corporate tiers to land on the walkway below.

Investigator Strait and Senior Deputy Sol Moon climbed out and stood on the reassuringly supportive walkway. Before them steps led up to the white Marblesque colonnade.

Inside, Investigator Strait and Senior Deputy Sol Moon made their way through the bustle of citizens milling around the vast lobby to one of the plastiglass skyvators.

'Welcome to Flush Away – the corporation that totally wastes your waste!' the skyvator intoned in an indeterminate, flawless accent. 'How may we be of service?'

'Investigator Strait and Senior Deputy Sol Moon to see Mr Francis Stein,' responded Investigator Strait officiously.

Without hesitation the skyvator closed its doors and whisked them skywards towards the plastiglass atrium many hundreds of levels above. On the way the skyvator recited a series of important safety announcements. And thus, with the occupants' tacit agreement – that is to say they were present in the skyvator when the announcements were made – the Flush Away Corporation was absolved from any liability in the event of accident, asteroid impact, cosmic collision, supernova or other acts of whoever the prevalent deity happened to be.

The skyvator glided effortlessly to a halt and opened onto a wide concourse of unmarked doors. Third on the left had been the skyvator's instruction. Investigator Strait and Senior Deputy Sol Moon walked the corridor and entered what they hoped was Mr Stein's workspace.

Inside, the room was almost empty, save a workhub, some seating and another door directly opposite. A smart, efficient-looking female sat at the workhub.

'Deputies, please take a seat, Mr Stein will be with you momentarily.' Mrs Shelley continued being smart and efficient.

Investigator Strait and Senior Deputy Sol Moon sat as instructed and admired the view of the featureless wall in front of them – as only experienced members of a law enforcement agency can do. And then the other door slid open.

Out stepped Mr Francis Stein looking particularly resplendent in his business attire; business attire that didn't just shine it positively glowed. 'Welcome. I appreciate that you've been able to come at such short notice; I know how busy you must be. Please, step into my workspace where things are a little more comfortable and where we can talk.'

Investigator Strait and Senior Deputy Sol Moon entered Francis Stein's workspace.

'Call me Francis,' instructed Francis Stein as he outstretched his hand. Investigator Strait and Senior Deputy Sol Moon pressed it in turn and introduced themselves, although not by their first names – for after all, law enforcement business is formal business.

To Investigator Strait, Mr Stein's workspace seemed more like an upmarket beverage emporium than any workspace he'd ever seen. There was an impressive view of the skyline – a clear measure of status in business – images on the wall, comfortable furniture and that all important row of very expensive drink cartons sat behind an unobtrusive beverage counter in the corner of the room. One glance at the images told Investigator Strait all he needed to know about Mr Francis Stein: connected and self-important.

Francis Stein indicated to the opposing antiquarian ottomans in the centre of the room. 'Take a seat. Can I tempt you with a drink?'

'No thank you, sir. On duty, sir.' Investigator Strait and Senior Deputy Sol Moon sat.

'You're probably right, perhaps it is a tad too early in the rotation.' Francis Stein turned from the beverage counter and sat opposite Investigator Strait and Senior Deputy Sol Moon. 'I don't know how much Hank has been able to tell you.'

'Hank, sir?' replied Investigator Strait knowing full well who 'Hank' was.

'Apologies Investigator, Law Enforcement Chief Garett. I forget myself, law enforcement is a little more regimented than I'm used to.' Francis Stein smiled.

'Perhaps best to start from the beginning, sir. Assume we know nothing.' Investigator Strait searched for that tell-tale superior look that often glinted in a person's eye when he made that statement during an interview: 'Law enforcement, know nothing – nothing unusual there!' but Mr Stein's face was a mask.

Investigator Strait indicated to Senior Deputy Sol Moon. 'My colleague will now turn on the Tell-It-All auto-transcriptor, just a formality during interviews, sir.'

'Fine. The beginning – ah yes. The first I knew that anything was up was when I had a little deputation appear from my customer-relationships and promotions team early this rotation. Lucretia, my head of customer-relationships and promotions, came to see me with this.' Francis Stein projected the message he had been given, over the table for all to see.

Senior Deputy Sol Moon then carefully and painstakingly read it aloud. 'Flush Away. Your employee is with us. Requests organic restitution. You have the time of creation. The Children Of The Soil.'

'And this,' added Francis Stein projecting the image of a male leant back in a chair set against a blank wall.

'And the male in the image, you believe him to be one of your employees?' enquired Senior Deputy Sol Moon.

'Yes, Johnson, one of our customer-relationship and promotions specialists,' replied Francis Stein.

Investigator Strait froze inside. Johnson, Johnson! It couldn't be. The suspected leaf trafficker he'd chased halfway across the Spiral Arm. The 'master of disguise' was now masquerading as a Flush Away employee pretending to be kidnapped? It couldn't be.

'And you're certain about the identity, sir?' asked a superficially calm Investigator Strait.

'I don't know the male personally, Investigator, but Lucretia, his boss, can confirm that it's him in the image and, as you can see, the message was sent from his holocom.' Francis Stein sat back, observing Investigator Strait. It was always important to know to whom you were talking.

Senior Deputy Sol Moon pressed on with the questioning. 'Prior to receiving this message, sir, when did your organisation last have contact with Johnson?'

'My understanding is that Johnson had just been sent on a business trip to Nova Vega a couple of rotations ago, so I guess we last had contact with him then. You'll have to ask Lucretia, she'll be able to give you the exact details,' replied Francis Stein who had now switched his attention to Senior Deputy Sol Moon.

'And Nova Vega is where you'd expect him to be, sir?' continued Senior Deputy Sol Moon.

'No. I'd expect him to be here. He should have returned to the workplace by now. To check, I sent someone to meet him at the spaceport, but he didn't get off that transit shuttle. We've tried his holocom and his co-op, but no sign of him. So I decided to holo the authorities. That's why I holoed Hank, I mean Chief Garett, for advice.' Francis Stein leant forward. 'Although I must say my initial thoughts were that it must be some kind of workplace prank. Who would want to kidnap one of our employees?'

'You did the right thing, sir,' commended Senior Deputy Sol Moon.

'Now, returning to the message. I am unfamiliar with the term "organic restitution", can you explain what it means?'

'I'm afraid your guess is as good as mine on that one, senior deputy,' replied Francis Stein. 'Lucretia thinks it means some kind of payment, a ransom of some sort. But I think if you want payment why not just put down the amount of credits you're demanding?'

'So "organic restitution" is not a term particular to your industry, sir?' queried Senior Deputy Sol Moon.

Francis Stein shook his head. 'Not as far as I'm aware, and I've been in the sanitation business for the best part of thirty solar cycles.'

'How about the Children Of The Soil, sir, do you know who they might be?' continued Senior Deputy Sol Moon.

'No, you've got me there again. That's what makes it all so odd: a ransom demand that's at best cryptic from an organisation no one's heard of. I hope you can sort it all out.' Francis Stein sat back.

'No need to worry there, sir. The law enforcement chief has put his best team on the case. I'm sure we'll get this resolved in a photon's phase,' replied a confident Senior Deputy Sol Moon. 'Now, if I may, sir, we'll need all the personal details you have on Johnson and copies of this message and image. Also we will need to interview his boss, Lucretia...?'

'D'Baliere,' added Francis Stein.

'Now, if you'd just approve your statement, sir, and touch there, sir, and there, sir, and there and a – just there, sir. Thank you.' Senior Deputy Sol Moon handed Francis Stein the transcript of the interview. 'You know how it is, sir, administration, administration, administration!'

Francis Stein read the auto-generated transcript, touched in the places indicated and returned it to Senior Deputy Sol Moon.

'Thank you, sir, and here's your copy.' Senior Deputy Sol Moon handed Francis Stein a copy of the transcript.

Francis Stein put the transcript on his workhub. 'Thank you, senior deputy. Now, unless there is anything else I can help you with, I must take my leave. Unfortunately, or fortunately depending upon one's cosmic perspective, the demand for sanitation products never stops.'

*　*　*　*　*

Investigator Strait sat before Chief Garett. Each looked at the other, but said nothing. The air was uncomfortable, confused, and were it not for the self-conscious embarrassment that such activity would bring, heads would be scratched.

The cause of confusion, and the very subject of Chief Garett's newly initiated kidnap enquiry, also appeared to be the suspect at the centre of Investigator Strait's recently, and in his view, ill advisedly terminated

Operation Kicking Butt: Johnson.

The additional interviews Investigator Strait had held at Flush Away's headquarters had yielded nothing further.

The analysis of the message and image also gave little additional information about the whereabouts of Johnson, 'The kidnap victim', other than to determine that the message had been sent from the Liberty Discount starliner inbound from Nova Vega; the very starliner that Investigator Strait had been on whilst unsuccessfully tailing Johnson, 'The leaf trafficker'!

Investigator Strait was not happy. He was not happy because he did not like coincidence. His many solar cycles of law enforcement experience told him that coincidence rarely existed.

Chief Garett began to mark time by tapping on his workhub. He too was not happy. He was not happy for he too did not like coincidence. His many solar cycles of law enforcement experience told him that coincidence rarely existed. He leant forward and looked directly at Investigator Strait.

'So let me see if I've determined the indeterminate, Investigator. Five rotations ago Operation Kicking Butt's surveillance activities detected leaf being trafficked through the spaceport by this Johnson, who was disguised as a jump associate off an inbound starliner from Old MacDonald's World.'

'Yes, sir,' replied Investigator Strait.

The chief of law enforcement continued, 'Rather than apprehend the suspect and the leaf, there and then, you allowed him to continue on his way, believing that he would lead you to the rest of the leaf-trafficking ring.'

'Yes, sir,' replied Investigator Strait.

'Your team then promptly lost Johnson.' Chief Garett sighed.

Investigator Strait had little choice but to reply, 'Yes, sir.'

'However, after what you described as "rapid and exhaustive enquiries", you and your team determined that your suspect had left for Nova Vega on a business trip, whereupon you mounted an unauthorised, covert operation to follow your suspect, apprehend him and repatriate him back to Pacifica.' The chief of law enforcement paused to ensure that his words had been heard and understood.

'Yes, sir.' Investigator Strait could only go with the solar stream.

Chief Garett maintained eye contact. 'Whilst on Nova Vega your suspect met with persons you also suspected of being involved in leaf trafficking.'

'Yes, sir,' replied Investigator Strait.

'Then Johnson made an attempt to evade capture, but you and your team managed to, and I believe these are your own words, "with commitment above and beyond the call of duty", track him to a starliner bound for Pacifica. However, being a "master of disguise" and despite the large law enforcement reception party you had arranged for him,

Johnson evaded arrest – again.' Chief Garett awaited Investigator Strait's confirmation.

Investigator Strait responded reluctantly, 'Yes, sir.'

Chief Garett failed to detect anything in Investigator Strait's demeanour that disagreed with what he'd said. 'Please correct me if anything I have said so far is wrong.'

'Yes, sir,' replied Investigator Strait.

The chief of law enforcement then turned his eyes from Investigator Strait to look out of his window at the forest of skybreakers that populated Pacifica's skyline. 'And then I was holoed by Francis Stein, over at the Flush Away Corporation, saying that he thinks one of his employees has been kidnapped by an organisation called the Children Of The Soil – whoever they are – requesting "organic restitution" – whatever that is. But best of all, the person who's been kidnapped just happens to be your prime leaf trafficking suspect, one Johnson!'

'Yes, sir,' replied Investigator Strait.

Chief Garett returned his gaze to Investigator Strait. 'Coincidence?'

Investigator Strait just managed to stifle back a 'What do you think?' reply and responded with the much less confrontational, 'Don't know, sir.'

'So what do *you* plan to do to unravel these seemingly interlinked lawbreaking activities?' asked Chief Garett.

Investigator Strait sensed that Johnson had become pivotal to his career. Anything other than a successful conclusion would undoubtedly be detrimental to any future aspirations he had. He drew breath. He had his hunch, his sixth sense, that Johnson was truly a master lawbreaker, a leaf trafficker, but he had no evidence to substantiate his suspicions – a fact that the law enforcement chief had made only too clear when terminating his beloved Operation Kicking Butt. And to confuse matters, a personal friend of the chief had reported Johnson to be a kidnap victim and had evidence to go with it. However, more importantly, Investigator Strait knew it was the status of reported lawbreaking that would be uppermost in Chief Garett's mind, for it was an electoral solar cycle and such numbers always seemed to surface in debate. In the hierarchy of life the law enforcement chief would only have a singular quest: to keep the First Citizen happy. And, in the hierarchy of life, Investigator Strait knew he should have only one singular quest: to keep Chief Garett happy. Thus he spoke, 'Putting any unsubstantiated suspicions of leaf trafficking in stasis, at this point in the space-time continuum, it is clear, based on the evidence, we need to solve the kidnapping.'

Investigator Strait looked up and saw that his law enforcement chief was smiling. He then continued, 'I suggest we share this with the electorate. We know nothing about the kidnappers and have next to no leads. A request for information may just give us the break we're looking for.'

'And a high profile, *successful* law enforcement operation during an electoral campaign would, I'm sure, be viewed very positively by the First Citizen,' added Chief Garett.

So it was agreed. Investigator Strait would front this request for 'information leading to...' at the earliest opportunity, with Chief Garett's support.

Investigator Strait was no fan of the media, but he knew that they could be a useful tool – in certain circumstances. He also knew that what the media reported to the electorate carried immense momentum with his superiors, whether it was fact or, as was more often the case, fiction.

[27] Finding The Answer

Johnson, head cleared and hangover-less, sat in his cell and wondered quite what had led him to this. For one brief but memorable point in the space-time continuum he was a successful sales representative living the stellarlife with the best that the traditions of Nova Vega had to offer, and then, in the flicker of a falling star, he was sat dressed in a suspiciously yellow, hessian-like robe, not a possession in the universe and staring at four walls and a door.

The cell was surprisingly cool and lighted by a narrow shaft of sunlight casting down from a single slit, high up on the door-facing wall. Ground, walls and ceiling all shared the same bare sandstone theme, and the hardened metal door had a certain inescapable, captive quality about it. With an achernarian rush mat serving as the only piece of furniture: lavishness, opulence and sumptuousness were not words to be found in this cell's description.

What was it the monk had said? 'Sit in thy cell and it will teach thee all.' Well, Johnson's cell seemed remarkably silent on the teaching front. He was sat in it, and it hadn't said a word. Although, given the fragility of Johnson's head, that was probably all to the good.

However, the monastery had certainly delivered on the 'no gambling, no alcohol and no females' promise – so far. And it seemed that the monastery was going out of its way to meet its offer of 'a simpler life without temptation' with the removal of such enticements as conversation, entertainment and any other form of sensory stimulation, unless, of course, you considered the hessian-like nature of the yellow robe, or the endless opportunity to count grains of sand, as stimulation.

The only thing that Johnson did find absent from the commitments the Order Of The New Desert Brethren had made in their promotional material was the Holy One. Not that Johnson truly expected to find the Holy One, or even had the presumption to believe that the Holy One would ordain to find him – if, of course, the Holy One existed, something that, based on his life's experiences, Johnson increasingly doubted. In truth he'd never been a believer. To Johnson things mostly didn't make sense and, at best, had something of the ridiculous about them. It wouldn't surprise him if the whole thing – life, existence, time, space, matter, love, death – was one almighty mistake and the harder the universe tried to correct itself, the more it all went wrong.

This uncharacteristic thinking was starting to give Johnson a headache again. He took a drink of water, hoping to wash his contemplations away. It didn't work. The fabric of reality started to churn in his head.

Life, existence, time, space, matter, love, death, the Holy One; what did it all mean?

Where was the sense, the logic?

Why was he here?

How had he got here?

Who was he?

Questions, questions, it was if his mind had been awoken after a lifetime of hibernation. It was a strange and uncomfortable sensation for Johnson. He put his head in his hands and swayed back and forth, hoping that the motion would somehow send his thoughts back to sleep. It didn't work, and the claustrophobia of the four walls started to become oppressive.

Johnson stood, turned and, with some effort, pushed open the door. He stepped outside. A walk, that's what he needed to clear his head. And some food too, to redress the alcohol imbalance he'd put his body through these last couple of rotations.

Johnson made his way to the refectory. Within the first few steps his mind started to cloud back to its natural, confused state – what a relief!

In the refectory he found many of his fellow visitors sat at the long trestle tables. It was hard to tell anyone apart, as all wore hooded yellow robes. He surveyed the scene. Whilst most looked vaguely into the distance, some were looking up at the gold five-pointed star suspended from the ceiling; others were looking at the flagstones. None spoke.

At the far end of the hall there stood a monk, in a white robe and wearing a gold five-pointed star. Johnson could not see Mr Jones or William Robert. He wondered where they were. He did not need to wonder for long.

With a noise not heard since the Big Bang, the two of them thundered into the refectory. William Robert was pushing Mr Jones, who had his hands firmly pressed to his ears, and William Robert was singing, 'Oh Holy One, Let me spread my muck all around, Oh Holy One, Let me sow my seed to your sound...'

All looked and stared as the wheelchair and its reluctant occupant were danced across the refectory to the tune of an easily misquoted, if not misinterpreted, holy tune.

Billy Bob ended the dance by pushing the wheelchair away, sliding to his knees in a crescendo of hand-raising 'Glory be's, and proclaiming, 'I have seen the light.'

Jones, whose wheelchair had come to a stop at the feet of the white-robed monk, cautiously pulled his hands from his ears and asked, 'Has he stopped yet?'

The white-robed monk, who appeared completely un-phased by Billy Bob's antics, spoke to those gathered, 'Brothers, through this last sunfall you will have experienced a taste of what devotion to the calling can bring.

Some of you will have sensed its flavour whilst others,' and he looked directly at Billy Bob, 'may have gorged themselves without thought.'

'Brothers, let us now turn from matters of the spiritual to matters of the physical, come, you are our guests, please eat.' And the white-robed monk gestured for food to be served.

The grey liquid ladled into Johnson's bowl was just viscous enough for his eating utensil to stand unaided and remain vertical. Johnson didn't doubt that the gruel satisfied all of his nutritional needs: it surely had to for nothing that tasted this bland could be anything other than good for you. It was also clear to him that the food being served wasn't going to attract anyone, other than the most devout, to monastic life.

When he and his fellow monastic visitors had eaten their fill they were encouraged to wash their crockery and utensils in a large stone water-trough situated at the refectory exit and wait to be taken on the obligatory sightseeing tour, or as the hooded monk had phrased things, 'The path to enlightenment'.

Jones leant across and asked if the monastery was what Johnson had expected.

Johnson just smiled. However, their conversation was interrupted by a loud 'So be it' as Billy Bob dropped his hands and looked up, presumably in the direction of his heaven.

'Come on, William Robert, time to make a move.' Jones tapped Billy Bob on the shoulder. 'You'll have plenty of time to offer devotion later no doubt.'

Billy Bob stared skywards. He did not move.

'William Robert.'

Billy Bob continued to stare skywards.

'William Robert?' Jones shook Billy Bob's arm. 'It's me, Mr Jones, and our new friend, Johnson. Are you alright?'

No response.

In frustration, and forgetting who he was pretending to be, Jones reverted to type and ordered, 'By the heavens, let's get movin' star trooper!'

But this was to no avail and Billy Bob did not respond. It was only when the hooded monk rose that Billy Bob stood, and it was only when the hooded monk went to leave that Billy Bob followed in his footsteps, and, as they all exited the visitors' refectory, Billy Bob continued to stare skywards.

Arched corridor passed into arched corridor, sparsely lighted by shafts of natural light. To mark the pace the hooded monk swung an incense burner, half-filling the passageway with smoke; and to fill the silence, he chanted. The monastic visitors followed each other, one after another, with Johnson and Jones at the precession's tail.

And then all was flooded with light. Blinded, the precession came to a halt. Eyes adjusted. A large double door had been opened at the end of the corridor. The precession stepped out into a chequered quadrangle. Around the edge of the quadrangle ran a colonnade that marked the inner perimeter of a closed, covered walkway.

When all had filed out, the hooded monk began to explain the purpose of the cloister.

Johnson listened with half-interest. Whilst he had no intention of becoming a monk, his visit was certainly giving him time to reflect on the frantic activity of his life and, more particularly, the events of the last few rotations.

As he reflected he realised he had more questions than answers: why had Chad let him do the deal with the Creation Corporation so easily? And why had Chad gone to Old MacDonald's World? – Which, at best, Johnson considered to be the cesspit of the Spiral Arm.

And then Johnson puzzled: it wasn't like him to miss his starliner back to Pacifica, and it wasn't like him to lose his holocom.

There were too many unfortunate events occurring. Yes, he liked his drink, but he'd never drunk so much as to not remember what had happened, well not often anyway – as far as he could remember.

Perhaps most unsettling of all, Johnson was beginning to feel that he was being followed. Was this the natural, evolving paranoia that came with the bitterness of life's experiences, or was there really someone out there after him?

As the hooded monk turned and left the quadrangle, Johnson could see William Robert pushing a fervently gesticulating Mr Jones around the cloister.

Chad, the Creation Corporation deal, Old MacDonald's World; what was it all about?

What was really going on?

And who were these two characters he'd managed to tag along with? Were they really who they said they were?

Johnson wanted some answers.

[28] Is There Anyone Out There?

After a brief conversation with Chief Garett, Francis Stein felt forced to call an extraordinary executive board meeting. This was something he would never normally choose to do. Other executive board members were to be avoided; little good ever came from interaction with them. However, he sensed that things might start to go open loop. And he wasn't about to take that kind of responsibility and subsequent blame himself, best to share it with the others.

It was clear that the authorities had little idea about who the kidnappers were, or why they'd kidnapped Johnson. However, what was of real concern to Francis Stein was that the authorities wanted to make the details of the kidnap open to the electorate to solicit further information, and for Flush Away to offer a reward.

Francis Stein thought for a while. To call any kind of meeting with Flush Away's board usually took endless dialogue, discussion, bartering and cajoling. The board members needed to be persuaded that there was something in it for them. Then it came to him. Two simple words, used judiciously, would definitely engender a much more rapid and amenable response than would be the case under normal circumstances: 'electorate' and 'scrutiny'. And, if required, he could always add 'by the media'.

And so, at the end of the rotation, the boardroom's ancient oak-panelled doors were opened and then closed. Inside, the executive board were seated at the ancient oak table, under an equally unhappy, flickering holo-image of Flush Away's founder.

Chief Executive & President Joseph Firtop waited impassively for the last of the small talk to die down. When silence came, he addressed his fellow executive board members in a solemn tone, 'Our vice-president of customer-relationships and promotions has gathered us here to update us, briefly, on an unfortunate issue that has occurred within *his* department, and the subsequent actions *he* is taking to resolve the concerns that have arisen. In normal circumstances I would expect such an issue to be a purely internal departmental matter. However, events have transpired that will affect us all.'

All turned to look at Francis Stein whilst ensuring physically that they drew away. No one wanted to be associated with bad news. But before Francis was able to speak, the ever-eager vice-president of merchandising, Luton Touch – who was always keen to exact advantage, particularly at the expense of one of his fellow board members – interjected, 'Perhaps I should carry out the task of minute taking?'

'For the benefit of the vice-president of merchandising, and the rest of you, there will be no minutes taken from this meeting, just a statement that our vice-president of customer-relationships and promotions will draft.' Joseph Firtop always expressed any displeasure he had with employees by addressing them using their job title, rather than their given name. It emphasised their responsibilities and yet, somehow, also managed to underline the fragility of their tenure.

Francis Stein, the current incumbent of the post of vice-president of customer-relationships and promotions, spoke slowly and clearly as he delivered his news. 'It appears that one of *our* employees has been kidnapped.'

His announcement was met with hush initially, and then muttering broke out.

'That is unfortunate,' commented Aron Grace, vice-president of conception and evolution. 'How did *you* let it happen?'

Francis Stein decided to let Aron Grace's inference drop; he had a battle to win and wasn't going to be distracted by every offer of a skirmish along the way. He waved his hands over the ancient oak table, and the image of a reclining Johnson appeared together with the somewhat cryptic message from the Children Of The Soil.

'We received this earlier. Johnson, one of our customer-relationship and promotions specialists, was sent to close a deal with the Creation Corporation on Nova Vega three rotations ago. He hasn't been heard from since, except for this message and image,' explained Francis Stein.

'Isn't the Creation Corporation one of Chad Edger's clients?' Aron Grace asked, persisting in his quest to find an angle to exploit.

'Correct,' replied Francis Stein. He then returned to addressing the rest of the board. 'As you can see, the message, whilst thankfully short, does raise some questions.'

'So why did *you* send Johnson instead of Chad to do the deal with our *most* important client? If I understand correctly, this Johnson has a less than glowing record?' continued the vice-president of conception and evolution.

Realising that Aron Grace wasn't going to let go, Francis Stein responded, 'I believe Ms D'Baliere felt that Chad could better serve our business needs by seeking market penetration on Old MacDonald's World, and that she felt Johnson was more than capable of landing the Creation Corporation deal. "Teamwork" was how she phrased it to me.'

'And the results are?' pressed the vice-president of conception and evolution.

'Chad has delivered a ten thousand unit deal on Old MacDonald's World, something which I think you will all agree is a wonderful result. This is the first time we've achieved any substantive sales in that system.' Francis Stein smiled as he saw the nods of approval from those around the ancient oak table.

'And the Creation Corporation deal?' Aron Grace was not about to give up.

'Ah... with the disappearance of Johnson, um... we're just awaiting confirmation of a satisfactory conclusion,' admitted Francis Stein.

Sensing blood, the vice-president of conception and evolution rounded on his colleague. 'So, if I understand the situation correctly, *you* have left the deal with our biggest and *most* valued customer potentially unsecured. In fact, *you* may not have yet done the deal at all! Surely this is the real issue here, not whether some second-rate sales representative has gone and got himself lost in space!'

Joseph Firtop looked at his vice-president of conception and evolution with newfound respect – perhaps he'd underestimated him. 'I think you've raised a very pertinent point, Aron.'

Francis Stein began to feel somewhat beleaguered as he saw nods of approval turn to hardened, arm-crossed stares. But as with every naturally begotten survivor, Francis Stein's defence mechanism cut in and he rallied in his ever-positive way. 'Good point, Aron, we'll make a customer-relationship and promotions specialist of you yet! Team's on it right away.'

'As vice-president of customer-relationships and promotions you need to be sure that *your* team is,' added Joseph Firtop.

'Francis, what is "organic restitution" and who are the Children Of The Soil?' asked Chief Fiscal Officer Tobe Milton.

'Ah, good questions, Tobe, and therein lies the epicentre of *our* current problem,' replied Francis Stein, relieved to be back on trajectory. 'We have consulted with the authorities and, unfortunately, they too are in deep space as to who the kidnappers are, or what their demand actually means, which brings me to why I have called us all together.'

Francis Stein paused. Then, when he was sure he had everyone's attention, continued, 'Pacifica's law enforcement agency has advised us that they are going to call a media conference at sunrise to raise the profile of this case. The media conference is timed to catch the early newscasts. They are going to make the details of the kidnapping open to the electorate in order to ask for information and to request that the kidnappers return Johnson.'

Francis Stein paused again to allow everyone to digest what he'd said and, to help those who were a little slow on the uptake, added, 'This will, of course, bring Flush Away right into the electorate's awareness.'

Silence now descended on the room as each thought what may come of this.

It took Joseph Firtop to break the silence. 'Hm... whilst I welcome anything that increases the electorate's awareness of our products, I think our vice-president of customer-relationships and promotions may have gone a little too far this time.'

At this, several board members nodded their heads with considered agreement – it never hurt to agree with the boss.

'It's bad enough having the auditors here each solar cycle, but the scrutiny of the media, that's not good news.' Joseph Firtop was definitely unhappy.

'Can't we stop them?' asked Aron Grace.

'Unfortunately not. According to our litigation department once law enforcement have an approved transcript alleging that a law has been broken it is then added to the statistics holobase and they are legally bound to investigate it,' replied Francis Stein.

'And they have such an approved transcript?' enquired Joseph Firtop.

'Ah, yes. Yes they do.' Francis Stein knew what was coming next.

'Signed by?' sighed Joseph Firtop.

'Me.' Francis Stein looked to the ground. He was not having a good rotation, and he made a mental note to pass his feelings on to his team, in particular to Johnson who would repent for his very existence – if he were ever found.

Francis Stein drew breath, he might as well continue with the bad news. 'In addition the authorities have asked us to post a reward for information received.'

And silence again lumbered into the boardroom.

'On the star-lit side I must congratulate the vice-president of customer-relationships and promotions. At our last board meeting I asked for someone to blame for our current fiscal predicament. Given the events that are about to unfold, I believe that our vice-president of customer-relationships and promotions has just presented himself front and centre for that particular honour,' concluded Joseph Firtop.

All eyes turned, and the members of Flush Away's executive board drew even further away from the now estranged vice-president of customer-relationships and promotions.

Francis Stein pictured himself carrying his beloved images, descending the steps that led outside, stripped of his precious golden key to the executive toilet. He shuddered.

Feeling without hope, cast adrift in the void, was that a voice he could hear? Could someone be throwing him a survival pod?

'Perhaps, if I may, I might give the fiscal perspective on this, after all it is all that is important,' ventured Chief Fiscal Officer Tobe Milton. He took control of the holoplay and, with a deft series of hand motions, projected a series of graphs and columns above the ancient oak table.

'Whilst I'm sure we all appreciate the risks that scrutiny by the media could have, this kidnapping could potentially be fiscally advantageous,' stated the chief fiscal officer.

This was a statement that caught everyone's attention, particularly the vice-president of customer-relationships and promotions who thanked providence for his good fortune and added his support with renewed positivity. 'Fine news, Tobe, fine news.'

'My initial estimation shows that we could achieve the following projected increase in revenue, based on an approximate assessment of the potential effectiveness of the inadvertent promotional opportunity that this situation could bring. This could translate to the highlighted improvement in our gross margin.' The holoplay flashed, and underlined numbers and columns hypnotically grew through the bottom line from red to green – a colour rarely seen at Flush Away's board meetings in recent solar cycles.

Tobe Milton continued, 'In addition, our cost base will be positively enhanced by the nett reduction in our salary burden due to the aforementioned employee's absence. In fact if the employee were to remain absent permanently not only would our free promotional opportunity be extended, but we would have achieved organisational downsizing without having to bare the normal restructuring costs and other associated charges.'

'Tobe, I knew there was a reason you were *my* right-hand male.' Chief Executive & President Joseph Firtop positively beamed, and there was a smattering of applause from the other executive board members, relieved that their, previously 'at risk', bonuses could be recovered.

Even the vice-president of fabrication, Tim Moontide, together with Luton Touch, the vice-president of merchandising, ventured their full support. They had recognised that Tobe Milton had identified an opportunity where they could share in the glory, but not have to take the responsibility.

'However,' expanded Chief Fiscal Officer Tobe Milton, who always felt that it was incumbent on him to detail the negative as well as the positive to the balance sheet of life, 'paying a reward would adversely affect this fiscal analysis, both in its direct nett deduction from the bottom line and, if the kidnap victim were to be found, the requirement to pay his salary burden. It should also be noted that there would be a negative impact on the projected increase in revenue, due to the reduced amount of free promotion.' And, with a practiced flick of his wrist, the recently green holoplay numbers and columns sank to red, much to the horror of Flush Away's board.

'Then our course of action is clear,' summarised Joseph Firtop, buoyed by this turnaround. 'Francis, draft an appropriate statement detailing who we are at Flush Away and what essential services we provide to the electorate. You know, all that good stuff about our products, whilst quietly stating that it is, unfortunately, against our corporate social responsibility policy to offer a reward. It would be good if you could get a reference or two in about the Empress irradiating sanitation unit, it's not selling as well as it might. Oh, and you'd better run it past our litigation department, I'm

223

sure they'll want to add some legalese sub-clause or other. You can then pass it on to the authorities to be included in the media conference next sunrise. Good work everybody, bonuses earnt!'

No one felt greater relief than Francis Stein, not least because he'd been referred to as 'Francis' by Joseph Firtop and not the 'vice-president of customer-relationships and promotions'.

* * * * *

Sunrise came, and at the appointed time slot Investigator Strait walked out to the waiting throng of reporters with their holocoms and hovering Eye Sight holocast bots. In a clear, unambiguous tone he announced he had a pre-prepared statement to read out and would take questions afterwards. He knew all he was about to say would be breaking news, projected across Pacifica, and then eventually jumped out to all the local systems this side of the Spiral Arm.

'We have reason to believe that this male,' Investigator Strait paused and looked up, amid a barrage of flashes, questions and calls, to the very much larger-than-life image cast behind him, 'that this male, one Johnson, a customer-relationship and promotions specialist employed by the Flush Away Corporation, has been kidnapped by an organisation calling themselves the Children Of The Soil.'

Investigator Strait thought he detected a certain amount of stifled sniggering among the reporters as they worked out the acronym of Johnson's job title, and with it an endless variety of 'catchy' headlines.

'We ask that the aforesaid organisation, the Children Of The Soil, release their captive immediately and turn themselves over to the nearest law enforcement agency. Failure to do so will only make their situation worse.' Investigator Strait again paused, this time casting his eye directly at the gathered media.

'And we ask all our good citizens out there, if you have any information that may help bring an end to this human tragedy, please step forward.' Investigator Strait put his pre-prepared statement down, signalling that he would take questions.

'Just some details, Investigator. Can you confirm when Johnson was so brutally kidnapped by this vicious gang of ruthless desperados?' enquired the first reporter.

'As far as we are aware, he was kidnapped during the last rotation or so. Next.' Investigator Strait selected the next reporter.

'Does Johnson have any immediate family? A distraught wife? Kids? Pets? Or any other relative dependant on him for their survival, someone who may die as a consequence of his cruel kidnap?' probed the next reporter.

224

'No. Next.' Investigator Strait's answer seemed to disappoint.

'Have Johnson's employers posted a reward for information leading to the victim's rescue, after what will be a doubtlessly bloody operation to capture and arrest these despicable kidnappers?' asked the next reporter.

Investigator Strait sighed and referred to the notes he had been given and told to read word for word. 'The Flush Away Corporation offers the Spiral Arm's most comprehensive range of ever-popular irradiating sanitation units. So why not plumb for the Dante and its Warm-It-For-Me posterior temperature sensing capability? Or, perhaps, you should plumb for the spectacular Empress and its unique Mould-It-To-Me seat. All available at a price to suit you, and what's this I read here? In fact there is no need to plumb: all irradiating sanitation units are standalone! What more could you ask?' Investigator Strait shook his head. He wondered whether he'd been given the wrong statement to read, but continued on with the unquestioning diligence that only twenty-five solar cycles of law enforcement service could bring. 'Suffice to say Flush Away is an organisation that's ethically committed, and, as such, believes that to make payments, or other such awards of goods or services deemed to be of value, whether for reward or ransom, is contrary to its corporate social responsibilities.'

There was now a unpleasant air of dissatisfaction among the gathered reporters: not because they'd just been subjected to a brazen and somewhat inopportune holovert on behalf of the Flush Away Corporation – after all, if it weren't for product propagation they'd all be out of a job – but because they'd been deprived of the offer of a reward. Every reporter knew a reward improved viewing figures. One reporter was heard to mutter, 'Never mind contrary to its social responsibilities, contrary to its profit statement more like!'

Investigator Strait coughed, took a deep breath and persevered amid the growing unrest. 'And furthermore the Flush Away Corporation wishes to thank all those agencies, planetary administrative bodies, media and members of the electorate who have, or will have, provided support and expressed good will. However, in summary, and under legal guidance, the Flush Away Corporation must confirm and clarify that it can accept no responsibility for, or liability from, the actions of third parties, arbitrary events or other acts of deities towards its employees, employee's families or other associated interests. A full transcript of this statement, together with a full exposition of all legally applicable references, will be made available on provision of acceptance of the terms and conditions detailed therein.'

'So no reward then,' précised the reporter who'd asked the question.

The rest of the reporters stared at Investigator Strait.

Investigator Strait said nothing.

And then, regaining the thread of the media conference, a voice asked, 'And where was our hapless victim so mercilessly taken from?'

'He was returning from a business meeting on Nova Vega. Next.' Investigator Strait nodded to the next reporter.

'Do the authorities believe the kidnap victim to be alive, or are they expecting his tortured and dismembered body to be forever lost, floating through the vast emptiness of space?' asked the next reporter expectantly.

'We have no information on that. Next,' replied Investigator Strait.

'Who are the Children Of The Soil, and what other monstrous acts have this murderous faction committed against the hard-working, law abiding and innocent citizens of Pacifica?' enquired the next reporter.

'Good question. Next.' Investigator Strait passed on to the next reporter.

'Have these pitiless, hard-hearted kidnappers demanded the release of yet more callous lawbreakers onto our already unsafe skyways and walkways, or a First Citizen's ransom in credits and a fast space-yacht to make their getaway with their ill-gotten gains?' ventured the next reporter.

'No. Next,' replied Investigator Strait.

The gathered reporters stopped jostling. There was a pause in the questioning. This was not the answer that the throng of baying reporters had expected. A lone voice uncharacteristically asked an unloaded question, 'So what have they demanded?'

'They have requested "organic restitution". Next.' Investigator Strait nodded to another reporter.

All remained silent and the last voice repeated his question. '*What* have they requested?'

'They have requested "organic restitution". Next.' Investigator Strait waited for the usual barrage of attention-grabbing noises and gestures, but none came.

The last voice continued, 'And as far as the authorities understand what does "organic restitution" mean?'

'We're seeking further clarification. Next.' Investigator Strait scanned the crowd; no one came forth with a question. He waited.

The gathered reporters were clearly disappointed and began to murmur among themselves as they disbanded. This kidnapping was proving to be less than interesting.

A voice emerged from the disbanding collective. 'So correct me if I'm wrong, the story is: you suspect a male has been kidnapped, but you don't know who by, or what they actually want; either way no reward or ransom will be paid, and as far as anyone can figure out no one will actually miss him.'

'Not an unreasonable summary,' thought Investigator Strait. However, he needed their help. The media conference hadn't quite gone to plan. He decided to appeal to their inner nature. 'I think what we have here is a *mystery*: a mystery with much speculative opportunity. Trying to solve the mystery is surely a story in itself.'

The disbanding collective of reporters stopped disbanding. 'And?'

Investigator Strait waited until he had their full attention. 'I doubt I could barely imagine the journalistic scope for reporting on a mysterious organisation that abducts an unknown male for a mysterious ransom demand. But I'm sure that reporters of your talents will be able to bring a whole new insight into this abduction.'

And, as a virus spreads, so the holocoms reappeared. Amid the ensuing hubbub Investigator Strait picked out the odd, well-worn phrase:

'Celebrity concerns…'

'Viewers poll…'

'Ten things to do when you're held hostage…'

'Hostage helplink…'

'Can you spot a kidnapper?'

And then, there it was, the inevitable: 'Could this be an alien abduction?'

And Investigator Strait just shook his head as the media feeding frenzy began.

[29] Seeing The Light

Chad did a double scan as he passed the holoplay. He stopped and then retraced his steps backwards as if rewinding in slow motion. His eyes were wide-open so as not to blink and risk not seeing what he was watching.

He was totally fixed on an image of Johnson and a commentary using words like 'Hostage', 'Kidnap', 'Demand' and 'Mystery'. No wonder Johnson hadn't arrived at the spaceport. Chad re-rolled the newscast, gasping with disbelief each time Johnson's name was mentioned. It turned out he'd been kidnapped by a group calling themselves the Children Of The Soil, and they were demanding 'organic restitution' – whatever that meant. As ever, the authorities hadn't a clue and were asking the good citizens of Pacifica for help. And the media were speculating over the possibility of alien abduction, as they did whenever there was the slightest chance that something inexplicable may have happened.

Johnson had certainly done Chad proud in drawing law enforcement attention away from his little sideline – not that Johnson knew anything about it.

It was never too early to celebrate. Chad poured himself a strong one and raised his plastiglass tumbler to Johnson's image projected from the holoplay. 'To absent friends, long may they remain so.'

Down in one. Chad chuckled and poured himself another. He raised his tumbler again. 'To Johnson, great stuff!'

From Chad's cosmic perspective the rotation couldn't have started any better. Johnson's kidnap would distract Pacifica's law enforcement agency away from anything he might do. What better time for his first, newly-routed delivery to arrive from Old MacDonald's World.

Chad finished dressing and left for work. And then it started: his holocom buzzed and buzzed, again and again. Messages were flooding in. Nothing travels faster than bad news. His workplace would be awash with gossip and supposition, a fertile environment for an experienced operator like Chad to sow the seeds of suspicion about Johnson. He couldn't wait to get there!

On arrival at Flush Away's reception Chad had barely managed to make a single tasteful innuendo at the ever-appealing Miranda's expense, before he was called into Ms D'Baliere's workspace for what he assumed would be a team debriefing about Johnson. But instead he found himself standing alone, door closed, plastiglass opaque.

Ms D'Baliere seemed uncharacteristically anxious. She paced the length of her workspace, occasionally stopping to pick imaginary specks from her immaculate business attire and muttered repeatedly, 'We are a team: what are we?' under her breath. She turned to Chad. 'Ah, Chad, take a seat, the team has a situation.'

Chad relaxed into the chair, coolly – even if he had to say so himself.

Ms D'Baliere looked directly at Chad. 'I'll come straight to the nucleus. Johnson's been kidnapped by a group calling themselves the Children Of The Soil.'

'I know, it's all over the media. Poor male. Who'd a thought he'd manage to get himself kidnapped? And just when you gave him the chance to do the deal of his life,' mused Chad.

'Yes, and therein lies the reason I've called you into my workspace,' interjected Ms D'Baliere. 'We do not know whether he did the deal or not. Suffice to say the executive board are somewhat anxious about the current state of our relationship with our number one customer. Mr Stein has made it clear he wants to be sure the deal is entered, coded and transacted as soon as possible. It's not an exaggeration to say that careers are at risk.'

'Mostly yours,' thought Chad.

'The team needs you out on the next starliner to Nova Vega.' Ms D'Baliere finally allowed herself to breathe.

'No problem, I'll get right on it.' Chad smiled.

The rotation was getting better and better. He had the fate of Ms D'Baliere in his hands. If the deal were to fall through, then it would all be Ms D'Baliere's fault for insisting that Johnson went in his place. If he were to secure the deal, then it would be Chad to the rescue! Fantastic job, Chad! He could feel the kudos surging through his veins already.

Great Stuff!

* * * * *

Jones managed to wheel himself past the file of monastic visitors. He was trying to catch up with Johnson. It was a relief to be inside; just spending a few photon phases outside had become unbearable under the churning heat of Nova Vega's intense yellow sun.

Johnson sensed the approach of Jones's rolling wheels, and looked back. Jones pulled alongside and matched Johnson's pace. 'By the heavens, it's an amazing place. Who'd 'a thought somewhere like this existed on a planet like Nova Vega, eh?'

'Yeah, who'd 'a thought?' Johnson seemed disinterested, distant.

Jones continued, 'It's certainly lived up to its promises so far. I haven't seen any females, nor gambling, nor alcohol, and I don't much expect to see any, though a long, cool carton of Drinkers' Delight would sure go down well right about now.'

Johnson nodded.

Jones pressed on with the conversation. 'Looks like this place has been a real revelation for William Robert, perhaps too much of a revelation, but

I'm sure he'll re-engage with reality soon enough.'

Both Jones and Johnson glanced behind to see William Robert trailing the file of visitors, his head lifted skywards, his arms outstretched.

'Or perhaps not,' concluded Jones.

The hooded monk drew to a halt outside a row of four large, imposing double doors. 'Brothers, we are about to enter the chapter house. In our monastery this is the one place where the spoken word is encouraged and debate promoted. All are welcome to share their thoughts or discuss whatever is on their mind. Once inside, feel free to listen to what is being said. You may contribute if you wish, but we suggest that you contain your contributions to those of a relevant nature.'

The hooded monk raised his hand and, aided by the wonders of infrared sensing and remote iono-hydraulic actuation, the four double doors opened. Inside, all was light and space. A vast open area extended out under a white domed roof. Light emanated from star-shaped windows that littered the whitewashed ceiling. And circling the walls were tiers of plain benches upon which monks sat. 'Brothers, you are truly fortunate. We are graced by the presence of Sigmund The Sane. Please be seated, you may find what he has to say enlightening. Unfortunately I have to take my leave of you temporarily, but I shall return.'

In the very centre of the chapter house an old male sat cross-legged on a star-shaped plinth, sporting a long white beard and little else.

'And all I have learnt is as nothing to the love I have for all. For there is nothing other than love. It is only through abandonment of all worldly ties, whether manifestly physical, or sensed, that the true purity of love can be found. Though the discarding of one's possessions and the casting off of one's attire may ease our load on the path to enlightenment; and though the solitude of the unbound desert may clear our senses, there can be only one step that will take us to our journey's destination.'

The old male looked from face to face as he scanned the attendant monks and novices until his eyes fell upon the yellow visitors' robes. He stood and ambled over, his lengthy white beard covering his pride.

Sigmund The Sane smiled a warm, fatherly smile. 'Ah, we have visitors. Welcome brothers, welcome. Forgive the idle ramblings of an old male who is surely beset by the effects of sunstroke. It's an occupational hazard if you spend your life seeking closeness to the Holy One at the top of a pole in the heat of the desert sun.'

He leant forward and, with a wink, confided, 'However, whilst such an occupation is holy and entirely commendable; as a life choice, if I may say, it leaves little to recommend itself.'

Sigmund The Sane looked around and, ensuring the monks were not listening, whispered casually, 'I don't suppose any of you have brought a drop of moonblaze with you?' Taken aback heads shook. 'A deck of cards perhaps?' Heads shook again.

'Now this may be a bit off the light barrier, I know, but are any of you females who've come disguised as males? It has been known to happen you know.' And again heads shook.

Sigmund The Sane seemed disappointed. 'No harm in asking. What is it they say? "If you don't ask you won't receive". I've always thought that to be one of life's more useful sayings. A lot more useful than some of the drivel I've spouted in my time.'

He began to turn away, but then added, 'Enjoy your stay, and a word to the wise from the wise, so as to speak: our little conversation is just between you and me. We don't want to go upsetting the monks now, do we? They work so hard at their beliefs you know, and I wouldn't want them to be let down. They take it all so seriously. Anyway, it's been a pleasure. Take care, and you should do what I say about the truth of life: "Enjoy it while you can."'

And, with the slightest of waves, Sigmund The Sane ambled back to the plinth and resumed his cross-legged position.

The hooded monk returned with open arms. Were his face visible he'd surely be smiling. 'Brothers, you've been blessed to have a personal audience with Sigmund The Sane. I regret that I missed what he had to say. He so rarely returns to the monastery, although when he does he always makes an effort to speak to our visitors. I do so hope you found enlightenment in the wisdom of his words.'

* * * * *

Investigator Strait was relieved he'd managed to recover the media conference – although that reporter had definitely put his sensor on it. They didn't know the identity of the kidnapper, or kidnappers, or what they wanted. All they knew was that the last time they'd seen Johnson was on the Liberty Discount starliner, planetbound from Nova Vega. They hadn't a clue how the kidnappers had managed to snatch Johnson from under their very scanners. Perhaps the appeal to the good citizenry of Pacifica would yield something.

Investigator Strait wondered whether the kidnappers might be back in contact after his media conference. Often the attention such holocasts brought was exactly what extremist groups looked for.

Anyway, the team was on it: Senior Deputy Sol Moon, Deputies Hildale and Ossman. Perhaps not the largest or strongest team he'd ever had the pleasure to lead, but you had to make the most of what you were given.

Deputy Ossman had already set up a multi-fragmented, cross-linked, multi-referenced virtual simulation evidence holobase. A task that, even

231

for the fastidious Deputy Ossman, was accomplished all-too-quickly. He then busied himself by issuing instructions on the holobase's use, application and interpretation, much to the disinterest of the rest of the team.

Meanwhile, Deputy Hildale was locked in a pointless argument about the benefits of youth over experience with Senior Deputy Sol Moon: he said he'd seen it all before, but she didn't believe him.

Investigator Strait stood and addressed his team. 'Right then, listen up! For those of you who know me, you'll know that I'm an uncompromising law enforcer. For those of you who don't know me, you do now. The only thing I care about is bringing lawbreakers to justice. And, as far as I'm concerned, everyone is a lawbreaker – it's just that some haven't broken the law: yet.'

Investigator Strait then proceeded to outline the case. Using the holobase he took the team through the time line and associated evidence. 'Any questions?'

Time passed, time that consisted of a painfully long, extended silence. The team had pretty much failed to ask any pertinent questions.

Investigator Strait sighed. The team sat with feigned attention, mostly bored. Eventually one of their number raised her hand and asked, 'So what do we do next?'

'Good question, Hildale. Firstly, Deputy Ossman will be in charge of recording, categorising and assessing all incoming evidence. I want a regular summarised update.'

'Yes, Investigator,' replied Deputy Ossman, glad that he wasn't going to be parted from his precious holobase.

'Secondly, we need to retrace Johnson's movements. If we can see the events that have happened through his eyes, we may find our way to him, and then to his kidnappers. I need a volunteer to act as Johnson's double.'

Having surveyed the mostly empty room, Investigator Strait decided to forgo the waste of time that waiting for a volunteer would be. 'Deputy Hildale, well volunteered. Senior Deputy Sol Moon and me will shadow and support you, coordinating all information gathered back to Deputy Ossman.'

'Yes, Investigator,' replied Deputy Hildale. At least she'd get some field experience, even if it was with a pair of old relics like Moon and Strait.

* * * * *

The monastic visitors continued to follow the hooded monk as he guided them on their tour of the monastery.

Johnson was pressed into being Mr Jones's aide when they came

232

upon the many stairs they had to negotiate. William Robert now followed directly in the footsteps of the hooded monk, staring skywards, hands apart. And, except for the occasional 'So be it', he remained unresponsive to any attempt at communication.

It seemed to Johnson that the monastery was a place where an unknowing visitor could easily become lost. The vast complex of buildings was a confusion of direction. Even when returning along a route previously taken it all seemed to be new ground. How the monks ever found their way around was a mystery.

The tour introduced them to the many different areas of the monastery. Johnson learnt new words that he knew would be of no use to him whatsoever in the future. However, one word hit a resonant frequency – call it professional interest if you will: 'garderobe'.

Time lost all meaning, as Johnson stood transfixed in admiration, oblivious to the group moving on. There was elegance to that hole cut into stone. For Johnson, whose life consisted of promoting the features and benefits of irradiating sanitation units, the garderobe had a purity, a simplicity not found in the products Flush Away offered. It was all you needed.

Behind him the group turned the corner and disappeared from view. He took a step forward and peered into the hole. Blackness and silence. And, with the confidence of the skilled specialist he was, Johnson sniffed the air. And there it was! One of Nature's truly unmistakable smells.

Johnson knew he had to experience the garderobe. He closed the door, turned, lifted his monastic attire and sat. The well-worn stone was cold and hard, but surprisingly comfortable. The posture it created had that perfect balance between positioning, for the necessities of bodily function, and being conducive to that other essential lavatorial requirement: contemplation. Had Johnson a holozine he knew he would be set for the duration. Why seek inner tranquillity and oneness with the Holy One, at the top of a pole in the desert, when it could be found so much more easily here.

Johnson jumped, his contemplation interrupted by a rap at the door, it began to open. He managed a 'Busy in here!' and the door closed quickly.

After Johnson had finished his 'contemplation', he left the garderobe with a twinge of sadness. He knew that he would have fond memories of his experience, an experience that was unlikely to be equalled in his professional career.

Waiting outside stood a hooded figure in a coarse brown robe. Johnson nodded to the figure as he passed, and the figure returned his acknowledgement by raising a hand to his head and giving a salute. The figure then entered the garderobe and closed the door.

Johnson proceeded along the passageway and turned the corner. He climbed some stairs and turned left, unconsciously choosing the second of three archways. This way ran straight for some distance, with adjoining corridors coming off either side. At the end the passageway opened out into a hallway with several doors and corridors radiating in different directions. Johnson turned left and soon found himself ascending spiral stairs that led to another hallway. Johnson followed the right-hand passage that gently curved away.

It was then that he stopped, as if woken from a trance. Where were the rest of the group? And more to the nucleus, where in the cosmos was he? He always seemed to be in a dream these rotations. It was time to re-sync with reality.

Realising he was lost, Johnson decided to return to the place he'd last seen the group and the place the group had last seen him; the garderobe. He turned around and followed the gently curving passageway back to the hallway to turn... Which way had he come? Surely he couldn't have forgotten the way back already!

Johnson thought. He then made a decision. He turned left and found himself descending spiral stairs. This seemed familiar – a thought he felt confirmed when he found himself in a hallway with several doors and corridors radiating in different directions. He turned right and walked along a straight passageway, passing adjoining corridors on either side. He emerged from the middle archway and turned right, down some stairs into a passageway. The passageway turned a corner and there, in front of Johnson, was a door. The garderobe? He knocked on the door and, not hearing a response, entered.

*   *   *   *   *

Chad had to depart for Nova Vega in haste. The only passage available was first class on the Silver Service Star Line, much to the ever-assiduous Miranda's annoyance and Chad's delight.

As he sat in the executive lounge, at Pacifica's U-Tan-U Spaceport, Chad allowed himself to fold back into the faux art cube-o seating. He looked, but could not see the charming Lucinda. Perhaps she wasn't on duty. No matter, there were more than enough other attractive hostesses to service his needs!

But time was short and, before Chad had a chance to order his favourite drink, he was called to his passage by a hostess holding a silver tray that bore a card with his name and seat number on it.

As was his way, Chad smiled at every one of the hostesses who had lined up to see the passengers onto the executive transit shuttle, and each smiled back. He still had the charm. He would make sure that, when next he travelled, he would have more time to share with them. After all they deserved it.

Following a short but comfortable shuttle transfer, Chad boarded the orbiting starliner. The starliner, named the Palladium, was described in the Silver Service Star Line's promotional literature as 'The Nova Vega Express, the discriminating traveller's choice' – although it was referred to by many as the 'Nova Vega Excess'.

Awaiting Chad, and all embarking passengers, was a line of well-presented crew together with an officer in full-dress uniform, who saluted as Chad passed. This was how the Silver Service Star Line had always greeted its passengers, and it was how the Silver Service Star Line would always greet its passengers.

The Palladium, whilst retaining much of its majesty from the halcyon era of grand interstellar tours, had now been made over to short-jump, high turnover entertainment in a bid to recover its ever-mounting operating costs. And whilst the themeing was deliciously subtle – in the eyes of the interior designer who had been commissioned to do the work – passengers were left in no doubt that they were being transported in a world singularly devoted to pandering to their vices.

Amid the recently installed gaming tables Chad felt more than happy. Here he was travelling through the heavens in his own personal heaven. Life didn't get much more enjoyable than this. After a few drinks he found himself betting on the outcome of a card about to be turned over; a bet he won, but not big – Chad never bet big.

Chad drifted on to the next table, and placed his winnings on the spin of a ball; a bet he lost. With a smile Chad moved on: never put good credits after bad. And so the passage was, for Chad, pleasantly amusing, but with no great gamble taken.

Time passed easily and, in what seemed like only a pulsar's pulse, Chad found that he was disembarking from the Palladium and landing in the executive transit shuttle at Nova Vega's austere spaceport.

On planetfall he managed to arrange a meeting with Ms Carlsson, head of the resources department, sanitation section, at the Creation Corporation. With the little luggage he'd brought, he ventured out into the overwhelming sensory assault that was historic Nova Vega to catch a taxi-skyrider to the Creation Corporation's headquarters.

Standing amid the bustle, Chad's eyes were captivated by the holoverts that hinted at Nova Vega's untold delights. Through their merest suggestion he found himself astride a bull in an arena surrounded by cheering crowds. He rose and fell with every toss of the bull's head, plumes of condensed breath billowing, its horns twisting in rage. The bull then charged for the gate. Chad involuntarily closed his eyes to avoid impact, only to find that he was standing in a vast gaming hall and a voice was declaring, 'For the ride of your life come on down to the Raging Bull Casino'. And then the images faded.

Chad looked to see where the taxi rank was and joined the queue. It was while he was waiting that a Go-To-Show novelty bot jumped down in front of him. Shaped like a pair of large inter-connected red dice, the Go-To-Show novelty bot danced in the air to attract his attention. It stopped, moved close and whispered something. Chad leant forward to hear what it was saying. It said, 'Touch me and see.'

Chad touched and the two dice of the Go-To-Show novelty bot's body span faster and faster, causing the bot to gyrate almost uncontrollably, until it seemed to hit an invisible wall and come to an abrupt stop. 'Lucky seven, you're in heaven, play me ag'in and you could win!'

Why not? Chad touched the Go-To-Show novelty bot and again it span turbulently before coming to a sudden halt. 'Lucky seven, you're in heaven, do it once more and you could soar!'

And so Chad repeated his action and the Go-To-Show novelty bot again span. 'Lucky seven, you're in heaven, you're a winner, one free dinner!' At which point the large inter-connected red dice flashed and the bot spat out a golden ticket. The ticket floated to the ground. Chad bent down and picked it up. By the time he had straightened he found that the Go-To-Show novelty bot had moved on. Who said there wasn't such a thing as a 'free lunch' or, in this case, dinner?

Chad boarded the next taxi-skyrider, which then lifted off and sped on towards the forest of skybreakers emerging on the horizon. It headed directly for their centre where stood his destination, the five golden towers of the Creation Corporation with their enormous, rotating 'CC' logo.

After the taxi-skyrider had descended to the ground, Chad exited and stood admiring the immense golden towers. They were simply breath taking. Chad checked himself – always be sure your attire is correctly fastened before meeting with a customer, particularly if the customer is female! He then stepped forward to pass through the light-screen doorway at the base of the southern tower and entered the marble expanse of the Creation Corporation's foyer.

The greetings associate was as efficient as the skybreaker suggested and soon the young, smart, and rather delicious – as Chad said to himself – form of Ms Carlsson strode across to meet him. They pressed hands and Chad, and his eyes, followed her to the skyvator to ascend to the resources department level and a meeting-room.

Ms Carlsson went to fetch Chad a caff-o whilst Chad sat waiting in the meeting-room.

The face of an anxious young male appeared at the door.

'Like, Chad, where have you been, man?' asked the anxious young male.

'Busy, Adam, very busy,' replied Chad.

'Like, I saw that other dude, man, the one who said he was you, but he left before I could like get any s**t, man.' Adam looked behind. 'I need some, man.'

'Adam, you're gonna' have to wait. There's a lot of law enforcement interest at this particular point in the space-time continuum.' Chad relaxed back into his chair. He liked desperate customers; they never worried about the price.

'I like really need some s**t, man.' Adam seemed increasingly anxious and disappeared behind the doorway only to reappear a pulsar's pulse later.

'I'm sorry, Adam, but the best I can do is later.' Chad shrugged his shoulders as sympathetically as he could.

'Oh, man! Like, when later, man?' Adam dived back out of the room again. Chad waited. Then, on cue, Adam returned to view.

'Don't worry, Adam, by the time the rotation is out. You know when it comes to s**t there's no need to plead, I've always got all the s**t you need,' smarmed Chad.

'OK, man. Usual place, just holo me. Don't forget, man.' And Adam bowed out for a final time.

Ms Carlsson re-entered the room bearing caff-o. 'Nice to see you again, Chad. I wondered when Flush Away was going to get back in touch. I had expected Johnson to confirm delivery details last rotation.'

'Ah, yes. Unfortunately Johnson is unavailable. But have no fear; I shall pick up where he left off. You can be rest assured that Flush Away will deliver everything promised for its most favoured customer.' Chad smiled.

Ms Carlsson was a busy female. 'OK, Chad, here are the details I arranged with Johnson. I expect confirmation in two rotations otherwise I will need to review the Poseidon Corporation's very price competitive tender. The Great Cosmic Chronometer ticks.'

'Of course, no problem, Ms Carlsson.' Chad inwardly gasped at the size of the order, but squirmed at the giveaway prices Johnson had agreed. However, to Ms Carlsson, Chad's outward persona remained as professional as ever. He showed that smooth, ever-present smile. He was too shrewd a player to ever give the game away. On the star-lit side, it was the largest sale he'd ever seen, and with the volume, even at these prices, there'd be some margin. 'I shall be on it straightaway. Great stuff!'

Ms Carlsson stood and wished him well. Chad hadn't had a chance to drink his caff-o, but he knew not to outstay his welcome. He too stood, thanked Ms Carlsson, bowed and took his leave from the meeting-room. He knew the way out.

As soon as Chad had left the skybreaker, he pulled out his holocom and made sure the order was sent via Galactic Union back to Pacifica. The order would arrive next rotation.

He smiled and then allowed himself to chuckle. The order would clearly have his name on it as the winning customer-relationship and promotions specialist. It would be an order for which he would be accredited. His chuckle turned into a self-satisfied snigger. Oh, and by the way, Johnson, it was an order for which he, Chad, would see the commission. His self-satisfied snigger bellowed into out and out laughter.

Eventually he managed to stifle his laughter and got into a waiting taxi-skyrider. Though he had to wonder, why hadn't Johnson sent in the order? Probably waiting to gloat when he got back to Pacifica. Big mistake Johnson! Take it from the master, when the deal's done you make sure you get it transacted with your name on it as fast as possible.

Chad felt pleased with himself; who wouldn't be pleased with being Chad?

* * * * *

It was confusing. The door sure looked the same. The room sure looked the same. And though the garderobe looked the same it was not the same. Johnson had an eye for these things. The curvature of the seat just wasn't quite correct. He gathered up his robe and decided to sit. No, it definitely wasn't right. He stood and then, after repositioning himself, sat down once again. No, it just wasn't comfortable. He arose, turned and eyed the seat. One last try. And with a deliberate, more forceful movement sat for a third time. There was a clunk then silence, and just as Johnson was wondering whether he'd broken something he felt the garderobe start to move, downwards, rather too rapidly.

Johnson grabbed the edge of the seat as he and the garderobe descended. He closed his eyes. This was a new experience. The bottom, in fact to be precise, the whole garderobe had fallen out of his world, and he was hanging on for his life.

He tensed, preparing himself for what he was sure would be a sudden and terminal impact, but instead he sensed his rate of descent slow. And then he and the garderobe came to an unexpected, cushioned rest. He opened his eyes. All was darkness save for a small, garderobe-shaped hole high above him.

Johnson stood. He was visibly shaking. Whilst relieved to be standing, on what appeared to be firm ground, his recent experience had taught him you never could be too sure. He wondered whether he would ever be able to sit on a toilet seat again without the trauma of what had just happened coming back to him.

Eventually he stopped shaking and sighed. It would be typical of his luck in life if he now started suffering traumatic flashbacks every time he sat on a toilet seat – it was not the kind of handicap he needed in his line of work!

Unwilling to succumb to such an irony, a more resolute Johnson pulled himself together. He was not going to let the little inconveniences that life dropped on him get him down anymore. He was going to face up to life's challenges with his head held high. And the first challenge he was going to face up to was to find out why he felt there was something not quite right about this monastery.

In the dim pool of light he could make out a door in front of him. He opened the door. He could see a corridor that extended into the shadows, lighted by glow globes. The corridor looked dark, but having survived the freefall garderobe, Johnson was determined to press on.

The corridor ended. He stopped. He could hear the faintest sound of voices, but where? There was no door, just a facing sandstone wall. He stepped forward and pressed his ear to the wall and, to his surprise, felt a rush of air. Suddenly he found himself bathed in bright light. The wall had slid away to reveal a large, open room and several hooded, white-robed monks talking to a figure in a coarse brown robe. A figure that had his hood lowered. A figure that Johnson recognised. A figure that…

And then, for Johnson, there was a flash of ionic blue light, the faintest twinge, and darkness.

[30] A Sign Of Things To Come

Jones rolled on, following the group of yellow-robed visitors who trailed after the hooded monk. Passageway followed corridor followed archway followed doorway, all cut in red sandstone block, their path lighted by sunlight from high-set windows. There was something deeply captivating about the grandeur and the solidity of the monastery. Every turn presented a chance to marvel at what seemed to be a timeless building created from the very fabric of the desert and its mountains.

It was proving to be a long tour though, and Jones was beginning to tire of pushing himself. He looked along at the group. Where was Johnson? Which one was he? With their hoods up he could not tell them apart, except for Billy Bob, of course, who'd taken station as the hooded monk's shadow, and was on what must have been his thousandth 'Glory be, praise the Holy One'.

Jones passed the group one-by-one, looking up to see which was Johnson. When he reached the devotional Billy Bob it was clear that Johnson was no longer among their number. Where could he be? What had happened to him? He tugged at Billy Bob's sleeve and made a pushing motion with his hands, which Billy Bob chose to ignore until Jones deliberately rolled over his foot.

'Ow! What y'all go 'n do that for?' stammered a hobbling Billy Bob.

'To get your attention, William Robert. Ever since we changed into these ridiculous yellow robes you've gone monastic and seem to have forgotten we're on a mission,' whispered Jones as loudly as he dared.

'I'm just tryin' to blend on in is all.' There was a hint of hurt pride in Billy Bob's voice.

'It may have dropped off your scanners, but we appear to have lost our charge,' continued Jones through gritted teeth.

'Y'all sure?' Billy Bob looked back at the group of yellow-robed visitors and then added, less than helpfully, 'They all look the same to me.'

Had Jones the reach he would have clipped Billy Bob around the head, but had to settle for a much less satisfying sigh of frustration instead. 'By the cosmos we'd better find him, or the Children Of The Soil's first *kidnapping* will have truly burnt up on re-entry. Come on let's let the monk know Johnson's missing, I'm sure he'll do something about it, after all I shouldn't think they'll want to mislay any of their visitors.'

'Brother, how may I be of assistance?' responded the hooded monk on having his robe tugged by Jones.

'We've lost one of our number, our colleague, the one who had a touch of...' Jones searched for the right word, 'sunstroke on our arrival, if you remember.'

240

'Brother, I do remember. The one who had a little too much, shall we say, spirituality? Let me count our group to check.' The hooded monk quickly counted off the group who had now drawn to a halt. He then checked them off again. 'Brother, I fear you are mistaken for I count as many as I counted when we started our tour. Are you sure he came with us? I would have thought, given the amount of *spirituality* he had imbibed, he may have chosen to remain and rest in his cell.'

'I'm absolutely certain he came with us. By the heavens, he was with us but a few photon phases ago,' insisted Jones.

'Brother, I have counted and checked our number, and we are as we started. Perhaps you too have suffered a little sunstroke.' And that was that. The hooded monk turned and continued the tour.

This was not good. Things were not going to plan. Star Trooper Jonah Jones began to feel that his 'Jonah' by nature was returning. 'Come on, William Robert, we don't want to get lost as well.'

* * * * *

Chad checked in and freshened up. The Tumbling Dice Casino was not his usual choice, but a free dinner was a free dinner. He just had to go and do a little something on the side before he commenced with the main business of the sunfall: having a good time at corporate expense! After all, he'd just sent in the largest order in Flush Away's history.

Chad picked up a taxi-skyrider outside the casino. The red, die-shaped taxi-skyrider, despite its un-aerodynamic exterior, was surprisingly fleet and nimble as it negotiated the poorly lighted skyways of one of Nova Vega's few industrial zones. Below were grid upon grid of desolate, easy-to-construct, prefabricated buildings, each titled with their business names: 'Screw-U Fastening Supplies', 'Big Jobs Interior Design', 'Bite Me Caterers', 'Paperette Clips – Your Stationery Movers', 'Aardbot & Soare – Furniture To Relax In'… If denebian driftbush had been indigenous to Nova Vega's ecosystem then it would have surely blown between these buildings.

Chad's taxi-skyrider stopped outside a warehouse identified by a simple sign, 'Flush Away Holding & Distribution', which, on closer inspection, went on to further explain to persons considering unauthorised entry, that there was nothing of value inside the said workplace, and that should said persons enter, then the Flush Away Corporation could accept no responsibility, or liability, for their well-being and welfare under any circumstance.

'Nothing of value,' Chad read aloud. Now that was not entirely true. The taxi-skyrider waited whilst he went inside.

In a seldom accessed, dusty aisle there sat sealed crates marked 'Do

Not Open – Bio-material – Sample Sanitation Unit Contaminants For Demonstration Use Only!'

It was in these containers that examples of all that humankind chooses to flush away were kept. The crates were deemed to be indispensable aids for any customer-relationship and promotions specialist seeking to evidence the capabilities of Flush Away's irradiating sanitation products.

Chad opened a crate and removed a cleverly disguised, irregular, cylindrical, brown package; a package that concealed leaf. Chad considered it somewhat ironic that he had managed to conceal his s**t amongst real s**t right under the noses of the authorities – even if those noses were pinched firmly at the time.

Chad slipped out of the warehouse the way he'd come in and walked to his taxi-skyrider. A few photon phases later and he was bound skywards, heading towards his next destination.

As expected, Adam was waiting outside the usual place, if pacing up and down like an expectant parent could be called waiting. The usual place was a hall of conveniences sited off one of the many concourses in Nova Vega's mass-transit hub.

Chad considered such a meeting place ideal. Those in need of relief did not stay long and certainly didn't look at their fellow convenience users. Not only did Chad feel comfortable, surrounded by the very objects of his trade, but also he could quickly put them to use if a potentially embarrassing package needed to be disposed of in a rapid manner.

And so the deal was made. Each party was careful not to be seen entering their adjacent cubicles at the same time. Once doors were closed the exchange was completed under the separating partition. As Chad left his cubicle he was less than amused by the rather loud, and all-too-audible, 'Man, I really needed that' pronouncement, together with the upwardly drifting smoke ring that came from Adam's side of the partition. Chad made a mental note that he'd have to have a word with Adam on how not to behave suspiciously.

Chad patted the credits he had put in his attire and strolled, as large as the cosmos, out to the taxi rank. It was now time for his free dinner back at the Tumbling Dice Casino, and then who knows what. Great stuff!

*   *   *   *   *

Under Pacifica's ever-grey sky there was much excitement among the junior team members of the Flush Away Corporation. It wasn't often that a law enforcement re-enactment occurred in your very own workplace. Of course, what added to the entertainment was the fact that the affable but befuddled, and some would say less than attractive, Johnson was being played by a strikingly eye-catching female law enforcement deputy.

To ensure that Deputy Hildale bore a passing resemblance to their suspect, the other law enforcement deputies used a floating holoprojector to cast a jerky, but still recognisable, holographic image of Johnson over her. As she moved so Johnson's image moved, giving a very passable facsimile. And above this projected image a rotating sentence of argon-violet words flashed in the air, 'ALL CITIZENS – SPECIAL BULLETIN – DID YOU NOTICE THIS MALE?'

And so Ms D'Baliere guided Deputy Hildale through Johnson's place of work. They retraced Johnson's steps. The starting point was Johnson's departure from Ms D'Baliere's workspace.

Senior Deputy Sol Moon stood on hand, with his Tell-It-All auto-transcriptor, ready to take a statement, should anyone come forward with new information, and Investigator Strait observed, recording events for future reference with his holocom.

As Deputy Hildale walked through the main workplace, Johnson's fellow employees looked on. They were supposed to be at their workhubs in the same place, doing the same thing as they did on the rotation that Johnson left for Nova Vega. However, many had chosen to line the route and, despite several focussed glares from Johnson's holographic image, just smiled and waved.

Several onlookers remembered what they had said to Johnson and similarly quipped at Johnson's holographic image, 'Hey, Johnson, been shown the door?' and, 'They've finally found you out have they?'

As Johnson's holographic image passed Flush Away's reception workhub, an ever-supportive Miranda wished it the best of providence, as she'd done to Johnson on that fateful rotation.

Noticing that someone actually seemed to care that Johnson had been kidnapped, Senior Deputy Sol Moon descended on the ever-courteous Miranda and made sure her statement was taken.

Outside, drifting rain washed across the steps that descended from Flush Away's grand colonnade. Johnson's holographic image became disrupted and appeared to blister, but then reform, with the slightest flash of light, after each raindrop passed through. The overall effect was to give an ethereal shimmer to Johnson's image, and for the image to positively effervesce. A further effect of the rain was to cause many of the letters in the sentence that rotated above the image's head to spark and then disappear, so that:

'ALL CITIZENS – SPECIAL BULLETIN – DID YOU NOTICE THIS MALE?'

Now reduced to:

'AL• •I•••ENS • •••••A• B•••••••• • ••D ••U ••••C• T••• MALE•'

Such can be the effects of random probability!

This deconstructed message, together with the other-worldliness of

Johnson's image, certainly attracted attention. There was a buzz among onlookers, who stopped and raised their holocoms to capture the scene.

Investigator Strait and Senior Deputy Sol Moon were too busy working their way through the crowd to notice the image's message had inadvertently changed.

One member of the crowd asked if the 'abduction' was true. Investigator Strait said that Pacifica's law enforcement agency was proceeding on the basis that the male in question had, indeed, been kidnapped.

Much to Investigator Strait's surprise, the citizen, and those around her, gasped. Normally you had to compel members of the electorate to show any interest; they were always too busy being busy.

However, it didn't take a countdown before the crowd had holoed the news, that an alien abduction had taken place, to everyone they knew, and everyone they knew had holoed everyone they knew, and everyone they knew had holoed everyone they knew... For hadn't a member of Pacifica's law enforcement agency just said that there had been an alien abduction?

And soon the media knew too.

[31] As Luck Would Have It

Despite the interest the re-enactment caused, Investigator Strait and Senior Deputy Sol Moon found that few citizens remembered seeing Johnson. However, one good citizen, wearing very smart footwear, did comment that he hadn't seen the male in the wheelchair for a while – the one who was usually drunk and hanging around begging. In fact the citizen was sure that the rotation Johnson had left was the last rotation he'd seen the male in the wheelchair. Investigator Strait nodded knowingly: Star Trooper Jonah Jones. He showed the good citizen an image, and the good citizen nodded. 'Yeah, that's him.'

It may be a small piece of evidence, but it could be vital. Jones, one of Pacifica's most persistent vagrants, had been seen in the same place as Johnson the last time Johnson was on Pacifica. Then, a couple of rotations later, he was seen again with Johnson in the Black Hole Casino on Nova Vega. This time it was Jones in the guise of a stellar gamblestar.

The rain eased to drizzle, and Johnson's semi-transparent holographic image, together with its message, returned to normal. The argon-violet words displayed their request in letters too large to miss, 'ALL CITIZENS – SPECIAL BULLETIN – DID YOU NOTICE THIS MALE?'

The law enforcement team arrived at the Sun Rise Cooperative Skybreaker, level six hundred and sixty-five, Johnson's level. After spending a few photon phases inside Johnson's co-op, they then left. Johnson's holographic image was now carrying luggage. However, Johnson's neighbours were conspicuous by their absence. Outside, the team hailed a taxi-skyrider, as Johnson had done, and travelled to the U-Tan-U Spaceport.

The law enforcement team made their way through the crowd towards the Liberty Discount Star Line check-in. Many watched, none came forward. The team passed eateries and retail outlets, customer service counters and administrative facilities.

It was as they passed the concourse conveniences, showers and left-luggage hall that, at last, someone approached. A spaceport security associate snapped a smart salute to Investigator Strait who returned it. 'I believe I have seen this male before.'

Investigator Strait looked the spaceport security associate up and down. 'When?'

The spaceport security associate straightened to attention and looked across at the crackling holo-image of Johnson. 'A few rotations ago, here in the left-luggage hall. He was in the process of committing a number of minor offences when I intervened. I issued him with a warning, and made a record of it at the time.'

Investigator Strait listened. 'You're sure it was the same male?'

'Certain, Investigator. Never forget a face.' The spaceport security associate beamed, and was clearly proud and excited to be involved in real law enforcement business rather than the petty trivialities he usually had to deal with.

'You said minor offences?' prompted Investigator Strait.

'Yes, Investigator.' The spaceport security associate referred to his holocom. 'Ah yes, here it is. Leaving an item unattended, dropping an item and playing ball games with said item.'

Investigator Strait looked up. 'And the item?'

'A uniform, Investigator, if I remember correctly. Struck me as rather odd at the time, but you get all sorts in this job so you tend to go with the solar stream.' The spaceport security associate remained at attention. He dreamed of becoming a law enforcement deputy, but despite many attempts he'd never quite made it. Perhaps this would be the opportunity he'd been waiting for. He'd heard that sometimes citizens got in because of what they'd done in the real world rather than answering a bunch of questions in a test.

Connections were being made in Investigator Strait's mind. 'A white full-dress uniform?'

'Yes, Investigator.' The spaceport security associate was impressed.

'You didn't happen to see what he did with it did you?' Investigator Strait was desperate for a providential break.

'He put it in one of the compartments, Investigator.'

'Which one? Show me.' Investigator Strait immediately strode towards the left-luggage hall. The others followed.

'What's this all about, Investigator? If you don't mind me asking,' asked the slightly breathless spaceport security associate, who was clearly not up on the events currently being played out in the media.

Investigator Strait turned and replied, 'Son, I don't mind you asking at all.' And then continued towards the left-luggage hall.

They arrived in the hall and the spaceport security associate led them to a row of compartments. 'I believe it was this one, Investigator.'

'Open it,' ordered Investigator Strait.

The young spaceport security associate looked nervous. 'Open it, Investigator?'

'Yes, open it,' commanded Investigator Strait.

'I can't without...' the spaceport security associate closed his eyes, clearly focusing on remembering the rules, 'the authority of the compartment's user, or the ratified instruction of two of the spaceport's vice-presidents, or unless there is a clear and defined emergency that may constitute significant risk to citizen or citizens; all in accordance with *Spaceport Security & Trade Transit Statutory Regulation A/781/D/897521,*

Investigator.'

Investigator Strait looked straight at the spaceport security associate. 'You forgot one.'

The spaceport security associate seemed confused. 'Are you sure? I thought I listed all of the reasons. Which one did I miss, Investigator?'

'The one that says because I said so!' erupted Investigator Strait. 'Open it, now!'

Visibly shaken, the spaceport security associate leant over and hastily opened the compartment. Investigator Strait pushed him aside and, with a look of pure satisfaction, pulled out the uniform. It was as he had hoped: the white full-dress uniform that Johnson had been wearing when, what seemed a lifetime ago, Operation Kicking Butt was all systems go.

Right then, if all their stars had lined up in conjunction... and there it was, in the uniform! A neatly wrapped but unidentified package. Investigator Strait held it out in his hand, and Senior Deputy Sol Moon instinctively passed his holocom over it. With one simple 'beep' the package contents were confirmed.

Investigator Strait held the package to his nose: leaf, odious leaf. He'd been right all along. There was a leaf-trafficking ring. Johnson was clearly part of it and he had evidence to prove it! Though, unfortunately, the evidence hadn't been found on Johnson. Anyway, he couldn't wait to see the look on Chief Garett's face when he dropped this package of 'beeping' evidence on his workhub.

He punched the air. Operation Kicking Butt was back.

* * * * *

Chad had no worries. Having eaten and drunk surprisingly well, for what was a free dinner, he rubbed his hands together and contemplated what pleasures Nova Vega's Tumbling Dice Casino might have to offer.

Chad liked risk, so long as someone else took it. And Chad loved credits, particularly if they were his. He strolled out into the casino's main hall as if he owned all he surveyed. He clicked his fingers and, on cue, a dice-like Made-4-U serving bot zipped across to him bearing a freshly filled plastiglass tumbler on a tray. One of its pencil-thin arms lifted the tumbler and handed it to Chad who, with a flourish, downed the drink in one.

With a confidence that only Chad could assume, he then meandered across to the Snake Eyes Beverage Emporium and eyed the females who reclined there, females who elegantly sipped their cocktails, idly passing their time. He sidled his way closer and offered an arm. A female dressed in iridescent cobalt-blue, with matching veiled pillar-box hat and complementary krypton-white gloves, accepted with a radon-red smile.

'How would you like to be lucky, my dear?' asked Chad.

And with a well-polished, professional air she replied, 'I'll be whoever you want me to be.'

'Great stuff!' Chad smiled.

Thus, with a female, who wanted to be lucky, on his arm, Chad walked across the low-lighted hall to be faced with three entrances signposted 'Heaven', 'Sea' and 'Hades' in phasing holo-imagery.

Chad turned to the female on his arm and, with a slight bow, said, 'Let me take you to heaven, my dear.'

She returned a smile and wished she'd had another drink.

Heaven had a predictably cloudy theme; supported by togas, lyres and gods. Its gaming tables were set adrift from each other, floating free, each guided by an individual god. To play customers approached a central pedestal upon which stood an old male in pearl-white drapes, matching beard and a lapel badge that proclaimed him to be 'Zeus'. Zeus then consulted a 'book', presumably checking credit ratings, and gestured skywards by holding his staff aloft with both arms. There followed a flash of simulated lightning and a crack of recorded thunder, and then one of the clouds descended upon which the customers were invited to embark.

Chad rolled and rolled again, and, as only Chad could, he won against the odds, much to the disgruntlement of the cloud's god. The name displayed on the god's crown of ivy was 'Dionysus', and he bore a drinking cup from which he drank and drank. Each time Chad won, Dionysus would issue forth a threat, or a curse, ranging from, 'May you be beset by passing flatulence,' to, 'By Zeus I will turn you to a pillar of salt,' depending on how much was won.

Chad continued unabated, delighting his companion, who saw the potential for her own income to increase proportionally. By now Dionysus's ire had turned from threat and curse to rant and promise. His gesticulations were such that the cloud they were on was becoming unsettled. This had not gone unnoticed by Zeus who, with subtle swiftness, made the cloud descend, and the now apoplectic Dionysus found himself replaced by what could have been a clone.

Again the cloud rose, and Chad rolled and rolled, his good fortune did not miss a beat. His *lucky* companion clasped more and more tightly to his arm as the winnings mounted. And then, despite the encouragement of the new Dionysus, who knew that the odds must play out in the end, Chad stopped rolling, and the cloud descended.

For now Chad was satisfied. Yet again he'd proved to himself, and for all to see, how wonderful he was. He'd won enough, it was time to stop, not least because the micro force field generator in his ring had run out of power and would no longer tip the dice in his favour.

Chad bowed and bade farewell to his surprised but grateful companion with a handful of credits. He then made his way to his room. Whilst Chad enjoyed flirting he had never had the courage to step over that line.

* * * * *

Simply put, Chief Garett had had a busy time. It was a period of time that had started with a simple question, 'Is it true?' and ended with gratitude, 'Why thank you, sir.' Of course, what's missing, in this summary of Chief Garett's 'busy time', is the intervening dialogue, discussion and colourful phraseology, together with the characters that provided it. Suffice to say the First Citizen Of Pacifica, a fair number of reporters and Investigator Strait were involved; and the subjects discussed essentially centred on 'Alien abduction', 'The electoral race' and, perhaps by way of consequence, 'Suitable careers for ex-law enforcement chiefs' – although not all parties were involved in all discussions.

To begin.

In answering the First Citizen's hololink, Chief Garett couldn't help but notice that there was a queue of media stacked up behind, waiting to be linked. It was going to be another busy rotation.

The First Citizen Of Pacifica had holoed his law enforcement chief, as he often had the want to do – for political and law enforcement issues were often intertwined, particularly during an electoral race. His question was simple: 'Is it true?' Calmly stated as though no further elaboration was needed.

Chief Garett smiled his pleasant smile on the outside. However, on the inside he had a feeling that this wasn't going to be good news. He was clearly being tested to see if he was on top of events, but as far as he could think, other than the Johnson thing, nothing much was up, and the Johnson thing would hardly raise the temperature of the current political debate. Totality in totality, it was probably best to be honest and risk showing ignorance. 'Is what true, First Citizen?'

'That *your* law enforcement agency thinks that Johnson has been abducted by aliens?' There was a disarming lack of emotion in the First Citizen's question.

Chief Garett continued to smile his pleasant smile, though he felt like his star had just imploded. 'It is not something that I'm aware of, First Citizen, but I shall investigate the matter immediately. May I ask who the source is?'

The First Citizen's reply was short and to the nucleus. 'The media.'

Chief Garett felt a rush of relief, and scrambled for the obvious way out. 'First Citizen, I would suggest that these stories we see, read and hear from the media are more about entertainment value than factual content.'

'Perhaps you should look at your holoplay,' recommended the First

Citizen.

Any relief Chief Garett had been feeling dissipated, like the ejected matter from a star that had just gone supernova, as he watched Johnson's holographic image being paraded through the walkways of Pacifica with the words, 'AL• •I•••ENS • •••••A• B•••••• • ••D ••U ••••C• T••• MALE•', clear for all to read.

'Ah,' seemed a less than fitting response, but it was all that the law enforcement chief could manage.

'Beeping fix it.' The First Citizen terminated their conversation.

Chief Garett looked at his holoplay and the queue of increasingly insistent media, but before he could sequence his thoughts and link to the waiting reporters, Investigator Strait appeared at his doorway. Chief Garett maintained his pleasant smile and bid Investigator Strait enter. He decided to hear what Investigator Strait had to say for himself before relaying the First Citizen's concerns.

Investigator Strait stepped forward into the chief's workspace and, with an air of confidence, placed a package on the workhub. Chief Garett rolled his chair from side to side, then reclined in silence, a little way back from the workhub, looking at the package before him. Investigator Strait had attached a large hololabel projecting the word 'EVIDENCE' in equally large radon-red capital letters.

Chief Garett and Investigator Strait each had a trajectory to follow, but who would launch first?

If Investigator Strait was anything, he was a male of limitless patience. It was a patience that was borne out of many solar cycles of law enforcement, a patience borne of many long sunfalls of surveillance work, of endless one-sided interviews and of waiting tirelessly for verdicts to be given in justice halls. It was a patience borne out of being Investigator Strait. He could sit and say nothing with the best of them.

And so it was the over-burdened law enforcement chief who broke first and, with a sigh, spoke. 'Aliens?'

Investigator Strait hadn't expected this. 'Aliens?'

'Yes, aliens.' And Chief Garett projected the newscast of Johnson's holographic image being paraded through the walkways of Pacifica, for Investigator Strait to see.

Investigator Strait sat and stared. He then shook his head and, deflated, released every last breath in his body, to sigh, 'Oh, no...'

'Oh, yes,' confirmed an ascendant chief of law enforcement, leaning forward.

Investigator Strait buried his head in his hands. 'It must have been some kind of fault. It's supposed to have said, "All citizens – Special Bulletin – Did you notice this male?". The holoprojector must have not been working correctly. The media are going to have an absolute feeding frenzy.'

The chief of law enforcement was surprised by how calm he felt in the circumstances. Perhaps it was the sight of one of his most seasoned law enforcement investigators on the verge of emotional disintegration. 'I think we should concern ourselves with the First Citizen's thoughts on the matter.'

'The First Citizen knows?' Investigator Strait's head dropped further, as a male awaiting sentence.

'Yes, the First Citizen knows. In fact he has asked us to, "Fix it",' replied Chief Garett, uncharacteristically managing to avoid using the expletives that so often formed the foundation of the First Citizen's conversations with him.

'Indeed,' responded a subdued Investigator Strait.

It was in the silence that followed that Chief Garett happened to look upon the package on his workhub. He then looked at Investigator Strait.

'Leaf,' replied Investigator Strait.

'Leaf?' repeated Chief Garett.

'Leaf,' echoed Investigator Strait.

The law enforcement chief sat back in his chair and thought.

Investigator Strait remained as if in stasis. Given the spectre of being attributed with another 'unfortunate' incident, he half-expected to be on his way to the archiving department.

However, it was not just Investigator Strait's career that had reached critical mass. Chief Garett was under no illusion. He knew he might soon be looking for work suitable for an ex-law enforcement chief. He decided on a course of action. 'Leaf you say, Investigator Strait?'

'Yes, sir,' confirmed Investigator Strait.

'All I can say is good work, Investigator. I always knew you'd come up with the evidence in the end.' Chief Garett's ability to speak with absolute conviction, but without belief, was a key attribute required for his job. Though those with a less complex view of life simply called this particular ability 'lying'.

Investigator Strait was confused, perplexed. Praise was the last thing he'd expected.

Chief Garett continued, 'There's no point in going back and trying to deny alien abduction, that would just add to the media's conspiracy theories. The only thing that's going to fix this is the successful repatriation of Johnson to Pacifica, and the apprehension of those responsible for his kidnap.'

Investigator Strait sat up.

Chief Garett leant forward. 'Perhaps I should re-instigate Operation Kicking Butt, maybe that'll lead to Johnson. After all, the only tangible thing we have been able to come up with is your evidence. Perhaps that package of leaf will be enough to appease the First Citizen and keep the media satisfied.'

Feeling reprieved, Investigator Strait listened.

Chief Garett then nodded to himself and concluded, 'Yes, that's what we'll do. Investigator Strait go round up your team. Find Johnson. And the best of providence.'

'Why thank you, sir,' replied Investigator Strait with relish and a smartly delivered salute. He then turned and strode out through the doorway.

Chief Garett had realised that all he could do was put Investigator Strait at the epicentre of the enquiry and hope he'd get lucky, or, failing this, that the sacrifice of the investigator's career would be enough to satisfy the First Citizen and the media. Either way he'd done his best; Investigator Strait was clearly in the firing trajectory.

* * * * *

Jones and Billy Bob continued to follow the rest of the monastic visitors on their tour. Jones had managed to encourage Billy Bob to be less conspicuously fervent by getting him to push the wheelchair with both hands, thus preventing those unfortunate periodic 'Glory be, praise the Holy One' episodes Billy Bob seemed to be prone to having recently.

Billy Bob did continue to mutter to himself. However, his under-the-breath utterances had turned from being of the religiously minded to those of complaint about being in servitude.

By the time the group had returned to the visitors' refectory the rotation had drawn to a close, and the brightly illuminated corridors had turned to passageways of darkness.

Following devotion, food was to be served, something the whole group looked forward to – though perhaps more in hope than expectation if the plain utilitarian bowl, eating utensil and beaker laid before them were any indication of the culinary delights to come.

Unfortunately, as they sat at the long trestle tables, their expectations came to be realised when grey-robed monks ladled grey liquid into their bowls.

Billy Bob, used to the abundant produce of Old MacDonald's World, could scarcely believe that what was being offered was food. However, he accepted it with good grace because he appreciated that it was taking him one step closer to the Holy One. Jones simply ate it. He'd had worse. When you served in the Space Corps you ate everything that was put in front of you for you never knew where your next meal was coming from.

Throughout their repast there had been no sign of Johnson.

When all had finished, the hooded monk rose and, after they had

252

washed their utensils in the stone water-trough, he led the group from the refectory. With incense burner swinging, heads were lowered and hands were raised apart, as all followed, echoing his chant.

The discordant single file proceeded to the cloister to take a sunfall stroll of silence and contemplation.

Jones managed to roll after the hooded monk and catch his robe.

The hooded monk stopped and turned. 'Brother, what is it you ask in our time of peace and reflection?'

'Where is he?' Jones looked directly at where he thought the monk's eyes would be, though all he could see was darkness looking down on him from that hooded, white robe.

'Brother, of whom do you speak?' The hooded monk was calm and measured.

'My colleague. The one I enquired of earlier. He wasn't in the visitors' refectory. Where is he?' pressed Jones.

'Brother, there is no easy way for me to say this, so I shall speak directly and plainly about what I have been told.' The hooded monk paused. 'It is with great sadness that I must inform you that the one of whom you speak has departed.'

'Departed?' Jones was taken aback.

'Brother, his soul has departed us I'm sorry to say,' replied the hooded monk in grave tones. 'He left us earlier I believe, despite our best efforts. I fear that he has gone to a much darker place. We offer devotion and hope that, in time, his soul may be saved and that he may eventually rest in peace.'

'But couldn't you have saved him?' asked Jones, hardly believing what he was being told.

'Brother, had we had the time, perhaps, but he went so quickly.' The hooded monk lowered his head further.

'But how can that be? He only had a hangover,' questioned Jones.

'Brother, sometimes such things can be more than a mortal human can bear,' replied the hooded monk. 'Perhaps we should offer devotion.'

'It's a little too late for that don't you think?' retorted a perturbed Jones.

'Brother, it is never too late to offer devotion.' The hooded monk maintained his calm. 'Do not be despondent, I am sure you will join your friend soon enough.'

'Join my friend! By the stars, what kind of monk are you?' Jones became enraged and raised his voice. 'Do you wish death upon all your visitors, or is it just the ones in wheelchairs you single out for that particular pleasure?'

All in the cloister stopped. All had heard Jones's outburst.

The hooded monk considered what Jones had said, and then, in a very composed voice, asked, 'Brother, why do you speak of death so? I would not wish such a thing upon you or any other living soul.'

'But you said I would join my dead friend soon enough,' stated Jones adamantly.

'Brother, which dead friend do you speak of?' enquired the hooded monk.

'My colleague, the one with the fatal hangover, the one who *departed* us. You know, the one you were unable to save!' There was clear exasperation in Jones's voice.

'Brother, your friend is not dead,' replied the hooded monk.

'He's not dead?' echoed Jones.

'Brother, why would he be dead?' asked the hooded monk.

Jones was confused. 'But you said his soul had departed us for a darker place.'

'Brother, yes that is true, he departed us on a passing supply transport bound for Nova Vega,' clarified the hooded monk.

[32] Have A Nice Stay

All was darkness.

And then there was light.

Light that was a little too bright. Johnson squinted and the universe around him came into focus. He was in a room with a door, a room that seemed familiar, a room illuminated by a narrow shaft of sunlight. He lay on a mat and was dressed in a grey, hessian-like robe.

He tried to remember.

'Johnson'. At least he knew his name. He remembered wanting to go to a monastery to get away from it all. He remembered... not much more. Surely he must have some sort of past? But no matter how hard he thought, nothing more would come to him. Was his past so truly awful that his mind had blanked it out completely?

Johnson groaned as he sat up, every part of his body ached. He looked at the door.

Johnson stood and managed to push the door open. Outside, and an arched passageway led to a large room with long trestle tables at which others, dressed in grey robes, sat. And in the large room, above the flagstones, a gold five-pointed star was suspended from the ceiling.

A tall monk in white flowing robes approached. 'Brother, I am so glad you are able to join us. I hope you are feeling better after your turn. Come, sit. Nourish yourself on the Holy One's devotions and his munificent bounty.'

Johnson sat. Johnson was relieved to sit. He recognised no one, for all sat in anonymity with their hoods pulled over their faces. In front of each lay a bowl, eating utensil and beaker, plain and empty.

'Brothers, let us now stand and give praise.' The tall monk gestured with his arms, and all stood, raised their hands and lowered their heads in devotion.

After all had given praise, the tall monk clapped his hands. A line of monks dressed in grey robes, wearing gold five-pointed stars hung from their necks, entered the hall.

The monks bore yokes, from which roughly hewn buckets were suspended. One ladle of water went into the beaker and one ladle of a grey liquid went into the bowl. And though the liquid had little taste or texture it seemed somehow familiar. For Johnson, anything familiar was comforting. And so he ate it all, as did the others, in silence.

When all had finished, the tall monk in white flowing robes rose, took his utensils in hand, and walked to the large stone water-trough by the door. He then lifted an incense burner from the wall and left the hall, head lowered, hands raised apart.

255

The others then followed in seating order, Johnson too. And, as they walked in slow single file, deliberate step after deliberate step, the tall monk began to chant a low monotonous tone, swinging the billowing incense burner in time. With each chant the others responded with a subdued counter-call. But somehow these simple tones echoed and reverberated along the stone corridor to become much more.

It was a devout orchestration that welled from the shadowed figures as they stepped their way through the half-lighted incense smoke.

Johnson began to wonder if he had found a calling greater than his worldly life. The problem was that it was hard to know; he had no recollection of a worldly life whatsoever. For all he knew he was a monk, that would certainly account for his lack of a past to recall. But the more he thought about it the more it troubled him.

Thus, it was worry rather than devotion that filled Johnson's mind as he proceeded with his monastic journey.

*　*　*　*　*

It was more than Jez could believe. What had Cousin Billy Bob gone and done? Could it be true? Could Billy Bob have single-handedly and prematurely started the organic revolution that Jez dreamed of?

If what he saw and heard were true, Billy Bob had only gone and kidnapped Johnson. What could have got into that scratcher's mind?

Jez had always considered Billy Bob to barely have the wherewithal to fertilise his own soil never mind mastermind a kidnapping. And yet it appeared that he had gone and done it; and done it without discussing it with his kinfolk, and, more specifically, without Jez's own say so. Had Billy Bob's mind turned to mulch? This wasn't the organic way, what was Billy Bob thinking of?

As Jez watched the newscast play out over the holoplay, he could scarcely take it for truth. The masses' awareness of the Children Of The Soil had just gone supernova this side of the Spiral Arm. There was an image of Johnson. The holocast presenter said that the Children Of The Soil had kidnapped him and were demanding 'organic restitution'. However, Pacifica's law enforcement agency had now raised the possibility that aliens had abducted Johnson, and the Children Of The Soil were only a deception. At which point, Jez watched Johnson's holographic image walking through Pacifica with the words, 'AL• •I•••ENS • •••••A• B•••••••• • ••D ••U ••••C• T••• MALE•', clearly legible, rotating above his head.

But as Jez watched he realised that whilst the phrases, 'Children Of The Soil' and 'organic restitution', were being repeatedly transmitted, the media were making no attempt to explain who and what they were. The emphasis was on alien abduction.

And, to further rot his crops, their fundamental principles were being completely passed over in favour of what looked like a free holovert for the so-called benefits of Flush Away's irradiating sanitation products.

The more Jez watched the more he became incensed, and the more he became incensed the more he was convinced that he would have to deliver the 'organic word' directly to the masses himself. He would have to go offplanet. He would take a passage to Pacifica and make the true voice of organic fundamentalism heard. It was time to ensure the seeds of the organic revolution were sown properly, and that organic matters were propagated correctly.

*   *   *   *   *

Mary Usherman was more than surprised by her son's desire to travel to Pacifica. He had never expressed any interest in interstellar travel before. In fact he had often described it as 'unorganic', a term that she had come to understand to be dismissive and derogatory when used by Jez and his friends.

Jez had explained that he needed to meet with Mr Tree to discuss some concerns he had with the crop variant they were growing. Jez had said it was about time he stepped off Old MacDonald's World before he grew roots.

She could only agree. Perhaps, if he saw more of the universe, he would become a little less obsessive about all things organic. Whilst she was proud that he had his beliefs, and supported him fully, it was the lengths he would go to in the name of his principles that drove her to distraction: the organic toilet being a case in point. It was all very well and good, but when you needed to go in the depths of the fallow season, having to trudge through the snow to use it was a less than pleasant experience. Yes, you did get accustomed to the smell, but sometimes, during the intense heat of the growing season, it could be just a little too much even for her well-acclimatised olfactory sense.

However, Jez seemed a little disgruntled when she told him she wanted to go too – such is youth. She needed a change of scenery; she had not been to Pacifica since... since Jez was born. Wistfully she remembered how much she had wanted to travel the stars. Well, no time like the present. After all, she, like the rest of the universe, was not getting any younger.

Perhaps Amy Mae might like to come too; she would be good company whilst Jez met with Mr Tree.

*   *   *   *   *

Nova Vega's sun blazed bright in the red, fading-to-pink sky. Its heat fell heavy on the backs of those who toiled under it; a sensation that Billy Bob was all too aware of as he strained to push Star Trooper Jonah Jones onto the Starshine Tours dirigible.

Jones couldn't wait to leave. The monastic life was not for him. It felt good to be rid of the hessian-like robes. It felt even better to be returning to his 'spiritual' abode: the conurbation of Nova Vega and its cathedrals of entertainment, the casinos.

When all those who had chosen to leave were aboard, the droning ionic drives picked up pitch and, with a rasping scrape, the dirigible eased away from the tower to head out across the boundless dunes of the Red Sand Sea.

Billy Bob looked back. The vast complex of irregular red and white buildings, topped by its gold five-pointed star radiating in the sunlight, started to shrink from view. Whilst he missed Old MacDonald's World he could see the appeal of a monk's life: ordered routine, no distractions, and no surprises. What was the word? 'Simple.' 'Simple' suited Billy Bob; he'd even called his procyon hound dog 'Simple'.

Billy Bob knew that he'd promised Cousin Jez he'd see his mission through, and he would, but he longed for Old MacDonald's World. He so missed working on the farmstead. He so missed his family. He so missed his dog. He knew he was no organic revolutionary. He was a farmer. He'd get this mission harvested and in the silo, and then he was going back to his homeworld.

Across the aisle, with his head pressed against the window, and the Red Sand Sea passing by, Jones pondered how they were going to 'recapture' Johnson.

And time passed, and for those who couldn't wait the sprawled expanse of historic Nova Vega eventually came to view. A view that centred on the gathering of brightly lighted skybreakers that formed the core of the conurbation. And at their heart stood the five golden towers of the Creation Corporation, towers that arched together to form a single pinnacle pointing at an enormous, rotating 'CC'.

As the dirigible overflew the outskirts it began to slow, manoeuvring to dock at Nova Vega's mass-transit hub. From the sky the hub looked like an enormous spider's web radiating into the conurbation's very fabric.

The dirigible descended. Against the strained drone of its drives, and the intermittent beeps and buzzes of warning devices, Jones leant across to Billy Bob and said, 'It sure is good to be back. All we gotta' do now is find our friend Johnson and keep him entertained.'

Billy Bob was about to reply when, with a judder and a clang, the dirigible came to rest. But before he could speak, a voice boomed out, 'Valued passengers, we have arrived at our final destination, the Nova Vega mass-transit hub, and, on behalf of Starshine Tours, the corporation that "puts the shine in your star tours", I'd like to thank you for travelling with us and wish you a safe onwards journey. We hope to see you again on one of our many specialist tours for the discerning adventurer. And, as we like to say, "Have a nice stay!"'

Jones descended the disembarkation ramp under his own momentum and rolled at speed along the concourse. He looked back and with a sweep of his arm he signalled to Billy Bob, shouting, 'Come on, Billy Bob, we've got a reunion with the Prophet Of Providence at the Black Hole Casino!'

[33] Here We Come

Chad was a creature of executive lounges. It was his natural habitat. What he liked most, other than the word 'executive', was that they pandered to his desires, and Chad liked to have his desires pandered to. They couldn't do too much for him; his every whim would be satisfied – that is almost his every whim.

The Silver Service Star Line's executive lounge at Nova Vega's spaceport was particularly opulent. The faux art cube-o décor had a gilt-edged splendour to it, and the hostesses... well, it had to be said: the hostesses were simply celestial. Even the luscious Lucinda would struggle to hold a glow globe to these females. They had a glamour to them that just seemed to match Nova Vega's character. Chad was pleased he'd arrived with a time-slot surplus in his schedule.

Having surveyed his surroundings, Chad decided it was never too early to have a drink, and attracted the attention of a hostess named Genieve, who seemed to be able to maintain the perfect smile, even when speaking. He ordered his drink.

When she returned she placed the Skotch on a silver-coloured coaster in front of him. As he admired her he had to admit he could detect no imperfection in how she looked, how she spoke or how she moved. Everything was graceful, effortless, flawless, perfect: truly great stuff!

Chad simply had to have another drink just to watch her again. He winked at Genieve. She smiled back and positively floated over to him. He was transfixed. All he could hear were the words, 'For your pleasure, sir', as he gazed up at her. It was as if she could read his mind.

She reached down to take his empty plastiglass tumbler. He was so entranced he forgot to let go, however she continued to lift it, oblivious to the fact that Chad was attached. Chad found that he was being pulled up by a relentless force, and was half in the air before he relaxed his grip and fell back into his seat. Genieve carried on and walked to the beverage counter to get Chad's refill.

Now that was what Chad called attraction!

Chad looked around, feeling somewhat self-conscious at having been lifted clean out of his seat. No one, save a Silver Service Star Line technician, had seen the incident. Chad sat back, closed his eyes and, with a deliberately measured exhale, unwound. Perhaps it was too early in the rotation to have a drink.

When Chad opened his eyes it wasn't the perfect Genieve who stood before him, it was the Silver Service Star Line technician. The technician leant forward, giving a conspiratorial glance to either side, and whispered, 'On behalf of the Silver Service Star Line I'd like to apologise for that little mishap, sir. I'll make a note and get her adjusted. She is almost perfect though, isn't she?'

Chad was a little taken aback and just nodded.

The technician knelt down closer to Chad. 'You know I've seen that all males desire her, though each sees something different.'

Chad felt himself blush, his pale grey complexion registering a lesser shade of red on the embarrassment scale. But as he looked across at the beverage counter, expecting his drink to be brought forth, he saw Genieve and the other hostesses leave through an 'Associates Only' exit. Oddly they appeared to march in time in a very deliberate and regimented way. Once they'd gone from view, another file of hostesses ambled into the executive lounge in a most un-regimented way. A shift change perhaps?

Chad collected his thoughts. 'You said adjusted?'

'Yes, sir, adjusted so she doesn't use so much force. I'll get the servo control loop reset,' replied the technician in a more business-like tone.

There was something of a pause in the conversation whilst Chad tried to process the implications of what the technician had said.

'You're telling me she's not human, aren't you?'

'Why yes, sir, very real though, sir, a fabulous Sim-U-Sapien, crafted by the Creation Corporation. You know, it's simply amazing what they can do.' The technician handed Chad a Touchpaper sheet. 'May I say, sir, we would be most grateful if you would complete this questionnaire.'

Chad was floundering for words and resorted to repeating the last word spoken. 'Questionnaire?'

'Yes, sir, we'd like you to give us feedback on our Sim-U-Sapien hostesses. They're on trial at this juncture in the space-time continuum and we're evaluating their performance. Just touch the appropriate response against each of the questions, and the Touchpaper will record and send your comments for collation. When you've done, the Touchpaper will evaporate with just the smallest of puffs of non-toxic smoke, though that's really more for effect than anything else. We thank you for your assistance, sir.' The technician then gave a courteous bow.

Chad nodded open-mouthed, and the technician moved on to another customer. Thankfully, just as he really needed it, his drink was served, though this time by an all-too-human hostess who was clearly less than impressed by the whole affair. She scowled at his mesmerised face and said knowingly, and with bitter recrimination, 'Before you complete that questionnaire, sir, let me just say that they may look beautiful, but they are a little incomplete, if you know what I mean, sir.'

* * * * *

Having decamped from The Black and reoccupied their former incident-room in the U-Tan-U Spaceport, the members of the newly reconstituted, and somewhat enlarged, Operation Kicking Butt crowded round the holoplay.

Amid the clatter of boots, body armour, assault blasters and the loving unsheathing of combat knives Investigator Strait positively swelled with pride. He was back in charge of his operation. He even had extra resources. It couldn't have worked out better if he'd planned it himself. Operation Kicking Butt was alive and kicking again, and the air was agitated with the wit and banter that only a roomful of testosterone-pumped law enforcement deputies can bring.

'We're back!' announced Investigator Strait. 'Operation Kicking Butt kicks butt!'

Investigator Strait bathed in the adulation of his assembled team, who were more than pleased to be released from administrative duties.

'And this time we're bigger, better, stronger,' added Investigator Strait.

The cheering continued.

'We have evidence!' proclaimed Investigator Strait.

More cheering.

'And we have suspects,' declared Investigator Strait.

Yet more cheering.

'All we have to do is go and arrest them!' urged Investigator Strait.

Rapturous applause.

'I said it before and I'll say it again. We will not rest until this, the biggest leaf-trafficking ring of contemporary times, is broken, and the ruthless interstellar lawbreakers who run it are incarcerated.'

Investigator Strait held his arms aloft to a standing ovation.

He looked slowly across the team, and his gaze fell upon Deputy Hildale. 'This will be no vacation!'

After the initial euphoria had died down, Investigator Strait returned to business.

'Right then, for those of you who haven't had the pleasure we have retained the services of Senior Deputy Sol Moon, Deputy Ossman and Deputy Hildale.'

There were wolf-whistles, to which Deputy Ossman looked confused and Senior Deputy Sol Moon took, what he considered to be, a well-deserved bow. Whistles turned to jeers. Deputy Hildale turned red.

Investigator Strait coughed. 'Indeed, these deputies will continue to investigate the kidnapping of Johnson, the Flush Away employee who, by *coincidence*, also happens to be the principal suspect in our leaf-trafficking investigation.'

Deputies D'Angelis and Gilbrae sat at the back of the incident-room and said nothing. They had an underwhelming sense of déjà vu about

'Operation Kicking Butt 2', as they now termed the operation – though only among themselves. The investigation was being led by old, tried and trusted Investigator Strait. You knew where you were with Investigator Strait: always at the core of events, but mostly nowhere near solving the case!

Which wasn't exactly what Senior Deputy Aloysius O'Herd was thinking. He was beginning to believe he had only two types of luck: no luck and bad luck. Having just wasted half a solar cycle achieving nothing with Operation Kicking Butt the first time round, he could simply not understand how Investigator Strait could be put in charge for a second time. Who could figure the minds of those in authority? All Senior Deputy O'Herd knew was that it was about time someone recognised his abilities and gave him a chance.

'So first we must find Johnson and his accomplices: Star Trooper Jonah Jones, Billy Bob Brown and Paolo "Two Fingers" Cigstano.' And then, in an effort to be a little less dictatorial in his approach, Investigator Strait opened up the meeting to his assembled team for questions. 'Thoughts anyone?'

Deputy Hildale's arm went up immediately. Investigator Strait continued to survey the room in the hope of finding an alternative, but time did not come to his rescue. 'Yes, Deputy Hildale.'

Deputy Hildale stood. 'You know, if Johnson and his accomplices are leaf traffickers then this whole kidnap thing could be nothing more than a ruse to put us off the vapour trail of what's really going on.'

The gathered law enforcement deputies hushed.

Deputy Hildale continued, 'What better than to have the authorities chasing after some fictitious extremist group while they conduct their real business of leaf trafficking. I mean who in their right mind would call themselves the "Children Of The Soil" and demand "organic restitution"? It doesn't make sense. I think it's all a simple deception to throw us off their trail.'

The hush turned to silence.

'Ask yourselves: how can a male disappear from a starliner in the middle of the interstellar void?' Deputy Hildale revelled in her acuity.

At this there was much muttering, and an indistinct voice mumbled, 'Alien abduction.'

There was a rowdy cheer.

Investigator Strait leapt forward and demanded, 'Right then, who said that?' To which he received many stifled sniggers, but no answer.

Deputy Hildale shook her head and, with an exasperated roll of her eyes, sighed. 'Johnson didn't disappear in the middle of the interstellar void because he was never on the starliner in the first place.'

As a wave, confusion washed over the gathered law enforcement deputies. The pain of their thought processes struggling to understand was all-too-visible.

Deputy D'Angelis spoke up, 'But we saw him, we followed him from the casino to the spaceport and onto the starliner.'

'Are you sure? Did you see him clearly? Did you see his face?' questioned Deputy Hildale.

The conversation went into stasis, briefly, while Deputy D'Angelis considered his answer. Investigator Strait was still scanning the audience in search of who'd made the 'alien abduction' comment.

'Thinking back, I can't say that I did get a clear view, but Investigator Strait and Deputy Gilbrae were with me, they certainly did.' Deputy D'Angelis looked at Deputy Gilbrae and Investigator Strait. Their faces betrayed nothing. 'Didn't you?'

And then the bickering and recrimination started.

'Quiet!' bellowed Investigator Strait. 'So if he wasn't kidnapped from the starliner where is he?'

'I'd start at the last place you can confirm seeing him and take the trail from there.' Deputy Hildale sat down, pleased with herself.

Investigator Strait's mind went into hyperboost. A kidnapping that wasn't a kidnapping, a ransom demand that made no sense, and a victim who simply vanished. And, to eclipse it all, if anyone mentioned 'alien abduction' again he wasn't going to be responsible for his actions!

There must be a simple answer to all this. Investigator Strait entered his *concentrated cognitive thought* position. For those who had seen this before it was worrying.

* * * * *

With a puff of non-toxic smoke the Touchpaper evaporated. Chad had completed his Sim-U-Sapien hostess questionnaire. From an initially favourable impression, and after much deliberation, Chad decided to mark them down as a bad idea.

The dilemma over the hostesses had caused Chad's thoughts to scatter to the solar wind. He needed to collect them; he needed to focus.

Now, if there was one thing Chad could do quickly, it was focus. For Chad it was simple. He would concentrate on the epicentre of the universe: himself.

Chad's First Rule: it wasn't what he knew; it was who he knew.

He knew that Johnson getting 'lost in space' was sure to reflect badly on Ms D'Baliere's judgement; and if she looked bad so would Francis Stein. He needed to make more capital of that. If you can't rise up then bring them down. A few well-chosen words about how the Creation Corporation account had been handled, say in the ear of the vice-president of conception and evolution, and questions about her competence would surely be asked. All behind closed doors, of course.

Chad's Second Rule: it wasn't what he did; it was what others thought he did.

Chad had just secured Flush Away's biggest deal and, as far as the corporation was going to be concerned, he'd saved them from going down the pan. He needed to ensure that he was going to be portrayed as 'Chad The Saviour'.

Chad's Third Rule: always leave them with a smile.

Chad sat back and dreamed. He imagined being carried aloft through the workplace by his co-workers, applause echoing in his ears. And there, before all, he would be set down in front of Flush Away's executive board. In the quietened calm, amid the rapt attention of his colleagues, a small ceremony would be held. He saw a golden key torn from the neck of Francis Stein and passed to him on a cushion by a beaming Joseph Firtop. And he, Chad, would be flushed with pride as he received that golden key to the executive toilet, the key that opened the door to his future. Ms D'Baliere would be in tears, demoted to a mere customer-relationship and promotions specialist to be at his command and control. And, as he held the golden key aloft, there would be raucous cheers, and he would smile.

A now impatient Chad thought that it must be time to board the executive transit shuttle to rendezvous with the Deuterium, one of the Silver Service Star Line's most prestigious starliners. The executive lounge was crowded; historic Nova Vega was always popular. Finally, a hostess bearing a card on a silver tray approached. It was time to embark, time to return to Pacifica, time to return to his destiny.

Chad made his way to the shuttle departure point past the customary line of Silver Service Star Line hostesses. Not all were smiling, though Chad made sure he smiled at each and every one of them as he past, saving his most charming wink for the hostess who had scowled at him earlier. To his great relief she smiled back. The balance of order in the universe was restored.

Aboard the smart, sleek executive transit shuttle, Chad sat comfortably in his Save-Your-Soul passenger seat and admired the faux art cube-o interior. Chad relaxed as the executive transit shuttle lifted off.

With Nova Vega's Red Sand Sea well below, the red, fading-to-pink horizon darkened as the shuttle passed through the upper atmosphere. The shuttle broke into orbit and began to re-orientate itself towards a distant dot: a dot that barely stood out from the mosaic of stars that lighted space. As the shuttle approached, Chad recognized the familiar hemispherical outline of a Smith Starship Company starliner, presumably the Deuterium. Their rendezvous was imminent.

After the shuttle had docked, Chad marvelled at the shower of iridescent ice particles that floated past and the towering form of the Deuterium looming above. But this scene was dwarfed by the endless bounds of the Spiral Arm beyond, as it meandered across his panorama only to be lost, in turn, in the immense darkness of the void.

Chad nodded as he strolled past the line of well-presented crew and proceeded to the enormous central atrium of the starliner. A plastiglass skyvator took him to the main passenger deck where one of the awaiting hostesses showed him to his seat.

When all had embarked, and the transit shuttle decoupled itself, the Deuterium began its slow passage to draw a safe distance away from Nova Vega in readiness for the jump to Pacifica.

Chad closed his eyes and, with little effort, fell asleep.

*   *   *   *   *

There was no doubt in Investigator Strait's mind that Johnson was the key: whether to kidnapping, or leaf trafficking. And whilst it pained him to admit it, Deputy Hildale was right; they should go back to Johnson's last confirmed sighting and see if they could pick up the trail from there. Unfortunately that place was the gaming hall of the Black Hole Casino on Nova Vega.

He would have to go to Chief Garett and seek permission to mount an offplanet operation. That permission would undoubtedly mean administrative transactions to be agreed, approved, validated and ratified. He sighed, but was resigned. What had to be done, had to be done.

Investigator Strait looked up at The Black, the very edifice of law enforcement that so dominated Pacifica's skyline. It seemed to be the one immoveable object in an ever-changing universe, the constant that kept all things in check. Its merest presence moderated behaviour. However, he knew as soon as he stepped across its threshold he would become ensnared in the bureaucracy and politic he'd struggled so hard to keep away from. He took a breath and stepped inside.

Chief Garett smiled that pleasant smile that belied the true emotion he felt. His meetings with Investigator Strait were becoming more frequent and, with each meeting, he felt that his control was slipping away. Though, it had to be said, he much preferred his meetings with Investigator Strait to his short and stressful conversations with the First Citizen. He wondered what Investigator Strait would pull out of the ether this time.

'Nova Vega'. The words hung in the air for all to see. Chief Garett's mind cast back to the unfortunate incident involving the goodwill ambassador and Investigator Strait; he shuddered. He understood that it made sense to start searching from the place where Johnson was last confirmed to be. But what would the First Citizen think? Perhaps it would

266

be best not to trouble the First Citizen over Investigator Strait's request.

To get positronic, a high profile and successful law enforcement operation was always a vote-winner with the electorate. It always made a good story, and that in turn made him look good, which significantly increased his chance of retaining his tenure if the First Citizen were to be re-elected. Although the media had, in the past, maliciously and without good reason, hinted that such timely law enforcement operations were staged; something that he and the First Citizen always vigorously denied.

On the negative side there was the risk that the operation could go horribly wrong. This would be much to the media's amusement, and would thus be sure to receive plenty of adverse coverage leading to an unhappy First Citizen and the search for a new career.

Chief Garett's mind recalculated as he thought about giving approval to Investigator Strait's request. He pictured himself stood next to Johnson, the kidnap victim, who had been returned amid the euphoria of a media frenzy, or, in the event of operational failure, having to accept Investigator Strait's resignation, reluctantly and with deep regret.

Chief Garett smiled that pleasant smile. Hopefully it would be a win-win scenario, so long as Investigator Strait didn't cause another 'unfortunate' diplomatic incident.

And thus, after due consideration, he approved Investigator Strait's request.

* * * * *

It was an apprehensive but exciting time. Amy Mae stood nonchalantly in the contemporary surroundings of Old MacDonald's World's Insem-A-Sow Spaceport. She was dressed in her chicest attire, but her demeanour belied her youth and inexperience. This was going to be her first time offworld.

Jez was not apprehensive even though he, like Amy Mae, had never been offworld before. He stood resolute. His mission was clear. Guided by his organic principles he was going to make sure that the 'organic word' was spread. Organic restitution would prevail.

Surprisingly the most apprehensive of all was Jez's mother. Surprising because, unlike her charges, she had been offworld before. In fact she had made this very passage to Pacifica many times when she was young. But it was not the passage that made Mary Usherman nervous; it was the thought of what she might find when she arrived at her destination. Things rarely stayed the same when you had left them for almost twenty solar cycles. Who knows how it all may have changed. She needed to sit down. She needed a drink.

Whilst Jez stood self-absorbed, Mary asked if anyone would like a drink. Jez shook his head, and Amy Mae, after nudging Jez sharply in the ribs, politely declined.

Awoken from his deliberations, Jez offered to go instead.

'Why thank you, Jez, that is kind. I think I need to sit here for a while.' Mary Usherman sat.

Jez made his way to a small self-service beverage emporium, which had a garishly coloured Stiff One drinks dispense machine stood against the back wall. After selection, and a simple pass of his holocom, his mother's drink was served.

To pass away the time – and truth be told to ease her nerves – Mary Usherman began to tell tales of her time on Pacifica all those solar cycles ago. How excited she had been to be going to the Academy. She was the first in her family to ever win a scholarship. In fact she was the first to ever go to an academy. It was not a thing that folk did back then. Old MacDonald's World had just been terraformed, and it was all hands to the soil. Except, of course, for when the war came. Yes, the young males went offworld and did their part. Many came back, but somehow they were never quite the same. It seemed they were all so much older and had a little less light in their eyes.

She paused, lost in her thoughts. And then something must have drawn her back. She sipped her drink, smiled and spoke of the excitement she had felt. All those things to do: the parties, the concerts, new friends, falling in and out of love. It was a social whirl. And the studying, of course. How much she had learnt and how much she realised she did not know. And then she stopped.

'And?' Amy Mae wanted to know more.

For just a pulsar's pulse Mary looked at Amy Mae with eyes that had seen it all, she then looked across at Jez, who was again adrift in his own universe. 'Oh, you will find out soon enough, my dear, soon enough.'

Mary glanced at her holocom. 'Come on you two, it must be time to make our way to the shuttle departure point.'

Mary stood and, with Amy Mae, made to leave. Jez continued to stare into some distant place, he had not moved. Mary tapped him on the shoulder. 'Hello, Jez, are you with us?'

They joined the throng of passengers who milled around waiting to make their way up the embarkation ramp. A jovial jump associate stood by the transit shuttle's airlock, and welcomed each and every one as they boarded. He smiled the same smile, and bade that each should have the same pleasant trip.

Mary held Amy Mae's hand to reassure her, and with the slightest of half-grins added, 'Do not worry, my dear, this goes up in smoke every rotation.' And so it did, after the countdown was played out aloud – for all those who wished to count along – and after several unsettling, mechanical noises, and a slight judder.

Amy Mae looked past Jez and out of the porthole. She could see Old MacDonald's World dropping away below, getting smaller and smaller. She pushed her hand to his, and waited in hope for him to hold it.

The view darkened and then, with astounding brilliance, the stars appeared. Below, the green ball that was Old MacDonald's World fell away, encircled by a ring that glistened orange. And beyond were the moons in conjunction, Ei and EiO.

Amy Mae's attention was suddenly distracted by the sound of sporadic retching – weightlessness inevitably has its drawbacks. She could see that the jovial jump associate was busy, bearing a Go Suck portable suction pack and a familiar smile.

Time passed and the transit shuttle began to rotate, manoeuvring to dock with the starliner, adding to the commotion. There was a gentle thud, and the reassuring sense of orientation returned. In a flurry of activity the passengers made their way to the transit shuttle's airlock to be met, once again, by the jovial jump associate who, through his ever-present smile, hoped a pleasant trip had been had by all.

Inside the starliner, Mary, Amy Mae and Jez searched for their seats. Without portholes, and curving away to some hidden horizon, the passenger deck was a little disorientating to the uninitiated passenger. Amy Mae began to feel faint and dizzy. But just as she started to swoon, experienced hands reached out to catch her and suggested, 'Here, take a seat, miss.'

Amy Mae sat down gratefully and thanked the jump associate.

He nodded courteously and replied, 'No problem, miss.' It was, after all, what Rodger was there for.

The passage to Pacifica on Liberty Discount's Freedom Of The Stars proved to be uneventful. For the most part Amy Mae felt mildly nauseous. Jez had drifted off to where Jez drifted off to, and Mary managed to sleep. And whilst the passing universe could be watched on the holoplays in front of each passenger, it just wasn't quite the same as being able to idly view it ebb by through a proper porthole.

The jump too proved to be uneventful. A blink and the universe's stars shuffled. Every celestial body appeared to be in a different place, and yet they had not changed position; in reality, at that juncture in the space-time continuum, only the starliner had moved.

It was only after they arrived in orbit and made the transfer to the transit shuttle that the anticipation of planetfall began to grow. Amy Mae made sure she had a porthole seat, for she could look at space and planets and stars for eternity. And there it was: Pacifica, a vast ball of merging grey, not the blue she had imagined. But before she could take in all that the panorama had cast before her, the transit shuttle passed into Pacifica's clouded atmosphere and was descending to land through rain.

It was a cushioned, barely noticeable landing. Amy Mae, Mary and the distracted Jez followed the rest of the passengers along the disembarkation tunnel. With a sharp intake of breath, Amy Mae joined the river of travellers that filled the concourses of Pacifica's U-Tan-U Spaceport. All these folks. She had never seen so many. Where did they all come from?

Carried along by the crowd, bombarded by the endless holoverts for personal colour enhancement products, it was with relief that they stepped out into the grey rain.

Mary Usherman said that they would make their way to the Come On Inn Hotel, where she'd reserved their rooms prior to departure. However, she asked that they take a short sightseeing detour first. And so it was that Jez found himself sandwiched in the back of a Show-2-U rickshaw bot, signed 'See Pacifica By Dark'. A bot that, despite its folding roof, offered little protection from Pacifica's ever-pervasive precipitation.

With all strapped in, the Show 2 U rickshaw bot pulled up and began to climb vertically. Its surprising turn of speed caused Amy Mae to draw close to Jez, and even when the Show-2-U rickshaw bot had levelled out above Pacifica's crowded skyline Amy Mae remained close.

In a deliberately intoned local drawl, that was barely comprehensible, the Show-2-U rickshaw bot described the scene and explained that the metropolis of Pacifica was built on a solitary island in a vast, solitary ocean. Jez could just make out the coastline in the pallor of the dark, rain-filled sky.

After recanting Pacifica's brief history, and pointing out several illuminated skybreakers of note, the Show-2-U rickshaw bot began to descend, stopping on occasion when an explanation of a particular sight demanded.

Jez noticed that his mother said little but leant forward, looking intently, as if she was searching for something. It was when the Show-2-U rickshaw bot pointed out the up-lighted spires of Pacifica's Academy, half-hidden behind the packed skybreakers, that she sat back. And then she quietly dropped her head into her hands, and Jez could hear silent tears add to the falling rain. A few photon phases passed. She lifted her head and, as quickly as the rain had washed away the traces of her tears, she regained her composure.

[34] Hearing Is Believing

All was silence.

And then all was noise.

Noise that was so very loud.

Johnson pressed his hands to his ears, but it did not stop the noise. Loud, thundering clangs followed, each after the other, shaking the very foundations of the monastery. He opened his eyes. And just as he closed them again, to drift back to sleep, the cacophony resounded.

It wasn't going to stop. It was still dark. Who could be ringing bells at this time of sunfall? He heard muffled footsteps from the corridor outside, and glimpsed a flickering line of light passing under his door. What was going on?

He was awake now, and so he stood and fumbled for the door, his body achingly stiff in the places that only sleeping on a mat bedded on sandstone can achieve.

Silhouetted figures strode along the corridor, heads hung in hooded grey robes, hands raised apart in silent utterance, gold stars glittering.

With all this commotion he wasn't going to get any sleep. He joined the file and, after a few painful steps, the circulation returned to the parts of his body that had become numbed whilst sleeping.

The procession of figures disappeared into the distance, shadowed against the occasional feeble glow globe that barely gave shape to the corridor. And the bells rang and rang setting tempo to the procession. And then they stopped. Johnson and his fellow grey-robed novices entered the monastery's abbey.

Johnson craned his neck as he lifted his head to see the vast arched pillars of stone and marble disappear far above. Sandstone walls shimmered red with light. Haunting harmonics of incantation reverberated to his very core.

The procession of grey figures was lost in the vastness of the building. And with other processions, white, grey and black, they filled the abbey, forming a monochrome terrace of monks. The monks' gold five-pointed stars sparkled as if in the firmament. Whilst high above, visible in the darkness, a much, much larger gold star provided a focal point for all.

Then all was silence until a single voice spoke of contemplation and devotion and love, a single voice that gave praise for its very existence to the one true Holy One.

Johnson found himself saying 'So be it' together with a thousand other hushed voices.

And, after the single voice had spoken, silence returned, save for the monks' footfalls as they filed out of the abbey. Johnson followed, walking the return along the slowly enlightening corridor. The sun was rising, casting its light from windows high above.

And so Johnson sat with the others to eat bread from his bowl and drink water from his beaker. He felt relaxed. Was this how normality felt? But with his unremembered past, how would he know?

* * * * *

Pacifica's grey, intermittent drizzle had turned into a consistent, even rain; the kind of rain that stayed. Chad stood before the gleaming krypton-white steps that led up to the colonnade frontage of Flush Away's corporate headquarters. He had returned, but there was no one to greet him. Where was the radon-red walkway, the heralds trumpeting his arrival, the cordons of jubilant colleagues, and the traditional shower of silver and gold Paperette stars? He had just landed the biggest deal in Flush Away's corporate history. Did no one care?

Chad was truly disappointed. But he wasn't to be done out of his triumph. He'd just have to make it happen himself. In a way it was no surprise. If it weren't for his efforts this corporation would have gone down the toilet solar cycles ago.

As he climbed the steps he thought of the none-too-distant future where he, 'Chad The Saviour' as he surely would become known, would be in charge. There'd be changes; you bet there'd be changes. He had a list with names on it.

Past the colonnade, and Chad entered the skybreaker's foyer. Ever-vigilant Ever-On security drones bleeped and whirred above. A solitary old male, who looked as though he'd only come in for warmth and shelter, attended a floating sign, which flashed the words, 'Museum Guided Tour'.

Chad looked up, half-expecting, half-hoping to be surprised by his colleagues cheering, and dropping silver and gold Paperette stars on him from the grand circles that ascended above, but all he heard was the hollow sound of his own footsteps echoing in the emptiness.

Chad was never a male to be down for long. The wonder of living with his own ego soon saw to that. He entered the plastiglass skyvator which intoned, in its flawless accent, 'Welcome to Flush Away – the corporation that totally wastes your waste! How may we be of service?'

'Customer-relationships and promotions level, now,' ordered Chad.

One person who was certainly not on Chad's list of names was the ever-welcoming Miranda. As Chad approached her workhub he wore his best smile, as he always did for her. She looked up and then, after a hastily returned half-smile, looked down, her eyes were tearful, glistening red.

Chad saw them as tears of joy at his successful corporation-saving deal. 'There, there. There's no need to cry. I know it's wonderful news.

But really, even if I say so myself, it was only business.'

The ever-tireless Miranda looked up and, drawing from a strength somewhere within, replied, 'Only business?'

'Perhaps I am being a little too modest.' Chad assumed what he considered to be a contemplative pose. He stared to the distance, palm under chin, foot forward and, with his other hand resting on his hip, rephrased himself, 'Only the greatest piece of business ever!'

The ever-tranquil Miranda's jaw dropped. No words came out.

Chad, seeing that she was completely awestruck, added, 'I know, I know; words fail you. But it's true; Chad's gone and delivered again. Great stuff!'

The ever-selfless Miranda, who had managed initially to compose herself, erupted. 'Johnson's been kidnapped and you think it's wonderful news, only business! What kind of uncaring, self-centred, egotistical s**t are you?'

Chad took a step back. She was clearly distraught and emotional, overwhelmed by his achievements. He decided to press on and leave the ever-perceptive Miranda.

As he walked past the clusters of workhubs he received the odd nod of recognition, even a thumbs up and a 'Hi ya' Chad', but it was hardly the reception he'd hoped for. He knocked on Ms D'Baliere's door and entered.

Ms D'Baliere glanced up anxiously. 'Welcome back, Chad. I'm afraid the team's a little upset; Johnson's still missing.'

Chad deflated. 'You got my order?'

'Yes,' replied a clearly distracted Ms D'Baliere continuing with her work.

'The order from the Creation Corporation I sent via Galactic Union last rotation,' persisted Chad.

'Yes, it arrived late last workshift,' confirmed Ms D'Baliere.

Chad repeated himself, announcing each word between his teeth, 'The largest order in the history of the Flush Away Corporation!'

Ms D'Baliere looked up. 'Was it, Chad? Oh, well done, great teamwork! I'm sure Mr Stein will have a word or two to say about it, after this business with Johnson is concluded.' She returned to her work.

After a while, Chad realised he was standing in front of Ms D'Baliere's workhub for no apparent reason. He made a note to highlight her name on his list, and left the room.

*   *   *   *   *

Jez had holoed his contact.

His mother and Amy Mae were off enjoying being tourists; taking in

273

all that Pacifica had to offer. Amy Mae had spoken of nothing else since their arrival. The attire of Pacifica's indigenous population captivated her. It was an entirely different, stylish take on fashion from the utilitarian fit, form and function adopted by her agricultural kinfolk on Old MacDonald's World.

Jez had agreed to meet his contact and had asked for a backdrop of life, of greenery, not the cold grey of urban sprawl. The taxi-skyrider took him to Emerald Rise Park. He quickly found the meeting place he had been told about. There, before him, stood a smartly dressed, well-manicured female with a tethered Eye Sight holocast bot.

She stepped forward, confidently, with an outstretched hand. 'We meet at last.'

Jez nodded and pressed her hand. He looked about to check that she had come alone as promised. She explained what she wanted to do and how the process worked: the Eye Sight holocast bot would float between them, recording each simultaneously; he should speak clearly and slowly and, most importantly, she told him to keep it short and simple; after all this was light-time holoplay not dark-time debate. And, as agreed, she would not transmit until he had left the park. Also his identity and voice would be masked, though she would have editorial control. Jez understood.

Jez watched curiously as she closed her eyes, took a deep breath, and then drew her hands from the centre of her body up over her face whilst expelling the air she had just taken in.

It was as if she had been transformed, energised. And with the brightest of smiles she bounced into holoplay view. 'Respects Pacifica! Colette Wright reporting with an exclusive. That's right! Another sensational exclusive just for you! I have managed to track down a representative of the Children Of The Soil, and he has agreed to speak exclusively to you. That's right! An exclusive just for you!'

She paused and then continued, 'Sir, firstly, if you would tell our audience who the Children Of The Soil are.'

She nodded at Jez to prompt him to begin, and Jez spoke, 'We, the Children Of The Soil, are organic fundamentalists dedicated to returning to the soil that which comes from the soil.'

Colette Wright spoke to interject, 'Why thank you, sir...'

However, Jez continued regardless, 'We ask you all to abandon the yoke of corporate oppression, to discard the universisation and subjugation that corporate themeing has brought to your planets. It is time for us all to take a stand...'

Using her hand to make a rapid throat-cutting movement Colette Wright frantically indicated for Jez to stop. He did, and she managed to regain control of the interview. 'Thank you for that insight. Perhaps you could explain your organisation's role in the recent events concerning the disappearance of Johnson, the Flush Away employee.' She cued Jez to speak.

'Our only hope is to share the "organic word" with you, so that we can all save our planets. Johnson is with us and we wish him well, for like you and I, he is but a victim. Unfortunately, he has been employed by the Flush Away Corporation: a corporation who symbolise the very essence of what is wrong with humankind; a corporation that infests the planets we live on with their poisoning, unnatural products; a corporation driven by all-consuming greed; a corporation that is simply unorganic!'

Colette Wright was almost taken in by the rhetoric and fervour of Jez's speech, but the hardened scepticism of her media professionalism soon pulled her back. 'Thank you. Finally, and briefly for our audience, can you clarify what "organic restitution" means?'

Jez stared directly at the Eye Sight holocast bot. 'Organic restitution simply means: that which we take from the soil must be returned to the soil, for, if we wish for the soil to give unto us, we must give unto it.'

Colette Wright translated for the audience, 'So if I understand you correctly, our natural waste by-products should be returned to the soil.'

Jez nodded and added, 'And the Flush Away Corporation prevents us all from performing organic restitution by the very nature of their irradiating sanitation units. They need to stop fabricating what they fabricate and help us return back to Nature's way, or the soil will surely die and we will be no more. We request that the Flush Away Corporation turns from its unorganic path and joins us on our natural, organic way.'

Colette Wright clasped her hands together and summarised to the Eye Sight holocast bot, 'There you have it, electorate: no aliens, just a passionate belief, a missing male, a corporation, and the way we dispose of our natural waste. You decide. That's right! Signing off for now, this has been an exclusive just for you from your very own Colette Wright.'

She looked, but Jez was gone.

[35] Found Out

The sight of what could only be law enforcement deputies, dressed in 'plain attire', jogging two-by-two through Pacifica's U-Tan-U Spaceport did attract some attention from travellers, particularly when the law enforcement deputies started singing tunes that were perhaps best left in the changing-room. But Investigator Strait let it go. He and his Tactical Response Assault Patrol, together with the rest of Operation Kicking Butt, were planetbound, travelling to Nova Vega with permissions agreed, approved, validated and ratified. This time they'd get Johnson!

After an uneventful though somewhat boisterous starliner passage, the law enforcement team arrived in orbit around Nova Vega and descended to the planet's as yet unnamed spaceport.

Investigator Strait and his team were met by Liaison Deputy Germane from Nova Vega's law enforcement agency. The Tactical Response Assault Patrol, together with their matching holdalls of body armour, combat fatigues and associated paraphernalia, were directed to the Desert Bluff Law Enforcement Barracks. There they were to set up a command and control centre and get ready for whatever 'action' may be required.

Investigator Strait, his deputies and Liaison Deputy Germane headed for the place of Johnson's last confirmed sighting: the Black Hole Casino.

The sun shone hard as the law enforcement skyrider sped through the congested skyways of historic Nova Vega. Within the half-life of carbon-11, the skyrider drew up outside the very large, and very black, Black Hole Casino.

The attendant Do-4-U valet bots kowtowed into action. They bowed their heads dutifully and opened the skyrider's doors to allow the occupants to step out, offering their ball-jointed arms to aid egress. However, the Do-4-U valet bots became somewhat confused by the projecting of law enforcement identifications and the words, 'Law enforcement business,' spoken loudly and at haste. They did the bot equivalent of scratching their heads, and beeped frantically, circling the skyrider in a vain, pre-programmed hope that a random search pattern would resolve their confusion.

The law enforcement team strode purposefully through the casino's entrance, the thronging crowds parted before them. They headed straight for the gallery of associate and bot images with its casino ground plan. However, it was again apparent that Mr Paolo Cigstano, the casino manager, was not in attendance.

After some discussion, Liaison Deputy Germane suggested they head for the casino's reception. He added, with a sparkle in his eye that, given a quiet word in the right ear, the whereabouts of the absent casino manager would be forthcoming.

Investigator Strait nodded in agreement.

It was as the law enforcement team studied the ground plan of the casino, to determine the best route to reception, that a black spherical Hi-2-U greetings bot swooped down in front of them and dropped a fortuitous arrow-headed 'Reception' sign, crackling with blue ionic discharge.

'Beep – Respects, sirs and madam – beep.' There was a pause. 'Beep – On behalf of the management and associates of the Black Hole Casino please accept our most heartfelt welcome – beep.' Another pause followed. 'Beep – For rooms and all other services we offer please follow the sign – beep.'

Investigator Strait looked at Liaison Deputy Germane and, with an economy of effort, shrugged his shoulders as if to say, 'Shall we?'

In reply Liaison Deputy Germane shrugged his shoulders as if to say, 'Why not?'

'Beep – Would sirs and madam like me to carry their luggage? – Beep,' asked the Hi-2-U greetings bot.

'No luggage,' responded Investigator Strait curtly.

The law enforcement team then followed the Hi-2-U greetings bot past the rows of shimmering holographic gaming machines that populated the casino, walking on into its ever-darkening interior.

Several turnings, corridors and stairs later, and the law enforcement team was delivered to the casino's reception. They stood, waiting, amid a collection of exotic potted parasol plants. The Hi-2-U greetings bot bade them a fond farewell, expressing the hope that they thoroughly enjoy their stay, and with a final 'beep' departed.

Liaison Deputy Germane *suggested* to the casino's reception associates that full cooperation would be their best choice. Despite their all-too-apparent reluctance he walked them, one at a time, across the reception area to Investigator Strait for interview.

Investigator Strait reclined in a high-backed, faux-leather chair and, after asking the usual introductory confirmation questions, projected images of the suspects and pressed for details of their whereabouts.

Whilst the image of the casino manager drew a clearly nervous and adamant blank, the images of Johnson, Jones and Brown did trigger a better response. The reception associates remembered all three and were, eventually, able to furbish the law enforcement team with the three's arrival and departure times.

However, it was when Investigator Strait interviewed one particularly alert young female – who, upon viewing the projected images, simply looked up, pointed and said, 'You mean those two?' – that providence smiled.

Investigator Strait instinctively turned around and there they were:

277

Star Trooper Jonah Jones being pushed along by Billy Bob Brown.

He gestured with his arm, waving to Jones and Billy Bob to come over and join him.

With surprise Billy Bob pointed at himself, and Investigator Strait nodded. Jones tried to ignore him and, despite a valiant attempt to wheelie his way out of trouble, the closing ranks of law enforcement deputies, together with a broad smile from Investigator Strait, helped Star Trooper Jonah Jones fully understand his somewhat limited options.

* * * * *

When Jez returned to the Come On Inn Hotel, from his 'meeting' in the park, he had not expected his mother to be waiting for him in his room. She should be out enjoying all that Pacifica had to offer, but by the look on her face she clearly hadn't.

'Tell me, how was your business meeting?' she asked.

'Meeting?' echoed Jez, surprised by his mother's direct interest. 'No problem. In fact I think it went quite well.'

'Yes, and tell me, do you plan to have any more?' There was an edge to Mary Usherman's voice.

'Perhaps, if they are necessary. Why do you ask?' replied Jez.

'As Amy Mae and I sat for a much deserved rest, I happened to glance upon a holoplay.' Mary Usherman looked directly into her son's eyes and his star collapsed. 'You know I had to do a double scan. I thought to myself it could not be could it? And then I thought it must be. A mother knows her own son when she sees him, even if he is being digitally disguised.'

Jez stood uncomfortably, accused in silence.

Mary Usherman, with resignation, continued, 'The Children Of The Soil?'

Jez said nothing.

She then added, 'Kidnapping?'

Jez squirmed. 'But I didn't.'

She shook her head and looked away.

'Organic fundamentalists demanding "organic restitution"? Where do you get it all from? Yes, I know I brought you up to be principled and believe in living with Nature, but this.' She sighed and then, with forthright determination, turned to Jez. 'You are going to have to redress what you have done and apologise to everyone whose time you have wasted.'

* * * * *

Star Trooper Jonah Jones would not even confirm his name and, after demanding his right to representation, stared blankly at the wall refusing to even engage in eye contact. And so it remained, no matter what Investigator Strait said about 'leaf' or 'kidnapping' or 'Johnson'.

In his mind Investigator Strait had categorised Star Trooper Jonah Jones as a professional lawbreaker. Patience and negotiation would be the only way forward here. Even when confronted with irrefutable evidence it was Investigator Strait's experience that the hardened professional lawbreaker would always try to deny and lie his way out of any situation he found himself in.

By way of contrast, in the other interview-room, Billy Bob answered all the questions he was posed, and answered them as truthfully as he could, for he had been brought up to do so. It was discourteous not to answer when asked a question, and, of course, you had to answer truthfully. Billy Bob knew that lying was a sin. He trembled in the knowledge that such a transgression would lead him onto the path of temptation, and that would only lead to eternal fire and damnation in the Evil One's dominion – Preacher Jedidiah Grimthorpe had made that all to clear to Billy Bob over the solar cycles.

Unfortunately Investigator Strait did not believe him. It wasn't that he thought Billy Bob to be any more or any less untruthful than anyone else. Indeed, Investigator Strait was nothing if not consistent in his treatment of all lawbreakers. It was that Investigator Strait believed all lawbreakers to be untruthful and, as Billy Bob was sat on the wrong side of the interview, it thus must hold that he was not telling the truth.

The fact that Liaison Deputy Germane actually believed Billy Bob, was of no consequence, for, despite his best efforts to convince Investigator Strait otherwise, Investigator Strait was not to be swayed.

Although the ever-present Tell-It-All auto-transcriptor recorded everything said in absolute detail, Investigator Strait always made his own notes. It helped him distil what was said to what he considered to be the salient points. He often found that the more traditional justice tended to believe the noted word of a law enforcement investigator rather than the digitised output of a machine: no matter how scientifically proven that digitised output might be.

And so, with heavy patience and a steadfast determination – that only a law enforcer of Investigator Strait's vast experience could muster – the interview started again for what must have been the fifth time. 'OK. Let's take this from the beginning. Your name is Billy Bob Brown.'

Billy Bob thought for a while and then nodded.

Investigator Strait continued, 'A resident and citizen of Old MacDonald's World.'

Billy Bob again thought for a while and then nodded.

Investigator Strait carried on with the interview. 'You are a member of the Children Of The Soil, which you describe as an organic fundamentalist

279

group.'

This was a somewhat more complex proposition for Billy Bob to affirm. However, Billy Bob thought long and hard, and then, in time, nodded.

Investigator Strait took a deep breath and pressed on. 'You are here on Nova Vega on a mission – and please correct me if I get any of this wrong – a mission: "To spread the organic word and bring about the collapse of the unorganic corporations that infest the universe with their attempts to enslave the very masses they are meant to serve in themedom."'

Billy Bob thought, visibly checking that Investigator Strait's recited words were as Jez had spoken them to him, and then nodded.

Investigator Strait paused, so far so providential. 'And Johnson was the target of your mission. By discrediting him, and perhaps even turning him to your cause, you hoped to bring about the downfall of the said "unorganic corporations", as well as an end to irradiating sanitation facilities, and achieve "organic restitution".'

Billy Bob listened very carefully and only asked Investigator Strait to repeat what had been said twice this time. Billy Bob then nodded in agreement.

'You then say you didn't kidnap Johnson; you only *pretended* to kidnap him, and you did this to raise the profile of your cause. And you say that what you *actually* did was all go on a trip to the Simucalc Monastery here on Nova Vega.' Investigator Strait shook his head and then added, 'And it was whilst you were at the monastery that you last saw Johnson.'

Billy Bob sat back, considered carefully what had been said and then nodded, dutifully.

Investigator Strait gathered himself and continued, 'However, believing Johnson to have left the monastery, you returned to Nova Vega to search for him.'

Billy Bob thought, nodded and smiled.

Investigator Strait then tried that most ancient and practised of law enforcement interview techniques; the long hard cold stare. 'Are you a leaf grower?'

Billy Bob shook his head.

Investigator Strait's stare became longer. 'Have you ever been in possession of, or used, or sold, leaf in any form?'

Billy Bob shook his head again.

Investigator Strait's stare became harder. 'Are you part of a leaf-trafficking ring?'

Billy Bob continued to shake his head.

Investigator Strait's stare became colder. 'Do you know of any leaf traffickers?'

Billy Bob did not stop shaking his head.

Investigator Strait sighed. All in the room looked at each other with a sense of déjà vu, for the questions and answers had not changed since the last time the interview had been conducted, or, indeed, the three times before that.

Liaison Deputy Germane tapped Investigator Strait on the shoulder and motioned to the door, leaving Billy Bob and a duty deputy in silence in the room.

'He's telling the truth,' ventured Liaison Deputy Germane. 'He's no lawbreaker, he's just an offworlder out of his zone who has ended up in something that's got a lot out of control.'

Investigator Strait still remained unconvinced.

Liaison Deputy Germane glanced around and, trying another vector, leant in closely to whisper into Investigator Strait's ear, 'But I'll tell you what.'

Investigator Strait looked quizzically at Liaison Deputy Germane. 'What?'

'He's given us the chance we've been waiting for.' Liaison Deputy Germane hoped what he was about to say would stop Investigator Strait from carrying out another interview with Billy Bob Brown. 'We've been trying for an eternity to raid that monastery, but have never had just cause. We've suspected that it's been at the centre of the *financial redistribution* industry for some time. That kid's just given us the ideal opportunity to drop in unannounced and see what shakes out.'

Investigator Strait considered what Liaison Deputy Germane had said.

Liaison Deputy Germane put a conspiratorial arm around Investigator Strait's shoulders. 'If we were to believe what he has to say, Johnson's last confirmed sighting was in the monastery. I think we may have enough to get the search authority we need. Who knows what, or who, we might find?'

Liaison Deputy Germane had his eyes closed and was beseeching his lucky stars. The thought of having to sit through *yet another interview* with Billy Bob and the relentless Investigator Strait was more than any law enforcement deputy could reasonably be asked to endure.

Investigator Strait thought and thought some more. He then nodded, reluctantly.

Liaison Deputy Germane thanked his lucky stars.

[36] By The Stars

From a distance they were mere glistening specks tracing across the vast Red Sand Sea. They could just be seen against the sky, hugging the contours of the sand dune peaks, almost lost to the eye, distorted in the heat haze. And, above it all, Nova Vega's descending yellow sun glared.

The law enforcement assault craft raced; the Great Cosmic Chronometer was ticking. Which would reach the monastery first, the craft or the word? Such a large operation was bound to have drawn attention.

Inside the assault craft, all studied their plans. Each had an objective. Each had an area to cover. Each had an image of Johnson.

First in were the Eye Fly surveillance bots. These fly-like machines would buzz their way through every passage, corridor, room and chamber in the monastery; imaging and sensing everything, providing invaluable information for those who followed. Yes, there would be casualties; there were going to be spiders' webs, fly-traps, monks with fly-zappers, but it would be a debit that would be creditworthy.

Second in were Operation Kicking Butt's Tactical Response Assault Patrol, each partnered with a member of Nova Vega's elite Hunt And Neutralise Group. Once they had subdued any potential threats, they were to occupy the monastery and hold station, ensuring that no monastic personnel left.

Finally, the investigating deputies would disembark and begin their methodical enquiries. Objective one was Johnson. Objective two was evidence of *financial redistribution*.

Still, just visible in the half-light of Nova Vega's setting sun, the gold five-pointed star of the Simucalc Monastery glinted high above the desert. Through their imaging sensors the law enforcement team could see the vast complex of interconnected buildings and, at the centre, the domed citadel with its five towers.

Sunfall. The time had come. The assault craft slowed and spread out, encircling the monastery.

At last! Combat fatigues were donned, body armour strapped on, assault blasters checked and most lovingly of all, combat knives were affixed ready for action – just in case they were needed, of course, purely precautionary. The air was charged with testosterone; this was what the Tactical Response Assault Patrol had been waiting for all these long, desolate lunar cycles.

Under the watchful eye of Liaison Deputy Germane, Investigator Strait began his countdown. 'Five, four, three, two, one, go!' Then, from each craft, a multitude of Eye Fly surveillance bots swarmed and buzzed out across the dunes towards the monastery.

After this, lines of shadowed figures followed, step-in-step on the red sand, soon to be lost in the fading light.

It had begun.

The images from the Eye Fly surveillance bots were clear, the sensory returns concise. And, whilst there was the odd fateful screen of white noise, the majority of the bots accomplished their mission without incident.

Close behind, and armed with the knowledge of what was around every corner, law enforcement deputies overcame the startled, unprepared monks, corralling them, arms aloft, in groups at predefined locations.

The monastery was secured quickly and, much to the disappointment of the Tactical Response Assault Patrol and the Hunt And Neutralise Group, no resistance had been offered.

Investigator Strait gave the order for the monks to be marched to the chapter house. He then disembarked from his law enforcement assault craft and strode along the arched stone corridors and passageways. His footsteps were measured and deliberate, each made in the knowledge that they were taking him closer to the successful conclusion of Operation Kicking Butt and, in his mind, the certainty of promotion.

Side-by-side stood four massive double doors. It was through these that Investigator Strait led his team to an open area that extended outwards in all directions under a vast white domed roof. A star field of glow globes cast light down from the whitewashed walls, and row upon row of white-robed and grey-robed monks, interspersed with the occasional brown-robed and black-robed monk, sat in the tiers that circled the chapter house. At the heart, an inner circle of darkly dressed law enforcement deputies watched, fingers poised over triggers.

Investigator Strait strode to the very centre of the chapter house and stood on the star-shaped plinth. He looked around and then spoke. 'Right then, my name is Investigator Strait and these males and females, who have gathered you together here this rotation, are law enforcement deputies. They are deputies who are part of a joint operation being run by Nova Vega and Pacifica law enforcement agencies, an operation fully sanctioned by their respective authorities.'

Investigator Strait paused to allow this information to sink in to the assembled monks. 'To the vast majority of you, who I am sure are entirely innocent, I apologise for the inconvenience caused; we seek only those among you who are guilty of lawbreaking.'

The tension in the chapter house seemed to visibly ease.

'I would now ask that you stand, one-by-one, and lower your hoods.'

And so the process began. Each monk stood and lowered his hood. He was scanned, recorded. And so it was that Johnson stood, oblivious to the fact that he might be the central focus of the operation.

'Finally,' announced a beaming Investigator Strait, and signalled for two law enforcement deputies to step forward and escort Johnson down from his seat. There were audible gasps from the monks around the chapter house.

Johnson looked puzzled and pointed at himself. 'Brother, do you mean me?'

'Yes, you,' confirmed Investigator Strait. 'You have no idea of the trouble I have gone through to find you.'

'Brother, I think there must be some mistake; I'm just a monk, I've done nothing wrong,' said Johnson with true sincerity, though the worry of what his unremembered past might be was really starting to phase his photons.

Resigned to the fact that, in his experience, the guilty always denied their culpability, Investigator Strait replied, 'Indeed, that's something I think we can discuss.'

It was as Investigator Strait stepped down from the plinth, to follow the escorted Johnson, that a monk, wearing a coarse brown robe, stood quietly and, while all around were distracted, tried to take the opportunity to slip away.

Liaison Deputy Germane had been waiting in anticipation for such a move. He jumped up onto the plinth, and drawing his hand-zapper, shouted, 'You there, in the brown robe, stop or I'll zap you.'

All looked around. The figure in the brown robe stumbled forward, jostling through the monks, using them for cover. In desperation he grabbed and held a monk in front of him and made for the doorway.

All was noise and confusion. The brown-robed figure pushed his human shield forward into Johnson, who, together with his accompanying law enforcement deputies, tumbled to the ground. The brown-robed figure then bade farewell by snapping off a blast from his previously concealed blaster, whilst deftly stepping out through the doorway. The air was lighted with ionic blue blaster discharge ricocheting around the chapter house.

'After him!' bellowed Liaison Deputy Germane and joined the chase as several law enforcement deputies made for the door.

Investigator Strait looked down at the tumbled figures on the ground. The monk, who had been the human shield, and the two law enforcement deputies clambered to their feet, but there, eyes closed, prostrate on the ground was Johnson, not moving.

'Medibot!'

*   *   *   *   *

'You are one lucky male,' announced Investigator Strait, as he dangled a rather blackened and misshapen gold five-pointed star over Johnson, not that Johnson felt lucky. In fact he'd rather not be lucky if being lucky meant feeling like he felt.

Having regained consciousness, Johnson now looked around and wondered quite why he was lying on the ground surrounded by law enforcement deputies staring at him. He decided to lift himself up. Bad move. The whole universe began to spin. However, there was little chance he'd fall back as several well-exercised arms grabbed him.

Johnson wondered why he was dressed in grey robes – robes that itched badly by the way. And then, image-by-image, his memory returned, jumbled, disconnected and all-too-vivid: stepping off the transit shuttle; in a taxi-skyrider dodging the manic traffic that weaved among Nova Vega's skybreakers; doing a deal; having too good a time in the Black Hole Casino; crossing the desert; in a monastery!

Liaison Deputy Germane returned, out of breath. 'We've lost him, but I've set a full search pattern in place. He's sure to surface somewhere.'

'OK,' replied Investigator Strait. 'Right then, in the meantime let's continue vetting the monks. You two take Johnson to the temporary interview-room, I've got a few questions for him.'

A rather disorientated Johnson turned to Liaison Deputy Germane. 'Who did you say you lost?'

'The male who snapped off the blast that hit you,' replied a busy Liaison Deputy Germane.

'Mr Cigstano,' remarked Johnson.

'What? You know who that was?'

'Er – yes,' replied Johnson. 'I'm sure he's the reason I'm here dressed in these ridiculous grey robes and not on my way back to my workplace to claim my commission. It's the biggest deal I've ever done you know.'

Liaison Deputy Germane interrupted Johnson. 'Did you say Cigstano? As in Cigstano the general manager of the Black Hole Casino.'

'Yes,' said Johnson.

Liaison Deputy Germane turned to Investigator Strait and asked, 'I wonder what a casino manager is doing in a monastery? We need to find him. If he gets away he'll fabricate an alibi so airtight that even my own mother would swear to it.'

Investigator Strait nodded in agreement and began a hushed but heated debate with his law enforcement deputies.

Johnson tapped Investigator Strait on the shoulder and was ignored.

Johnson tapped again and was again ignored.

For a third time Johnson tapped the investigator's shoulder to be met with, 'Why hasn't this suspect been taken to the interview-room yet?'

Undaunted, Johnson announced to no one in particular, 'I bet *I know* where he's hiding.'

There was a pause.

'What? Is this some kind of petition trade?' asked an irritated

Investigator Strait.

'Petition trade?' Johnson was a little confused. Why should he, an innocent citizen and clearly a victim of some kind of wrongdoing or other, be asking to petition trade? 'Look, do you want me to show you where Mr Cigstano is or not?'

Investigator Strait looked at Liaison Deputy Germane who nodded vigorously. He then signalled to the law enforcement deputies holding Johnson to bring him back. 'OK then, show us, and don't forget we'll be behind you every parsec of the way.'

'Well, follow me.'

Released from the grip of his two accompanying law enforcement deputies the disorientated Johnson set off. All he needed to do now was remember where he was going.

Having backtracked several times, and having taken several wrong turnings, Johnson was now certain they'd arrived at the right door. He nodded to Liaison Deputy Germane.

Johnson was pushed out of the way as two law enforcement deputies assumed positions on either side of the door, a third kicked it open, and the rest flooded in, assault blasters at the ready, combat knives affixed.

It proved to be somewhat crushed as they all piled into the garderobe, a room that, whilst spacious for one, was cramped for ten.

Following Johnson's instructions, but looking sceptically at him, Investigator Strait sat on the garderobe's stone seat, and then stood, and then sat, and then stood, and then sat for a third time, much to the amusement of his deputies.

Clunk.

Unlike those around him, Johnson knew what was about to happen, as Investigator Strait and the garderobe, together with the law enforcement deputies, descended at speed.

Johnson looked at his fellow occupants and could see fear in their eyes. Knowingly he smiled.

Then, to everyone's relief the rate of descent slowed and they came to rest in a dim pool of light.

In front of them was a door.

When all had gathered their breath, and in some cases stopped shaking, Investigator Strait nodded and the door was opened, carefully this time. Through the door a corridor extended into the shadows, lighted by glow globes. They proceeded along the corridor. There were no exits left or right.

The corridor ended, no door, just a facing wall. Johnson pressed his finger to his mouth to hush the others, stepped forward and pushed one of the stones in the wall. To his disappointment nothing happened. He selected another stone and pushed, again nothing happened. A third stone:

nothing. Johnson turned to face his escorting law enforcement deputies.

Investigator Strait began to wear that look: the look of unhappiness at being led up a blind alley.

Sensing the gathering solar storm, Johnson involuntarily stepped back and brushed against the wall. And, to his relief, he felt a rush of air as the corridor became bathed in bright light. He then toppled backwards.

The wall had slid away to reveal a large, open room, several pallets of neatly wrapped and stacked credits and, sat upon one of the pallets, a figure in a coarse brown robe with his arms crossed, shaking his head.

The figure gave a resigned two-fingered salute.

[37] And So It Is

Francis Stein, vice-president of customer-relationships and promotions, was sat in his workspace. The sign on the door read, 'Mr Francis Stein – Vice-President Of Customer-Relationships & Promotions'; clear evidence that, in his view, the right male was in the right job.

Another clear indication that Francis Stein was the right male in the right job was the gallery of images on his workhub and across the wall, each unmistakably of himself with some important person or other.

But for Francis Stein the one absolute surety, that the right male was in the right job, was where it read 'Mr Francis Stein' under the words 'On behalf of the Flush Away Corporation by its appointed officer' on the fabrication release confirmation for the biggest order the Flush Away Corporation had ever received. With a smile he pushed his finger into the release confirmation holo-image to touch that dotted line. His approval then appeared. Job done!

Self-satisfied he sat back, drink in hand, shining in his shiniest business attire. He congratulated himself and waited patiently for others to do the same. Things couldn't be better.

As if on cue, the images flashed on his hololink.

So many colleagues wishing to link to him, whom should he select? He decided to start with Vice-President Of Merchandising Luton Touch. He was bound to want to take a slice of the credit.

'How are you, Francis?' asked Luton Touch.

'Couldn't be better,' replied Francis Stein.

'We've done it!' Luton smarmed. 'It really does go to show what power there is in the brilliantly conceived, marvellously run and wonderfully executed merchandising campaign I delivered. It just makes those sales happen.'

Francis Stein was feeling unusually magnanimous and decided it was better to keep Luton in his gravitational field, at this point in the space-time continuum, rather than tell him his true thoughts. 'I couldn't have done it without you, Luton, I couldn't have done it without you.'

The self-congratulatory Luton continued, 'That's what good teamwork delivers. Anyway, I've got to go now; I'm busy, busy, busy!'

And after Luton Touch had finished, Francis Stein selected the next person to link to; it was Vice-President Of Fabrication Tim Moontide. For a pulsar's pulse Francis thought there was something wrong with the hololink, for all he could hear was someone seemingly struggling for air. 'Tim, is that you? Are you all right?'

The rasping breath eventually subsided and Tim Moontide managed to speak, 'Francis, this can't be right, you must have put a zero or two in the wrong place.'

'Oh Tim, you do like your little jokes. It's right, true and proper. I checked the numbers myself. Gotta' keep you occupied,' Francis Stein replied.

'Right, OK, I'll um... I'll make sure my team get straight on it.' And, feeling somewhat burdened with the task of producing an unprecedented number of irradiating sanitation units, Tim Moontide closed the link.

Francis Stein revelled. It certainly was turning out to be a fine rotation.

But before Francis could select the next person to congratulate him, there was a rap at the door and a voice. The door slid open and Mrs Shelley stepped through looking uncharacteristically flustered. The door closed behind her and she whispered as loudly as she dared, 'Mr Stein, Ms D'Baliere is here and she has some visitors. She needs to see you urgently. I tried to buzz you, but you were busy.'

Francis Stein smiled, brushed himself down and made sure he struck a serious but informal, 'busy but my portal is always open' pose. It could only be one thing: the customer-relationships and promotions team was here to congratulate him. 'OK, just give me a pulsar's pulse, then show them in.'

'Yes, sir.' And Mrs Shelley left his workspace.

A pulsar's pulse passed and the door reopened. In came Ms D'Baliere, as smart and as professional as ever, but looking very tense; she seemed to be muttering something over and over under her breath.

'Why, Lucretia, good to see you,' Francis began. 'You didn't have to...' His sentence trailed off, for behind Ms D'Baliere came a colourfully dressed older female – clearly not a customer-relationship and promotions specialist – and a young male with a sparse grown beard and long hair – who was also clearly not a customer-relationship and promotions specialist.

Francis Stein returned to his smile and began again. 'Ms D'Baliere, I am at a disadvantage; I've not been introduced.' He stepped forward with outstretched hand. 'Mr Francis Stein, Flush Away's vice-president of customer-relationships and promotions. Call me Francis.'

The older, colourfully dressed female pressed his hand. 'Ms Usherman, Mary Usherman and this,' she paused and then continued with a less than happy edge to her voice, 'is my son, Jez.'

The young male nodded, but avoided eye contact.

'What can I do for you, Mary?' asked Francis Stein. He could see Ms D'Baliere wince.

'Mr Stein, my son has an apology to make.' Mary Usherman folded her arms.

'Sorry,' mumbled Jez, his head bowed.

'And,' prompted Mary Usherman.

'And we will not do it again,' concluded the humbled Jez.

'I don't think I quite follow what you're saying,' responded a confused Francis Stein.

'We did not do it,' continued Jez, trying to explain. 'We did not kidnap him. It was all a ruse for publicity. It is just that I do not think what you are doing is right. It is simply unorganic!'

Mary Usherman, sensing that Francis Stein was still confused, interrupted. 'My son, together with a few of his, shall we say less intellectually endowed, cousins decided in their wisdom to become organic fundamentalists. Not that there is anything wrong with organic principles mind you. They decided to call themselves the Children Of The Soil.'

'Ah.' Francis Stein began to understand. 'Though I appreciate your son's apology, perhaps this is a matter for the authorities.'

Mary Usherman agreed. 'They will be our next stop, but I thought it was important that my son made his amends in person before going to them. I have always taught him to be principled, but I think he has taken it a little too far this time. I wish you well.'

As Mary and her son turned to go, Francis asked, 'Just one question: where's Johnson?'

Jez shrugged and made to leave, but before he and his mother had reached the door, it slid open.

Joseph Firtop was not happy and was clearly in mid-rant. 'Mrs Shelley, is the vice-president of customer-relationships and promotions in here? Why doesn't anyone tell me what's going on? Do I have to find everything out through the media? I've just seen Colette Wright interview that Children Of The Soil person. He's mad; he wants us to go back to flushing toilets! What kind of ransom demand is that?'

'Ah.' Francis Stein sighed, then recovered. 'Joe, I have some breaking news for you.'

'A OK. It's about time! And it had better be good news or there'll be trouble!' bellowed Joseph Firtop, oblivious to the others in the room.

'Ah, in fact, as it turns out, this whole Johnson thing has been a bit of a publicity exercise,' grimaced Francis Stein.

'Publicity exercise!' Joseph Firtop's ire was absolutely focused on Francis Stein.

'It seems that this young male,' and Francis Stein indicated with his arm towards Jez, 'decided to pretend that he and his cousins had kidnapped Johnson. They did this to get media attention for their cause.'

Joseph was surprised to find that there were others in the room. He turned quickly towards Jez and then back again to Francis Stein. 'OK, so where's Johnson?'

'Good question, Joe, good question,' replied Francis Stein.

Joseph Firtop, who was now looking around the room, noticed Ms D'Baliere and a colourfully dressed female upon whom his gaze settled and stayed. In an entirely different tone he managed, 'Mary?'

'Joseph?' said Mary.

There was a long silence that eventually Francis Stein ventured to break. 'You two know one another?'

But their locked gaze remained unbroken. A tear ran from Mary's eye.

Jez looked between the two, and then he understood. 'Why, you are my...'

'Father,' interrupted Mary, turning to Jez. 'Yes Jez, he is your father.'

Joseph looked across at Jez and then back at Mary. 'Come again?'

Mary simply stated, 'It is true.'

At which both Joseph and Jez exclaimed, 'Oh my Holy One!'

*   *   *   *   *

Whilst events have a habit of unfolding rather too rapidly for those involved, their consequences necessarily don't.

Mr Cigstano turned planetside evidence and, in return for identity reassignment, implicated several members of Nova Vega's Chamber Of Commerce in credit laundering; an activity they'd been running through the New Desert Brethren into Pacifica's notoriously complex banking system for some time. Oh, and along the way he managed to allude to illicit campaign contributions, and, very nervously, mentioned the First Citizen Of Pacifica.

In this elaborate, tangled and often obscure network of lawbreaking and politics, the entropy of denial, allegation and counter-allegation ran and ran and ran, such that, over time: blame, guilt, innocence and justice became confused, dissipated and somewhat intangible. And so it was, and always will be, when those who rule are accused – such is a basic principle of the mechanics of this universe.

What disappointed Investigator Strait was the complete absence of leaf in the monastery. Indeed, according to Liaison Deputy Germane – who he suspected of telling the truth – all of this was simply about credits: the transfer of credits; the ownership of credits; the tax of credits; the trading of credits; the future trading of credits; the potential future trading of credits. Simply credits, not leaf.

Liaison Deputy Germane told him that the legal case was sure to go on and on and on, lucratively employing advocates and, in his experience, would never reach a conclusion, lost in legal arguments so convoluted that, if truth be known, no one actually understood them.

The only thing that was certain was that the pallets of used, unmarked credits, which sat in the evidence vaults of Nova Vega's law enforcement agency, must have surely burnt a hole in someone's stratosphere.

What further added to Investigator Strait's disappointment was that, no matter which angle he took, which vector he tried, nothing stuck: Johnson simply denied that he was a leaf trafficker. He also denied that he'd been kidnapped by the Children Of The Soil, though, much to Investigator Strait's annoyance, he didn't rule out having been abducted by aliens at some point.

Johnson remained adamant and consistent to the story he'd first told in that temporary interview-room back in the Simucalc Monastery on Nova Vega.

And, whilst Investigator Strait and his gut instinct could never believe Johnson's innocence, his head was forced to conclude that Johnson was simply a human with an uncanny ability to be spatially and chronologically misplaced.

It thus became next to impossible to bring any substantive charges against those who'd taken advantage of these apparent deceptions. The best that could be brought to bear was 'wasting law enforcement time' – although the presiding justice had said that the law enforcement agencies had done enough of that themselves without trying to implicate others.

And so it was, with little more than warnings, Jez Usherman, Billy Bob Brown and Star Trooper Jonah Jones were released to wreak their organic fundamentalism on an unknowing and uncaring universe – something that would, more than likely, pass completely unnoticed.

Perhaps the only citizens who truly profited from these events were the members of Flush Away's executive board. With all the additional media exposure of their products, their fiscal indicators turn from red to green, and, with self-congratulatory smiles, they collected their bonuses.

All Investigator Strait was left with was a package of leaf which, unlike his promotion prospects, had not gone up in smoke.

* * * * *

Johnson sat on the irradiating sanitation unit in Flush Away's visitors' convenience, and closed his eyes. He thought of what might have been. He sighed. Even the act of wiping with the corporate-embossed toilet Paperette brought no relief. He stood, operated the activation icon, and felt the ground shudder. Then, having exhausted all the other distractions that the visitors' convenience had to offer, he left his sanctuary to face the workshift.

And as he approached Flush Away's reception, the ever-caring Miranda stood, opened her arms and burst into tears. She held him so. She was delighted he was back, delighted he was safe.

He then took the long walk through the workplace towards his workhub, past his colleagues, who looked on with bemused silence. But before he was able to deposit his things, Ms D'Baliere's door slid open and a smiling Chad beckoned him forth.

Dutifully he did as he was requested. And, as he stepped inside, he found Chad sat at Ms D'Baliere's workhub with his feet up.

Chad pointed to the strategically positioned, solitary chair.

Johnson sat uncomfortably.

'Good trip?' enquired Chad with his all-pervasive smile. But before Johnson could answer, Chad continued, 'There've been a few changes around here since you went on your... trip.'

'Oh,' replied Johnson, knowing invariably that words delivered by Chad were not necessarily good news.

'There's a new head of customer-relationships and promotions,' announced Chad, maintaining his smile.

'Ah,' was all Johnson could say.

'Yes, Ms D'Baliere decided to leave, something about needing to find the "me" in "team". Anyway...' Chad paused, keeping Johnson in suspense for just a pulsar's pulse longer than necessary, 'I've been chosen to be her replacement. Great stuff, Johnson, you have a new boss!'

With good grace Johnson managed, 'Excellent.'

'Why thank you, Johnson.' Chad paused again and then added, 'That'll be all, the door will close behind you.'

It was an even longer walk back to his workhub and, as he put his things down, Johnson looked at the sign that told the universe who he was.

Johnson – Customer-Relationship And Promotions Specialist.

And that about summed it up.

Lightning Source UK Ltd.
Milton Keynes UK
UKOW031839160612

194557UK00004B/10/P